I0631589

The Rebel Christian Publishing

Copyright © 2022 Valicity Elaine
Original Copyright © 2015 Valicity Garris

Original Edition ISBN: 9781310975851
ISBN (eBook): 9781957290065
ISBN (Print): 9781957290072

This is a work of fiction. Any references to historical events, real people, or real places are used fictitiously. Names, characters, and places are products of the author's imagination. Inclusion of or reference to any Christian elements or themes are used in a fictitious manner and are not meant to be perceived or interpreted as an act of disrespect against such a wonderful and beautiful belief system.

Cover illustrated/designed by Valicity Elaine

The Rebel Christian Publishing LLC
350 Northern Blvd STE 324 – 1390
Albany, NY 12204

Visit us: http://www.therebelchristian.com/
Email us: rebel@therebelchristian.com

CONTENTS

ACKNOWLEDGEMENTS

The Rebel Christian Publishing

Series Order:

Cross Academy
Cross Academy: The Howler's Cry
Cross Academy: The Nine Births of Carnage
Cross Academy: Book IV

Other Books by Valicity Elaine:

Patches
The 'I' Word

I AM MAN series:

I AM MAN
I AM LOST
I AM BROKEN
I AM FREE
I AM COMPLETE (coming 2022)

Withered Rose series:

Withered Rose (coming 2022)
Clipping Thorns (coming 2022)
Starting Over (coming 2022)

This book is dedicated to JESUS CHRIST; Your plans were so much bigger than my own.

For our struggle is not against flesh and blood, but against the rulers, against the authorities, against the powers of this dark world and against the spiritual forces of evil in the heavenly realms.

Ephesians 6:12

Cross Academy

Book I

By Valicity Elaine

A Rebel Christian Publishing Book

X

Remember your training...

PART I

1

Roaring

We have to burn the bodies," Ryko said.

Roaring Fire stood silent, his vision forward but his thoughts scattered. He should have been used to this, to finding bodies in the forest. But each time it happened, it sent chills up his spine. Especially now when he couldn't even tell what sort of creature the body had once been. Arms twisted in one direction, legs bent and crooked, the head turned all the way around—mouth open. Screaming. It'd died screaming. Whatever it had been.

The rest were all the same; a tangle of limbs and parts and screaming faces. It was a pile of corpses, some thoroughly rotted, others recently dead. Whatever had killed these things hadn't done it all at once—it'd been hunting. Finding prey, killing them, eating them, and then going back for more.

Roaring knelt beside the blob of bodies and dared touch some of the goo seeping from it. Beside him, Ryko groaned in disgust; even his own hunting hound protested with a whimper, but he ignored them both. The liquid was deep red, darker than blood ... tainted. He smelled it and immediately regretted it; bitter poison burned his nostrils, nearly choking him. He wiped the goo onto the grass.

At least one of the bodies was human, Roaring noticed; a naked body with thick braids sprouting from the head. A red knot of thread had been woven into the braids; Roaring recognized it; a reward given only to those who made it through their Regiment training. His own knot was tied into his hair, mixed in with the kinky curls that kissed his shoulders each time he turned his head.

Roaring grimaced, staring at the head, at what was left of the face. He knew that man. Remembered when he'd gone missing during a hunt. That was days ago, when every member of the Regiment had vowed they would find him. They *had* finally found him. Except now there was nothing to bring back home. Beside a head full of braids.

"Chiefono," Ryko said.

Roaring turned, blinking. "Hmm?"

"We have to burn the bodies."

They had to. It wasn't barbaric tradition, it was survival. Burn the bodies; young and old, men and women. Burn them all. Roaring remembered the warnings of his elders; *burn them or the darklings will come and claim their empty flesh, put it on, and the dead would never rest.* Had to burn the darklings, too; sometimes their bodies would kill the soil; nearby trees

2

would decay, plants dry up and die. The whole area could get contaminated from just one dead monster—and if its corpse was left unchecked, it could bloat and burst and then you'd have miasma seeping into the air. Poisoning everything around it.

But there was nothing to worry about—these darklings were all ripped up and distorted and the part Roaring knew was human had barely any flesh left for the monsters to claim. And he couldn't let his own kinsmen burn outside the village. That wasn't their way; he deserved to be burned by the sacred flame, have the Holy Word read at his burial ignition. He was a member of the Fire Tribe; he deserved better.

"We can't burn them," Roaring finally said. He felt Ryko's eyes on him, studying him. They'd been friends since childhood, the brother Roaring never had, but Ryko knew better than to question his prince. Still, his curious eyes remained on him and it made the chiefono's skin prickle with sweat.

He exhaled a sigh; Roaring hated explaining himself. "There's a human in the pile. We can't burn it with the others."

Ryko shook his head. "Chiefono, we have to—"

"No, we don't."

"We *must.*"

"I am telling you; we aren't." Roaring stared at his companion, daring him to say more but it was his father's voice he heard instead.

"What's this about?" Wolf Fire asked, stepping into the clearing. "You're talking too loud. Like there aren't flesh-eating monsters crawling around." He was followed by the rest of their small team, Roaring's uncle and three other members of the Hunting Regiment. Each Hunter was a hardened warrior, hunting, scavenging, and fighting demons in the forest—surviving. But even they blanched at the sight in the woods. Naked, decaying bodies tangled together in a heap of flesh and limbs; the ground beneath the bleeding blob was black, tainted by the evil pouring into it. Roaring had seen horrible things outside the village before, but never anything like this.

Wolf Fire swallowed as he stood before the mass. "What on Earth is this?"

"Demons," Roaring answered. "Something's been hunting indiscriminately." He pointed to the Hunter's head. "That's the head of Aizol Fire. My own cousin."

"A distant cousin," his uncle quickly inserted.

"He is of the Flame, nonetheless," Roaring said. "So we aren't burning his body out here like he's some outsider. He deserves better."

His uncle frowned, eyeing the pile of bodies. "Aizol's body is tainted."

"Isn't much of a body—just a head—we could still touch it without getting ourselves tainted."

"Is it worth it, though?"

The rest of the men looked at Wolf Fire. Though this had been Roaring's expedition, the decision on Aizol's remains was left to the leader of the Hunting Regiment. Wolf Fire looked between his son and the men seeking guidance; Roaring could see the cogs churning in his head, considering his son's admirable compassion, but also knowing his uncle had a point. Digging out the body would take time and effort they weren't sure they could spare.

Roaring sensed his father's indecision. "He is our cousin," he said quietly. "Distant to me, but closer to you, Uncle Kato."

4

Kato rolled his eyes. "Whatever made this pile of bodies is still out there. We don't even know what it is—and you want us to go digging through its pile of leftovers while there's only a few hours of daylight left? We haven't even finished the hunt."

"Today wasn't about hunting," Roaring said. "It was about finding one of ours."

Kato knelt beside him in the tainted grass. "And what happens when the thing that did this finds us?"

"It could have been a bear," Ryko spoke up. He cleared his throat when the other men stared at him, waiting for more. "The monster who killed these darklings ... and Aizol."

"How do you know?" Roaring asked.

He pointed to the deep gashes in the earth and the scratches on the nearby trees. "Claw marks. And teeth marks on the bodies, too."

"Mighty big bear," Kato grunted. "Almost twice as big as any I've ever seen."

"That's not possible," Wolf Fire said.

"It is if the bear is possessed by a darkling," Roaring suggested.

Kato crossed his arms. "Where is it's cave?"

"If it is truly possessed, it likely abandoned the cave in a mindless search for flesh," Ryko explained.

"And, for some reason, a demon-possessed bear still doesn't deter you." His uncle was looking at him now, up close. Roaring could see the lines in his face, tugging away his youth and his kindness, too. Kato wasn't just a member of the Hunting Regiment, he was a *Kifu*, a master of his class and skill. He'd earned his knot at only twelve-years-old and then joined the Regiment immediately after. He'd seen more of the darkness

5

beyond the village than he cared to mention, and it made Roaring wonder if that was why he was so hard. So cold.

"Father can keep watch," Roaring said, rising from the tainted earth. He pointed to the three men beside him, "You three will go with Kifu Kato and track down the bear who did this while Ryko and I retrieve whatever remains of Aizol."

"You want us to go *looking* for that monster?" Kato asked, heavy eyebrows raised. "We should be heading back to the village—should have turned and high-tailed it out of here as soon as we saw this nightmare."

Roaring stood his ground. "That thing won't stop. It'll keep hunting until it's out of prey—or until it reaches the village. We have to find it and kill it before that happens."

Wolf Fire nodded agreement, though he cast a hesitant glance at Kato before he said, "Roaring is right. We can't let this darkling reach our home."

"It won't get past the Walls," Kato said.

"But it could get another one of us."

Kato set his jaw, trying to find the right argument but his nephew didn't give him the time. "You can take Chava with you if you're afraid." He leaned down to pet his hunting hound. The great beast was thrice the size of any of the other hounds in the village; sometimes even Roaring found it hard to believe she'd once been the runt of the litter.

"Being cautious is not the same as being afraid," his uncle informed.

When Roaring looked up, he saw the frown on Kato's face and had to keep himself from laughing. Kato did not like being beaten. But he rounded up his men and marched into the forest without another word. Chava followed in silence, stalking into the woods behind them.

"Was it wise to send them after the monster?" Roaring asked once they'd left. He peered into the forest, listening for their fading footsteps.

Wolf Fire sighed. "Humans have been fighting the darklings for over seven-hundred years. This is what we're raised to do. It's what we joined the Regiment for."

"We didn't join to get killed," Ryko muttered.

Wolf patted his shoulder the way he would his own son's. "Sometimes the monsters get the better of us. But we still have to try."

"Now we have to dig Aizol's head out of that." Ryko pointed to the grotesque mound of flesh, grimacing as if it hurt to look at.

"We'll get it done," Roaring promised.

It turned out, Aizol had more than just a head left; his neck and part of his torso, his right arm, too—down to the elbow. It was all buried beneath the other corpses; dead demons and animal carcasses mixed together. The blood and goo was thick and reeked of death and evil. Roaring gagged when they finally freed the body, covered in gunk to nearly his shoulders. Ryko took off the cross dangling around his neck and pressed it to Aizol's head, muttering a prayer.

"The Flame never dies, only flickers. God, light his way so he might rise again."

Roaring watched in silence, thinking of his childhood lessons from the village Magi. Before the bodies were burned, they were cleansed so any lingering spirits could be purged. Briefly, he wondered where Aizol really went. If heaven was a place he could actually go. But then the shrubbery shimmied, and his uncle appeared with Chava and the others by his side and his wonderings fizzled away.

"Did you find the beast?" he asked, eyes wide, noting their clean skin, free of bruises and injury.

Kato shook his head. "We picked up a trail about two miles out, but it went cold pretty quickly. This thing either moves faster than we thought or its hunting in a new area now."

"We won't know for sure until we find it or someone else gets eaten," Roaring sighed.

The walk home was silent and sullen, not just because they'd lost Aizol but because they'd found him and that meant they would have to return him to his family now. *Or what's left of him*, Roaring thought bitterly. He felt the muscles in his broad shoulders tense as he marched beside his men, the stench of his comrade's body riding on the gentle breeze. He hadn't been close to Aizol at all, but he'd known him since childhood. Could remember how bad he was at skinning a rabbit and how he'd had an innocent crush on Roaring's younger sister when they were just kids—he also remembered how she'd rejected him, too. That put a smile on his face, a sour, rueful smile.

There would be weeping tonight. When they presented Aizol's remains to the rest of the tribe and the elders and the Regiment Hunters. The Magi would clean and dress his body, whispering prayers of protection over themselves and the villagers. The servants would roast a lamb in honor of his sacrifice, and then they would burn his body until the smoke covered every little hut in the village and the smell of burning flesh was heavy on their clothes. When the smoke cleared, he would be nothing but a black stain in a firepit. And tomorrow they would go out again like none of this had ever happened.

The sunlight dimmed as they neared their home, the Village of Wi. Blocking the view was a giant wall over 40 meters tall and 5 meters thick. It was the village's first line of defense against the monsters that'd killed Roaring's cousin. For hundreds of years the Walls stood guard over the Children of the Sun; Roaring Fire was proud, they'd never had a breach, never had an invasion. They were safe. But he couldn't shake the feeling that his cousin's death was an omen of some sort. A sign that maybe they weren't safe anymore.

2

Fox Fire

I'm stronger than him. Fox clenched her jaw, watching her opponent closely. She stood on one end of the sparring mat, her legs spread apart in a 'ready' position, a dagger sheathed at her hip. On the sidelines, Kifu Kato detailed the rules of their match, but she was not listening. She'd heard the rules plenty of times, having trained twice a day every day for nearly all her life. Her attention was focused on the small boy on the other side of the ring; despite being an inch taller than her, he'd never beaten her before. Still, Fox wouldn't underestimate him. If she could win this match, she would finally earn her blade— something she'd been waiting sixteen years for.

"Fatal blows are minus one point each," Kifu Kato said. "The first to reach zero loses the match. Understood?"

Fox nodded. The boy twenty feet away nodded, too. He

looked nervous, she could tell, but she was nervous, too. Just last night she'd dawned her funeral attire for her own cousin. Had slathered makeup onto her face and ashes on her forehead as she watched his body burn. Now she had to push him from her thoughts so she could focus—but how could she? How could she ever forget the way her cousin looked with only half his body on the pyre?

"Begin!" Kato's voice snatched her back to reality with a jolt.

She took off running, her bare feet slapping the dirt floor. Her opponent met her fiercely and they greeted one another with their fists. She punched him in the jaw, but he recovered quickly and jabbed her hard in the gut. All the air went out of her in a shout of pain and before she knew it, Fox was on the ground looking up at him, his fist hovering over her throat, as if to snap it.

"Good, KI!" Kifu Kato shouted. From the corner of her eye, Fox could see his large frame pacing just a few feet out of reach. He stepped to the side and removed a red feather from the clay vase on display. Red feathers for Fox, brown for KI. That last move had cost her one point—but she still had nine left, and she didn't intend to lose them.

The other students cheered, pounding their fists on the ground where they sat just outside the ring. Fox rolled her eyes; no one ever cheered when she had the lead, then again, it wasn't impressive to beat up an orphan boy—but being able to flatten the *chiefana* of the village was something to brag about.

Focus! she told herself, trying to clear her head. But just as her thoughts vanished, an image of Aizol's face appeared in her mind and she gasped. *They said he'd been eaten.*

With a grunt, Fox slapped KI's fist out of her way and got to her feet. He moved in for an attack; instead of trying to evade, she shifted and knocked him onto the ground. Now it was her turn to take a point from him.

Kifu Kato did not shout in excitement when Fox thrust her elbow down, stopping *just* before making contact with KI's forehead. He only nodded approval and removed a brown feather from the vase.

They continued fighting, prying points away from each other until KI dropped to six points; that was when Kifu Kato shouted, "Weapons!" and they drew their daggers.

The *rahkai* was a curved blade carried by every member of the village's Hunting Regiment. It was used for hacking as well as slicing and was the first weapon every student mastered in their training. Fox Fire had learned to wield the rahkai before she could even braid her own hair.

A question burned in her head as the silver blade whispered against its sheath. *Did Aizol fight back?* She shook away her musings, it didn't matter. He was dead—no, not dead—*eaten*. **They said he'd been eaten**. Because that's what happens when you go beyond the Walls. *Shut up!* she screamed at herself.

Suddenly, KI was before her. With a clang, her rahkai met his as they danced together. The students shouted behind them, mad with excitement as he thrust his blade at her chest. Fox sidestepped and moved in to slice at his arm, but she stumbled and lost her footing—allowing him to claim another point. In her clumsiness, he lunged and jabbed his blade right at her heart while she was off balance.

Fox recovered from the mistake but not before KI managed to take two more points, earning more noise from their onlooking classmates. Fox had to get away from him; though she was stronger, KI was faster, and his speed gave him an advantage in close combat like this.

Swiftly, she shuffled around her enemy, making sure to stay in his blind spot; she could feel Kato's eyes on her, watching and critiquing her every move. The students weren't any help, openly cheering for KI's victory over hers, even though this fight would be her confirmation. Even though it would determine whether she could join the Regiment.

At age sixteen, Fox was the oldest in the class and a chiefana, at that. If she lost to KI, a lowly orphan two years her junior, she would never live this down. The pressure to win threatened to shake her—if the thoughts of her dead cousin weren't enough. This was her final fight; she couldn't simply win, she had to ruin her enemy.

Fox attacked quickly, aiming for a jab at KI's shoulder. He instinctively turned away to protect himself, but she feinted and shoved him hard in the chest instead. He lost his footing, his skinny arms grabbing wildly at the air. Fox rushed him, knocking him to the ground so she could point her rahkai at his exposed throat.

Kifu Kato gave a grunt of approval and adjusted KI's score. "Spears!" he shouted, throwing their ranged weapons into the ring.

Fox glanced down at KI and their eyes met for a heartbeat. Then she dived for her spear, bringing it up just in time to block his attack. Their weapons met with a *clack* that could have shattered bone—if she had been any slower, he would have knocked her unconscious.

She forced him away and got to her feet, keeping her spear

pointed at him. KI wasn't holding back; he knew the spear was her choice weapon—he had to finish her now or else the match was as good as over. A smirk crossed her lips, flattered by his effort.

"This is where you lose," she said.

KI snorted. "Don't talk to yourself that way."

Then he was on her, crossing the floor in rapid speed and slamming his spear against hers. She shuffled backward and blocked him, lashing out to keep him at bay. KI thrived in close combat, but the spear was long-range by nature. With a grunt, she thrust her weapon forward and swiped at the floor; forcing him to back away or get a good smack to the toes. KI stumbled and fell to the ground, instinctively raising his spear to protect himself. With a smirk, Fox smacked his weapon from his hands and pointed her spear in his face—earning a nod of approval from Kifu Kato.

KI gritted his teeth. Fox had three feathers left, the lowest she'd ever had in a match, but it was still more than KI's two points. This was her territory—she wouldn't lose with a spear in her hand. The wooden staff felt like an extension of her arm, the blade like her hand cutting down her enemy. As a young girl, she'd hated the spear; it was strange and awkward and almost taller than her. But her Uncle Kato had shown her it could be deadly.

"You are a small girl, little paws," he would say. "That puts you at a disadvantage in battle. So when you're facing an enemy bigger than you, it's best to keep them at a distance—that's what makes the spear such a beautiful weapon. You can disarm someone without getting close. You can keep your enemy at bay, tire them down, and then move in for the last strike."

14

Fox kept herself focused, watching KI closely as he rolled over and shoved himself to his feet. He wiped the dirt off his cutoff pants and then glanced at his spear just a few feet away. He dived for it, but Fox had predicted that; just before he reached his weapon, her spear crashed down on his hand with a loud *whack!*

She followed up with a swift kick to his ribs and then pointed her weapon in his face. "Surrender."

KI panted, glaring at her as he cradled his injured hand. The crowd around the ring had hushed to little more than a whisper.

"You are unarmed and injured. Surrender."

He waited another moment, as if weighing his options, then he sighed and gave a curt nod, giving Fox her victory.

A slow applause went off through the crowd of students. Moving as one, they stood and bowed, paying their respects to Fox as both the winner and the chiefana—the daughter of the Grand Chief. Kifu Kato stood amongst them, bent at the waist as he bowed before his own niece. Fox couldn't help but blush. She'd watched other students receive their graduating honor many times; had bowed before her elders, wished them good fortune on hunts beyond the Walls, prayed for their safety as members of the Regiment. And now it was her turn.

"Good job, both of you," Kato said. With a wave of his hand, he dismissed the other trainees and stepped into the ring.

Fox gripped her spear so tightly her knuckles turned red. "I won," she said. "That was my final fight. That means I get my blade."

"You only won because you nearly broke my hand," KI grumbled.

"It was a fair move," she shot back.

15

Kifu Kato agreed. "It was a fair move and it got you the win you needed."

"So, I'm getting my blade, right?"

He let out a laugh, but Fox didn't see what was funny. She'd been training under her uncle nearly her entire life, waiting for the day she could earn his approval and receive a weapon to call her own. Nearly everyone in the village went through this training; learning how to fight and master a weapon, preparing for the day the darklings would break through the Walls. Earning her blade was a rite of passage, a cold distinction between the fancies of childhood and the grim realities of adulthood. Fox was ready for it.

But Aizol had been ready, too. Aizol had earned his blade and it hadn't helped him. Hadn't kept him alive beyond the Walls.

Fox swallowed thickly, trying to ignore the fear growing inside. But there was something else mixed with the fear, something darker—dirtier. It was anger. Cold anger that set her hands to trembling and set her heart on revenge. **They said he'd been eaten**—and they hadn't caught the monster. But she could. Now that she'd earned her blade, she could go beyond the Walls and find the demon that'd taken her cousin.

Kifu Kato helped KI to his feet. "Yes, little paws, you're getting your blade."

"A blade of my choice." It wasn't a question. She knew what weapon she wanted, had known for years now. Most trainees had a sword made; a blade forged with fire and beaten until it glowed. Others designed a specialized bow with arrowheads carved from the finest metals. But Fox wanted a spear, one like no other; the staff made of hardwood—strong enough to crush

16

bones, and the sharp end made of animal bones reinforced with metal so it could slice through flesh.

"It will be a blade of your choice," Kato said, moving KI out of the ring to wrap his hand in bandages. "It doesn't look as bad as I thought. Just a dislocated thumb." He popped it back into place before the boy could protest, ignoring his sharp cry of pain. "I'll stop by the blacksmith today and give her your design," he said to his niece.

A smile split her face. "And my knot?"

"And your knot," Kato repeated.

Almost as exciting as getting a personally designed weapon was the moment a trainee received their knot. A thick cluster of an exquisite red thread woven together to form an intricate braid. The knot was distinct in its color and design, only worn by those who'd completed their training. Some had it braided into their hair, others tied it around their wrist as a bracelet, some had the knot untangled and the threads stitched into an article of clothing. Fox had no idea what she would do with hers; she'd thought about attaching charms to it or even tying it around the handle of her spear.

Kifu Kato pulled a knot of red thread from his pocket and held it out to her. "Today you've earned this."

Fox gasped and snatched it from his hands. She pressed it to her nose, inhaling the rosy fragrance of the hand-woven threads. It was said the knot was tied from one-thousand fine strands and then stained red from a bath in waters enriched by crushed roses. Fox could smell the herbal scent; *it's so strange,* she thought, inhaling deeply, *such a delicate smell can only be found on the fiercest men and women in the village.*

"Hold on to that," Kifu Kato instructed.

"I will."

"I mean it, Fox. You have to present that to your family tonight. They're all waiting to hear your results from today's match."

Fox's smile faltered. She had earned her knot but now she would have to present it to her family, a tribe of warriors, hunters, and leaders. Being a chiefana should have given her endless perks but it seemed all she ever faced was a crowd of sharp, scrutinizing eyes.

She closed her fingers around the knot. "I'll present it with pride, Uncle."

He crossed his meaty arms. "*Kifu*, we are still in class, young one."

"Yes, *Kifu*. May we be dismissed?"

He nodded. "Go in peace."

Outside Kifu Kato's classroom, the rest of the village waited. Dirt roads and wooden shacks, barefoot children running naked through the streets. The Village of Wi stood proud behind its high Walls, a settlement hundreds of years old, with hundreds more to go. Large cattle pushed through the roads, their hooves crushing the soft earth, leaving prints in the ground. Bells hung from their necks, ringing a song as they trotted along, their strong backs weighed down with sacks of grain and goods for trade. Merchants lined the roads shouting their sales, pretty-faced women modeled the latest robes and headscarves, tribal paint covering their arms, precious jewels glittering on their fingers.

The sun beat down on Fox as she walked beside her friend. She bumped him with her elbow. "Let's skip the rest of our classes."

KI frowned. "No. I need to focus on taking care of my hand." Then he mumbled, "Thanks to you."

Fox punched his shoulder. "You didn't hold back, either."

"But *I* never would have broken *your* hand."

"A dislocated thumb is not a broken hand."

KI grumbled something under his breath, but Fox ignored him. "You can't train with your hand or write with it, either."

He groaned. "I know where this is going."

"Might as well have lunch outside today!" Fox dangled her knot in front of his face. "Please? I want to celebrate with you."

"We can celebrate *inside* the village," KI said, annoyed. "You know I hate sneaking out."

"*Quiet*," she whispered, glancing around. "Or are you trying to get us caught?"

"I'm trying to get you to understand there are dangerous things outside. Why do you think they built walls around the village?"

"That's a stupid question."

"No, it isn't," KI went on. "But you don't care. You've just *got* to go outside for some crazy reason. Didn't you attend an ignition just last night? Did you notice half of Aizol's body was missing? Demons did that. Demons *outside* did that. That's why they built the Walls, Fox. To keep the darklings out." He brushed past her and trudged down the road, shaking his head in anger.

KI hated sneaking outside, but his anger over it never lasted long. He walked a few steps up the road and stopped, bunched his shoulders as he took a deep breath and then sighed. "I'm going to get something to numb my hand. Then I'll meet you

19

for lunch."

Fox stood alone in the road, watching her best friend leave. She clutched the knot in her hand, holding it against her heart. "No," she whispered. "They didn't build the Walls to keep the darklings out. They built them to keep us in."

3
Talon

The clang of metal resounded through the Red Garden. Talon watched the men spar from her perch atop the garden balcony. She was surrounded by red in every direction; red flowers woven together to form thick floral ropes were draped over the balcony with red paint spattered across the high walls. The flame of the Fire Tribe glowed red against its amber flag, flowing slowly in the gentle breeze. Even the men in the field wore red; the guards standing nearby were draped in red leather and the men sparring seemed bathed in a red hue, their brown skin glowing in the hot morning sun.

Red was the color of the Fire Tribe. Talon had to wear it every day of her life. She exhaled a sigh between red painted lips and rolled her amber eyes. Watching the Hunting Regiment go through their training had been exciting as a young girl, when

21

it was an honor and all the young men had wanted her attention. But now, as an adult, it was a duty—and the men never seemed to notice her hidden in the Grand Chief's shadow.

"He's getting better, isn't he?" an elderly voice asked behind her.

Talon turned to glance back at the Grand Chief seated on a red cushion behind her. "Yes, he is, Mother."

"He looks like he's improving," her mother said, smiling behind her veil.

Talon returned her gaze to the field below, unsure what to say.

"I think he looks great!" exclaimed a voice beside her. Cat Fire, the second chiefana, looped her slender arm through her elder sister's and gave her a wink. She dropped her voice to a whisper. "In more ways than one."

Talon gave her an icy look, hoping their mother hadn't overheard the comment. "Our *brother* has always looked his best with a weapon in his hand."

Cat smirked, whispering, "I wasn't talking about the *chiefono*. I meant his opponent, Ryko."

Talon kept her eyes forward, refusing to acknowledge her sister's teasing. She couldn't, however, ignore the two men trading blows twenty feet below. In the field, on display for everyone in the garden, the chiefono and one of the Regiment Hunters trained fiercely. Two rahkai met with a thunderous clap and in a few maneuvers, the Hunter was flat on his back. The rest of the guards cheered for the chiefono, but Talon's father grunted a command to the trainees, and they straightened immediately.

Talon watched quietly as Ryko and her brother began their

next match. It was strange to think of how sad they'd been the night before, how much weeping she'd heard during the ignition ceremony. Roaring Fire had stood silent, not shedding any tears, not showing any emotion. As proud as a chiefono could be. Ryko hadn't been much different; quiet and sullen. Now they shouted as their blades met, letting their anger and frustration out in their training.

They are men now. This is how they cry, Talon thought. She could remember when they were boys. When they were happy and goofy and always competing. Like when Ryko had asked her to bless his knot with a kiss before he'd braided it into his hair. Filled with jealousy, the chiefono had done the same, swearing he would marry her someday. It had been a cute gesture years ago, but then the boys had grown up; Ryko shaved his head and moved on. He wore his knot tied around his arm now, stretched against his muscles as he blocked and parried her brother's attacks. But the chiefono—the Prince of Fire—had never cut his hair. His knot remained neatly tied into his thick coils, a flash of red whipping by each time he turned his head.

Talon subconsciously reached up to play with the delicate thread looped into the string of her necklace. She had earned her own knot years ago and had turned it into a piece of jewelry, decorated with clay beads, feathers, and precious stones only a Grand Chiefana could wear. Her brother had told her she'd looked beautiful in the necklace.

"Can you believe he still wears that thing?" Cat made a face, motioning to Roaring.

"No," Talon whispered. "I can't."

"You think Fox earned her knot? Her final match was scheduled for today."

23

"If there's a fighter in our family, it's Fox. Or our brother."

Cat leaned over the balcony with a huff. "Who on Earth wants to be good at something you'll never get to do?"

Talon thought a moment. The chiefana trained like everyone else, earned their knots and their right to defend their village in the Regiment. But they weren't allowed to join the military force. Being daughters of the Grand Chief kept them focused on the Flaming Veil—the crown of the Fire Tribe. As the Grand Chiefana, Talon was expected to take her mother's place; fighting demons outside the village was too dangerous a job for her and younger sisters. They needed to be alive and healthy and ready to replace her should something ever prevent her from wearing the Veil.

Sometimes Talon wished one of them *would* replace her; Cat was far more confident in her decisions and Fox was certainly strong enough to handle the job, even at her young age. Talon could barely make it through the day without somehow feeling as if she'd disappointed everyone around her.

Cat nudged her. "You still there?" Her big eyes blinked open and shut, like lights flickering on and off.

"Yes," Talon replied. "Just lost in thought."

"Lost in thoughts about a *special someone*." She wiggled her perfectly arched eyebrows.

"Cat," the Grand Chief interrupted.

Both girls went rigid.

"Yes, Mother?" Cat said.

"Don't you have an engagement soon?"

She placed a hand on her lithe hip. "I forgot you're trying to marry me off."

"Cat," Talon scolded. "It's a date, be happier about it."

24

"It's an *arranged* date—the sixth one in ten days," Cat informed her. "Which means I'm either getting old or getting on everyone's nerves."

"You're being dramatic," Talon said.

"I'm being married off," Cat corrected. She turned on her heel, her flowing dress whirling around her, and marched away. A pair of handmaids scurried behind the princess, trying to keep up.

Silently, Talon returned to watching the match below. The chiefono was still trading blows with Ryko, his hunting hound lazily lounging outside the sparring ring.

"Marriage is what's best for her," the Grand Chief said.

"Of course, Mother," Talon murmured.

"You disagree."

She took a breath. "I think the stability of a marital partner is good for her. But I think she might be more cooperative if she could choose her spouse herself."

"I don't need her cooperation. I need her children—her ability to continue the family line."

"She could continue the family line with someone she actually loved."

Her mother made a noise between a laugh and a grunt. "This is why you are weak. You are far too emotional."

Talon sighed and returned her attention to the fighting below.

4

Fox Fire

Afternoons were always hot in the Village of Wi. Fox Fire tried to ignore the heat as she ran, sweat bubbling the back of her neck. It soaked the collar of her shirt, but she didn't mind, she was already covered in dirt and mud and grass. Silently, she weaved her way through the Square, the most crowded area in the village. She could feel the breeze dancing on her skin, hear merchants shouting trades over the wail of babes and the whinny of horses. She could smell fresh cornbread, hot and sweet as it was baked in clay ovens, and she could see the clouds floating high above the giant Walls which guarded her village. A rush of excitement gripped her as she ran, it wasn't every day the chiefana got to venture beyond the massive structure.

The great Walls of Wi was the village's ultimate defense system. Constructed by the Fire Tribe, the 40-meter Walls stood guard, silently watching for the enemy, daring them to march against one of the greatest tribes in all the region. When she was just a girl, the Five Defenses were drilled into Fox's brain day after day until she could recall them by heart.

In the case of a raid on the village, the First Defense is to lock every Official Gate and secure the outermost Wall.

Should the enemy infiltrate the first Wall, the Second Defense is to escort civilians from the first ring into the second ring.

Should the enemy approach the second Wall, The Third Defense is to deploy the Hunting Regiment for counterattack.

Should the counterattack fail, The Fourth Defense is to escort survivors to the innermost ring and begin emergency evacuations.

Should the attack persist, the Fifth and final Defense is to—

Fox's thoughts vanished as she neared a giant oakwood gate. The Village of Wi was divided into three sections; each Wall had an Official Gate monitored by a platoon of guards. As the daughter of the Grand Chief of Wi, Fox lived in the innermost ring, but she found ways to slip away, often with the help of her clever best friend.

Carefully, Fox scaled the massive beams supporting the oak gate and scanned the crowd flowing through the grand double doors. Hunched backs, limp legs, and tired faces approached the gate. Though they appeared haggard and weary, Fox could see a glimmer of pride twinkling behind every eye. The Village of Wi had a long and violent history, but it was one each villager remembered with dignity. No other village had walls as large or grand or old as Wi. No other village had as many living villagers.

Against all odds, the Children of the Sun survived the terrors of Black Day and the darkness that'd followed: a 750-year struggle with the vile creatures who'd climbed from beneath the earth and nearly destroyed humanity. The Walls of Wi stood as a symbol of hope—a massive reminder of just one of humanity's victories over evil. While other villages had been crushed from raids and attacks in the centuries to come, Wi prevailed, stubbornly and proudly living on to tell their tale.

A smirk claimed Fox's lips when she spied a familiar face in the crowd. With olive skin and strange golden hair, KI was easy to spot in this cinnamon-toned village.

"Took you long enough!" Fox called, gracefully hopping from the wooden support beams.

KI smiled, palmed the back of his neck with his good hand. "Well, you're in better shape."

"Injured hand means you can't run?"

His smile became a grin. "Maybe if I got a proper start like you."

"Is this a bet?"

He laughed. "Isn't it always?"

Fox stepped aside as the gate creaked to life and opened its mouth; a merchant and his carthorse slowly passed by. "Grab something for lunch and meet me by the third ring. Last one there has to pick firewood," she said.

"But—"

"Go!" Fox hopped onto the merchant's cart, laughing loudly as the mare took off in a fretful trot.

She rode the cart through the mass gathered at the gate, watching KI shrink behind her. They'd been having these races for as long as she could remember, charging through the village, gathering supplies for lunch, and meeting outside the Walls for a secret picnic together.

Fox hopped off the cart in front of an old wooden hovel covered in shredded animal skins and reeking of blood. Inside stood a tiny woman bent over with age, her knuckles fat and swollen, her skin tough as leather. She gave Fox a toothless grin and waved her over.

"Been too long, Fire child."

"I've been training, Lady Bolt." She held up her knot. "My final spar was today."

Lady Bolt's smile widened as she went into a string of compliments in the Old Tongue. Fox nodded politely, not understanding a single word—she'd never paid much attention to her lessons.

Bolt limped from behind the counter and pulled Fox into a hug, her grip unbelievably strong for her age. Then she kissed both her cheeks and hobbled back to the counter where she swiftly cut down two dead fish hanging on display above her head. She dashed a handful of salt over them and wrapped them in corn husks, shoved them at Fox.

"Take."

Fox stared at her gnarled hands, twisted from a century of hard work. Lady Bolt ran one of the best meat shops in the entire village; snake, raccoon, armadillo—she even traded rare meats like cow. But with all her success as a butcher, Lady Bolt never earned enough to move into the innermost ring. The Bolt Clan was too small—too insignificant—to take up dwelling with the rest of the old tribes of Wi.

"I'll pay for this," Fox reached for the sack slung over her shoulder, but Lady Bolt refused.

"You earned it, *Chiefana*."

Fox nodded. "Thank you."

* * *

Quietly, Fox trekked through the second ring of the village; enjoying the smells of spices and meat and herbs. This ring was full of traders and merchants and masters of all sorts; a woman who sold incense, a weaver who swore his silks were the finest in Wi, and a cook who could make the best oxtails Fox had ever tasted. The chiefana's favorite ring was the second—the one with all the life and color of Wi, unlike the rigid high-ranking tribes and councilmembers of the innermost ring.

The village changed as Fox walked through the second gate into the outermost ring; going from traders and merchants to thieves and beggars—dirty, hungry children with ragged clothes and matted hair. She ignored them as she walked, hoping none of them asked for her food, hoping none of them recognized her.

Moving swiftly, Fox was halfway to the last gate when she heard KI's voice behind her.

"Wait up!" he shouted, waving a sack over his head, his ponytail dancing in the wind.

Fox grinned at him and took off running toward the Wall. She never took the gate in the outermost wall, you had to have a permit to leave that way. Instead, she wove her way through a patch of woods, running past a cluster of trees, bushes, and a tiny creek. Fox's breath hitched as she raced, listening to KI's quick footsteps right behind her. From the day she'd first met him, a shy boy wrapped in a wolf's pelt, KI had always run behind her, following her wherever she went. She had never seen a living wolf or a fox in person, but she imagined they wouldn't look much different from herself and KI. A small, swift fox and a strong, agile wolf running together through the same woods. *Come, my wolf,* Fox thought, leaping over a boulder, *run with me.*

Fox found her way to the uneven stairs cut into the giant stone wall, taking them two at a time until she made it to the watchtower.

KI clambered up the steps behind her and fell to his knees. "Why do you always run so fast?" he panted. "You'd swear something was chasing you."

"Nothing is chasing me," she smiled, opening the door to the watchtower. "*I'm* chasing something."

The final wall of the Village of Wi greeted Fox outside. It was called *Yamina,* meaning, *three,* and had been constructed during the Great Demon War, back when there were traps, guardsmen, and weapons loaded atop the ledges to prevent any of the dark creatures from getting inside. Centuries later, demon raids subsided, and the Wall's defenses dwindled. Watchtowers were abandoned, guardsmen relocated to the inner-walls, and traps eventually rusted away.

Fox had found her way outside while playing hide and seek some years ago. She'd initially crawled into shrubbery to stay hidden but soon discovered the stone stairs that led to watchtower *Elim*, one of the many abandoned posts on Wall Yamina. After an hour of pleading, and a few fat tears, Fox convinced KI to climb the stairs up the wall, but it took another week of coaxing before she got him to take the stairs down into the woods below.

Fox's face split into a wide smile as she stepped toward the edge of the wall. The wind seemed stronger atop Yamina, like needles stabbing her cheeks with every gust. Still, the chiefana was happiest whenever she stood there, overlooking the rest of the world.

"Don't get so close to the edge," KI warned, wary as always.

Fox ignored him and tiptoed to the very edge until each of her toes peered over. "I'm on the edge of the world!" she screamed, thrusting her arms into the air—on top of Yamina, she might as well have been. Fox had never been far beyond her village Walls, but she could see what was out there from her stance. Lakes, wild animals, even the ruins of small settlements in the distance. She could see it, but she couldn't get there.

"One day," she promised.

"Fox," KI stood firmly beside the watchtower's doors—he never looked over the edge. "Come away from the edge," he told her. "Let's go now."

Reluctantly, Fox backed away and ran down the stairs, her bare feet leaving warm footprints on the cold stone. The two never ventured far from Yamina; demons weren't the only creatures lurking outside the Walls. There were also bears, wild boar, and even wolves, but it was other travelers the villagers of Wi feared most. Not many people ever left Wi but even fewer went *inside*.

Never trust the ones beyond Yamina, Fox had been taught

32

since childhood. She remembered the warnings of the Magi and the stories of the elders. How darklings could wear a person's skin, how they could use their flesh to sneak into villages and destroy them from the inside-out. That's why travelers were rare in Wi. Merchants were allowed inside with passes; they wore ashes on their foreheads and crucifixes around their necks to keep the evil at bay. Even then, guards checked them and doused them with holy water to make sure they were cleansed. Outsiders were dangerous in a world without trust.

But Fox had KI. He was the only one in Wi who came from the outside, the only one who hadn't been born within the Walls, the only one who could tell her about the world beyond. Except he couldn't remember a thing about his life before coming to Wi.

"It's like I woke up here one day," he used to tell her when she would ask about his past. "I'm sorry, Fox. I can't remember a thing."

At first, she thought he'd been lying but when even the village Magi couldn't trigger KI's memory, she gave up hope. No one knew if the boy would ever remember his past, but Fox didn't need his memories to be fascinated by him.

Everything about KI was different. He only went by his initials, never sharing his real name with anyone but Fox. He didn't enjoy the spicy foods of Wi, preferring dishes better suited for a gentler palette. And he looked nothing like the men and women of Wi, with his burning hazel eyes and perfectly smooth olive skin—the total opposite of the nut-brown villagers. Even his hair was unique; KI didn't have Fox's dark curls, instead he'd been born with straight golden locks—except for his eyebrows which were a deep shade of black. Fox always joked he was two different people sharing one body.

"You're collecting firewood again," she announced, eyeing his golden hair. She settled into the grass beside a small pond. KI groaned but didn't protest, he was used to gathering the wood.

"I got two fish this time; Lady Bolt was generous."

"That's nothing. I got a full batch of honey biscuits. Do you know how hard it is to get *a full batch* of biscuits in the second ring?"

He passed her his bag and smiled as she hungrily dug inside, the sweet smell of honey-butter saturated the air.

"What did you trade for this?" Fox held a biscuit to her nose and inhaled, rolling her eyes to the back of her head. As a chiefana, she could eat as many honey biscuits as she wanted in the innermost ring, but they seemed much sweeter and much flakier out here beyond the Walls.

"I'll have to give a portion of Kato's hunting rations to the baker for two weeks." KI laughed.

"My uncle is going to skin you alive." Fox split the biscuit in half and offered him some; he took it but didn't eat. "He won't really skin you alive," she muttered softly.

"I know."

Fox stared at the grass, trying to think of something to say. As much as she loved Kato for taking in KI all those years ago, she'd always wished someone else had adopted him. Someone who wasn't so short tempered. Wasn't so unkind. But no one had stepped up when KI appeared outside the Walls, bloody and naked and screaming mad. The elders had all but voted to send the boy back to where he'd come from when Kato spoke up, promising to take care of him and turn him into a man of

Fire. He'd been met with applause to his face but scowls to his back. He'd taken in the outsider, the foreigner, the one who didn't belong. And he'd been shamed for it ever since.

At first, Fox hadn't noticed the way he'd treated KI, how he would correct anyone who had called him his son. How he would keep his distance whenever they were home or at functions or ceremonies. It was when she'd found out KI wasn't allowed to take his meals at the same table as his adoptive father that she'd realized what'd been going on. KI had never eaten at her table, she was a member of the Head Family, and he was just an orphan, after all. But she'd thought he could at least share a meal with the man who'd taken him in. She had been wrong.

Outside of training, Kato wasn't her loving uncle; he was a Hunter of the Regiment—a hard man with tough skin and a horrible frown. He'd never hurt KI, but he'd never treated him well, either. And now KI had gone and promised his hunt to the baker for the next two weeks; Kato wouldn't punish him for it, not physically. But whatever he did do would be Fox's fault. KI hadn't wanted to come, hadn't wanted to go for lunch at all—let alone outside the Walls. But she was a chiefana and he was her personal guard. He would go any time she asked because that was his duty. But KI was more than a guard, he was Fox's only friend. And he hadn't just gone beyond the Walls out of loyalty, he'd gone for *her*. Had found honey biscuits for *her* that'd been sweet on her tongue but now tasted like poison. Fox swallowed slowly, her throat burning for water.

KI stood, wiped dirt from his pants. "I'm going ahead to collect the firewood."

"I'll help you," Fox said, hoping this would be enough of an

35

apology. "There's a patch of oaks not far from here."

* * *

A half-mile hike through the dark green trees brought them to a small burst of oaks tucked into the center of the forest. They'd walked in a stiff silence; KI trudging ahead with Fox following behind, ignoring the way he seemed to avoid her now. She'd thought about apologizing for dragging him out here and causing him trouble, but her pride got in the way. He'd known what he was getting himself into when he'd made that deal with the baker. *However Kato punishes him, it won't be my fault.* That's what she told herself and it managed to keep the guilt away—for a time.

"I guess I'll chop." KI pulled a rahkai from his tunic and Fox watched as he took a wild swing at the limbs of the tree. The branches shook violently, their leaves gently falling to the ground, but the rahkai did little more than graze the tough bark.

"KI," she said sympathetically, "hand me the blade."

He grunted, taking another swing. "I got this. I always chop the wood."

"And I'm always happy you do. But today you're one-handed, and I promised I would help, so pass me the blade."

He passed it to her and walked away.

"Maybe I should have a fancy rahkai designed for myself—instead of a spear." She tried starting a conversation.

KI leaned against the tree; half his face hidden in the shade. He didn't look at her as he said, "It's not like you'll be able to carry either one."

"I'm still happy to get a weapon of my own, whether I get to

36

use it or not."

Though she'd earned her knot, she wouldn't get to carry her weapon—or any weapon at all. Tradition prevented chiefana from handling blades outside of training. It was her duty to lead through diplomacy, not brute strength—that was the job of the Hunting Regiment.

What she wouldn't give to trade places with KI. It wasn't like she needed a personal guard anyway; he'd never even beaten her in training.

"I was thinking of asking the elders to allow me to join the Regiment. I'm a chiefana but I'm last in line—they don't really *need* me."

"They won't let you join," he said flatly, his face like stone—the half she could see. "You'll have to keep your spear in your room. On display or something."

"Or maybe I could sneak it out here. We could hunt for demons on our own."

"No. We can't."

She grunted, hacking at the branches with all her might. "You're my Shield, KI. Not my mother."

"Yeah, well, going hunting for demons makes it difficult to protect you."

"I'll only be hunting for one demon. One that looks like a bear."

He pushed off the tree and stepped into the light; now she could see the hard frown on his face, the irritation creasing his forehead. Everything about the goofy boy from before was hidden behind his anger. "You shouldn't go looking for trouble. You shouldn't break the rules on purpose."

"I'm not looking for *trouble*. I'm looking for a way to protect the people I love." She waved her hands around, at the woods, at the trees, at the outdoors. "Don't you want to see this every day? Aren't you tired of the Walls? We can't go out because of darklings—Aizol *died* because of darklings."

He heaved a sigh. "The Walls protect us, Fox Fire. Aizol didn't just die from darklings, he died because he was *outside*. And besides ... demons aren't the only monsters in this world."

She wanted to yell at him, scream at him for not caring more about Aizol, but when she looked at him, she couldn't summon the anger. KI wasn't frowning anymore, wasn't in a bad mood anymore. He was staring at the ground, his eyes full of a sadness she couldn't describe, and she knew the other monsters he was talking about had nothing to do with demons or Kato or the Walls at all.

Though he could not recall any details of the village he'd come from or the events that'd brought him to the gates of Wi, KI did have one gruesome memory of his life before: the murder of his parents. He'd told the story to the men who'd found him, how a tall man with a calm face had killed his father and mother, but no one had believed him. *People don't kill people*, Kifu Kato had said, *darklings kill people*. KI's story had been dismissed as the fearful ramblings of a lost child, but he'd never let go of his tale.

Silence replaced their argument. Fox studied the rahkai in her hand, the way the blade curved so smoothly and sharply. She pressed the tip into her finger, felt the prick of the metal and watched a red dot form on her skin. Fresh blood: she wondered what color darklings bled.

"I know people have been as cruel to you as demons have." An image of her uncle flashed in her head; she hated herself as much as him right now. "I'm sorry for that. And I'm sorry I dragged you out here again. I knew you didn't want to go but I wanted to celebrate—and I wanted to see if maybe we could find out something about the demon that killed my cousin."

KI sighed, every muscle in his body relaxing. He was small for his age, barely taller than Fox, but he was fit; nice and lean from all his training. Other girls in their lessons never spoke to him outside of class, he was the *outsider*, but Fox saw them staring when he wasn't looking, saw them glancing over their shoulders when he walked by. She tried not to stare when he sagged against the tree again and smiled at her.

"Don't apologize, Foxy. And ... don't think I hate people."

"Don't you?"

He shook his head and his golden ponytail moved with the motion. "I used to. Because of what happened to my parents and because of how hard it was to fit in at first. But you changed my mind. You were always kind to me; that's why I became your Shield when Kato asked me." He shrugged one shoulder. "I don't know. What I feel isn't hatred anymore; it's more like, I don't trust people. For hundreds of years this village has lived behind its Walls. The only evil you know are the demons outside. But I remember how cruel humans were to me when I first came here, and I remember the human who killed my parents. I've learned that demons aren't the only evil in this world."

Fox searched her mind for words. This afternoon wasn't supposed to go this way. She wasn't supposed to feel this terrible, and KI wasn't supposed to be staring at the ground, fighting to hold in the anger and the hatred he'd supposedly quelled over the years.

39

She opened her mouth to apologize again; to tell him to forget the firewood and the fish and just go home, but when she looked at him something over his shoulder caught her attention.

"What's wrong?" KI reached out to her. Fox grabbed his arm and jerked him toward her.

There wasn't much time for either person to react; a blur of darkness whooshed by and then a horrifying roar resounded through the forest. Fox shoved KI to the ground but not fast enough; she could hear his tunic ripping as the monster took a slash at her friend. It tore through his clothes and destroyed the tree beside him, shredding a giant oak into nothing but shards of flying bark and loose leaves. Fox inhaled very slowly, sweat prickling her forehead as she stared at the roaring creature in front of her.

A demon.

It stood well over eight feet tall with claws almost a foot in length and teeth sharp enough to pierce flesh down to the bone. Pitch black eyes stared at her as the monster growled a low rumbling noise that nearly shook the earth beneath her feet, but she didn't let it shake her. She glanced down at KI, knocked unconscious by the attack. He couldn't help her in this state, and no one would be coming to her aid; but she didn't need help.

They said he'd been eaten—by a monster that looked like a bear. *This* was the creature she'd heard about the night before. *This* was the devil that'd taken her cousin and injured her best friend. She wouldn't let it have her.

Fox lunged at the monster with her rahkai in hand; blinding anger blocking all sense and fear. Her blade met its razor claws but just as quick, she pulled away to throw it at the beast, smiling when it sank into the center of its face. The demon stumbled backwards, shrieking and spraying Fox with its gushing blood.

For half a second, Fox hesitated. Her and KI had taken years of combat in their courses together, but they'd never met such a beast as this. *This is real*, Fox glanced at KI again, limp and bleeding, *and it's nothing like we've learned.*

The monster struck the air in a panicked frenzy and clumsily stumbled backwards with the rahkai jutting out of its head. Fox darted forward, tackling it to the ground. A flurry of claws and blood and cries of rage rang through the trees. Fox grabbed hold of the rahkai plunged into its skull and yanked hard, earning another howl from the monster. A scream escaped her as she returned the blade to its skull, burying it in its flesh over and over until it stopped moving.

"I killed it," she breathed, staring at the demon's body.

A puff of black vapor expelled from the corpse, scaring her so badly she backpedaled away, kicking and crawling in the dirt.

The village Magi had taught her plenty of things about darklings; if you killed one, you had to burn it to get rid of any lingering evil. Some demons were so horrid their ashes were locked in an unholy shrine. But no one mentioned black vapors and hot air rising from demon carcasses.

A slight breeze shook the trees and Fox covered her face as the hot vapor licked at her skin. She gasped at what was left behind once the stirring wind had settled. It wasn't a demon or its corpse; it was a bear. A plain brown bear with normal claws and normal teeth lay dead beside her, the gap cratered in its head the only proof it was the same monster she'd just slain.

Fox leaned closer, noticing the wounds peppering its body. It was old and hurt, crusted blood on its fur and deep gashes all over. And it stank. Like death. If it hadn't been for the demon inside, the bear would've died long ago. It must have tried to fight it off when it'd first encountered the darkling. But it'd lost the fight and then lost its own body—mindlessly wandering through the forest in an uncontrollable bloodlust. A bloodlust that'd killed her cousin and had nearly killed her best friend.

Fox gasped and scrambled to her feet. "KI!" she screamed, running to his side. He did not respond. Blood gushed from the wounds on his side, his flesh shredded where the demon had struck him with its abnormally large claws.

Fox stooped and grabbed him beneath both arms; she managed to drag him back to Yamina; his wounds left a trail of blood through the woods, a wicked streak of red that stained every stair she climbed. Fox heaved for air as she pulled his body, praying that he would somehow live through this. It helped that he was unconscious, she couldn't fathom dragging him while he wept and panicked.

It'd been nine years since KI was discovered on the dark side of Yamina, but Fox still remembered the day her father introduced them. Covered in fresh wounds, his cries had filled the empty night like a haunting song. Fox had never heard such a terrible sound before. KI had been wrapped in a wolf's pelt so large it looked like the animal was still trying to eat him, even from the dead. Fox stared at him in shock, wondering how a child wearing a mighty wolf's pelt could be sobbing so hard. *You wear the skin of a beast, yet you cry like a child*, she'd thought, watching him weep. But then her father mused her curly hair and said, "Be kind to him, little paws, he has seen what lurks beyond Yamina. You can't blame him for his tears."

For nearly a decade, Fox had wondered what on earth beyond Yamina could make a boy dressed in the garb of a warrior appear so pathetic. It wasn't until she held KI in her arms, his body limp and clinging to life, that she realized exactly what could reduce a person to such a state.

Her best friend was right; demons weren't the only evil in the world. *But they're the worst of them all,* she told herself, grinding her teeth as she climbed the stairs of Yamina. *They are the monsters from the tales of our elders and the nightmares we dream of at night. They are evil.*

But I killed one. And I'll do it again.

5

Talon

Red drapes flowed from the ceiling to brush against the floor, matching the amber cushions placed neatly around small firepits. Talon stood on the dais as she watched servants put the Chief's Hall together. As the Grand Chiefana, it was her duty to make preparations for dinner. Talon enjoyed her job; the meal, the decorations—every little detail was left under her control. She could not compete with her brother or her baby sister in combat, or with Cat in social gatherings. She even struggled to impress her mother with her morals and politics, but *this* she could handle.

A proud smile crossed her face as she watched the Hall transform. Strong men from the Regiment rearranged the heads of bucks, bears, and wolves on the giant oak walls. They were spoils from their trips beyond the Walls, something

Talon's father and brother couldn't go a day without bragging about. Heavy furs carpeted the floor, leafy green plants sprouted between the seating arrangements, red flower petals were sprinkled throughout the grand Hall. Talon had done her job well, but she couldn't shake the unease winding up her spine.

"Something isn't right," she muttered, eyeing the young maid placing logs into a firepit.

"I think it looks lovely," Ryko said.

Talon turned to him, surprised by his presence. "You finished your training."

He straightened. "I got him in the last round."

Talon almost couldn't hide her smile. In all their years of training together, Ryko had only flattened the chiefono once. "And you rushed here to brag?" she asked, directing a group of servants carrying a bouquet of red flowers.

"I rushed here because I'm your personal guard."

She nodded. Ryko had been her Shield since childhood; the only time he left her side was for training or sleeping or bathing. "And what of my brother?" she asked.

"The chiefono returned to the Regiment headquarters."

"Of course."

Ryko lingered, hovering too close. She took a casual step to the side and preoccupied herself with the fluffy cushions on the dais—seats suitable for the Head Family. A pair of men shuffled into the Hall balancing a giant cauldron between them; Ryko raised his eyebrow.

"What's on the menu for the last meal?"

Dinner was always grand in Wi; most families in the outer rings ate in the privacy of their home with their own kin, but the Fire Tribe enjoyed their evening meal with dozens of guests. Councilmembers, smaller clan leaders, and head families of sister-tribes dined with the leaders of the village. Talon always aimed to make it an event.

She flashed Ryko a big smile. "We're having *potsu*."

His eyes widened. "In the middle of summer?"

"A little bird told me Fox Fire fought for her knot today."

Understanding relaxed his features. "She'll have to present it tonight."

"And I want that moment to be special for her. Besides, we could all use some cheering up after last night."

Ryko chewed his lip. "We'll be taking a team out tomorrow to track the monster. We'll find it and kill it. I swear, chiefana."

She gave him a small smile. "I know you will. I guess this is my way of offering comfort to those who are still mourning."

"But," he sighed, "*potsu?*"

She smiled again. Potsu was a traditional dish in the Region of Smoke and Ash; a soup deconstructed into various components—vegetables, meats, starches, and even seasoning—and prepared by its hungry consumers over an open fire. It was best served in colder weather but in the Village of Wi the sun always burned hot and bright.

Talon patted Ryko's shoulder. "You'll only have to endure the heat for one night."

"You're making a dozen cauldrons of potsu in one room."

"It'll be worth it once you're scooping out a bowl."

He couldn't argue against that. Potsu was laborious but fulfilling—and it would certainly impress the Grand Chief. To make this sort of arrangement at such short notice was worth something ... it had to be.

46

Talon turned to Ryko. "Do you know if my brother is preparing anything special for tonight?"

Ryko smiled, making her heart sink. If the Regiment was going to put on a show, then she'd already been outdone. "I've got strict orders to keep my mouth shut."

"No need to say anything anyway," she sighed. "Whatever you guys are doing, a pot of soup won't be enough to compete."

"Don't think of it that way, chiefana. We're trying to lift everyone's spirits—just like you. You know we aren't competing."

"I know. But I'll still be measured against my brother."

Ryko did not respond.

"You should go."

"Chiefana," he gave her a wounded look, "I'm your guard. You know I can't leave you."

"Then come with me, because I need a break from all this."

"Where are we going?"

She grinned, holding up her long dress as she hopped down from the dais. "To visit my little sister. I want to hear all about her date this morning."

Talon guided Ryko through the open gardens, past the hunting hounds training with the Regiment and through the Chief's Way. She went uphill on the trail she'd taken since childhood, ducking under low hanging trees, and stepping over clusters of flowers and bushes heavy with fresh, dark berries. She walked with Ryko right behind her, just as she'd done as a girl, when she was just a kid and he was just her friend. Now she was the Grand Chiefana and he was her Shield.

Ryko stopped to pick a handful of berries and passed them to her with a shy smile.

"You've got to be the kindest Hunter on the Regiment." Talon laughed through a mouthful of raspberries.

Ryko hesitated. "You are the one who is kind. You've always been good to me."

"You are deserving of kindness, Ryko," Talon said carefully. She knew where this was going but hoped she could steer the conversation away. This wouldn't be the first time Ryko had gotten too familiar with her. When she'd been a child this had all been nothing more than a crush, but she was a woman now and somehow that simple crush had become love. A very one-sided love.

"Chiefana," Ryko said, taking a step forward.

Talon turned away. She couldn't do this, not now. Not when she could still remember the pain of rejection from long ago—when she'd heard the rumors of Ryko and another and then saw how he'd shaved his head and removed the knot she'd tied into his locks. And all at once the new woman was gone and Ryko's gaze had landed on her again. But it was too late now. She had finally found peace. Had finally garnered the strength to move on.

His hand was on her arm, sliding down to her wrist, trying to grasp her hand the way he used to. "Talon," he said softly.

She looked up at him, at the gentle curls on his head—just a few inches of new growth—and she thought of the chiefono and how his hair brushed his shoulders. How his knot had never left his head. How he'd never left her.

"Ryko, this is not the time," Talon said, her voice shaky.

He held her hand, intertwining his fingers with hers. "I've been wanting to talk to you for a while now."

"Can't it wait?" said a voice from behind.

Talon turned to find her little sister waiting on the trail, arms crossed over her chest, a stupid grin on her face, like she knew exactly what she'd interrupted.

Ryko jerked away. "I—I apolo—"

"No need to apologize." Cat waved him off. "We all know you're sorry. *What for* is the question."

Ryko held his tongue.

"I was just coming to see you," Talon said.

Cat frowned. "I was at the temple, praying to God for forgiveness. I've clearly done something horrible and now I'm being punished for it."

"Was the date that bad?"

Cat looped her arm through her sister's. "I'm dying to tell you all about it." She turned to Ryko. "Leave us."

Ryko glanced at Talon. "Chiefana—"

"A chiefana has just spoken to you," Cat snapped. "Leave."

With an obedient nod, Ryko turned and left.

"Do you have to be so harsh?" Talon asked.

Cat sighed, slowly walking the Chief's Way. "He's the hound master's son, he doesn't even belong in this ring."

"He is a loyal Shield. He's been living in the innermost ring since he was a kid—he grew up with us. Don't you remember?"

"I remember never liking him. Especially after he dumped you."

Talon winced.

"I'm sorry," her sister said, patting her arm. "You should be happy about it, really. Mother would never allow you to marry him anyway. She wouldn't let me marry my Shield."

"That's because you got *caught* with your Shield," Talon said, thinking of all the drama that'd stirred when their mother

49

realized Cat's virtue had been broken.

Cat snorted. "And she's been trying to marry me off ever since."

"Maybe marriage would do you some good."

Another snort. "After today's date, I'm thinking of joining the temple and becoming a Magus. The only love they speak of is that of Christ. His sort is much less complicated."

"You are not meant for temple life."

Cat nodded. "I couldn't agree more. *You're* the pious one of the bunch."

Talon pinched her.

They spent the afternoon walking the Chief's Way and going over every detail of Cat's date. It had been dreadfully hot out, but Talon endured it, even though the heat made her hair shrink into an afro. When she arrived at her room to get dressed for dinner, her handmaid nearly fainted. Now she sat on a cushion while the girl fought her unruly mop of curls into a ribbon.

"I told him I don't care for flowers—all they do is stink," Cat was saying. She'd come for tea and more gossip about her terrible love life. Tea before dinner had been their ritual since childhood, back when the gossip was juicy, and the tea was always sweet. But now her sister was being married off—the gossip wasn't funny anymore and the peppermint tea left a sour taste in her mouth.

"So instead of bringing me flowers, this idiot caught half a dozen butterflies to give me. Except they died overnight so he left their dead, little bodies in the sun to bake and brought me their dried wings." Cat made a disgusted face. "Artists are the worst sort of men."

Talon tried her best to stay interested in Cat's story, but the heat left her agitated and dehydrated and her handmaid, Mohpa, was doing a terrible job with her hair. She was adorned in a long-sleeved, beaded *kataa* that flowed to the floor, covering her soft rabbit-skin slippers. The jewels on the bodice of her dress matched the pin Mohpa picked for her hair. A shock of feathers jutted from her neckline so large and gaudy it looked like she had a mane, and her hair was so tightly coiled you would never guess it could stretch to her waistline.

"How do you like it, chiefana?" Mohpa stepped back and offered the princess a polished mirror. She heard her sister snort before she looked.

Red. Talon saw nothing but the color red—on her lips, on the jewels of her bodice, the beading of her dress, the feathers about her neck, the pin in her hair and even the jewel that hung from it. She knew it was an honor to wear the colors of her tribe, but when she had on so much, it reminded her of blood.

Talon nodded and stiffly passed the mirror back. "I think you did a lovely job, Mohpa."

Cat cackled. "I think you look like a bleeding chicken."

"No one asked what you think, Cat. Mohpa, it is lovely. Now, please go and grab Fox Fire for dinner, I'd like all of us to arrive together."

Cat rolled her eyes, waited until Mohpa had gone before saying, "I'm the only one who tells you the truth around here."

"That is why I love you so much."

"And why you hate me."

Talon surrendered a smirk. "I do look like a chicken, don't I?"

"You've got to stop letting Mohpa pick out your clothes."

"I don't mind the clothes as much as I mind what she does with my hair."

Cat stood and removed the pin from Talon's afro. Talon had always adored her little sister. Cat had been the easy sibling; talkative and lively while their older brother was proud and too daring for his own good, and their youngest sister was wild and unruly. It was Cat who always took extra berries from the table and shared them later with Talon. It was Cat who convinced Talon to let Ryko kiss her in the open gardens when she was thirteen. And Cat who promised not to tell when Talon let Ryko touch her on her sixteenth birthday.

Cat had never been especially smart or wise; she didn't learn the Old Tongue and she couldn't recite many of the scriptures the girls learned in their teachings. She refused to take physical training after she sprained her ankle at age seven and hated learning how to fish or hunt. But she could cook all of Talon's favorite dishes, mend any garment, and she knew her way around men. Despite being the older sister, Talon often felt childlike whenever Cat turned her nightmarish gowns into something beautiful or her wrecked hair into something soft and silky.

Cat held up the mirror. "Looks good, doesn't it?"

Talon smiled at the elaborately twisted bun decorating her head now. "It looks amazing."

"All eyes will be on you during dinner."

Talon opened her mouth to reply but she was silenced by Mohpa calling from the hall. "My lady, may I enter?"

"Of course," Talon said.

"Chiefana, I'm terribly sorry to say this, but there's been

52

word about your youngest sister."

Talon sighed. "What is Fox up to now?"

"Well ... She isn't in her room. She's being held at the infirmary."

"What happened?"

"There was an attack by a bear—"

"Is she hurt?"

"I wasn't able to see her."

Talon rose, the beads of her dress clanking against one another with every movement. "I'll go see about this." She turned to Cat. "You'll have to host dinner tonight."

Cat wrinkled her small, round nose. "I hate hosting dinner. That's supposed to be your job."

"My job is keeping this news from reaching our parents—" she turned back to Mohpa, "this hasn't been reported to them, correct?"

Mohpa shook her head vigorously. "No. I came directly to you as soon as I found out."

"Good. Be sure that no one else hears this news. Inform my good parents Fox Fire and I will be late for dinner tonight. I'll catch up with both of you later."

Talon walked as briskly as she could in her floor-sweeping kataa, careful not to step on any of the beads. Servants and guards stepped aside, nodding hello as she passed. There were a number of perks to being the daughter of the Grand Chief but Talon enjoyed none of them. As the eldest daughter in a matriarchal village, her nobility was a *responsibility*—for her sisters it was a privilege. Only Talon had to master reading, writing, and praying in the Old and New Tongue. Only Talon was required to maintain the image of perfection—not her sisters nor her older brother. Her life was controlled by her birthright and cursed by her irresponsible siblings.

Fox, she thought, crossing the open gardens with Ryko trotting close behind, *what have you done now?*

Two guards stood outside the infirmary clad in armor and armed with a rahkai and a shield. They nodded at Talon when she approached and parted without words. Fox was held in one of the back rooms, away from the rest of the patients. Talon tried her best not to wonder why as she passed each room one by one, the sickly-sweet smell of blood and death filling her nose.

"Good evening, chiefana," greeted the Magus outside Fox's room. She was a small woman dressed in all white with her head veiled and her nose and mouth covered by a large white cloth. A small part of Talon envied the Magus's attire, that cloth over her nose kept out the horrible smell of illness.

"Good evening." The princess politely inclined her head. "I came to see my little sister and her Shield."

Though Talon could not see the look on the Magus's face, she could sense the change in her demeanor. The small woman cleared her throat and tugged at the tight collar of her white cloak. "My lady, Fox Fire and KI have been quarantined—"

"I did not ask you about quarantine, Magus...?"

"Magus Illenna."

"Magus *Illenna*, please allow me to see my sister and her guard now. I'd like to have this incident cleaned up before nightfall."

Magus Illenna nodded and stepped aside. "As you wish, Grand Chiefana."

Inside, the room was plain and incredibly bare; there were four brown walls with a black curtain pulled to cut the room in half. Fox sat on a stuffed cushion, stringing beads together, while a guard stood silent in the corner by the curtain. Talon could hear the chatter of half a dozen Magi on the other side of the curtain, but her attention rested on her sister first.

"Fox Fire," Talon said. "What's been going on?"

Fox dropped the beads to the floor at her sister's voice. "Talon! Talon, they won't let me see him." Though the room was dimly lit, the eldest princess could see the tears forming in her little sister's eyes as she wrapped her small arms around her waist.

Talon patted Fox on the head. "Calm down, little paws. Tell me what happened."

"I came to the guards for help—KI was in *trouble*—and all they did was lock me up here. They won't let me see him." She gave the guard beside the curtain a foul look. "Not even when I *commanded* them to."

"Chiefana—" the guard tried to explain but Talon interrupted.

"How serious are KI's injuries?"

He responded by bunching his shoulders and staring open-mouthed at Magus Illenna who stood silently in the doorway. "Magus?" Talon turned toward the woman.

"Well, his wounds have been treated."

"Then why won't you let my sister see him?"

Magus Illenna swallowed. "That is a complicated question."

"It's honestly a very simple one."

"If we could discuss this without so many ears around us—"

"If you won't tell me, I'll just go see for myself." Talon pushed

55

Fox aside and marched over to the curtain, ignoring the protests of Magus Illenna and the guard as she shoved the curtain aside.

A small crowd of Magi stood hunched over a table in the middle of the floor; elbow to elbow they were packed into the room staring intently at the body sprawled before them. Talon stood on her tiptoes to peer over them and gasped at what she saw.

A small boy lay unconscious on his backside with purple bruises staining his skin from neck to groin. His veins were thick and filled with black liquid, forming a twisted dark web over his skin, as if a net of ink had been cast over him. Talon's hand covered her mouth but not before a fearful cry filled the air. It wasn't until she'd turned to see Fox Fire standing beside her that she realized the cry hadn't come from herself.

Talon grabbed her sister by the shoulders and shoved her behind the curtain. "Keep her away!" she shouted as the guard rushed to grab the struggling little girl.

"What's wrong with him!?" Fox shouted. "Let me *see*!"

Talon watched them struggle, chewing her lip as she tried to think of what to do next.

"Grand Chiefana." Magus Illenna stepped behind the curtain, meekly inclining her head. "Please let me explain the situation."

"Tell me what on Earth I'm looking at." Talon motioned to the body splayed on the table. "It shouldn't take a dozen Magi to realize the injuries on this boy's body are obviously not the result of a bear attack."

One of the Magi shoved his way through the crowd and removed the cloth from his nose and mouth. "Chiefana, we found evidence that supports the story Fox told us about the bear." He pointed to the injury on KI's side; three gaping slashes starting at his navel and crawling around his waist to his back. "The wounds are deep but not serious. But there is no evidence the bear who attacked KI could have caused the ... the blackness in his veins."

Large amber eyes gaped at the orphan's body, taking in the thick, inky veins, the bloody welts on his side, and the blanket of sweat that veiled his unconscious body. *If he were awake right now*, she thought, *he wouldn't be lying here so peacefully.* "This is not the result of a bear attack." Talon turned on her heel and thrust the curtain back to find her sister restrained by two guards. "Leave her," she instructed.

Fox gave them a sour look before turning to her sister. "What's going on?"

"You know *exactly* what's going on!" Talon spat. "You weren't attacked by a bear at all, were you?"

Fox's shoulders slumped in defeat. "It—it was inside a bear."

"*Inside.*"

"Once I killed it, the real monster came out."

"And where did this monster go?"

"Back into the woods."

Talon blinked, sucking in a sharp breath of air. "Where were you and KI attacked?"

"Talon—"

"Just tell me!" she shouted, panic cracking in her voice. She grabbed her small sister by the shoulders and gave her a shake. "Don't lie to me, not now!"

Fox lowered her gaze to the floor, her mouth pressed into a tight line. "About one mile beyond Yamina."

A high shriek escaped Magus Illenna at Fox's words, even the herd of Magi behind Talon hushed their anxious squabbling. "Ryko," Talon said to her Shield. "Please go and find my older brother. Right away."

A thick silence settled in the room, only lifting when Talon cleared her throat and demanded of her sister, "Tell me what happened. From beginning to end."

All eyes were on the young princess as she tried to explain what'd really happened outside the village Walls, stuttering and stumbling over her words. "It was just outside the Wall, Talon. Not far at all. We went to look for firewood and the monster attacked us—"

Fox's words became muffled in Talon's ears. Suddenly the room felt far too small and the smell of sickness much too strong. Talon could feel her peppermint tea clawing its way back up her throat as the floor spun beneath her feet. She swallowed thickly, wiping the nervous sweat from her forehead as she tried to focus on what was happening around her. Ryko had returned with a dozen more men, they tried to take KI's body, but the Magi refused. A fight broke out just over the princess's shoulder but all she could hear was a ringing in her ears.

"Talon! *Talon!*" a familiar voice called her name, but she could not respond until she felt strong arms gripping her. "Look at me!"

The face of the voice slowly morphed from a tall brown blur into the striking figure that was Talon's older brother: Roaring Fire. "Brother," she whispered weakly.

He touched her cheek and surprised her when he pulled away a wet hand. "What's made my sweet sister cry?"

"Fox Fire," she said, and the name shook her back to reality. With a gasp, she exhaled the story, feeling faint all over again by the time she reached the end. One look at Roaring's face and she knew he understood the severity of the situation.

Smooth brown skin with a mane of chocolate coils and eyes that always seemed much too serious, Roaring Fire was the thunderous oldest child of the Fire Tribe's Head Family and one of the well-esteemed leaders of the Hunting Regiment. But even he could not keep a straight face when presented with the news of KI's injuries.

He turned to Fox Fire who'd been cowering in a corner, his dark cloak twirling behind him. "You went beyond the Walls?"

She swallowed, buckling under the heat of her brother's gaze. It was a look that could stop the rain but here it only caused a nervous girl to bite her tongue and refuse to speak.

Roaring had no time for games. He turned to the quarreling guards and Magi, his voice a loud bark as he shouted for order. "Quiet down! Who is the Magus in charge here?"

"I am." Magus Illenna had removed the cloth from her nose and mouth, exposing her pinched face and crooked teeth. "My name is Magus Illenna, I treated KI's wounds when he was first discovered."

"And where was that?"

"The princess and the boy were found just inside Yamina, near an abandoned shack. KI was already unconscious when I arrived. It seems Chiefana Fox was able to drag him back into the village by herself."

"Are you certain there's no other way this boy could have been injured?"

Magus Illenna nodded slowly. "Yes, chiefono. The markings

on KI's body could have only come from ... a demon."

Talon gasped, covering her mouth with one hand, and reaching for her brother's arm with the other. "It's going to wake up," she said. "It's going to come back to life."

"What's going to wake up?" Fox found her voice, though it was filled with fear. "What will happen to KI?"

"Dispatch a team into the woods," Roaring ordered his guards. "Take the hunting hounds with you and find the corpse of the bear that attacked my sister. I want it examined thoroughly."

"That won't help anything," Talon said. "You haven't looked at him, Roaring. That boy isn't KI anymore."

"What does that mean?" Fox took a step, but Roaring pointed at her, stopping her in her tracks.

"Don't move!" he ordered.

"Why not?"

"We don't know if this demon touched you at all."

"I'm fine," she insisted.

"You will be quarantined here until further notice. Magus Illenna will keep watch over you as well as KI."

"Yes, chiefono." Illenna nodded obediently but Fox crossed her arms, her fear turning to anger.

"I'm *not* infected. I don't have the same injuries as KI. Can't you see I'm fine?"

"Your health is not my only concern. I'm taking the safety of the entire village into consideration." Roaring clenched his jaw, the veins in his thick neck swelled as his anger mounted but his words came out strangely calm. "Do you have any idea what you've done, Fox Fire?"

"I—I didn't know there would be a demon."

60

"Roaring," Talon said, trying to calm him down. "We can still handle this situation."

He turned to her. "You're right. Every Magus in this building is now assigned the task in keeping KI monitored every second of every day. I will leave a hand-picked squadron of guards to keep watch over this area. And, as of this very moment, the Village of Wi is under the restrictions of the First Defense."

Talon's eyes grew large. "You're closing the Gates. No one will be able to travel between rings now."

"That's a good thing. We don't know what may happen from this point on—"

"We don't know what's happening *now*," Fox said angrily. "What's wrong with KI? Why does the village need to be on lockdown?"

Talon looked at her sympathetically, her voice full of sorrow. "Because we're in danger now."

6

Roaring

Smoke wafted from the blunt ends of what used to be thick rolls of sage. The aromatic herb had burned down nearly an hour ago, leaving a bitter smell behind. Roaring Fire sat cross-legged on a cushion beside Talon; they were in a circle of men and women far too old to be awake at this hour. Even Chava seemed dreary. The hunting hound lay in a corner of the room, only stirring whenever she heard Roaring's voice over the squabbling elders. A few of the village nobles harrumphed at Chava's presence but the Prince of Fire had refused to leave her behind. He'd raised her since birth, carrying the pup around the village in his own arms. Now, Chava followed Roaring everywhere he went and listened only to his command. It was said the hound could shred a dozen demons alone and with Roaring fighting at her side, they could slay a hundred.

The Prince of Fire straightened his back, stifled a yawn. This meeting had crept past its third hour two hours ago. *We will be here until morning*, he thought. With the village under the First Defense, the Grand Chief had made it her business to call Council meetings every night since Fox and KI's encounter. The first night had been locked in a heated debate about what to do with the boy. Half the Council wanted KI out of the village, the other half wanted him put to death—Roaring didn't see the difference.

"He is a *child*," Talon had passionately argued. She was the only one to speak up in KI's defense, not even the boy's adoptive father voiced any concerns.

Roaring spoke not a word during the heated debate; closing the village gates and securing defense squadrons along every Wall was his only concern and since he'd done that over a week ago, he considered his job well done. The decision in the matter of the boy's life was well beyond his interest. Still, it pained him to see his sweet sister so upset, not to mention Fox Fire's reaction. The young chiefana spent her first night in quarantine without a fuss but when the nights ticked by and she received no news of KI, her patience whittled away. There was an incident where she tried to fight her way out her quarters with a sharpened chicken bone; she was eventually apprehended but not before drawing blood from two of her guards. Roaring ordered the servants to give her a vegetarian diet after that.

"What do you think?" an aged voice asked. It wasn't until Roaring noticed the pair of grey eyes trained on his face that he realized the question had been directed at him.

"Think about what?" he said, clearing his throat.

Lady Minga, an elder on the village Council and leader of the

Modon Clan, frowned at him. "What do you think about the boy's situation? Should he be cast out or put to death?"

"That is of no concern to me." Roaring crossed his arms, his large muscles straining against the giant bangles around his biceps. The prince of the Fire Tribe sat bare-chested with a string of wolf claws hanging around his neck; simple leggings covered his lower half and—despite the heat—a brown cloak sat on his shoulders. Made from the pelt of a wolf, it was a souvenir from the life-threatening battle he'd had with the great beast years ago. Roaring kept the head perfectly intact, it sat on one shoulder with dark, beady eyes staring back at the onlooking crowd, its mouth pulled back in a snarl, teeth bared in aggression. Sometimes Chava would stare at the wolf, sometimes she would growl.

Kifa Modon glanced at the dead wolf before speaking. "Chiefono, as second in command of the Hunting Regiment, the safety of this village is your responsibility."

"You said as much the day you enacted the First Defense," Talon agreed, watching her brother closely.

Roaring suppressed the urge to sigh—he did not enjoy explaining himself. "Seven days ago, I enacted the First Defense once we realized Fox Fire and KI had gone beyond Wall Yamina and faced a demon. During the attack, KI received a wound from the demon which we believe is responsible for the black veins covering his body and his current comatose state. Initially, I believed KI had been infected by the demon, so I enacted the First Defense to prevent this infection from spreading."

"Initially," Kifa Modon repeated. "You sound as if you've changed your mind. Have you learned something new?"

"KI is still unconscious," Talon said, regret in her voice.

"Actually," Roaring leaned forward, one hand on each knee, "KI has been unconscious for seven days now. During that time, the Hunting Regiment delivered reports of demon hordes spotted miles off from Wi."

Sudden gasps and murmurs rippled through the Council.

"These hordes are far off, but their path is very clear: There is a legion of demons heading straight for this village. And that's not all."

"No?" Kifa Modon questioned.

Roaring met her gaze. "It isn't just a horde coming to the village; they're being led—*drawn*—by a demon the size of our Walls."

More gasps and murmurs, even Talon covered her delicate mouth with a hand.

"I do not know where the giant darkling is coming from," Roaring went on. "But it has not changed its course since it was spotted three days ago. To me, the connection is clear; just days after KI and Fox battled a demon which managed to cause strange injuries to KI, a horde of dark creatures appeared and began the long march to our village. I don't know exactly why the demons are coming, but they're on their way and it's got something to do with KI or Fox Fire."

Kifa Modon raised a swollen, arthritic hand to her mouth, shaking as it covered her toothless face. "This is horrible."

"Something should be done," Talon said.

"That's your job," Kifu Kato snapped from across the circle.

The chiefana blinked dumbly at her uncle. "Kifu, I have been doing my best—"

"You have done nothing but faint and cry since your sister

65

and the outsider scrambled back behind the Walls." Kato folded his arms, the tribal tattoos inked onto his dark brown skin stretched across his muscles. "If that is your best then our village is doomed, Grand Chiefana."

Silence captured the room. Through the haze of smoke from the burnt sage, Roaring eyed his uncle quietly. The Hunter had always been hard on his nieces and nephew—especially Talon. She was the Grand Chiefana, she needed to be strong, stern, confident—like her mother. But Chiefana Talon was nothing like the small woman in the Flaming Veil across the room.

The Grand Chief sat on a cushion separate from the group, observing the Council in silence. She hadn't spoken a word in five hours and didn't raise any care or concern at her brother's tone with the Grand Chiefana. The rest of the room watched raptly, unsure how to respond.

It suddenly felt too hot; though he'd grown up in Wi, Roaring had never enjoyed the endless heat. Legends said the First Flames built the village over a volcano—and each time it erupted a Sunrider was born. But that was hundreds of years ago, when people had unimaginable powers and the Great Demon War was a fairer fight. Now all they had were walls and memories.

Roaring swallowed, keeping his eyes on his uncle. Kifu Kato sat up perfectly straight, a head taller than every other man in the room. His dark skin glowed in the hue of the burning embers in the firepit. The room was red all over, drapes hanging from the ceilings, whispering against the redwood floor. The red flag of the Fire Tribe hung above a carving in the wall; an enormous, winged beast erupting from a volcano. Red lava and flames were painted onto the walls around the carving, bringing

66

it to life. The Grand Chief sat beneath the mouth of the Sunrider, its sharpened teeth jutting out around her, as if it'd spit her out onto her cushion.

Roaring peeled his eyes from his uncle to his mother; they were just alike in so many ways—unbent, unbowed—but Talon was not like them at all. She was not built for chiefdom; she lacked any sort of confidence and hesitated too much. Roaring could think of a dozen others who'd be a better fit to take their mother's place. *He* would love to take his mother's place, but he'd been born the wrong gender. The perfect son in a matriarchal village. The jealousy burned within him; to have all the talents and be unable to use them. To be limited by foolish tradition. But he'd made his peace years ago, resigned to leading wherever he could.

He'd found success in the Hunting Regiment, becoming a Kifu before turning sixteen. He'd known his blade before he'd known a woman. Had taken life before he'd given it. But for all his glories beyond the Walls, Roaring knew his place—knew where his leadership ended and his submission began. His uncle, however, had never learned this lesson.

Kifu Debo Hawt, leader of the Hawt Tribe, leaned forward, stroking his long, white beard as he spoke. "Give the young Grand Chiefana more credit than that. She did argue on behalf of the boy's life. That's more than you've done for your own child, Kifu Kato."

Kato bristled. "The outsider is *not* my child."

"You raised him, did you not?"

"My role in the monster's life has nothing to do with this. The question at hand is what will the Grand Chiefana do to save her own village?"

Talon took a shaky breath. "Kifu Kato, Kifu Hawt, I understand your concerns—"

"I'm afraid you don't, girl," Kato said. "Have you ever gone beyond the Walls? Have you ever fought a demon? Have you ever *seen* one?"

"No, I haven't. But—"

"Then you don't understand at all."

"If you would let me speak—"

"You have nothing to say worth listening to, little niece." Kato stood and approached the Grand Chiefana. "Now be quiet and learn how to be a leader."

Talon's hands curled into fists, bunching the fabric of her hand-stitched kataa. This wasn't the first time their uncle made a point in shaming her, especially in front of their mother— *always* in front of their mother. Undermining her authority seemed to give the Hunter a sense of power he didn't need or deserve, yet no one felt inclined to stop him.

Roaring glanced about the room, taking in the nodding heads, the tiny smirks, and bored eyes watching the disrespect unfold. *They aren't going to say anything because they don't disagree*, Roaring realized. *They don't believe in Talon.* And why should they? It'd been Roaring who'd initiated the lockdown in the village, Roaring who had ordered the bear carcass to be examined, Roaring who kept Fox under surveillance, and Roaring who stood atop the Walls each day. He'd gone beyond Yamina, he'd seen darklings face to face, he'd gotten the reports of the demon horde—and he knew what to do about it.

As if realizing this herself, Talon deflated before her uncle. Her shoulders slumped in defeat, her fists uncurled; she was not a Grand Chiefana, she was nothing more than a lost little girl.

Kifu Kato smiled, victorious. "I will take command of the village now, with your permission, Grand Chief?" He glanced at his sister in the corner of the room. All eyes shifted to the Grand Chief, but it was Roaring who answered.

"You will return to your seat and quiet down, Kifu Kato."

His uncle glared at him; rage barely contained. "Come again?"

"Talon is the Grand Chiefana, it is her duty to rule in the Grand Chief's stead. Not yours."

"The Grand Chiefana is not ruling."

"Then the Grand Chief will appoint a new leader of her choosing." He lowered his voice, dangerously calm. "And it will not be you."

"You speak out of term, nephew."

"Perhaps we should vote on this," Wolf Fire interjected.

Roaring glanced to his father, stunned by his input. He'd trained with his father for years but had heard his thoughts at Council meetings only a handful of times. Like most of the great Hunters, he spoke better with his weapons than his words.

Now, he leaned forward and offered peace. His dark eyes scanned the crowd quickly, the scar over his eyebrow lifting as he quirked it. Roaring shifted on his cushion. He recognized that look on his father's face—the nervous way he regarded the group. Anger bloomed in his chest, and he nearly groaned; his father was afraid of Kato. *He would rather take a vote than a stand.*

Roaring sighed.

"A vote," he repeated. "Good idea."

Wolf Fire glanced between his son and daughter. "Talon has not performed her best, but appointing a new leader is hasty. Let us vote to give her another three days to take care of this matter."

Kifa Modon and Kifu Hawt nodded agreement, along with the rest of the village leaders seated around the glowing embers of the firepit.

"And so, you are *not* taking command of the village." Roaring smiled up at his uncle. "Now, return to your seat and quiet down."

Kifu Kato glared daggers at his nephew as he crossed the floor, but Roaring was unfazed. He'd sat quietly while his uncle had shamed his sister—his *favorite* sister—but he would not remain quiet as he wrested the Veil from her brow.

"Now that the voting is done," Kifa Modon said, "what will you do about this issue, Grand Chiefana?"

Talon gulped but Roaring was there to save her yet again. "I have dispatched messenger hawks to the nearest villages asking for their aid, but we've gotten no reply as of this morning," he explained. "I'll be honest, this horde may be the devastation of this settlement."

A tense silence stretched taut over the room, even Kifu Kato shifted uncomfortably.

Roaring stood, his cloak swaying behind him; in the hazy smoke, he appeared a silhouette—a shadow hissing nightmares into the ears of the fretful crowd. "I don't care about the boy. Toss him out, kill him, cut him to pieces. I. Don't. Care. My one and only concern is the safety of Wi; what happens to the child that brought about its doom is the last thought on my mind. If anyone has input on how to save the village, feel free to fetch

70

me from my chambers. Until then, I'm going to get some sleep."

Roaring made his exit in just a few strides, his long legs crossing the room with all the elegance a prince should have. Chava followed close behind, her oversized head loomed over some of the sitting nobles. No one protested Roaring's leave except the Grand Chief.

"You don't care what happens to the orphan, no one here faults you for that, but suppose you are right: the horde marching toward Wi is coming for KI *and* Fox Fire. What should we do with your sweet little sister?"

After becoming the Grand Chief of Wi, the Lady Fire renounced the name she was born with and became Lady Reign of Fire, leader of the Village of Wi. Lady Reign was half the size of her mighty son, drowning in a tunic much too large for her small frame. Her head was adorned by a crown of wrought gold, shaped like a flame; a veil hung low enough to cover the top half of her face, leaving only her mouth and chin exposed. She appeared the least intimidating person in attendance, almost childlike in her size. Still, her voice managed to silence the room and seize Roaring Fire where he stood. "What will you do, Roaring?" she asked, a small smirk the only visible expression on her face. Roaring stared at her, wondering what her eyes looked like. Though Lady Reign was his mother, even he had few memories of her entire face.

Lost for words, the prince huffed and left the room with Chava right behind.

In the darkness, he found his way across the open garden back to his chambers where he was happy to change his clothes. He'd just settled beneath a mound of furs when the pelt in his doorway shook, and a slender figure entered his room.

71

"For someone who is praised for being so polite, you're mighty rude for entering without knocking," Roaring said.

Talon surrendered a laugh and moved to sit beside her brother, gently nudging Chava aside. "I came to check on you."

"As you always do."

Roaring couldn't see her clearly in the grey darkness, but he knew she was smiling. "It's your duty to look after the safety of Wi," she said, "but it's mine to look after you." Talon extended a hand and delicately stroked his cheek; he reached up and caught it, kissed her palm.

"I don't deserve a sister as sweet as you."

"I am not your only sister."

He dropped her hand. "Fox Fire can be such a fool."

"That's beside the point right now. Fox was not infected; we should let her see KI."

"*No,* we shouldn't." Roaring's voice was firm. "I'm the one who's been beyond Yamina, not you. I know what can happen to people who've been infected by demons. We don't want Fox anywhere near KI—we shouldn't even let him remain in the village."

Talon sighed. She could not argue with her brother; as a member of the Hunting Regiment, Roaring was one of few people allowed outside Wi. The Regiment found access to resources beyond Yamina and prevented demons from roaming too close to the Walls. Because of people like Roaring and Ryko and Kifu Kato, there weren't more children suffering, lying unconscious just like KI. While the villagers inside hadn't seen a living demon in their lifetime, the Regiment saw them nearly every few days. Roaring had a collection of scars from encounters with the creatures; without Chava, he'd likely have

72

a collection of missing limbs.

Even with all his experience fighting the darklings, Roaring knew the Regiment was not ready to face the threat marching towards Wi. The monsters he'd grown up fighting had been fearsome creatures, but the horde and the giant would flatten the village and there was nothing the young prince could do.

At only nineteen, Roaring had managed to become second in command of the Hunting Regiment; his reputation was known in all three rings, his hound was feared by men and demons alike—yet he felt powerless against the monsters. He grunted in disapproval.

"I know what I'm doing."

"As you so wonderfully demonstrated by walking out of a Council meeting."

"And what strength did *you* demonstrate today?" he snapped. "You let Kato make a fool of you."

Talon exhaled. "I know that."

Roaring looked away, embarrassed of his temper.

"I know you would make a much better Grand Chief," his sister said. "I realized that a long time ago—when Chava chose you as her master and the Regiment chose you as their leader. Man and beast alike flock to you for leadership, no one even asks me what they should have for breakfast." Talon laughed, though Roaring only heard sadness in her voice. "But for better or worse, tradition has named me the next Grand Chief and the next in command of our village. So, no matter how you feel about the situation, I will not allow KI to be killed or exiled by the Council." Angrily, she rose and made her way to the door, but Roaring called out to her.

"What will you do, Talon?" He could just make out the crease in her forehead, the downward curve of her lips when she turned back to face him.

"Lady Reign has left KI's life in the hands of the Council, but the least you could do is allow Fox to see him. If she isn't infected, it won't hurt anything."

Roaring tightened his jaw. He knew how Fox felt about her Shield; KI was more of a brother to her than he'd ever been. Still ... could he really put his youngest sister in danger? Was there nothing he could do to help KI?

"I thought you didn't care what happened to the boy," Talon teased. Of all the Fire children, Talon was the only one Roaring allowed to get close to him. It was no surprise she could read his emotions, even in the darkness.

"I *don't* care," he lied. "The safety of the village—"

"Is your only concern. I know." Talon moved to the open window across the room, where the moonlight poured in to shine a spotlight on her. Though she'd changed into a plain nightdress, she still managed to hold an air of regality with her hair stretched so it could cascade to her waist, her long neck bare, and her face painted by the ashen moonlight. Roaring did not have to wonder why the village had named her the Beauty of Fire.

"I'm not strong enough to take my mother's place but I *am* strong enough to admit that," Talon said. "It's all right to care, Roaring. Convincing yourself that you don't only makes the pain worse later."

He sighed. "We have a day—maybe two—before the demons arrive. When the hordes reach Yamina, we won't be able to withstand them for long. Demons *will* get inside."

"Then we'll fight inside."

"It won't be enough. What about the giant?"

Talon paused, peering out the window in thought. "Maybe ... Maybe you could dance."

"*Dance*," Roaring scoffed. "There hasn't been a sundancer in hundreds of years, sister. You know that."

"But there has." She turned to him, and the moonlight cast a shadow over half her face. "Our mother was the first to appear in the last few centuries. And you were the second. Together you could—"

"Set a few demons on fire," Roaring interrupted, agitation clear in his tone. He held out his hand for her to see, fingers flexing as he spoke. "You want me to use my gift." A spark flashed, crackling in the darkness. It lit up the room for an instant before bursting to life as a flame flickering in Roaring's palm. Greedily, it ate away the dark, licking at the air, dancing in his hand. Talon watched in awe.

When the Great Demon War first began, humans were completely helpless. The tales of the elders say the demons appeared all at once—in *every* part of the world. Monsters crawled from beneath the earth and devoured nearly all of humanity. The survivors of the Great Demon War dispersed into only a handful of remaining villages in four separate regions. The Village of Wi settled in the Region of Smoke and Ash, the Region of Ice was in the north, the Region of the Lion in the east, and the Region of Shadows in the west.

Before the Regions were established, humans were mercilessly devoured by the dark beasts. It wasn't until they were able to fight back that they gained their footing in the War. Silly earthly weapons had little effect on the demons; spears, swords, and arrows could only cut down so many. This was a

75

supernatural war, humans had to learn to use supernatural weapons to survive.

The Fire Tribe quickly adapted to the rules of this War. Blessed by God, they were gifted an *anointing*; the power to manipulate the flames of the sun. They called it *sundancing*. With this anointing, the Children of the Sun defended themselves against the monsters and established the Village of Wi. But as time passed, their power faded until sundancing became obsolete. Lady Reign of Fire was the first dancer born in Wi in the last two centuries. Roaring Fire was the second.

Talon's eyes were trained on the flame in Roaring's hand; he could feel the heat of her gaze just as much as the warmth of the fire in his palm. Sunfire was different from nature's fire—hotter, angrier, hungrier. In an instant it could become a wildfire large enough to devour Wi, but Roaring had learned to control his flames as a child—he still remembered the day his abilities awakened.

After spending the afternoon sparring with Kifu Kato, young Roaring wanted to show off his skills to his adoring little sister.

"Does Lady Reign know you're spending your lunch break swinging that thing around?" Talon asked, popping a sweet berry into her mouth. Cat snorted, sitting in the grass beside her as she bounced Fox Fire in her lap.

"You know you can call her *Mama*, right?" Roaring pointed his rahkai at her, the metal shined in the sunlight. "Why are you such a stick in the mud?"

"Talon's *not* a stick!" Cat shouted, upsetting Fox.

Talon sighed as their toddler sister began to cry. "Ryko, will you take my baby sister back to her wetnurse?" The young boy who'd been sitting quietly in the grass stirred to life; Ryko had only recently been assigned the personal guard to all three of the young princesses despite being just two years older than Talon.

Roaring eyed him closely. "Wait a minute," he said. "Ryko, why don't we fight for a bit?"

"I—uh—chiefono, I don't think that's a good idea."

"Why not? Are you scared?"

"N—No. It's just—"

"If you aren't scared, then fight me. Kifu Kato taught me this new trick today, I want to see how it works against someone puny like you." Roaring took a few swings at the air; the metal sang as it sliced.

"Ryko is not puny," Cat said. "He doesn't want to fight you because he's a trained guard and you're a spoiled brat. He could kick your butt."

Ryko turned three different shades of red but didn't speak.

"Shut up, Cat. If I want him to fight me then he's *got* to fight me. I *command* him." Roaring smirked, defiant.

"I can command him *not* to," Talon challenged.

"I'm the oldest here."

"But I'm the oldest *girl*, so my command is higher than yours."

Roaring stomped his foot. "Just let me fight him! All I want to do is show you my new move!"

"Fine." Talon waved a dismissive hand. "If it'll make you stop yelling. Just don't cry once you end up on the ground."

He smiled, showing off the gap in his mouth from a missing tooth. "Let's go, Ryko."

Reluctantly, the boy drew his club and held it out to fight. The sparring didn't last very long at all; just as the girls

77

predicted, Prince Roaring ended up on his backside staring up at Ryko after just a few moments.

The boy pointed his club in Roaring's face. "I—I've defeated you, chiefono."

The chiefana erupted in a fit of giggles, even Fox squealed in joy.

"I'm sorry," Ryko said, extending a hand to help the chiefono to his feet. Roaring slapped the hand away and shoved Ryko as he hollered, "You think you're better than me!"

"Stop it! The fight is over!" Talon leapt to her feet and stood between the two boys. "You lost, Roaring. Don't be angry—it wasn't even a serious fight."

"I am the son of the *Grand Chief*!" he shouted. "I won't let someone from the *second* ring beat me."

Roaring stepped around his sister, his fist pulled back, ready to punch Ryko right in the face. But Talon was faster—and more stubborn—than he thought; she managed to get in front of him again, blocking his charge. Roaring tried to pull his punch but there was no time, all he could do was shift his weight so he wouldn't hit her face. He closed his eyes and his anger turned to raw panic as his fist collided with her shoulder instead.

Talon screamed but it sounded different. It sounded horrible. He hadn't hit her hard, not hard enough for her to shriek so loudly. And then he opened his eyes; saw the flames in his own hand, engulfing his small fist, and he screamed, too. Except he wasn't in pain. He screamed because he saw what he'd done to his own sister—his favorite sister. And there was nothing he could do to make it better.

"Roaring, calm down!" The sound of Talon's panic shook him back to reality. The flame in his hand had nearly tripled in

78

size, but he put it out by simply closing his palm. Smoke rolled from between his fingers, black ribbons streaming in the hazy night; he hated the smell of it.

"What were you thinking about?" Talon sat in front of him now, her wide eyes filled with concern. She looked so young and innocent to him, no matter how old they grew, she would always be the young girl he'd naively loved as a child.

Roaring reached up and brushed her thick hair behind her ear; lazily, his hand traced her neck to her shoulder to tug at the strap of her dress. It clung to her skin for a moment, sticky with sweat. Roaring tugged a little harder, his eyes on his sister's, silently asking permission.

Talon didn't move.

The material slipped free, falling away from her body to expose her bare shoulder.

What'd once been a smooth expanse of brown skin was now a bubbled, black mess. The fleshy scar went down Talon's shoulder to eat up part of her left arm. Only a handful of people had ever seen the burn before—even less knew the story behind it.

After that day, Roaring's mother personally overlooked much of his training and his sundancing became the best kept secret of Wi. Ryko had been rewarded a permanent home in the innermost ring for his silence. No one ever spoke of the incident again; Talon made sure to keep her scar covered except when she was around her family. In public she wore long sleeved dresses, no matter how intense the heat, and in the privacy of her home, she let her hair hang loose to cover her shoulders in case she bumped into a servant. Cat and Fox, the youngest of the family, eventually lost memory of the fight but Roaring

79

never forgot.

"It was over ten years ago." Talon's voice was just a whisper.

"Still..." Roaring lifted his gaze from her scar to her eyes. "I've never forgiven myself."

"Things are different now. You can control your flames. You can help the village. It doesn't have to be a shameful secret anymore."

"It still won't be enough."

"But it'll be *something*."

He chuckled, abruptly standing to cross the room. Dancing always made him hot, he could feel steam rising from his bare chest as he stood in front of the open window, willing a breeze to soothe the tingling of his skin. "Together, Lady Reign and I could probably melt a thousand demons. But what will the village look like afterward? *Who* else and *what* else will burn in the process?"

"No one will care if their homes are burned down as long as they're still alive."

"*If* they're still alive," Roaring emphasized. He turned to look at her. "Did you know a dancer cannot be burned? Not by nature's flames or their own." His eyes drifted to her shoulder again. "It's like insurance, something to keep dancers from turning against each other. That's why mother and I have never used our dancing in front of others. No one else in the village can dance; if they knew of our powers, they would fear us— some might even suggest we got these gifts from the demons outside. We don't want to rule that way. We don't want to control through fear."

"I'm not afraid of you." Talon's voice was unwavering. "I've never been afraid of you."

"What if I'm afraid of myself?"

"You can only be brave when you *are* afraid," Talon said. "So, it's a good thing to feel fear. I'd find it queer if you didn't."

Roaring chuckled. "And you said you weren't strong enough to replace our mother."

"I'm sorry, brother." She blushed.

"Don't be sorry." Roaring waved her off. "I'm glad you can be so honest with me. Now, why don't you get some sleep? You'll need plenty of rest if you're going to take Fox to see her Shield tomorrow."

Her face lit up. "Will that be all right with you?"

He shrugged, let go of held breath. "I suppose it will."

"What will you do?"

He smiled. "I think I'll spend a few hours training."

"We'll make it through this."

"I know."

Talon kissed her brother on the cheek, but he grabbed her wrist as she pulled away. "One last thing," he said, adjusting the strap to her dress. "Please cover up again."

She smirked at him. "Goodnight, brother."

The room felt darker without his sister there, but Roaring was used to the grim solitude. His isolation helped him concentrate on his training, enjoying the bursts of light from his flames as he danced in the darkness. His muscles tensed, straining as the searing heat pulsed through his veins. It burned, from the inside out. But it was a sweet pain that Roaring couldn't explain. Like pulling out a splinter or yanking out a bad tooth. Pain and relief all mixed into one.

The fire wanted him, called out to him, screamed for his summons, and he gave in through the night. Releasing all his pinned-up tension in raging balls of fire. He was slick with sweat when he finished, curly hair sticking to his neck and forehead. Steam rose from his body as the sweat evaporated. Sundancing made him so hot, he almost couldn't stand it. He wanted to rest. Wanted to eat a meal big enough for three and then sleep for two days and dream of a beautiful woman—but he couldn't. He had a village to save and sisters to protect. His training had given him some courage, some hope that maybe Wi could survive this. But as quickly as hope arrived, it was snuffed out by dark anxiety.

Roaring settled in his bed, kicking his fur blankets onto the floor as he stared at the ceiling. The darkness around him felt ominous; his room was a shade of black that came not because it was night but because Wi had suddenly become void of light. Roaring forced himself to concentrate on sleep, but he couldn't find it, especially not with the trembling he felt—not in his hands or his knees.

In the late hours of the night, the Prince of Fire sat with his legs hanging over the edge of his bed, his feet planted firmly on the ground. Beneath the calloused skin of his heels, he felt the slightest tremble. At first, he'd been confused—*is this an earthquake?* But it was too rhythmic, too unnatural, to be a shake of the earth. Then he gasped, realization hitting him hard. This wasn't a natural earthquake, the ground was shaking from something heavy, something huge. Something *giant*.

These are footsteps, he realized, *and they're getting closer.*

Thump ... Thump ... Thump ...

7

Evelyn

Lieutenant Diaz sat in his tent with his weapons displayed in front of him, a pair of hook swords in desperate need of a good shine. An eerie red glow settled over them as the sunset cast a carmine shadow against his tent. Beyond the thin walls of his meager dwelling, the lieutenant could hear his men setting up camp; a tiny squad of less than fifteen starved soldiers. A week ago, they'd been the prize of the Academy, war hardened Hunters who had no fear. Today they were scared, fussy, and unsure of their next meal or day.

Thump ... Thump ... Thump ...

Diaz shifted as he sat on the hard ground, the feeling of the earth quaking beneath him made him uneasy. He had fought the monsters more times than he could count but something felt different this evening, something felt **dark**. Days ago, he'd gotten reports of an ambush on a small village nearby; since he was a Hunter of the Academy, he had to jump into action. At age 24, the young Hunter had managed to climb the ranks to First Lieutenant. He'd been proud when the badge was first pinned to his shoulder—now he was only tired.

What'd fueled the lieutenant's fiery passion years ago had whittled down to a hopeless flicker. The quaking beneath him threatened to stamp out even that. *And then what?* he pondered, staring at his bloodstained weapons—whose blood it was, he did not know. Darklings and humans bled the same color. *Red is red*, he told himself.

Thump ... Thump ... Thump ...

This was supposed to be a simple ambush. Diaz's superiors had made the mission sound easy. "We've got reports of a nearby village calling for help. It's a simple ambush, no worries," Major Marshall had told him. "You wanna take care of that, or should I?" Though the major had been smiling, the lieutenant knew he didn't have a choice.

"I'll do it as long as I can choose my own team."

A squad of fifty men and women had set out a week ago. They'd done their part in squashing the *simple ambush*, but things got complicated when they spotted the beast responsible for the attack; a massive monster that stood 40 meters tall. The darkling had walked right over the settlement, squashing houses and shacks and livestock without care or concern. Diaz left half his squad to deal with the few demons left in the village and help survivors find shelter while he led the rest of his men to chase after the giant.

Thump ... Thump ... Thump ...

"Why don't we just let it go?" Second Lieutenant Kotaro had

84

asked him on the fourth night of pursuit. "The men are tired, and we'll run out of rations if we keep going like this."

"It's only been four days," Diaz had replied. He gave her a sideways glance, his dark eyes scanning her. "Do you want to turn back?"

"Of course not, Evelyn. I just don't want things to go south."

Lieutenant Kotaro was Diaz's closest companion and the only one bold enough to speak to him so casually. The sound of his first name on her lips softened him. "Things will be fine," he muttered, looking away.

"If you say so."

"Haven't you noticed?" Diaz asked.

She nodded, adjusting in her saddle. "The giant monster didn't attack that village: it walked *through* it. We've been trailing it for days now and it hasn't shown any interest in us. This demon isn't aimlessly walking—it's going somewhere."

Diaz smiled, impressed by her deduction.

"But," she continued, "what are you going to do? Follow it until it stops?"

If I turn back, I can at least report everything I've learned, Diaz thought, but that idea didn't please him. He had to know where this monster was going. And then what? He couldn't bring it down with his few soldiers. *Maybe we can ride ahead of the monster and warn the next village.* Days ago, that'd seemed like a good idea until they began their rush forward. That was the only time the monster *did* pay them any mind. With one stomp of its foot, the beast sent a shockwave through the earth, summoning gusts of wind so powerful it sent a dozen men and horses flying. *It isn't going to let us ride ahead,* Diaz had realized, *it doesn't care if we follow but it won't let us interfere with its travel.*

The lieutenant leaned back in his saddle, staring up at the dark sky. His muscles ached. His stomach growled. He sighed. "Yes."

"What if it *doesn't* stop? Not for a week? Not for a month?" Kotaro had asked.

Each time the giant walked through a village he would leave a few Hunters to help survivors or lose a few Hunters in the fight. They were low on rations and a small herd of darklings had begun following the giant, chasing off any wildlife they might have hunted in the surrounding forest. The giant's trail was easy enough to pick up but since it never stopped walking, Diaz and his team could not rest for long. They were tired and hungry and had a day or two left in them.

Diaz looked at Kotaro riding beside him; her brown eyes seemed dull against her tan skin, void of all the bravery and hope they'd once held. She had never been one for fighting— she'd only joined the Academy to watch over him, he knew that, but where she lacked grit, she made up for in wit. She had twice the brains and instinct of even the deadliest of Hunters. Diaz needed her by his side; if she could just hold on a little longer...

Kotaro cut into his thoughts, shocking him with a smile. "However long you ride behind this darkling, I'll be riding beside you."

Meaning, I'll be dying beside you. Diaz smiled back—he hoped it looked like a smile.

Thump ... Thump ... Thump ...

In his tent, the lieutenant spat on the ground, filled with anger. *This was supposed to be a simple ambush.* Now he faced two horrible choices: chase the demon to his own doom or leave it and suffer the guilt of allowing countless other villages to fall. They had no hawks to send back a request for reinforcements; *maybe one of the men I left behind had the sense to relay a message,* he hoped, grinding his teeth. Even so, any forces the Academy sent to aid them would be a few days' ride behind. They were alone in this darkness.

The red glow against his tent dimmed as the sun finished its goodbye. Lieutenant Diaz reached for his weapons and sheathed them at his sides before he stood to leave. Outside, small fires lit up the night—meager little flames desperately licking at the air. Weak Hunters sat warming their hands over the flickering flames; one group had a tiny rabbit on a spit, slowly roasting for dinner. It was the only successful hunt his team had gotten since leaving the Academy. Another group sat in silence but watched him closely, their eyes glowed against the heavy black of night as they wondered what his orders would be. Kotaro was among this group, her eyes round and full of wonder.

Thump ... Thump ... Thump ...

The quaking of the monster shook Diaz where he stood, rattling the trees and echoing endlessly through the darkness. The world was so black the sound seemed to come from every direction.

"Everyone," the lieutenant said quietly.

A howl of excitement rang through the camp. The men roasting the rabbit began to cheer and clap; dinner was ready. One by one they moved to gather around the small cut of meat, ignoring their leader.

Diaz tried again. "Everyone, listen."

The cheering grew louder as the rabbit passed from person

to person; mouths smeared with grease and fingers covered in charred meat, the team seemed alive for the briefest moment. Their hoots and cries grew so loud they nearly drowned out the giant's *thumping*.

Lieutenant Diaz watched, his frustration bubbling. "Everyone, shut up!" he yelled and suddenly every pair of eyes was on him, the rabbit forgotten, the cheers lost on their lips. "Mount your horses," he instructed. "We're riding through the night."

Thump ... Thump ... Thump ...

8

Fox Fire

Fox played with the thread of her knot as she stared at her chilly cup of peppermint tea. Her eyes traced the ripples, watching them form and fade; tiny wrinkles started in the center and stretched outward, madly racing to the rim. *There is no escape,* she thought as the ground beneath her began to quake.

Thump ... Thump ... Thump ...

The shaking had begun the night before; barely noticeable at first—Fox wasn't even sure she'd felt it when she woke in the middle of the night. That was something she'd been doing the past week: alluding sleep. Most nights she would lay on a mound of furs, clutching her knot and willing herself to rest, but nothing would happen for hours. Horrible images of KI's unconscious figure would fade in and out of her mind's eye until, mercifully, sleep called out to her. With the voice of a maid, it would sing her a sweet song and she would succumb until the horrible images became horrible nightmares. That was when sleep would lose its grip and Fox would wake cold and shaking.

Last night had been no different; Fox gave in to her exhaustion only to be met face to face with the black demon from the woods. Just like before, she fought it with all her strength until she was out of weapons and energy but, unlike before, the demon of her dreams never went down. No matter what Fox did, she could not save her dear friend.

A terrible vision of KI sprawled dead in front of her, black veins webbed over his body, shook her from her nightmare. Wiping sweat from her brow, Fox had stood in the open window of her small room and inhaled deeply. For a moment, she enjoyed the stillness of the night; she loved the salty smell in the air and the way the wind tasted, she liked the sound of the crickets in the ground and longed to feel the grass beneath her feet. Reflexively, she stretched her legs—standing on the tips of her toes, digging them into the dirt. That's when she felt the *thumping*. The gentle quaking had been so light—so far away—Fox thought she'd imagined the vibration beneath her feet.

Silently, she waited by her window to feel the quaking again. It seemed like half the night had passed with her on her tiptoes standing perfectly still, but just as she'd given in to her cramping calves and set her heels to the ground, she felt it once more.

Thump ... Thump ... Thump ...

"I'm not allowed to attend Council meetings," a bored voice was saying. Fox pulled her vision from her shaky tea to her older sister sitting on a cushion across from her. Cat didn't visit

Fox for the first three days of her confinement—Fox never complained—but as the second youngest in the family, Cat held no significant position beside her status as the Grand Chief's daughter. Unfortunately for her, this meant she was not privy to sensitive information regarding KI's condition. Unfortunately for Fox, this meant Cat would eventually stop by once she'd finished squeezing information out of Talon—her preferred gossip gal.

"We shouldn't be kept in the dark, you know?" Cat blinked at her, waiting for a reply.

"Uh—right."

"You're not even listening to me."

"I don't think you've been in the dark nearly as much as I have." Fox waved at her surroundings. "I've been kept in this little shack for a week now. No one tells me anything; the guards bring me food three times a day and Talon visits me in the afternoons but says nothing of KI. I haven't even seen Roaring since he had me imprisoned here."

Cat rolled her eyes. "No surprise there. He's been going nuts—got the whole village on lockdown, had your dead bear dragged in from the woods to be examined. Didn't find anything—just a regular bear. Whatever demon had been inside must have escaped and took Roaring's sanity with it. I heard he walked out of a Council meeting last night."

"Why?"

Cat smirked, took a long sip of tea. "There's been debate over what to do with KI."

"What do you mean?"

"Half the Council wants him exiled; the other half wants him dead."

"Dead?" Fox choked on the word, clutching her knot as the bloody images from her nightmares flashed in her head.

"Don't look so surprised." Cat placed a hand over hers. "I know you've felt the shaking, Fox. This morning, Talon told me KI is the reason—"

"That's not true," Fox cut her off, she would have said more but a guard let himself into her room just then with Talon following close behind.

Cat jumped to her feet and rushed to her older sister; Fox remained seated, greeting the future Grand Chief with an icy glare. "Greetings, ladies," Talon said warily.

"Is it true, Talon?"

"Is what true?"

"The Council is thinking about killing KI."

"I am not going to let them condemn a child to death—"

"It *is* true." Fox stood, then sat, unsure what to do. "Take me to him. You have to let me see him."

"That's what I came to do."

"Wait," Cat cut in, "is it safe for anyone to be around him? Isn't he infected?"

"The Magi say he is not contagious."

"How can they know for certain?"

"Well," Talon sighed. "There are no black markings on Fox's body and none of the Magi who've been overseeing him have developed black markings, either. I've been to visit him a few times and I'm perfectly fine."

Cat chewed her lip.

Fox pushed to her feet, nearly knocking her tea over. "Take me to him. Now."

KI had been moved from the infirmary to a small cabin nearby; it was large enough to house the boy and four Magi and was conveniently located across from Fox's quarters. The young princess hadn't been allowed to visit her companion, but she'd found some comfort in watching his cabin from her window. Her heart seemed to quicken as she neared the small shack; she kept calm by thinking of the last time she'd seen her best friend conscious and smiling. It felt as if that were months ago.

Magus Illenna greeted the princesses as soon as they entered the room. "Chiefana, Cat, Fox—I was not expecting any visitors for the boy today." Illenna pulled the cloth from her face to smile at them. "He is doing well."

"That's good, all things considered." Talon brushed past the Magus and guided her sisters to the unconscious boy. His wounds had been wrapped in bandages and his body covered in a long tunic to hide the black veins. "He looks like he's sleeping," Talon said.

"But he isn't." Fox moved closer. She sat beside him and took a deep breath, daring to touch him. His skin felt hot, but she refused to flinch away, instead she held his hand and tied her knot around his wrist. She couldn't remember the last time she'd prayed but she whispered one then, hoping God would hear and protect her friend somehow.

"You never got to present your knot to the tribe," Talon said behind her.

"It doesn't matter now."

"I'm proud of you anyway. And I'm sure KI is proud of you, too. You earned your knot, you're strong, Fox Fire."

Fox stared at KI's face, at the smoothness of his skin and the way his nose curved and how his lips looked much fuller now.

"He looks different," she muttered. "What is he infected with?"

"Well... it's hard to say," Talon replied.

"Then put it simply."

"Don't be a brat," Cat snapped.

"It's all right." Talon smiled gently, a pitiful smile full of sympathy. Fox hated that smile. It was a smile that said everything was not all right. Everything was doomed.

"KI is infected with a demon," Talon said.

Magus Illenna gasped from across the room.

"Please say you're trying to scare us!" Cat shrieked, clutching her necklace.

"I wish that were so." Talon gazed at KI. "He's infected with a demon. And we believe that is what's drawing the giant and its herd towards the village."

"Chiefana, this is sensitive information." Magus Illenna nervously sanded her hands together. "Please be mindful of what you are saying."

"Why didn't you tell us this before? Why hasn't KI been exiled or killed yet?" Cat yelled.

"Neither exiling him nor killing him guarantees the demon hordes will suddenly vanish. At this point, it's very likely they will swarm the village just for the sake of it."

"Can't we at least evacuate?"

"If we leave, we risk attracting stragglers from the horde. The safest thing for us to do is sit and wait and fight when the time comes. As of this morning, the Village of Wi is under the restriction of the Fourth Defense. I initiated it myself and personally overlooked the evacuation of the first Wing of Wi. Roaring has been busy preparing measures of counterattack should the Regiment fail at Wall Yamina. Every able body has

94

been given a weapon."

"I don't understand. I saw the demon, Talon, it came out of the bear and *left*. There's no way it could have infected KI."

"Possession is the only thing that would explain the markings or this state of unconsciousness he's been locked in."

"Will he ever wake up?"

"If he does," Talon peered at the boy's body with a painful look in her eye, "he'll likely be someone else entirely."

"*Something* else, you mean." Cat looked at the door. "I'm ready to leave now. This is creeping me out."

"Perhaps we should go," Talon said but Fox paid her no mind.

KI may never wake up. But if he does ... he'll be someone else entirely.

Fox bit her lip, trying to hold back the tears. KI hadn't wanted to leave in the first place—he'd only come because of her pleading. How could she ever forgive herself for killing her own best friend?

Guilt flooded her like a storm, and she gripped KI's arm, shaking him violently. "Get up!" she screamed.

Talon tried to pull her away, but Fox was stronger; just like her battle in the woods, instincts took over and she moved without thought—swiftly, fiercely, even deadly.

When a guard tried to yank her from KI's body she shoved him so hard he fell backwards into Magus Illenna. When he tried again, she used a pin from her hair to stab him in the arm and even scratched Talon when she came too close. It took four guards to apprehend her and even then, she managed to break someone's nose in her madness.

"You can't let him die!" she screamed as a guard forced her

arms behind her back. She tried to twist away but he grabbed her by her dress and slammed her into the ground so hard the world went black before she could even register the pain of impact.

* * *

It was cold when Fox opened her eyes. A heavy pain throbbed in her temple; she rubbed at it as she sat up from her cushions.

"You're awake," a gentle voice spoke across the room.

Fox blinked at the inky darkness. "Talon."

"It's nice to see you."

"How long—" a rumble cut her off.

Thump ... Thump ... Thump ...

Fox could feel the rumbling in her bones. Decorations beat against the walls, trinkets lining the shelves fell and clanked to the ground. Even the wind began to howl, crying out in anger as it charged through the small window, making the curtain clap.

"Eight hours," Talon said. She stepped into the moonlight. "You were knocked out for eight hours. It's the middle of the night."

"What happened to KI?"

Thump ... Thump ... Thump ...

Talon waited for the fit to end before replying, "He's being protected by a handful of guards. I haven't been to see him in a few hours, though."

"Why not?"

"We are under the Fifth Defense now."

"No—" Fox tossed her blankets aside and rushed to the door,

but the ***thumping*** started again and knocked her off balance. She heard Talon chuckle as she struggled to her feet. "What's so funny right now? What *on Earth* is funny?" Fox bit out.

"Your stubbornness. I only wish I could be as fierce and fearless as you, my sweet little sister."

Fox blinked.

"Roaring and the Grand Chief are out there fighting, along with our father, Ryko, Kifu Kato, and every man or woman who can yield a weapon. Two hours ago, the Village of Wi witnessed its first demon raid. One hour ago, Wall Yamina fell to the enemy forces. The battle has now made its way into the first wing, headed straight toward Wall Nunpi. It's only a matter of time before we are overtaken. Everyone else is running toward the fight—even Cat tried to take up arms, but I ordered her guards to take her and flee the village." Talon let out a rueful laugh. "I ordered guards to carry KI out of the village, but they refused to touch him. I convinced them to at least stay and guard him for as long as they could. I knew you would hate me if I let them take you and not him—but I couldn't let both of you stay here alone. So here I am."

"You should have left." Fox waited for the next wave of ***thumping*** to pass before she made another attempt for the door.

"You shouldn't go; you won't come back if you do," Talon warned.

"There won't be anything to come back to if I don't."

The trembling started again; this time Fox didn't get back up when she fell but instead crawled the short distance to the doorway. "I'm going to protect KI. If I can help it, I'll save at least *one* person."

97

"What will you do when the demons reach you? What will you do when the giant makes it to the innermost ring?"

Fox smiled at her sister, their features oddly similar in the darkness. Talon was known for her beauty, Cat for her sensuality, but Fox had only ever been known for her ferocity—something she shared with Roaring. Sitting in the darkness, however, with the sound of death all around her and the determination to live beating back her gripping fear, Fox was the mirror image of the Grand Chiefana, Talon Fire. Her tight curls hung loose, forming a kinky mane around her angled face, her almond shaped eyes softened with her smile, and her brown skin—a few shades lighter than her eldest sister's—glowed in the moonlight. "When the demons come," Fox said, "I'll fight."

"Wait—" Talon called, slowly crossing the room. "If you're that determined, let me fight with you." She retrieved a small dagger from her sleeve and pressed it into Fox's hand. "Something to fight with. And something to help defend." Talon removed a necklace from her own neck and tied it around Fox's, smiling wanly as she inspected it.

The pendant was a small piece of wood, hand-carved into the shape of a cross. There was nothing special about it at all, a cross with twine tied around one end. The silent Priests of the village, and some of the more pious Magi, often wore the little trinkets; Fox had never cared much for the Faith, but she knew enough of it to understand the pendant's significance.

"Thank you, Talon." Fox closed her fingers around the crucifix, *have you become so desperate?*

Together, the chiefana made their way from the small room to the foyer and then out into the courtyard. Shrieks and cries echoed around them, muffled by a heavy rumbling that shook them so cruelly Fox could barely stand without gripping her sister's arm for support. Fire crackled in the distance, lighting up the dark night as ribbons of smoke danced from the roofs of burning houses.

A hunting hound skirted past the girls headed toward the gate with a trail of younger hounds, half a dozen messenger hawks, and the scrawny hound keeper running behind. "They're escaping," Fox said, thinking of Chava and her giant paws and razor-sharp teeth. She wondered if she was fighting beside Roaring now; tearing demons to shreds, howling in anger, using her mighty strength to protect her brother.

Talon tugged her arm. "KI is this way!"

The fires and the demons hadn't made it into Wi's innermost ring yet, but Fox could hear the chaos well enough. The cries for help and the high-pitched squeals of the dark creatures drowned even the sound of her own thoughts. Madness crawled up the back of Fox's neck as she ran, forcing her legs to move faster, erasing all sense of sanity until nothing but raw panic remained.

"Slow down!" Talon shouted over the chaos, but Fox didn't hear. She jerked her arm from her sister's grip and ran ahead, closing the distance between herself and KI's shack.

Please be there.

The **thumping** knocked her to the ground, but she rolled and got to her feet, keeping up her sprint without missing a beat—her body moved without thought now, functioning on pure instinct. She was just a few feet away, her lungs crying for oxygen, when she heard a deafening roar that brought her to a halt almost immediately. Fox covered her ears, hoping she would still be able to hear when the noise ceased. She thought the monsters had broken through the gate but when she glanced up, she realized the gate hadn't been forced open at all, it'd been crushed by a giant.

The Village of Wi had three giant Walls; they'd been constructed from the inside out. The first Wall had been erected at the beginning of the Great Demon War and was the shortest and weakest of the three, while the others had been expansions made as the village's population grew. Wall Yamina had been the greatest of the three and had fallen within the first hour. Wall Nunpi had been the best guarded and fell shortly after. Wall *Wi* was the last Wall standing.

Fox Fire watched in horror as the wall crumbled beneath the weight of the giant as it pummeled its way through. Stone debris showered into the wing, killing the guards and servants who'd remained to protect the elders and high-ranking families of the village. In a rush to escape, dozens of tribesmen had run towards the gates only to come face to face with the nightmare itself. One man was crushed by a stone the size of a horse, another lay crying for help as he bled out, his legs shredded by the flying debris.

Up close, Fox could see the giant clearly; this was the monster who'd caused all the quaking for an entire day and night, the type of monster from the tales of the elders. The black beast was so dark it nearly blended into the night but the fires burning wildly through the village left a menacing glow on its face and body. Three massive horns protruded from the top of its head, its eyes were black and unblinking, and its mouth gaped open, a dark hole in its face; thick black drool fell from its sagging lips to splash upon the ground 40 meters below. It landed with a thud, melting the earth and rocks beneath like acid. Its hands were large enough to wield a tree like a weapon, just as easily as Fox could wield the dagger in her hand. It ripped a nearby oak from the earth and used it to smash a hole in the wall, but it was too small for the beast to climb through, so it moved toward the wooden gate and gave it three mighty kicks. The giant oak gates splintered and screamed in agony as the monster tore through; hordes of smaller demons poured in through the hole in the wall and the broken gates, devouring the escapees who'd survived the hailstorm of stone.

The demons tore through the crowd effortlessly and ran about looking for more. Fox turned to run to KI's cabin, determined to get there before the demons but her sister's voice stopped her.

"Fox Fire! HELP!"

Talon had fallen to the ground, her leg twisted at a horrible angle, and a swarm of demons rushed right at her. Fox couldn't take her eyes off her sister as she watched the dark creatures move in. Talon's eyes were so wide they were like to pop from their sockets. The demons circled her like little children, and danced about scratching at her, kicking her, ripping out fistfuls of her hair. Talon fought as best she could, punching and swinging. Through a sheer will to live, she forced herself to her feet and stumbled back and forth as the creatures pummeled her. Though her leg was twisted and useless, the chiefana remained standing on her good foot, madly swinging and screaming as she tried her best to fight—to *live*. She grabbed a darkling by the face as it tried to jump on top of her and ripped its horn from its head, wildly using it to stab and slice a few demons open. Red liquid spurted everywhere.

Red. Their blood is red. Just like ours.

101

Fox fell to her knees. KI lay in the cabin behind her, just a few feet away, with demons pounding at the door and digging through the roof and walls. But her sister was being devoured right in front of her. *I can't save them both, but I can't pick one, either. What can I do? What can I do?*

"FIGHT!" Talon screamed, her voice piercing. "Fox Fire, FIGHT!"

Talon stabbed another demon as it lunged at her, but her hands were sweaty, and the horn was slick with blood—hers and the demon's. The makeshift weapon barely scratched the monster. It dove to the left and tackled the princess to the ground. The rest of the demons poured in, swarming Talon like flies on the dead. Fox could see her hand reaching out, stabbing here and there as she went down, screaming bloody murder. A demon grabbed her hand and swung its blade-like claws to cut it off. Blood squirted from the wound and spattered Fox's cheek. It was then that she realized the blood was not her sister's, nor had the demon cut off her hand.

The monster howled in pain and drew back its stump, thick red liquid gushing from the wound. Fox shifted and swung, slicing at the creature again—this time, she cut off its head. *When did I move?* she thought, swinging again, pivoting, dodging, slicing, grabbing, biting, turning, jumping back, lunging in. Fox moved without thinking, her desire to protect her sister taking over. Slowly, the scene before her began to make sense; she could see the demons throwing themselves at her, could feel her arm swinging the dagger, hear the metal whispering in the air as it landed a sweet bloody kiss on a darkling's arm, throat, or head. Beneath that, she could hear her sister's voice. Somewhere in this storm of darkness, Talon was alive.

Fight.

Fox forced her way through the demons as best she could. When she was knocked down, she fought on her knees. When the dagger was taken from her hands, she punched and scratched and bit the creatures. When she was grabbed and dragged away, she screamed at them, cursing them, damning them to hell. And when she realized there was nothing else she could do, Fox cried out in a loud voice, "Help!" *Anyone, someone, God!* "Lord, help!"

A flash of silver darted past and tore through the demons. Fox's heart nearly stopped as she watched in awe, wondering what creature had come to her aid—what sort of demon turned on its own kind. But this was no demon.

The great beast ripped the darklings to shreds and the ones it missed were suddenly set afire, bursting into flames before Fox's eyes. The demons holding her down ran to join the fray, but they too were devoured and set aflame, their bodies reduced to ash in mere seconds. Through the smoke, Fox saw figures emerge.

A hound with grey fur stood on all fours, it looked like a demon itself but when the dog knelt and licked her cheek, Fox's eyes filled with tears. "Chava!" she cried as Roaring appeared beside his fearsome hound. Ryko emerged from the smoke as well, carrying Talon in his arms while Kifu Kato and Cat stood by his side.

"Cat?" Fox couldn't believe it. "I thought you fled the village."

She harrumphed. "Did you really think I would leave without my sisters?"

"Cat and her guards came to find us instead of fleeing."

Roaring stooped, handing the little dagger back to Fox. "If they hadn't, you'd be dead."

She took the dagger with shaking hands. "What about Talon?"

"Still breathing," Ryko said, though Fox knew the words he was thinking. *But not for long.*

The giant demon roared again, making everyone wince in pain. "We're not done here." Roaring turned, his wolf's cloak sweeping the ground behind him, smearing blood in the dirt. "Lady Reign and Kifu Wolf Fire are both fighting that beast. They won't be able to hold it off for long. We have lost Wall Yamina. We have lost Wall Nunpi. The enemy has just breached Wall Wi. Our Walls are gone but we can still save the village within and once the dust has settled, we can *rise again.*"

The words of the Fire Tribe rang in the air; they were words Fox had heard thousands of times, but they'd never held more significance than they did that moment. The Fire Tribe had risen from the carnage of the Great Demon War just as Christ had risen from the grave. Now, they would rise again after this attack. They would clean themselves off and they would get on with it. First, they had to kill this monster.

Roaring turned to his companions, his voice firm and commanding. "Kifu Kato, gather what men you can and go assist the Grand Chief in defeating that giant."

Kato nodded and left without a word.

"Ryko, take Cat and the Grand Chiefana and find a way out of the village. Survivors are gathering in the woods a mile off; Chava will go with you."

"Of course," Ryko left immediately, moving so swiftly it confirmed Fox's worries: *there isn't much time left for Talon.*

"Fox," Roaring's voice was flat now, void of all emotion, but his face was wrought in anger. He didn't look at her as he spoke, he simply turned and walked toward KI's cabin, issuing a single order over his shoulder, "Get up."

Fox stood by her brother's side on the steps of the cabin. The demons had destroyed part of the roof and one of the walls had caved in from the hail of stone debris, but the door remained. Roaring extended his hand and from his palm came a blast of fire that shredded the door and the wall with it.

Fox blinked.

"How did you—" she began but her brother cut her off.

"There's a lot you don't know about the Fire Tribe, Fox Fire. There's a lot you don't know about the world."

Dust and debris covered the inside of the little cabin; part of the debris had landed on KI, leaving the unconscious boy partially buried in wood and stone and the bodies of charred demons. Fox gasped and ran to his side, wildly digging through the rubble to get to him.

"Help me!" she hollered to her brother.

They dug frantically, throwing rocks and wood aside. Roaring lifted KI into his arms and turned to where the door used to be but froze in place. Fox shoved him. "We have to go!" she screamed but Roaring didn't move; he was too distracted by the armored woman standing on the steps before him.

She was at least seven feet tall with silver hair and glowing brown skin stained by a black inverted cross in the center of her forehead. It was a demon, that much Fox could tell, but she couldn't understand why it looked so human or wore human clothes and carried human weapons. The demon was dressed like a dark warrior; black greaves hugged her legs while a black skirt clung to her waist. Four swords were sheathed at her hips, two on each side, and a black breastplate shielded her torso with a floor-sweeping red cloak clasped to her shoulders by glowing red pins molded into an IX symbol.

Roaring knelt and gingerly placed KI on the floor. "Fox Fire." His voice was flat again. "Take the boy and go."

"What about you?"

The demon unsheathed one of her swords.

"Just go," Roaring said.

Fox moved to pick up KI, but the demon warrior swung her blade and the force of it sent a sudden storm of wind crashing into her, knocking her across the cabin. Roaring dodged the attack and side-stepped to block the next blow, punching at the air to counter. Fire met wind and a burst of heat and light erupted around them. Fox scrambled to her feet, trying to crawl back to KI but as she moved, she heard the giant roar once again and was paralyzed by the thunderous noise.

Roaring dropped to his knees, even the warrior stopped and bunched her shoulders, disturbed by the sound. Suddenly, the ground began to shake, and the roof of the cabin *crunched*. Fox looked up to glimpse the giant standing above her, holding what was left of the roof in its massive hand. It tossed the ceiling to the side the same way Fox would toss a rag and reached its black hand into the cabin.

Unconscious, the boy hung limp as the demon closed its monstrous fingers around him. Fox screamed madly, stabbing at the hand with her dagger, but it was useless; the giant moved without flinching, even Roaring's flames had no effect. But the wind of the warrior *did*. She swung her sword again, and the air reacted, slicing through the giant's arm like a bloody razor. The

106

creature roared and stumbled backwards, its fluids flooding the cabin. Fox clumsily waded through the liquid to the severed hand and pried its ugly fingers back. KI lay inside, curled up so peacefully he looked to be sleeping.

A smiled broke Fox's face and she reached to take hold of her friend, but something grabbed her by the hair and jerked her away. The dark warrior had forced her way past Roaring and meant to do the same to Fox. Gasping, Fox struck wildly with her dagger and then struck again when she felt the demon's grip loosen. The demon let go when a burst of fire kissed her backside, burning her red cloak away.

"Get KI and run!" Fox heard Roaring scream as he shot flames at the silver-haired woman.

Fox turned and ran toward KI without looking back. *I won't get another chance*, she thought, rushing to scoop the small boy into her arms. She had him with her, his body pressed against hers, the little dagger held tightly in her hand. KI was safe. And then the warrior was on her again. She grabbed her arm as she tried to run, forcing her to let go of KI.

Fox turned and swung, this time, the demon caught her wrist and twisted the blade free. Her long fingers were suddenly around Fox's throat but when the demon's hand began to sear and burn, she dropped Fox to the floor and cradled her hand against her chest.

Fox landed with a thud, staring up at the demon-warrior; black eyes glared back, shifting slowly to gaze at the pendant tied around her neck. Pale lips peeled back, as if to speak, but a blast of fire hit her hard and knocked her off her feet. Fox tore the pendant from her neck and threw herself at the demon, pinning her to the ground. *I don't know how, but this pendant*

107

can somehow hurt her. Shouting in anger, she shoved the cross into the warrior's throat and gasped as it let out a vicious, gurgling howl.

"Shoot her!" Fox yelled, glancing at Roaring who stood watching in shock.

He moved to throw a punch, his fist glowing with flames, but stopped. The demon struggled beneath Fox, trying desperately to get the pendant away from her burning flesh but Fox held on.

"Shoot her, now!" she screamed at Roaring. She looked at her brother's face and knew what he was thinking: *It'll kill you, too*. But she didn't care. "We can't let them win!"

Roaring took a deep breath and threw a mighty punch. Fox watched as the flames swirled toward her, a curtain of bright red and yellow storming through the air. It lit up what was left of the cabin, devoured the straggling demons, scorched the giant's hand. Fox could feel the heat kissing her cheeks before it consumed her. Just as she closed her eyes, a figure appeared in the flames.

And then everything went black.

PART II

9
Evelyn

When you shoot an animal, make sure you kill it. Those were the words his father had told him the first time he went out for a hunt. *Don't take the shot if it isn't a kill-shot or else you're just being cruel, Lyn. You hear me?*

That afternoon they shot a buck, a single arrow through the eye. It wasn't fun.

Lyn's father had pat him on the back, knelt beside him to whisper, "That's how you do it, Lyn. One clean shot." His breath smelled rank.

"Dad told me you shot a buck?"

Lyn lifted his gaze to find his mother in the doorway, her hands behind her back; she glanced away as their eyes met, half her face hidden behind a curtain of chocolate waves. She always looked that way; shy, as if she didn't want to interrupt.

"Yes. A single shot through the eye."

"The first one is always hard, Eve." She always called him Eve and he hated it; it was too girly.

"Right."

"Why don't you come with me? I want to show you something by the lake."

Lyn grunted. He didn't have time for the lake, not today. He had to skin this buck.

"It'll be quick," his mother said.

He glanced at the buck splayed on the table, the arrow exploding from its eye. "I only have an hour."

The lake had been frozen for a month now; winter had angrily reclaimed the forest this year, digging its icy teeth into everything. Lyn tripped over a rock as he tromped through the snow, cursing under his breath. His mother giggled ahead of him, walking across the frozen lake with her arms swinging out at her sides.

"Come on!" she urged with a laugh.

Lyn grunted, swinging his bow over his shoulder—he always brought it, just in case. "I only have an hour, Mom."

"This won't take long. I promise."

But it'd already been half an hour. Lyn tried not to roll his eyes as he inched toward his mother. When he reached her, she took his hand, her fat mitten fitting perfectly into his.

"Look at this," she said, kneeling to wipe away some of the snow on the surface of the iced lake.

Lyn knelt, his eyes squinting. For a moment, all he saw was the grey-blue color of the frozen water, then—slowly—his reflection morphed into view, a thin face with sad eyes. He stared at himself, leaning closer to the ice until another face

111

appeared; this one old and disfigured, its skin broken and its mouth frozen open in a soundless cry.

Gasping, Lyn jerked away and fell onto the ice. "Th—there's a body!"

His mother laughed. It sounded haunting. "Each year winter comes and claims the forest. We try to keep our storehouses full of grain and dried meat to get us through, but there are some who aren't as fortunate, Eve; some who choose to come here." She glanced at the body frozen beneath the surface. "It's quicker this way."

It took Lyn a moment to realize she meant *death*. Death was quicker in the lake than in the village, starving and whittling away. Though he didn't want to look again, his eyes betrayed him and roved over the ice, over the dead person's face, the frozen tears that kissed their cheeks.

He shivered.

"I don't understand."

His mother smiled down at him, brushing aside her hair so he could see her entire face. She looked like him, with more hair and happier eyes, though her joy was hidden more carefully, as if it were a secret. Behind her curtain of hair, between the sad lines of her aging face, beneath the downward curve of her lips, was a smile reserved for his eyes only. In her large snowsuit, with her fat mittens, and her fur-lined boots, and the dagger sheathed at her hip, she looked like she always did, like he would always remember her.

"What I'm trying to tell you," she explained, "is that you don't have to feel guilty when you hunt. You're taking an animal's life, but it's given in exchange for your own. Live or die, Eve, that's the choice you make every time you fit an arrow to that bow."

112

He shifted, feeling the weight of the large bow on his shoulder for the first time. The arrows from his quiver had scattered when he fell; he reached to gather them but stopped short, his hand hovering over a single arrow.

"I didn't mean to scare you, hon," his mother said, but Lyn shook his head.

"I'm not afraid."

"Then what is it?"

Quickly, Lyn removed his glove and flexed his fingers open and shut, turned his palm up to catch the black powder showering from the sky. He'd expected it to be cold, like snow, but instead it was warm—it was *hot*, nearly burning his hand when it touched his flesh. Lyn inhaled sharply and glanced at his mother; a flurry of the black snow descended around her.

"It's snowing," he said. "It's snowing black snow."

His mother frowned and glanced about, noticing the dark flakes for the first time. Like her son, she took off her thick mitten and held out a palm to catch the snow. A gasp escaped her. "This isn't snow," she said, suddenly taking off—sprinting toward the village. She left her single mitten on the frozen lake before Lyn, he stared at it as he scrambled to his feet. He wanted to call out to his mother, to ask what the black snow could be, but he already knew the answer. Ahead of him, thick clouds of smoke rose from his village. It was snowing soot.

Lyn ran as hard as his nine-year-old legs could go, trying his best to catch up to his mother. The bow on his shoulder made his stride awkward but he pressed on anyway, certain he would have to use it. Smoke meant fire and fire meant *darklings*. Darklings meant death. Suddenly, he remembered his mother's words: *live or die, Eve.*

A terrible scream rang through the trees. Lyn halted, eyes large and open wide as he scanned the forest, trying to discern which direction the cry had come from. When he heard it again, he took off running and found his mother slouched against a tree up ahead. Her head hung low and her hair covered her face, but he didn't need to see her expression to know that something was wrong. The snow at her feet was stained red, a thick liquid trickled from beneath her heavy fur coat.

Lyn ran to her side. "Mom?"

She coughed up blood and whispered one word, "Behind—"

Before she could say more, Lyn pulled away, drew his bow, and aimed over her shoulder—where part of the tree line appeared ... *unnatural.* What'd looked like a crooked, twisted tree shifted and stepped into view; a tall, skinny demon with skin hard as bark and eyes just as dark. Lyn clenched his jaw, steadied his breathing.

When you shoot an animal, make sure you kill it.

But this was not an animal and if Lyn missed, he wouldn't be cruel, he'd be dead.

He swallowed and exhaled a shaky breath. The demon charged. He released the arrow.

* * *

It felt hot inside the conference room. Nearly a dozen leaders of the Academy had gathered for this meeting but after an hour of discussion, nothing had been accomplished. First Lieutenant Evelyn Diaz flexed his fingers open and close, ignoring the pain that shot up his arm. He remembered the battle that'd earned his injury just days prior; the way he'd recklessly charged a demon, the silver-haired woman with four swords. She'd been standing in a vortex of fire when he stumbled onto the scene, unsure who'd been the enemy; the woman or the man of flames who'd shot her. But then he saw the inverted cross on her forehead and rushed forward without thinking.

The man of fire screamed for him to stay away from the flames, but he ignored the warning and continued to charge, swinging his hook swords just as he neared the demon. He'd had every intent to take the monster's head from her shoulders but when he sliced through the flames, he felt only a biting, burning pain as his arm caught fire.

"Did you kill it?" A pair of dark brown eyes stared at the lieutenant from across the table. They belonged to Lady Shakira, a Priestess and high-ranking leader of the Cross.

Diaz blinked, coming back from his thoughts. "Excuse me?"

"Second Lieutenant Kotaro turned in a report stating you charged the silver-haired demon we believe is responsible for the attack on the Village of Wi. Did you kill it?"

He clenched his jaw, biting out the words, "No. I *missed*."

There was an audible shift in the room, murmurs rose from the crowd just as heavy and thick as the smoke wafting from the burnt rolls of sage in the center of the table.

"Well," Lady Shakira scanned the pile of papers in front of her, "it seems we've got another issue to discuss today; our rapidly growing Most Wanted list."

"First we must address the issue at hand," Captain Priscilla Payne of the Academy's military spoke up. Her eyes narrowed on the array of Priests seated across from her. "We rescued over two thousand people from Wi. We need to discuss how we're going to provide for all of them."

Lady Shakira nodded agreement. "Providing for these people is our top priority, captain. Giving is the Church's duty."

"But you're not asking for the *Church's* money, are you?" Captain Payne eyed the Priestess, harrumphing at Lady Shakira's silence when she did not respond. Diaz could not help but roll his eyes; it was not unlike the captain to get straight to the point, oddly enjoying the awkward silence left behind her candor. Of all his comrades at the Academy, he'd always liked Captain Payne the least.

"You're asking for the *military* to fund a refugee operation that'll cost somewhere in the millions," Captain Payne went on. "Rescuing people is one thing—that's the Academy's job and we've done that! But providing for them, well that's the Cross's responsibility."

"Have you forgotten the military was founded by the Church, captain?" Lady Shakira leaned forward, and an enormous wave of golden curls fell over her light brown face.

Captain Payne bristled. "Is the military founded or *owned*?"

"There is no distinction between the Church's finances and that of the military. All of our provisions have come from God, after all."

Beside Captain Payne, Major Marshall cleared his throat. "If that's the case, then use the Church's money."

"The Church's money *is* the military's money," Lady Shakira said sharply. "Cross Academy has two divisions; the Cross represents the Church, and the Academy represents our military force. But let's never forget they *are* one in the same— with the same agenda, serving the same God." She clutched the silver crucifix hanging from her neck, the long black sleeves of her cassock swept the table with her movement. Her eyes

116

narrowed on the blade-shaped pendant tied around Major Marshall's neck. "You and I graduated side by side, Major. Everyone in this room received the same training to serve the same purpose."

The Cross leader had expected an argument from the Major. Each of his three subordinates sat with watchful eyes, waiting for a rebuttal, but the old man simply sighed, palmed the back of his neck with a scarred hand and said, "I completely agree, my lady."

Captain Payne inhaled sharply. "Major—"

"Lady Shakira is right," he continued. "We shouldn't bicker about money right now; we rescued two-thousand refugees, one of the largest missions we've accomplished in years. Let's be proud of ourselves and move forward. We've always had enough provisions before, nothing's going to stop that now."

"The *Academy* rescued those people—let's at least be honest about *that*." Captain Payne crossed her arms.

"Excuse me," Lady Shakira said. "Priests of the Cross were deployed to fight by your side during the attack on Wi." She motioned to her three subordinates, each dressed in like manner—black, floor-sweeping gowns and other Church ornaments. "We may not hold a position in the Academy's military, as you Hunters do, but do not make the mistake of underestimating the Priests of the Cross."

The four Hunters heaved a collective sigh, but it was Major Marshall who spoke up on their behalf. "Lady Shakira is correct; we don't have the luxury of picking and choosing who we help and how we help them. Cross Academy is on *humanity's* side, we defend and protect *everyone* against the darklings. No matter the cost, we *will* provide for the refugees of Wi."

Lady Shakira dipped her head in thanks. "Since that's settled, I think it's time we move on to the attack itself." She turned to Lieutenant Kotaro. "You have a report?"

The mousey lieutenant gasped, as if realizing where she was for the first time. A gentle pink tint crept up her cheeks, staining her flesh with an embarrassing blush. "Y—yes, I made the report on the initial attack." She fumbled through her papers. "W—well, First Lieutenant Diaz was assigned the task of deescalating a simple ambush—"

The lieutenant winced at the words, his arm throbbing in pain at the memories of the ambush, the demons, what remained of Wi. Abruptly, he stood and excused himself. "Sorry to leave the party early," he muttered, "but I have important business elsewhere."

"Lieutenant," Lady Shakira began but her husband, Lord Razzle Shoren, interrupted.

"Diaz, we all have someplace else to be, but this issue is dire—"

"Demons attacked, we killed them. There's nothing else to discuss." Diaz made his way to the door.

"I'm afraid there is *much* to discuss, lieutenant." Lord Razzle's voice teetered between anger and fear. He had fought beside the lieutenant in Wi, commanding part of the squad of reinforcements rushed out by the Academy. Together, they'd realized it'd been too late when they reached the village and saw the flames and the demons and the rampaging giant.

"You saw the silver-haired demon." Lord Razzle's voice softened. He ran a thick hand, thrice the size of a normal one, through an equally large head of hair. The Shoren Clan was known for their abnormally large bodies and incredible strength, some called them giants—but not to their faces. "You saw the giant; you saw the demons that destroyed one of the largest villages of that Region in just one night. There is *much* to discuss."

"Um." Lieutenant Kotaro shyly raised a hand. "It's just a theory, but I think I can find out who the demon is. The silver-haired woman, I mean."

Lord Razzle choked on his words. "W—what makes you so sure?"

"I interviewed some of the refugees; they described the silver-haired demon as having an inverted cross in the center of her forehead. According to Academy records, that sort of tattoo is worn by members of the Nine."

"*The Nine*," Razzle spat the words like poison then paused to let them sink in. Even Lieutenant Diaz stood still, his attempt to escape the conference room suddenly forgotten.

"Cross Academy has been battling the Nine since the start of the Great Demon War—hundreds of years ago, Lieutenant Kotaro. Are you absolutely sure about this?" Razzle asked.

Shrinking beneath his stare, Kotaro adjusted her glasses and said softly, "I'll have to speak with more of the refugees—particularly the ones who fought the demon—but I'm certain of it."

The Nine had been longstanding enemies of Cross Academy—their conflict could be traced back to Black Day, the beginning of the War. Some scholars theorized the Nine had existed long before the War. Some claimed they started it.

The enemies of the Cross called themselves *The Nine Births of Carnage*—nine powerful demons who claimed to be the very pillars of darkness, the embodiment and manifestation of the hatred, violence, and rejection of light in the heart of humanity. The extent of their power was unknown, their mission just as much a mystery. The only thing the Academy knew for certain was that the Nine was not just *their* enemy but an enemy to all of humanity.

Despite their reputation, not every act of violence could be linked to the Nine, but members of Cross Academy had grown familiar with the IX insignia, the red cloaks, and the inverted cross worn by members of the group. When Lieutenant Kotaro had learned a demon wearing each of those elements had been spotted in Wi, the connection was clear.

Nervously, she splayed her papers on the table in front of her. Her voice came out soft, almost a whisper, Hunters and Priests alike leaned forward, straining to hear her speak. "In the history of the Academy, we have only been able to gather a minuscule amount of data on the Nine. While multiple sightings have been recorded, this elite group of powerful demons have somehow managed to elude capture for centuries. Little is known about their members—even less about their objective, but over the centuries, the Academy has managed to positively identify two members: *Jareth*, the Second Birth of Carnage, and *Kajenbol*, a dark figure who calls herself the Fourth Birth of Carnage."

Captain Payne spoke up first. "Why would the Nine attack this old village? Wi was a stone settlement; incredibly large, but pitifully frozen in time. Their people relied on walls and traps to combat demons; they still lived in a hunter-gatherer society and have never heard of the Academy."

"That's true," Lord Izzy spoke up—a young, boyish looking

Priest whose eyes glimmered wildly with intrigue. "It seems the Village of Wi cut themselves off from the outside world at the start of the Great Demon War. I don't think many of them ever left their walls and the ones who did, never went more than a few hours' march."

Major Marshall rubbed his chin, the stubby growth of a shy beard prickled his fingers. "What could the Nine have possibly wanted or gained in Wi?"

"The Nine was not the only force to attack Wi," Vehenort answered, a young Priest who served as Izzy's assistant. She glanced at him for support, and he finished her statement without missing a beat. "The giant who rampaged and destroyed multiple villages before getting to Wi, that monster was the workings of a *witch*."

Major Marshall frowned, disliking every part of this case. "It seems like there's a lot more to this attack that we don't know or understand."

"I can continue my investigation," Lieutenant Kotaro offered weakly.

"They aren't going to talk to you," Diaz said. "Everyone gave brief statements when they were first rescued but I've been trying to get a follow-up interview for days and no one is speaking—the ones who do talk don't know a thing."

"I was thinking of targeting the leaders of Wi," Kotaro replied. "The man we saw fighting the silver-haired demon and his siblings are all somehow involved in this case."

"They're also guarded by their eldest sister—Lady Talon— she's not letting anyone get to them. I don't know what they're hiding but unless you find a way around their guard dog, you can kiss any interviews goodbye."

Kotaro chewed her lip and shot a glance at Lady Shakira. "It might help if a Priest joined me—"

"I don't think it's a good idea to have so many people involved," Captain Payne said.

Major Marshall disagreed. "There was a crucifix found at the scene where the Silver-haired demon attacked. Wi might have been stuck in time, but they knew something about fighting demons. I think a Priest's presence might help smooth things over."

Kotaro adjusted her glasses again. "Lord Izzy's the one who realized a witch had been involved in the first place."

"Right," Marshall nodded. "We Hunters spend our days killing demons, but the Priests are the ones who study them and other supernatural evils."

Izzy smiled. "Darklings of that caliber normally dwell in vast, flat lands, not places like Wi—surrounded by forests and mountains that would slow it down. I figured it had to have been summoned there. As far as our records can tell, witches are famous for summoning demons to come to their aid in battle."

"Then what about the silver-haired demon from the Nine?" Marshall questioned.

Izzy grinned, excited to share his findings. "According to a statement from one of the Fire siblings, the Nine warrior *attacked* the demon giant. These two forces were not working together, but they somehow had the same goal. We don't know exactly what that goal was, but we do know it has something to do with the orphan we took into our care."

Major Marshall leaned back in his chair. "I think you've found your partner, Lieutenant Kotaro."

"Agreed," Lady Shakira said. "You and Lord Izzy have permission from both the Cross and the Academy to speak with whomever you need to gather information about what exactly happened to the Village of Wi. We'll call another meeting should more details emerge, for now our work here is done."

"All right." Major Marshall stood, stretched, and nodded as the Priests left. He grabbed Lieutenant Diaz by the wrist before he could slip away. "I know you've got something planned, Lyn."

Diaz couldn't help but roll his eyes. No one besides his father had ever called him Lyn, then again, he'd only spent nine years with his real father and nearly fourteen with Major Marshall. He sighed, ignoring the nickname. "What makes you think that, old man?"

"I know you."

"I don't think Kotaro will mind me sitting in on some of her interviews. That's all."

He squinted. "You know you can't lie to me, right?"

Of course Evelyn knew that. The major was from the Marshall Clan, a family known for their anointing which gave them the ability to see the truth. They called it *Discernment*. Growing up in the major's care, Diaz had learned the hard way that it was impossible to lie to the man. He'd found the anointing as irritating as it was impressive. But it wasn't until the lieutenant joined the Academy that he saw the power's true gift. Major Marshall specialized in interrogations. Extracting information from his enemies. He would make a great addition to Lieutenant Kotaro's team, but a major with a reputation as grand as Marshall's was too busy to handle grunt work.

Which was why Diaz decided to sit in on the interviews

himself. He might not have the anointing of Discernment, but he was good at his job. He would get the answers he needed. First, he had to convince his adoptive father that he wasn't up to any mischief.

Diaz held up his injured arm. "It's not like I'll be of use on the ground right now."

"We have healers who could stitch you up in seconds. You're wearing that sling because you want to."

He flexed his burned hand open and close. There were a number of clans in Babel with gifts of healing; Lieutenant Diaz could have been back in the field within hours if he'd wanted, but he'd declined treatment and instead chose to recover the 'old-fashioned' way. "I'm wearing this sling as a reminder," he explained.

"Reminder?"

"Not to be so reckless."

Marshall chuckled. "Let's see if you've learned your lesson."

10

Evelyn

Talon Fire sat with her legs crossed at her ankles, nervously clutching her cup of warm peppermint tea. She kept her eyes trained at the floor as she spoke, sometimes squeezing them shut, trying to remember details of the night of the attack. Lieutenant Diaz watched her quietly; it was an effort to keep his emotions hidden, masked behind his neutral expression. When he'd heard his team had rescued the Grand Chief of the village, he'd expected to find a mighty warrior lying in the infirmary. Instead, he pushed aside doctors and found Talon's delicate frame unconscious on the white sheets. Her leg had been badly broken, her hair ripped from the scalp. He thought she would die.

When the healers released Talon, the lieutenant immediately wanted to see her, but she made it very clear that she would not cooperate. Talon refused to answer Diaz's questions and did everything in her power to keep him away from her siblings, too. The brother, Roaring, had been somewhat communicative at first but when Talon sank her claws into him, he shut down too. Suddenly, no one had any answers for the lieutenant's questions. His investigation had come to a halt.

And then Fox Fire woke up.

Lady Talon had been by her youngest sister's side each day of her three-week coma. When the girl woke, groggy and delirious, she was holding her hand and weeping into tissues. Out of respect for her recovery, Lieutenant Diaz waited three agonizing days before stopping by Fox's room; of course, Talon had been there and had tried to chase him away, but it was the Grand Chief he'd wanted to speak to.

"Fox Fire doesn't know anything," Talon had whispered fiercely, dragging the lieutenant into the hallway, away from her sister.

Diaz straightened his wrinkled sleeve where Talon had grabbed him. "I know she doesn't."

Talon blinked at him.

"Fox Fire has no idea why her village was attacked. And she has no idea what's wrong with the young boy from her village. But I have an idea as to why Wi was attacked, and I know what's wrong with the boy, and I know *you* know as well."

Talon swallowed nervously but her face remained hard and unmoved. "What are you saying, lieutenant?"

"I will tell her everything I know if you don't answer my questions." Diaz didn't need to say the rest, he could tell Talon already knew what he was thinking. It had been her own overprotectiveness that had given him the idea. Talon had put so much effort and energy into chasing him away from her siblings—it wasn't that she didn't want them to tell him anything, he'd realized, it was that she didn't want the lieutenant to tell her family anything.

What was the Grand Chief hiding from her siblings? What did she know that everyone else did not?

Both Lady Talon and the lieutenant winced at his words. He hated threatening her, hated the look of anger in her eyes as she glared at him, but he needed answers and he was willing to become a villain to one pretty woman if it meant saving thousands of others.

Talon Fire relented and agreed to meet for an interview.

"I saw the giant demon when I was trying to escape with Fox," Talon was saying now. She paused to sip her tea, dabbed at her mouth with a handkerchief. "We were running to find KI; he was unconscious and had been kept in his own cabin."

"Unconscious from what?" Diaz asked.

"He came into contact with a demon outside the Walls. After their interaction, he was rendered unconscious. I don't know why."

"Yes, you do," Diaz said bluntly and when she didn't respond he added, "Our people have looked at KI. We've found what you've been trying to hide. I just want to know why."

Talon peeled her wide eyes from the floor to look at Lieutenant Diaz. A sigh blew from her lips, the last of her will petering out. "We had no other choice," she whispered.

Diaz blinked. She'd spoken so softly he wasn't sure what he'd heard but then she said it again, this time so he could hear. "We had no other choice. We did what we thought was best at the time." Lady Talon sat up a little straighter. "And if I could go

127

back, I'd do it again."

He narrowed his eyes. "Do what again, Lady Talon?"

"Protect my family."

Diaz clenched his jaw. He hated playing games like this, beating around the bush, wading through all this buildup for a confession he'd known was coming weeks ago. His team had studied KI as soon as they'd brought him in; his veins had been stained black, his skin was so hot it was nearly steaming, and when one of the doctor's peeled his eyelids back, his pupils had completely dilated. Black orbs filled the boy's sockets, as if his eyes had been replaced by glowing ebony marbles. And then the research team turned him over and found the source of all the madness.

The inky black veins webbed over his body were thicker on his backside, as if all the dark matter inside was being pumped into a focal point. In the center of his back was a marking—a *seal*.

Lieutenant Diaz stole a glance at his comrades, Lieutenant Kotaro and Lord Izzy. Kotaro took notes on a scroll, nervously scribbling down every word Talon spoke while Izzy watched in silence. It had been Kotaro's team who'd examined the boy, but Izzy had been able to decipher the seal. The Priest and Hunter were Diaz's closest allies, but even he had a hard time believing them when they'd explained KI's condition.

Diaz leaned forward, put his elbows on his knees, and tried to level his voice. "The boy is demon possessed," he said, reading Talon's face for any sort of reaction. She was just as cold as him, though he suspected it was for a much different reason.

Lady Talon had grown up in a stone village, a princess hidden from the horrors beyond her village walls. She had never seen a demon face to face until the night of the attack. She had never seen a village rampaged by the monsters, heard the screams of their prey being devoured alive. Lieutenant Diaz had no choice but to suppress what he truly felt or risk going mad. But the Grand Chief was not hiding how she truly felt—she was not surprised or shocked by the revelation. *She doesn't feel anything*, Diaz realized, *because she already knew*.

"How long has he been that way?"

"Since he arrived at the village."

"What did you do when you found him?"

"What I had to."

He wanted to hit something. Instead, he breathed in and out and decided on a different approach. "Tell me how KI arrived in Wi."

She seemed to relax a little. "One day he showed up outside the Walls: hysterical, naked, and covered in blood. The Hunting Regiment found him; there was an argument over what to do with him, but they decided to bring him in and at least question him. The nearest village to Wi is at least a days' ride; we wanted to know how he'd gotten outside our Walls all alone at such a young age."

"What did he tell you?"

"Nonsense. That his village had been attacked and that he'd fled."

"How was that nonsense?"

Talon looked uncomfortable for a moment. "He said his village had been attacked by humans ... not demons."

Now Diaz looked uncomfortable. It wasn't unheard of for humans to commit crimes; the Academy had a public safety division designed to deal with small cases like this—break-ins,

129

fights, local disturbances. But for a group of humans to attack an entire village ... that was difficult to believe. Demons attacked villages; demons killed people; demons were always the culprit.

The lieutenant glanced at his comrades again; Kotaro had stopped writing, her hand hovering over the scroll, dripping ink onto the parchment. But Izzy was stony, his expression unreadable. Diaz didn't want to know what he was thinking.

"Was he sure the attackers were humans?" Kotaro asked Talon.

"He's never changed his story in all the time he's lived in Wi; he's always insisted it was humans. But he was just a child; he could have been confused; he could have been wrong. We never believed him, but we had nothing else to go on and our Regiment never found any evidence to corroborate his story."

"So they went out looking for his village?" the lieutenant asked.

"They did. And they found a small village that had been burned to the ground, but we weren't able to tell if it was the work of demons or humans. In the end, we had to take KI's words with a grain of salt and move on. We had bigger issues to deal with."

"Issues like what?"

"Like KI's condition." Talon set her cup of tea on the table beside her and shivered.

Diaz tried to sound sincere. "Go on," he urged.

Talon took a shaky breath. "When KI was brought to me, it was very obvious that something was wrong. I could sense his spiritual energy and I could tell it was tainted by something dark, even though I'm not as well-trained as your Academy

130

Priests." She motioned to Izzy in his floor sweeping cassock and stark white zucchetto, the white gloves covering his hands, and the silver crucifix hanging around his neck. With his boyish face and baggy robes, Izzy didn't look intimidating at all, but Diaz noticed the way Talon's gaze lingered on the black cross stained in the center of his forehead. It wasn't uncommon for Priest's to bear such a marking, but it typically appeared in battle, forming on a Priest's head when they were fully powered up and exerting an immense amount of spiritual energy. The Priest's Mark was what they called it and it was not something you saw every day unless you were fortunate enough to be near Izzy. Though he was one of the youngest Priests of the Cross, his potent spiritual energy allowed him to bear the Priest's Mark at all times. Izzy was in a league of his own.

The young Priest shifted uncomfortably beneath Talon's stare. "Well, you must be very good at sensing energy if you were able to tell the boy was tainted without having any training," he said, fidgeting.

"Our village Magi trained me as well as they could."

"Village Magi," Diaz repeated, thinking of the men and women from his own village before coming to Babel. The Magi were the Wise Men of most villages, leaders who were well-versed in the Word of God and had mastered other subjects such as healing, crafting, and history. Magi always wore white and kept their faces masked—their identities weren't important, only the knowledge they offered. Babel didn't have Magi; the city had been built around the Academy where Priests and Hunters did all the teaching and children who didn't go to the prestigious school joined family trades or took up apprenticeships instead.

131

"Why didn't you become a Magus?" Diaz asked Talon.

She said, "Because I was raised to become the Grand Chief."

"Is that why the boy was brought to you instead of someone else?"

She hesitated. "There were other village leaders there, too, of course. But since I realized the child's predicament, I was given the task of handling it."

"At the age of nine?"

Talon nodded. "I was honored by how much respect my elders had for me. But also..." she hesitated, "I was the only one in the village who could tell just how dire the situation was."

Diaz rubbed his chin. It wasn't shocking, considering Talon had come from a stone village. The Magi themselves were likely limited in their knowledge and training. Talon had been a prodigy in their eyes.

He squinted. She would have been a prodigy even by Academy standards. To be able to sense the boy's tainted energy at her young age. If she had grown up in Babel, she would be standing side by side with Izzy by now. Instead, she was being questioned about the part she played in covering all this up.

"How did you handle the situation?" the lieutenant asked.

"I made the decision to seal away the demon."

Diaz didn't speak for a moment, letting the confession sink in. "If KI was telling the truth; if humans attacked his village, then those humans were responsible for putting the demon inside of him. And you decided to leave the demon there—to seal it away."

"I had no other choice. Performing an exorcism to take the demon out was too risky. Even if I had done it successfully—

132

without harming KI—there was a chance the demon could overpower me once released. Who knows what would have happened then?"

"So, you decided to suppress the demon instead?"

"What would you have done?" Talon challenged.

The lieutenant chewed his lip, unable to answer. Talon was right, as messed up as it sounded, she really had done the best she could—especially since she had only been a child. When Izzy had discovered the seal and realized there was a demon suppressed within the boy, even he'd had his doubts about performing an exorcism. They were tricky procedures and could easily lead to someone's death if performed incorrectly. But sealing the demon away left a bad taste in Diaz's mouth.

"When you placed that seal on KI's back," he explained, "you locked away the demon and its dark energy, so KI appeared as a normal boy. Perfectly fine. But since you weren't well-trained, you didn't just seal away the demon, you accidentally locked away part of the boy's memories, too. His spiritual energy—even part of his *soul* had been dampened by that seal."

"*I didn't have a choice,*" Talon said again, angrier this time.

Lieutenant Diaz didn't care. "Every day KI lived with that seal on his back was another day you risked your entire village. Wi wasn't destroyed by a random raid; our reports say the monsters appeared *after* KI accidentally came in contact with another demon. When that happened, the creature inside of him woke up and every dark being around the globe heard the alarm. Whoever put the demon inside that boy had finally come to get it back and it was that broken seal that led them there."

Talon dropped her head, defeated by the information. The lieutenant watched her quietly, noticing the way her shoulders bunched when the tears began to fall. Silently, he pulled the red handkerchief from his uniform's breast pocket and passed it to her.

"There is good news," he muttered. "The demon inside KI happened to be in a dormant state when the boy showed up outside your village Walls. So even though the seal you placed on KI's back was weak and poorly done, it still managed to do its job. When the darkling outside the walls broke the seal, it awakened the demon inside but because it had been asleep for so long, it wasn't able to take total control of the boy—instead, the monster's dark energy began to seep out, staining his veins black."

Talon had lifted her head now, dabbing at her fat tears with the red cloth. "I don't understand," she whispered.

"We've placed a new seal on KI," Diaz said. He glanced at his companion. "Izzy put it on him; it's much stronger and will not break easily. But whatever's inside *has* awakened. Dark energy continues to seep into his body—it's only a matter of time before KI is filled with it, before the monster inside begins to take over. The new seal slows down the process, but it doesn't stop it— now that the process has begun, we *can't* stop it. But there is a chance he'll overcome the demon."

"What will you do with him?" Talon asked.

Diaz stood and gathered his things. "We're going to keep him in our facility, his foster father has given us full custody. It's safer for everyone if KI is kept here; that way we can monitor him and protect him at the same time."

Talon let go of held breath.

Diaz smiled but it was a crooked smile that gave the air of laughter. "We could kill him—end his life along with the demon fighting to take over his body. But don't worry," he said, one corner of his mouth raised, "the Academy is good at killing demons—but we don't kill kids. I guess we're alike in that manner."

"We are not alike," Talon said sharply. "The Academy kills demons for sport—the people of Wi fought demons to *survive*."

"The people of Wi cowered behind their ancient Walls," Diaz replied, waving a dismissive hand, as if to wipe away the entire history of Wi. "You didn't fight the demons; you *hid* from them. Your Walls didn't keep the demons out, they kept you *in*; chipping away at you, starving you of the world around you. KI may have cost thousands their lives, but he tore down the Walls in the process." The anger in Diaz's eyes glowed as he glared at the Grand Chief. He exhaled a hot breath and regained his composure. "Do understand the weight of this situation?"

She nodded slowly.

"The demon inside of KI must be powerful if its owners want it back. They destroyed your village to *get* it back. How long do you think we have before they come looking here?"

She sucked in a breath, hiccupping on the tears she didn't want to shed.

"You have brought death to our doorstep. And we welcomed you with open arms."

"I'm sorry."

"Talon," he said, his voice softer—gentler. She glanced up at him, but he looked away, eyes cast to the floor, staring down at nothing. "Like the claws of a bird."

"Yes," she agreed.

"A bird in a cage."

"Excuse me?"

"You were like a bird in a cage behind those walls. Aren't you glad you've been set free?"

Talon opened her mouth to speak but no words came.

Lieutenant Diaz gave his crooked, laughing smile again. It made Talon uncomfortable. "Don't worry, little bird, maybe here in Babel you'll learn to fly."

11

Fox Fire

A strange bird sang overhead. Fox did not recognize the song, but she knew it was not a love song—it was a song of mourning. *How fitting.* She shifted her weight from one foot to the other and ignored the pain in her hip, a dull ache from her tussle with the silver-haired demon. A dislocated hip was the only injury she took from that battle; though she'd expected to die when Roaring threw a fireball at her, she woke weeks later without so much as the smell of smoke upon her.

Talon sat beside her bed weeping buckets of tears when she'd first opened her eyes. The poor girl cried enough for Fox and herself and their lost parents. *My mother and father died in Wi,* Fox thought, staring at the two coffins before her.

Roaring had wanted to hold all the bodies of the fallen until they could be buried in Wi but there was nowhere to keep so many. The Council of Wi—what was left of it—decided to hold a mass funeral in Babel until they could return home. The late Lady Reign of Fire and her husband, Wolf Fire, were buried first. Fox and her siblings watched from their stance on the dais as men and women dressed in priestly garb stood in line before the bodies. In unison, they stepped forward and took an odd position Fox had never seen—as if to fight but without a sword in their hands. Their bodies shifted as they changed position, thrusting a fist down at the ground. It wasn't until the caskets disappeared beneath the surface of the earth that Fox realized the men and women were *controlling* the earth.

When they stomped their heavy feet, the ground shook in response, coming alive as if called into the realm of the living. The earth opened its mouth and hungrily devoured the coffins resting in the grass. Fox watched in awe, thinking of the night of the attack, the night she saw her brother shoot flames from his fists.

There's a lot you don't know about the world. She remembered Roaring's words as if he were by her side whispering them in her ear. She shivered as images of fire licking at his flesh came into her mind. Roaring had been right; there was so much out there that Fox had never seen—had never even imagined could be real.

She stole a glance at her siblings; Cat clung to Roaring, weeping uncontrollably while he stared blankly at the fresh graves. Chava maintained that same stony composure, sitting quietly on the dais, a silver shadow resting by his side. Talon dabbed at her tears with a handkerchief, reaching beneath the Flaming Veil she now called her own.

You could not see her eyes, but you could see the young

138

Grand Chief keeping her head held high. In her long red gown and crown of auburn feathers, she looked every bit the tribal leader she was—amidst terror and tragedy. It was weird for Fox to see her sister in the Veil, to watch her step forward to deliver a speech as the Grand Chief.

Talon wasn't supposed to be the Grand Chief just yet. She wasn't supposed to say the Last Prayer over their parents so soon. But Talon was determined to show her strength, now more than ever. *"They need to see that we are still strong, they need to see that we will one day rise again,"* she'd told young Fox Fire when she'd asked about the funeral.

Rise again. How could the mighty Fire Tribe resurrect their destroyed village, a foundation that'd been laid hundreds of years ago? Here, in this strange land amongst its strange people, Fox wanted nothing more than to go back home to Wi. But Wi was just a pile of dirt now—smoldering dirt.

Fox exhaled as a wash of fear and wonder overcame her; there were so many questions left unanswered about the night her village was destroyed. How did her brother have these powers? Why hadn't she been killed by his fire? And, most important, where was KI? She hadn't seen her friend since the day she fought off demons trying to protect him. KI had always been small for his age; he'd seemed even smaller that night when all Fox could do was watch as the giant curled its mighty fingers around his body as if holding a mere pebble in the palm of its hand. Fox thought that would be the last time she'd ever see KI—in some ways, she'd been right.

The last coffin closed with a *thunk,* making Fox jump in surprise. The men in uniform did their dance and the casket disappeared beneath the earth, just like all the rest.

Solemnly, Talon closed the ceremony by reading a scripture:

We glory in our sufferings, because we know that suffering produces perseverance; perseverance, character; and character, hope.

Romans, Fox remembered her Bible well, though the words had held no significant meaning to her until now. *I suffered that night, but I survived. I am alive for a reason—KI is alive for a reason. I intend to find out what that reason is.*

Dinner was served after the ceremony, Babel had been kind enough to provide a great hall to the Council, the Head Family, and over 500 guests. Fox and her siblings sat on a dais, this time with other Council members and honored guests while everyone else ate below. There was roasted lamb crusted in herbs and then eggs poached in a spicy tomato sauce, buttery braided bread was served next with a chicken soup full of vegetables and giant balls of dough floating in the broth. Fresh fruit came last, served on trays with little bowls of ice-cold yogurt and as much honey as the young chiefana desired. Fox picked around the strange foods, taking tiny bird bites here and there. Though her stomach growled, she could not get herself to enjoy very much, stricken with a painful craving for food from home. Fox had never missed simmered mustard greens and sweet cornbread so much.

It's so strange ... No one here eats with their hands, Fox frowned, watching the man beside her spear his fruit with a fork and carefully place it in his mouth. Sensing her staring, he turned to her and raised an eyebrow. "Not hungry?" He was a thin man with honey-toned skin wearing a beige and red uniform—*a Hunter's uniform,* Fox remembered.

140

A few guests from the famed Academy had been invited to the dinner. Fox noticed the small scar on the left side of the Hunter's face; a patch of skin darker than the rest of his body, it started near his chin and ran down his neck to hide beneath his collar. Though she couldn't see the rest of it, Fox knew the scar was a burn.

Vaguely, she remembered a man from the night her village was destroyed—a lunatic who'd jumped between her and Roaring's flames at the last second. She'd seen his face for only a moment before the fire had engulfed them both.

Just as recognition hit her, the man suddenly shifted so Fox couldn't see his burn anymore. "I am sorry for your loss, my lady."

Fox cringed. "I am not a *lady*."

"Then what are you?"

"A Chiefana."

He made a noise—something like a laugh. "I took you for a warrior, maybe even a demon slayer."

"Don't mock me," she said. "I fought for my village. I did everything I could—I was willing to die for my family that night."

The Hunter nodded. "Then I wasn't mocking you at all. I was telling the truth; you are a demon slayer." With that, he stood and left her with her family as he pressed into the crowd below, disappearing into the sea of red. No one seemed to notice.

Tribesmen mingled at the foot of the dais as the Head Family enjoyed their fruit and yogurt; some men had gathered near Cat Fire, vying for her affection, offering comfort in whatever way they could. Talon was surrounded by leaders from Babel and Wi alike, Roaring sat simmering in his anger. No one dared speak to him. If Fox was going to sneak away, this was the perfect time.

What am I doing? she wondered, easing from her chair. She peered over the crowd below and saw the Hunter in the back corner, leaning against a wall. He caught her eye and something like a smile formed on his lips, the very corner of his mouth turning up. Then he peeled from the wall and disappeared into the crowd again.

Fox followed. Up close, the dinner looked less like a funeral and more like a terribly sad party. Scraps of food lay strewn across tables with people crying into their plates. A man stood on his chair singing a melody Fox had heard ringing through the streets of Wi countless times, a small crowd gathered at his feet to listen. The air was hot, almost difficult to breathe, with the thick smell of boiled blackberry wine lingering at the end of every breath. You could almost taste the sweet flavor if you stuck out your tongue.

Fox pushed her way through the mourning folk as she searched for the Hunter. He should have been easy to spot in his uniform and leather boots, surrounded by tribesmen and women dressed in tunics and headwraps and tribal paint. Yet Fox could not find him.

Not until he wants to be found, she realized, spotting him against another wall just a few feet ahead. He was looking right at her, eyes lazy and half-lidded, as if he weren't interested in this silly game—as if he hadn't started it in the first place. When she neared him, he pushed from the wall and walked away, turning the nearest corner.

Fox gasped and shoved past weeping soldiers and singing women. When she rounded the corner, anger swelled within

142

her; the Hunter was nowhere in sight. But she *knew* he'd gone this way, so she walked down the empty hallway, searching every doorway and shadow. When she came to the end of the hall, she found a locked door on her left and total darkness on her right. The hallway curved into another hall; Fox blinked into the inky shadows, trying to make out shapes or patterns.

In the darkness, a line of silver twinkled; before Fox realized what it was, it shot towards her. Suddenly, she had a blade pointed at her throat. The curved end of a hook-sword shimmered a white-ish silver as it emerged from the shadows, its wielder remained hidden, but Fox knew who stood at the other end of the weapon.

"Why did you follow me?" a voice spoke from the darkness.

Fox made a face. "Because you wanted me to!" It couldn't have been more obvious with the way he'd made eye contact and made sure she'd seen him before sneaking away. Fox suddenly felt dumb; *the real question here is, why did he want me to follow him?*

The Hunter stepped into the light, that lazy smirk still spread on his face. His sword remained at her throat, forcing Fox to step back. "I guess you did have some training."

"What do you want with me?"

He brought his sword higher, and Fox felt a sudden sting on her chin, the burning sensation of a fresh wound. "To be honest, it was your brother I wanted. He's the one with the gift."

Roaring and his flames.

"Then you should have lured him out here."

The Hunter chuckled. "You seemed an easier target. Plus, I was told you *wanted* to fight demons."

"Who told you that?"

He stared at her in silence, his eyes regarding her almost cautiously, as if his next words might scare her off. "Someone very close to you."

Fox inhaled sharply, tears pricking the backs of her eyes. "KI..."

"That's him."

"You have to take me to him—" she began but a voice over her shoulder cut her off.

"Fox! There you are!"

Cat Fire trotted down the hall, the click of her shoes echoed off the high walls.

"If you want to see him, go to the Academy tomorrow and ask for Lieutenant Diaz," the Hunter whispered, pressing something into her hand. Fox stared at it in shock before her sister grabbed her by the arm and pulled her away.

"We've been looking for you," she said, her breath sour from wine. "Talon's about to make her closing remarks—hey, you're bleeding!"

Fox blinked, absently touching her chin. When she pulled back a red-stained fingertip, she sighed. *He actually cut me.*

"Are you hurt?" Cat asked, leaning down to look at the wound.

Fox shook her head. "I'll be fine. Let's go back now."

During Talon's speech, she clutched the object from the Hunter, running her fingers along the woven design, enjoying the feel of the material. It was a cord of red thread; the knot she'd received the day she'd snuck out with KI. She'd nearly forgotten about her knot, something she'd worked almost her entire life to get suddenly seemed so insignificant. So small. But it was hers and she'd earned it and she'd given it away, tying it around KI's wrist when she'd seen him in the infirmary. For that Hunter to have her knot in his possession—he must have been with KI at some point. Lieutenant Diaz was the first person to even mention him since Fox had arrived in Babel. She *had* to find him again. That meant going to the Academy.

Fox looked at the crowd below her; the Fire Tribe had found a new land in a new region, but they had not settled. Every day, Roaring spoke of leaving, counting the days until he could go home and rebuild what was lost—*rise again*. Fox had no idea how he planned to do it, but she vowed she'd be right by his side the moment he marched beyond the gates of Babel. *Now*, she thought, *I can take KI home, too.*

There had been a time when Fox had wanted nothing more than to get out and see what lay beyond the Walls of her village. But now, hundreds of miles away, her heart and mind had changed. *I have gone beyond the Walls. I have seen the world; it is not a pretty place.*

12

Fox Fire

There was loud banging outside the window. Fox sighed as she rolled over in bed; the banging had been going on for hours, making it impossible to sleep, not that she'd gotten much during the night. *KI ... He is here, in this village ... somewhere.*

KI had been the first thing she'd asked about as soon as she'd regained consciousness. But Talon had avoided the topic, murmuring and making empty promises to see him soon.

"The City of Babel is our home now," Talon had said that with a smile when she'd first shown Fox their new home; it was a crooked smile since the darklings had knocked out three of the teeth in the back of her mouth. Talon had suffered the worst injuries of the four siblings; a broken leg and arm, six fractured ribs, and all the hair on the left side of her head had been ripped out. "The city is very different from home, but it's incredible. I promise."

So far, Talon had been wrong. Babel *was* different from Wi, but it was not incredible; there were lights *everywhere*—even at night—firelit torches lined the streets and hung on lamps outside every building to keep the city alive. Babel was always lit up and it was always busy; people were everywhere—in every corner, crevice, and alley. It was nearly ten times the size of Wi with people who'd come from clans and tribes Fox had never heard of, villages she'd never seen, and from other regions across the globe. *All this time, I thought demons were the only thing beyond the Walls.*

There was much beyond the Walls, Fox learned. Demons and humans and some things in between. There were more people like Roaring, too; the man who delivered mail to their apartment never came to the door, he simply flicked his wrist, and the papers would levitate from the bag at his hip and float safely to their mailbox. One time, there was a boy who'd tripped and scraped his knee as he ran down the street, nearly knocking Fox over. When she stooped to see if he was all right, he waved a dismissive hand and hopped back to his feet—the scrape had healed before he'd taken off running again.

There's a lot you don't know about the world.

The banging outside grew louder and Fox sighed, staring at her window. "It's so noisy." It was never quiet in Babel; she had learned that the first night she'd moved into her new home. Their neighborhood was *under construction*, Talon had explained, leaning on a crutch as she'd given her sister a tour of their new home.

In Wi, the buildings had been made of wood or mud and brick, covered in turf and tied together on great wooden beams.

Animal skins hung in doorways and furs lined the floor as carpeting or were thrown over the bed as a blanket. Here, everything was made of stone; perfectly square homes were squeezed side by side and stacked on top of each other. Some buildings were so high Fox had to squint to look up at them. Rickety wooden bridges stretched between buildings dozens of feet above Fox's head; when she looked up, she could see children running across them, playing and screaming as if they hadn't a care in the world.

Some parts of the city reminded Fox of home; lakes and patches of woods on the outskirts of Babel surrounded by wildlife and farming families. Some sectors of the city had been claimed by entire tribes, forced to resettle like Fox and her family; tired faces worked the earth, trying to harvest what they could from this foreign soil. Their banners and flags and sigils hung outside their homes, faint echoes of the cultures lost or destroyed by demons.

"You should be grateful," her eldest sister had said. "The City of Babel has given us a new home and a new kind of security Wi never had."

That much was true. Babel had an army and horses and swords and shields, and other weapons Fox couldn't name. There was an institution dedicated to training people to fight demons—*they must be really good*, Fox thought, because Babel had only *one* great wall surrounding the entire city, unlike Wi which had multiple walls and gates and *still* fell to demons.

Someone knocked on the door.

"Fox? It's time for breakfast."

In the kitchen a table was set for four with matching plates and cutlery; Fox could smell meat frying and tried to ignore the

148

involuntary growl of her stomach.

Talon laughed. "Hungry?" she chirped, plating the meat. "I got my hands on some salted fish! The eggs will be done in a minute."

Fox watched her shuffle through the kitchen, preparing the food. Talon's leg had been twisted so badly she'd nearly lost it, mercifully, she was only left with a limp after she'd put the crutches away. Talon adjusted the wood beneath their stove and started a fire to roast the peppers she would chop for the eggs. The sudden rush of heat caught Fox's attention; she snapped her vision to the flames beneath the pan, licking at the shining copper. They seemed to call her name, to draw her in as they danced wildly, begging to be released from their prison.

A radiant heat swelled in Fox's chest, as if in response to the fire. Sweat bubbled on her forehead and her mouth began to water as an unnatural urge to touch the fire seized her. Lazily, her feet carried her toward the stove, her eyes glued to the flames, but a heavy voice called out to her.

"Fox!" Roaring said loudly. He squinted at her; his shaggy head cocked to the side. "Are you there?"

"Uh, yes," she blinked.

"You're standing in the middle of the kitchen," he said. Chava appeared by Roaring's side, she licked at his large hand and then groaned when he ruffled her fur.

"I'm sorry, I was just thinking."

"Think at the table."

Roaring pointed her to a cushion to sit and then moved to help Talon with the pot of boiled eggs, insisting she let him do it. Though they now lived in a new city with a new culture and new people, Roaring had insisted they eat together the way they had in Wi. He refused to let the men who'd moved their furniture into their new apartment bring in the tall wooden table from their wagon. Instead, the Fire siblings gathered around a short table and sat cross-legged on cushions as Talon served the meal; pieces of simmered salt-fish, its skin burned crisp at the edges, with boiled eggs and a spicy salsa of chopped onions and roasted peppers.

Talon called for Cat while she served her other two siblings. When she finally arrived and took her seat, the Grand Chief led the small family in prayer and then began to eat. They enjoyed their food in silence until Roaring announced, "Some of the Academy leaders want to meet with the Council to discuss what's going to happen next for the village. They want to talk this morning."

"The *Council*," Cat echoed. "You mean, you, Talon, Ryko, and Kifu Kato?"

Roaring finished chewing, washed down his food with sweet tea, and said, "The Council is small for now, but we can't just sit here and forget about the home we left."

"Not everyone wants to go back home," Cat said.

Fox put down her piece of fish. "Not everyone wants to stay."

"That's why there's going to be a meeting," Roaring wisely interjected. "To discuss what's best for everyone."

Fox did care about what was best for everyone, but she had other reasons to visit the Academy today. Her knot rested in her pocket, she felt for it in the folds of her skirt as she finished breakfast. *Ask for Lieutenant Diaz.*

* * *

In Wi you had to walk everywhere you went—wealthier tribes had horses, the wealthiest had carriages for tribal leaders. Fox had her own hand-painted palanquin—though she'd only rode in it a handful of times, she'd always preferred to walk. In Babel, there were carriages for everyone everywhere, you could even arrange a carriage from a stranger and pay them coin for a ride. Fox and her siblings piled into a carriage to ride to the Academy; Roaring had wanted to take Chava, but she scared the horses so badly he was forced to leave her behind.

"I'll be back soon, girl, wait inside," he said, petting her solemnly. "She's restless. Misses the hunt."

"Don't you miss it, too?" Fox asked.

Roaring only groaned in response, yanking at his tie as he took a seat. Talon complained that he would loosen it too much, but Roaring didn't seem to care—he hated ties and dress shirts and the uncomfortable trousers all the men wore. Babel was full of strange fashion; a mix of tribal clothing and face paint and headgear with shirts that buttoned from top to bottom—even the women wore them with floor-sweeping skirts and shoes that click-clacked when they walked. Some of the prettier girls wore jewels, gold in their ears and ribbons in their hair. Talon wore a scarf wrapped around her head to cover the baldness.

When Fox asked why she didn't wear the Flaming Veil, she laughed and said, "In a way, I *am* veiled, aren't I?"

"At least it's a red scarf," Fox had said.

The Academy was a building that stood taller than any of the Walls of Wi; it was completely black and shimmered in the sunlight as if inset with dark diamonds. Fox's mouth hung open as she took in the view of it; it was the shape that truly took her breath away. Cross Academy was shaped like a giant cross.

"How?" Fox whispered as the carriage pulled to a stop at the entrance. The driver chuckled and tipped his hat at her.

"We call it the Tower of Babel. It's been standing longer than the walls themselves."

Talon inhaled sharply. "That sort of name seems like an omen."

"Maybe," the driver began but Talon shuffled them away before he could say more.

"It's just a name," Fox muttered.

Inside, Kifu Kato waited on a bench, nervously sanding his hands together with Ryko and two women from Wi by his side. They were all dressed in the same odd clothes of Babel; the women in dresses and shiny jewels, and the men in trousers and button-down shirts. Kato looked especially out of place as he hadn't bothered to wear a tie or give himself a shave. Fox could see the beginning of a thick black beard shadowing his dark brown skin. This was not the Kato she remembered; the Kifu with scars across his chest and a necklace beaded with the claws and teeth of demons he'd slain with his own rahkai. Kato had never worn trousers, nor had he ever bothered with a shirt—especially not one with buttons. *We have to get out of here*, Fox thought, *we have to get out of here fast.*

"Grand Chief," Kifu Kato inclined his head when Talon approached.

"How long have you been waiting?" she asked.

"Not long. A woman came by earlier and said she'd be back to take us into the meeting room."

"Good. Before we go inside, I want to introduce these ladies to my family." Talon turned to her siblings, though she only spoke to Cat and Fox. "We lost many great people in Wi—tribal

152

leaders and members of the Council were not exempt. Still, we must move forward and fill those positions; Kato, Roaring, Ryko, and I were each tasked with finding one member to add to the Council. You four ladies were chosen."

Fox flushed red, her cheeks burning. How could she, a sixteen-year-old girl, be admitted to the Village Council? It was unthinkable; not even Talon became an official member until she'd turned eighteen. By then, she'd already learned the Old and New Tongue, could recite hundreds of passages from the Bible, and had sat in on dozens of meetings alongside the Grand Chief herself. Fox Fire had never even seen the inside of the Council's meeting room.

Talon smiled at her, sensing her unease. "We would not have approved of you as a member if we did not think you were ready, little paws."

Exhaling, Fox said, "This is a lot to take in."

Cat agreed. "Being on the Council means I have a say in what happens in our village, are you sure you trust me with that position?"

There was laughter in the group, something Fox had not heard since before the attack. "That is why you were chosen," Talon explained. "Because you are the only honest person in Wi." She turned to the two other young ladies. "This is the daughter of Kifa Minga, an elder who'd served on the Village Council and leader of the Modon Clan. Since her mother's passing, Ina Modon has taken over as leader of the Modon Clan and will now assume her mother's position on the new Council."

Ina inclined her head; a wave of micro dreadlocks fell into her face. "I am honored, Grand Chief."

Talon motioned to the other woman. "You all know the Bolt Clan was very small, but it was well-known throughout the village because of the meat shop ran by Lady Bolt. She had two sons who served bravely on the Regiment and gave their lives protecting the village. Her daughter is now the only survivor of the three children." Talon smiled at the girl; a brown-skinned woman barely older than Roaring. "Thunder Bolt, will you accept a position on the Council and the Hunting Regiment?"

Thunder's eyes watered but she found the strength to nod and declare, "I humbly accept!"

"Now that that's over," Talon continued, "let's decide here and now; our goal in this meeting is to discuss the future of Wi. Do not let your emotions cloud your thinking or your judgement. These people have been kind to us, but we must think of ourselves now."

No one voiced a word of disagreement. Talon gave a firm nod and sat down to wait for the meeting to begin. Fox stood idly beside her, picking at the bandage on her chin. She wondered if she should go search for the Hunter from dinner, but there was no way she could abandon the meeting now, not after being named a member of the Council.

"How long will the meeting be?" she asked.

Roaring shrugged and leaned against the wall, anger coming off him in waves—Roaring Fire was not one who enjoyed waiting. Talon shot a nervous glance at their brother before answering, "I doubt it will be longer than an hour."

The door beside Kifu Kato swung open to reveal an exceptionally tall woman in a cassock. *A Priest*, Fox noted. She smiled at them. "Good morning, you must be the leaders of Wi? I am Lady Shakira Shoren, leader of the Priests of the Cross.

Would you all come inside?"

The group shuffled into the room in silence, a small room with too many chairs and not enough sunlight. There were two tables set up; one with a cluster of Hunters and Priests sitting quietly, and another with several empty chairs placed around it. Shakira guided Fox and her comrades to the empty chairs and took a seat at the head of the other table.

"These men and women beside me are esteemed Hunters and Priests from Cross Academy," she began. Fox looked at each of them, carefully studying their features. "As you know, Cross Academy is the center of our great city and faith is the founder. If I'm told correctly, *rise again* are the words of the Fire Tribe—*for faith and freedom* are the words of the Academy. I hope you can see our faith throughout the city, and I hope you can have faith in us, that we will do our best to provide for you and aid you in rebuilding Wi."

He isn't here, Fox frowned, staring at the men and women beside Lady Shakira. *The Hunter from last night is not here.* This meeting would be a waste of time if she didn't get to speak with the man who'd returned her knot. He seemed to be the only person willing to talk about KI. But how could Fox get to him now? How could she go on making plans for the future of Wi without her dearest companion by her side?

"Over two-thousand refugees were rescued from Wi," Lady Shakira said. "To our understanding, Wi was the largest village in the Region of Smoke and Ash, it was home to over ten-thousand people."

"That is correct," Talon agreed. "And now, because of demons, it is nothing but rubble. We owe it to the dead, and to the few thousand who remain living, to return home and

155

rebuild what was lost."

And I owe it to KI to make sure he is safe. Fox balled her hands into fists.

"The City of Babel welcomes you permanently, if you desire to stay." Lady Shakira's words cut through her thoughts. "But if you are intent on returning home, we will certainly assist as best we can."

"Is *everyone* allowed to leave?" Fox spoke up, surprising even herself.

Lady Shakira looked at her strangely. "W—Well, yes, everyone who wants to."

"What about KI?"

A pregnant silence hung in the air.

"Why isn't anyone talking about him?" Fox said.

"Fox, you are out of line," Talon warned.

Fox looked at her, snapping her head up in anger. "KI was rescued from Wi just like all of us, but I haven't been allowed to see him or speak with him."

"KI is a special case," Lady Shakira explained.

"Where is Lieutenant Diaz?" Fox asked.

Lady Shakira made a puzzled face. "The lieutenant?"

"He's the only one who'll speak to me about my friend."

"He has business elsewhere—"

"Then I'll go find him."

Before anyone could protest, Fox bolted from the room. She ran down the hall without thought or direction, pushing through the crowd, trying to get as far away as possible. Talon's voice pierced through her frantic thoughts, shouting for her to come back, but Fox ignored her and kept running.

Panting, she came to a halt in an empty hall, yanking her

knot out of her pocket—like it could somehow give her guidance. It didn't bring her any closer to the lieutenant, but it did give her comfort. *KI is alive*, she told herself, rubbing her fingers over the thread. *I've just got to find him.*

She walked aimlessly for what seemed like ever, passing large doors too heavy for her to pry open. There weren't many people in this part of the Academy—the halls were grand and empty and cold. Fox touched the wall, running her hand along the stone as she walked. It felt alive, like a living, breathing creature. *What is this place?* she wondered, halting as her fingers lingered on the cool stone. *Why is this city so different?*

"Are you lost?" a voice asked.

Fox glanced up to find a small woman staring at her from behind large round glasses. "I could help you, if you'd like," she offered.

Fox thrusted her knot at her. "Lieutenant Diaz gave this to me last night. Do you know where I can find him?"

The woman chewed her lip, shifting her weight from one foot to the other. She had on the same leather boots and the same beige and red uniform as the Hunter from before. "I can take you to him."

Fox tried to hide her unease as she walked. She distracted herself with thoughts of finally seeing KI. The last time she'd spoken to him was right before they were attacked; *we'd been fighting*, she remembered.

"Lieutenant Diaz shouldn't have given you that object," the woman was saying. She'd introduced herself as Lieutenant Kotaro. "It's an artifact—evidence from the case. For him to do something so reckless must mean that thread belongs to you. Which means you're Fox Fire." She stopped in front of a heavy door and smiled at Fox. "He's in here."

Fox had expected to find the lieutenant running military drills or hunched over a pile of complicated paperwork. Instead, she found First Lieutenant Diaz sitting at a table with a bowl of soup, whispering quietly to a man seated across from him. He looked up when Kotaro cranked open the door, his eyes bored and void of all emotion, but something inside him flickered to life when he spotted Fox.

"You came," he said, his face forming something like a smile.

Kotaro shut the door behind her. Fox tried to ignore the sound of the lock clicking in place. A shiver tiptoed down her spine as she realized her own foolishness. The lieutenant had sought her out at the dinner, mentioned KI to make sure she would listen. Kotaro had led her here without question. No one knew where she was. *She* didn't even know where she was.

Her hand found the knot in the pocket of her skirt; she clutched the thread tightly, forcing herself to calm down and remember why she was here.

"Where is KI?"

Diaz pushed his soup away. "About that."

"Where is he?"

"I see you've met Kotaro, she's a close friend of mine." He motioned to the man across the table. "Along with Lord Izzy."

Fox stared at him, at the cross in the center of his forehead. "That mark," she whispered.

"You've seen it before," Diaz said—not a question but a statement.

She shook her head. "No. I mean, yes, but it was different."

"Different how?"

The silver-haired demon appeared in her head, with her four

swords and the razor-sharp wind. She shivered. "It was inverted."

A smile ghosted the lieutenant's lips, crooked, as if he were holding back laughter. Fox grew angry at the sight of it. The silver-haired demon was nothing to laugh at. The destruction of her village was nothing to laugh at.

"Where is KI?" she repeated.

"The cross you saw was inverted because the person who wore it was not a human," Diaz replied, ignoring her question.

"I want to see my friend."

"You'll get to see him. But only after you do me a favor."

Fox bristled. "That's not what you said last night."

"I didn't have time to explain."

"Where is KI?" she repeated.

Kotaro placed a hand on her shoulder. Bad idea. Fox turned and grabbed it, twisting her wrist at a bad angle.

"Don't touch me!" she spat.

Diaz stood so abruptly his chair fell over, but he didn't move to attack. He remained at the table, staring at Lieutenant Kotaro with those dead eyes.

"You let a child grab you," he said flatly.

She grimaced. "I—I wasn't paying attention."

Fox twisted her wrist further, earning a cry of pain from the second lieutenant. "Are you paying attention now?"

"Let her go, Fox Fire," Diaz said calmly.

"Where is KI!" she yelled.

"I won't say it again."

She gripped Kotaro's wrist firmly, ready to break it. "Neither will I."

Diaz sighed. "Kotaro."

The second lieutenant obeyed his command, rolling her shoulder and turning to face Fox Fire. It happened so quickly the young girl didn't have time to react. Before she could even gasp in shock, Kotaro slipped from her grasp and punched her in the stomach.

Fox dropped to her knees, vomiting from the pain. Her eyes watered as she stared at the floor, her nose stung from the bile that burned her throat. She wiped her mouth with her sleeve and looked up at Lieutenant Diaz.

"I trusted you. I just want to see my friend."

"And you will," Diaz said, returning to his chair. He nodded at Kotaro who crossed the room to stand beside him, rubbing her wrist the entire time.

"When?" Fox asked.

"After you do me a favor."

She squinted. "What is it?"

"I need you to answer one question."

"Go on."

"The inverted cross is an *anti-symbol*—something that represents evil. It was on the silver-haired demon because she is part of a dark organization called the Nine Births of Carnage. The Nine have been enemies of the Cross since the beginning of our world, but they have been relatively inactive until now. I don't know what their goal is but that doesn't matter—they must be destroyed, nonetheless."

Fox's breathing steadied as the pain in her gut slowly subsided. Her knot lay on the floor a few inches away, dropped during her scuffle with Lieutenant Kotaro. She reached for it and clutched it to her chest, still on her knees.

"What is your question?" Fox interrupted Diaz.

160

He took a breath. "Your brother is a sundancer. He has powers to fight the demons—you possess those same powers."

She opened her mouth to object, but he spoke over her.

"Sundancing was considered a lost anointing until your village walls came crashing down. There is a reason the Nine are on the move and there is a reason your powers have awakened. You're meant to fight the demons, Fox Fire, and we can train you here. At the Academy."

She quirked an eyebrow. "What do you mean?"

"I mean we need you. The Academy specializes in training people with extraordinary talents—talents meant for fighting the darklings. With the Nine on the move, we need every strong anointing we can find. I told you last night I preferred your brother, but I'm willing to settle for the next best thing. That means you." He narrowed his eyes. "So, my question is this; if I allow you to see KI as often as you'd like, will you join Cross Academy?"

Fox rubbed her knot between her fingers, feeling the silky thread on her skin. Her stomach still ached from her fight with Kotaro. Her breath smelled sour from vomiting. She struggled to her feet and shook her kinky hair over her shoulders.

"Yes, I will."

13

Fox Fire

The lieutenant called for someone to clean up Fox's mess and offered her a bowl of soup. She declined.

"I want to see KI now."

Diaz rested his chin on a fist, tried to hide his vulpine smirk. "Are you always this rigid?"

Fox leaned across the table. "I've answered your question. I'm done playing your games. Let me see KI."

"This isn't a game."

She slammed a fist on the table. "Where is he?"

Diaz leaned back; his smirk vanished. "You're as stubborn as your sister and as fiery as your brother. The Academy will be glad to have you." He quickly held up his hands when she bared her teeth. "Calm down—you'll see him in a moment." He glanced to his comrade. "Kotaro."

Lieutenant Kotaro excused herself and stepped into the hall. Diaz's gaze returned to Fox as soon as the door shut behind her. "Tell me more about the silver-haired demon."

"I don't remember much."

"Tell me what you can."

She hesitated. "My sister told me I shouldn't—"

"I'm aware she may have warned you about talking to me. But this information could help us with KI."

Fox stared at her hands clasped in her lap, the knot squeezed in her grip. She had embarrassed and defied her sister once already on behalf of KI, but she'd convinced herself it was worth it—this was for her closest friend. Talon would understand. But she wasn't sure her sister's understanding would stretch so far as to excuse her sharing information about the attack on the village. Talon had never explained why Fox had to keep her mouth shut but she'd made it clear that talking to Diaz was not okay.

"How can it help KI?" she asked.

"We believe the demons attacked Wi because of him. It will help us find out why if we know exactly who attacked."

"It was a woman. She had four swords but only fought with one—and even when she used her blade, it didn't behave as a normal sword."

"What do you mean?"

Fox chewed her lip. "Whenever she swung her blade, the air reacted to it. It sliced the hand off the giant demon, almost like she'd been conducting it."

Diaz glanced across the table at the Priest. Izzy shook his head. "I've never heard of these powers before. It could be anything."

163

"Are you sure she fought against the giant? They weren't allies at all?"

"No," Fox answered. "They both wanted KI—but only for themselves."

"Huh," Diaz said. He thrummed his fingers on the table, the sound reverberated through his cold bowl of soup. "That is interesting."

"Will it help KI at all?"

He opened his mouth to answer but the door cranked open, and Lieutenant Kotaro returned with a man shuffling behind.

He approached the table with a crooked smile on his face. "Fox Fire," he said.

The voice was familiar, unmistakable, but the face and body did not match. KI had a boyish face, like that of a young teenager, and a small, scrawny body of a child. He'd always been tiny for his age and fragile, too, never making it through a training session without bruising. This man who stood before her was nothing like KI; he was tall, *much* taller than her for the first time, with strong muscles and a sturdy frame. He had a confidence Fox had never seen before but the most shocking thing about him was his hair; it'd grown a few inches, brushing his shoulders now, and its distinctive golden color had somehow turned jet black—finally matching his ebony eyebrows.

Fox's mouth hung open. "K—KI?"

Before she could convince herself she was dreaming, he leaned down and hugged her, lifting her from the chair in his strong arms. He smelled of water, like a glassful, cold as ice. She squirmed against him, and he set her on her feet, holding her at arm's length.

164

"I'm so glad you weren't hurt."

Without thinking, she reached up and touched his face, feeling the curve of his jaw. He smiled and in that flicker of joy that passed over his features, she recognized the boy she'd known in Wi. The little boy who'd always run behind her, following her wherever she went. He was hidden within this stranger with bright white teeth and muscles that strained against his shirt—nearly gone—save for his voice that betrayed his image. But Fox could see him clearly when he smiled at her, as if nothing at all had changed between them.

She smiled back. "Who are you?"

"That's an interesting question," Lieutenant Diaz said behind them. "I was hoping you could help us answer that."

"What do you mean?"

KI took her hand from his cheek and held it in his own. "Fox Fire," he said, "I remember now. I remember my past."

*　*　*

Fox sat and listened to KI's story; how the darklings raided his village—a tiny village named Toté with only three little clans. KI's father was taken from him first, by a tall man with hair the color of fire and a face calm like still water. His mother was taken next, right before his eyes, and then he woke up in Wi—surrounded by faces he'd never seen before.

Parts of his memory were still fuzzy but that was because his seal had been suddenly and violently corrupted—Lieutenant Diaz had explained.

"Your village was attacked because whoever forced that demon into KI knows it's awake now and wants it back."

165

Fox inhaled deeply, filling her lungs until she nearly choked. She wished none of this were true, but no amount of wishing could make this go away. Since childhood, she'd trained side by side with KI in slaying demons—what was she supposed to do now that one was inside of him?

She stole a glance at his face, noting his almond shaped eyes, the long lashes that hid them like heavy curtains. Watching his cheeks, how they dimpled when he spoke, and tracing the outline of his jaw. *Is this face even yours?*

"He's taller and stronger now because the dark energy flowing through his veins is changing him." Diaz seemed to read her mind. "He will continue to get stronger as the demon inside fights to take over."

"Take over?" her voice was barely a whisper.

"We've placed another seal on him, one that's better than what he had before but the demon is still awake. KI can fight it, but the monster will always be there, pouring its dark energy into him and sapping out his humanity."

"Why don't you just take it out? Isn't this *Cross Academy*? Don't you specialize in slaying demons?"

KI reached for her hand to calm her. "It's okay," he said. "It isn't as bad as you think."

"It's true, this is Cross Academy," the lieutenant said. "But we specialize in *slaying* demons, not extracting them from people. This is a special case."

"How?"

"Before Black Day," Diaz answered, "the physical realm and the spiritual realm were separate. Demons could not freely roam the earth; they had to inhabit a vessel in order to stay in the physical realm. This meant they had to possess something—

166

dolls, plants, animals, humans. Back then, the only people who fought demons of that nature were those of the Faith—Christians—far and few as the world had been shrouded in darkness.

"But then something changed. The barrier between the physical and spiritual realm was severed, allowing demons to freely roam the Earth in their spiritual form without need of a vessel. Christianity changed; we weren't only fighting on our knees in prayer. Our prayers became living weapons and supernatural abilities were born. That's how people like Roaring are able to manipulate fire."

Fox swallowed, reminded of the night she'd witnessed her brother's flames, and of the earthdancers who'd buried the bodies from Wi, she even thought of her mailman who could make his letters float.

"Since demons no longer required a vessel to roam the earth, things like demon possession became obsolete. It's rare that a demon inhabits a living human, so not many Believers today are able to handle the situation. That's why we haven't taken the demon out of him; it isn't a simple task, and we don't want to risk hurting KI in the process."

"But we're running out of time," Fox said, her voice soft and pleading. She'd already lost KI once, when he'd fallen unconscious for days on end, she couldn't lose him again—not to a darkling.

"Trust me, we know we're running out of time," Diaz said, his voice irritated. "Demons destroyed your village trying to get to KI—their search isn't over yet. The only thing that gives me rest at night is knowing that he's been re-sealed. Even if demons know the monster inside is awake, they won't be able

167

to find him here. Not so easily, at least."

"What can we do now?" Fox asked.

"Until we can get the demon out of him, we're keeping KI here. He's safe here."

"He's safe at *home*," Fox snapped. "KI should come back home with the rest of us."

"Fox Fire," he said, reaching for her hand again but she pulled away.

"You're coming back with us, right?"

"I—I think I should stay here."

Her eyes widened in disbelief. Of all the things she'd experienced in the past few weeks, KI's desire to stay in Babel shocked her the most. Not the demon sealed inside of him, not even the attack itself. Since leaving Wi, all she'd wanted was to go back home, to take KI away from this foreign place with these strange people and protect him forever. But KI didn't want to leave.

"What have they done to you?" Fox whispered.

KI looked away. "It isn't what you think, Fox. I do want to go home; I just think it's better that I stay."

"You agreed to stay, too," Diaz reminded her. "Don't forget the deal we made."

KI glanced between the two of them. "What deal?"

"Don't worry about it."

He squinted. "Don't worry?"

"Fox agreed to join the Academy in exchange for visiting rights with you."

His shoulders slumped. "No..."

"Now you two can train together." The lieutenant smirked.

Fox's vision snapped to him. "What are you talking about?"

"Tell her," Diaz ordered KI.

"I'm training at the Academy."

"Why?" Her brows furrowed in confusion. "I did all this to *protect* you. Why would you join the Academy and put yourself in danger?"

KI wouldn't look at her, his eyes glued to the floor.

"There is a blessing here, if you can believe it," Lieutenant Kotaro spoke up. "KI's body will be constantly changing because of the dark energy inside him. But we can train him at the Academy and use his strength to our advantage."

"You mean turn him into a weapon," Fox whispered.

Diaz nodded. "Yes. He will be a weapon—a powerful one—but there's more to it than that. KI is taller now and stronger, too, but if you look closely, you'll see he's still short for his age and his muscles are new and unused. He needs to be trained so he can handle his new body and learn how to protect himself from all the forces that *will* come for him. There may come a time where even we cannot save him from the monster inside. He'll have to fight on his own."

"No, he won't," Fox said calmly. "I'm here, too. I'll fight for him."

"Fox," KI said. His gaze rose from the floor. "The Academy isn't like the Regiment at all."

"He's right." Diaz leaned across the table. "There are only two Academies in existence—people will be coming from across the Four Regions to take the entrance exam. There'll be people with supernatural gifts who've trained their entire lives for this test—they won't hold back just because you're new here."

"I've been training my entire life, too," Fox argued. "I may not be as strong as my brother, and I may come from a village that isn't as flashy as Babel, but I have seen demons face to face. I have killed them with my own hands."

Diaz smiled. "I hope you're ready."

14

Evelyn

The white of the walls seemed much brighter with all the sunlight pouring in, illuminating the room. Lieutenant Diaz sat on a table with his shirt unbuttoned and hanging off; today he would finally get his bandages removed. The nurse had run all her tests and rubbed all her creams and applied all her ointments—all with a pink, blushing face and shy eyes that would never meet his gaze. The lieutenant pretended not to notice; he was used to the attention.

"You must be happy to finally get these removed," she said, unwrapping the last of his bandages, her hands lingered on his flesh a moment too long. "Don't forget to flex your hand often— just open and close your fingers to work the muscles." She stared at the burn; her eyes following the dark, wrinkled skin up his arm, to his neck, to his chin.

"I'm happy," Diaz replied.

She smiled and nodded. Gathered her supplies. "I'll leave you a moment to dress." And then she said her goodbye, trying hard not to let her gaze linger on his half-naked chest.

Major Marshall snorted when the door shut.

"What are you laughing at?" Diaz asked, gingerly sliding his arm into the sleeve of his Academy uniform. The material rubbed against his bruise, making him grunt.

"*You must be happy to finally get these removed,*" Major Marshall mocked, his voice high-pitched and shy.

Diaz rolled his eyes. "Well, I am happy."

"Does this mean you'll be back in the field?"

"You'd like that wouldn't you, old man?"

Marshall shrugged and lazily leaned against the wall. "I heard you've been busy interviewing the refugees. Kotaro says it's going well; Izzy says you're being too forward."

"We don't have time to be so polite."

That's true—Major Marshall *would* have said, but before the words could leave his mouth a commotion unfolded outside their door. There was shouting and shrieking, voices barking back and forth—then the door crashed open, and Talon Fire stormed inside, seething in anger.

"How dare you!?" she shouted, marching right up to Lieutenant Diaz.

"Speaking of being polite," he said. "When a door is closed, you're supposed to knock, Lady Talon."

"How dare you!" she shouted again, this time pointing a finger. "How dare you speak to my little sister behind my back!"

Major Marshall moved to intervene, but the door crashed open again, making him jump in surprise. An anxious nurse ran inside. "I'm sorry, lieutenant!" he apologized, his eyes darting back and forth between Diaz and Lady Talon. "We tried to stop her! We told her you were still dressing!"

Talon gasped, taking in Diaz's appearance for the first time; one arm halfway in his sleeve, his shirt unbuttoned, chest exposed. Her eyes roved over the wicked scars carved into his flesh, the muscles that formed his frame. A blush crept up her neck to her cheeks and all at once her rage became shame as she covered her eyes and turned away.

"I—I didn't know!" she sputtered.

The lieutenant sighed tiredly. "Get out."

The nurse ran for the door with Talon close behind, but Diaz called out to her. "Not you, Lady Talon."

Talon stopped at the door but kept her back to him. "You didn't have permission to speak with Fox Fire—to tell her all those things about KI."

"She has a right to know."

"She's a *child*," Talon said hotly, her anger returning. "She doesn't have a right."

Lieutenant Diaz remained quiet as he fumbled with his buttons; he'd expected Talon to be angry once she'd realized he'd spoken with her sister, but he hadn't expected her to bombard into his room at the doctor's office. This was a side of her he'd never seen.

"Why don't we discuss this somewhere else?" Major Marshall suggested.

"Are you hungry?" Diaz asked.

"I could definitely go for some lunch—"

"Not you." He rolled his eyes at the old man. "I mean our guest. Are you hungry, little bird?"

173

Talon bristled. "My name is—"

"Lady Talon Fire. The Grand Chief of Wi. The Beauty of Fire." His eyes lingered on her. "I know your name."

"Then use it when you address me!"

Diaz didn't respond, watching Talon shout at the wall. She looked quite silly, despite her anger.

"I apologize, *Lady Talon*," he finally said. "Shall we go?"

Lieutenant Diaz arranged for a lunch at a small shack just a few blocks from the infirmary; smoked fish simmered in tomato broth with flat bread and cheese and pomegranates to nibble on. Lady Talon picked at the fruit, wrinkling her nose at the fish soup.

"It was only a matter of time before Fox found out the truth about KI—I'm sure you knew that," Diaz said.

Talon put down her pomegranate. "I did know. I am not some airheaded little girl."

"I know you aren't," he said quietly. "You're a woman."

Talon opened her mouth. And then shut it.

"You aren't upset I told Fox about KI," Diaz continued. "You're upset at her response to that news—that she decided to enroll in the Academy."

"Of course I am."

"She needs to learn how to use her gift."

Talon stared at her half-eaten pomegranate, a hundred unasked questions ghosting her lips.

"I saw her the night of the attack; she was engulfed in her brother's flames, but she wasn't burned. I don't know much about her gift, but you can't deny she's got one. Fox Fire is a sundancer."

"You planned this, didn't you? You wanted Fox to join the Academy."

Diaz sighed, leaning back in his chair. He flexed the fingers on his burned hand, opening and closing them like the nurse had advised. Lady Talon was as smart as she looked, figuring out his plan in just a few moments. Here he'd thought their conversation would mostly consist of her shouting at him, but it seemed his little bird wasn't as hasty as he'd first assumed— not that her fiasco at the hospital had helped at all. Silently, he watched her play with the fruit in her hand, wondering what she would say next.

With eyes that shined like the sun, she looked up at him and smiled sadly. "I can't hold on to her forever, can I?"

Diaz didn't know how to respond. "Well—no, you can't."

"At the Academy, she can learn how to use her gift," Major Marshall interjected. "We'll train her to get stronger so she can learn to protect herself and defeat her enemies."

"You mean *your* enemies," Talon corrected.

Marshall shook his head. "Demons are the enemies of *humanity*, not just of Babel or Wi. Fox needs to train with us, she needs someone to teach her how to use her blessing. Cross Academy can do that for her."

"Stop acting like you care about her wellbeing." Talon glared at him; accusation glowing in her eyes. "You coaxed my sister into joining your program—you used KI as bait! And you want me to think it's for her own benefit?"

"You're right," Lieutenant Diaz confessed. "I did want Fox to join the Academy because of her power. And I did use KI as bait. With someone like her at the Academy, humanity stands a fighting chance. But she also needs this training for herself; if

175

she wants to go back home, she'll want to be able to protect you. In the meantime, Cross Academy gets a strong new recruit and, when she's ready, she can leave and use her gift to help defend her village."

Talon frowned at Diaz, trying to hold on to her anger but it fizzled out as the truth in his words set in. "Why couldn't you go after Roaring instead?" she asked, shoulders slumping in defeat. "Fox is so young."

The Grand Chief wasn't much older—only eighteen, compared to her little sister's sixteen. But Evelyn didn't comment on that. Besides, he'd already told her she was a *woman*. He was glad she was a woman. It made him feel less guilty about staring at her lips as she pressed them together and said, "She's the youngest."

He nodded. "I'd preferred Roaring. But he seemed so angry and unapproachable; Fox Fire was an easier target."

"With Fox enrolled, he won't want to be outdone. You might get what you wished for," Talon said, a rueful smile on her face.

"All the better."

"Except," her voice broke a little. For a moment, Lieutenant Diaz thought she might cry, but Lady Talon composed herself and spoke with the regality of the queen she was. "I am the Grand Chief—it will always be my duty to protect them, no matter how powerful they become."

The lieutenant didn't speak. *I guess it's only natural to want to protect the people you love,* he thought, watching Lady Talon closely. *Even if you are the weakest of the bunch.*

"There is a way you can help them—a way that doesn't involve training at the Academy or using special gifts."

"How?"

He leaned over. "Come away with me."

Talon's face turned six different shades of red before she blurted, "What do you mean!? I cannot!"

Diaz laughed. "For business, little bird. I'm taking a team back to Wi—just to assess the damage to the village and determine how long reconstruction will take. Maybe we'll find some clues that'll help us understand the situation a little better. We'll need someone from Wi to help us out. Who could be of more help than the Grand Chief herself?"

Pride flashed in Talon's eyes. "I'll help in any way I can."

Lieutenant Diaz nodded, allowing a smile to form on his face. He finished his lunch in silence, ignoring the idle chatter between Talon and Major Marshall. He needed to focus, to think about what would happen next; how many men did he need for this trip? Should they be prepared for encounters? Could Talon fight if she needed to? *Perhaps*, he thought, eyeing the scarf wrapped around her head. If he remembered correctly, her hair had been torn out in a fight she'd had with demons; she'd also suffered a few broken bones. *She isn't gifted like her siblings, but she's tougher than I thought,* Diaz rubbed his chin, *maybe tougher than she realizes.*

After lunch, Talon said her goodbyes with a shy smile, her previous rage long forgotten. She happily shook hands with Major Marshall, promising to deliver a recipe for *perfect* sweet beans the next time they met.

"I'm sorry for what happened at the hospital," she said to Diaz.

"Don't worry about it."

She smiled. "Goodbye, then."

"I'll see you soon," he said, watching her leave.

Major Marshall chuckled beside him. "That's strange."

"What is?"

"You're smiling."

Diaz squinted at him. "No. I'm not."

"You are," he insisted, his face splitting in a teasing grin. "And I think—I *think*—you were flirting with her."

The lieutenant stepped back, his brows lowered, his smile gone "You're getting old, major," he said. "You're seeing things."

Major Marshall laughed. "Perhaps, Evelyn. Perhaps."

15

Fox Fire

It was hot out, nowhere near as hot as Wi, but after standing in direct sunlight for nearly two hours, Fox felt as if she were melting. There was a boy standing in front of her, his ponytail kept whacking her in the face whenever he turned his head, which was often because he was friends with the boy standing behind her and they decided to have a conversation *around* her. For two hours. Fox sighed as she dug her heels into the hot earth, she knew there would be a line—KI had warned her about it when she'd told him she was going to sign up for the Academy today—but she hadn't expected this.

Students lined the streets leading to the cross-shaped building for miles, winding through the city. They came from every part of the Region of the Lion—even beyond that, from places Fox had never heard of. There were students much older,

179

much younger, much taller, and undoubtedly much stronger than her. The boy behind Fox said the school accepted new students only once every three years. *That would explain all the people,* Fox thought, glancing over her shoulder. Merchants pushed carts through the crowd, selling biscuits and sweets and hushpuppies. Fox had been tempted to buy something to eat but she only had a single silver coin; it was a lot of money but every bit of it had to go to her entry fee for the Academy—another thing KI had warned her about. She had one coin and nothing else, and it'd been hard to get her hands on that.

After being scolded for running out of the meeting, Fox had worked up the courage to approach her eldest sister about enrolling in the prestigious school. Talon hadn't liked the idea at all, but Roaring had cheered her on, Cat hadn't cared. She'd almost lost that argument with the Grand Chief, but it was Roaring's enthusiasm that'd won her over, reminding her family of her gift and how much training Fox would need to master it.

And then Fox brought up the entry fee.

A single silver coin had nearly torn her family apart. Back in Wi, they hadn't thought about money—they were members of the Head Family, they'd never needed money. Plus, the village functioned mostly on a bartering system. Cross Academy had been generous in gifting them a small allowance after settling into the city but however much they'd been given had dwindled faster than expected. Talon had all but revoked her hesitant *yes* when Roaring stepped in yet again to change her mind; though, even he seemed reluctant to hand over the coin.

Fox squeezed the piece of silver in her palm; all she had to do was hand this over to the lady at the table and answer her questions. There were only four students ahead of her now, if she concentrated, she could hear the lady asking her inquiries. *Name, age, height, weight, gift...*

Fox swallowed. What was her gift exactly? Roaring had called it *Sundancing*—a term she'd heard throughout her childhood. The First Flames had possessed the gift of sundancing, the ability to manipulate fire and bend it to their will. It was a gift from God to help humans fight back in the Great Demon War; but that anointing had disappeared hundreds of years ago. Sundancing was just another part of all the crazy tales her elders used to whisper to her at night— bedtime stories at best, myths, and insanity at worse.

But the demons were real, so the stories had to be real, too. At least that's what Fox thought, at least that's what the sundancing convinced her. But how much of the stories was true? Were there truly giants roaming the earth? Were there people who could ride the wind? Did the First Flames really tame the mighty Sunriders born of the volcano? Fox shook her head, none of that mattered right now. If she was truly a sundancer then she was exactly where she needed to be.

The line moved forward, and Fox's stomach turned knots. It would be her turn soon. Just three more students ... two more students ... one more student. The boy ahead turned around to grin at his friend before he stepped up to the table. His ponytail whipped Fox across the face as he said, "I hope we're placed in the same group."

His friend laughed. "If they even accept your enrollment request."

Fox gasped. *They could deny my enrollment request?* She opened her palm to stare at the coin, *then what is this for?* After waiting all day in the sun, she could end up returning home without anything to show for herself. And what about KI? How could she protect him if she didn't get any training? How could she hold up her end of the bargain she'd made with the lieutenant if they didn't accept her enrollment request?

Part of her wasn't surprised. A school that only accepted students once every three years had to be picky. And they weren't training students to become fishermen or teachers, they were training warriors. Demon slayers. Hunters and Priests. They needed the best in the Region—the best in the world. *Am I the best?* Fox wondered as the lady called for the next student.

A group of two Hunters and two Priests sat at the table, discussing the previous students and organizing their files. One of the Priests glanced up from a thick scroll and beckoned for Fox. She stepped forward with a forced smile.

"Hello! How are you today?"

"Hot," Fox answered with a nervous chuckle.

The Priest laughed. "The line is quite long. Can you believe enrollment has been open for weeks now?"

She gulped. "There are a lot of students here."

"Don't be nervous. I'm sure you'll be just fine."

"Right."

"What's your name?"

"Fox of the Fire Tribe."

The Priest whispered Fox's reply and the words appeared on the scroll before her. Fox tried not to look surprised, but she couldn't help herself. The Priest laughed at her gaping expression. "I'm from the Paulson Clan. We're a small people, but our anointing comes in handy for things like this. It's called

Permanent, it means our words have the power to take form—usually we just whisper into parchment but if we speak to a stone or a slab of wood, our words will be etched into it."

"Wow," Fox breathed. "That's incredible."

She shrugged one shoulder; her black robe shifted with the movement. "Not compared to some of the students I've seen today. But that's what makes the Academy so amazing. You don't have to possess a flashy gift to get in; we'll put you to use no matter what!" She laughed again, this time like she was genuinely humored. "If I could get in, then so can you, Fox of the Fire Tribe."

Fox exhaled some of her nerves. "Thank you."

"You're welcome. Now, where are you from?"

"The Village of Wi, in the Region of Smoke and Ash."

She leaned over to whisper into her scroll but stopped as the words sank in. "You're a refugee," she said.

Fox nodded. "I was told to join the Academy by a man named Lieutenant Diaz."

"I see." She whispered into the paper and a black check mark appeared on the parchment. Fox tried not to stare at it, wondering what it meant.

"How old are you?"

"Sixteen."

"Your height?"

"Um," she fidgeted.

"You don't have to know all this information; these questions are for our records more than anything."

"Oh," Fox said, shifting her weight from one foot to the other.

The Priest looked her over. "You look pretty short."

"Thanks?"

"Weight?" she asked.

"Uh—"

"Let's say you're well fed."

Fox frowned, unsure how to interpret that.

"What's your gift, Fox?"

"The gift of the flame," she replied. "We call it sundancing."

"And why do you want to join the Academy?"

"To get stronger. So I can protect the people I love."

The Priest nodded, whispering more words into the paper. She sat up with a smile stretched across her full lips. "Do you have the entry fee?"

Fox handed over the silver coin and wiped her sweaty palm on her pants. "Excellent," the Priest said. "You can grab your uniform from over there—" Fox glanced to the table with piles of folded white clothes guarded by a stern looking Hunter. "Congratulations," she gushed. "The first step is done."

Fox made her way to the display of clothing. An assortment of white pants, socks, and shirts lay before her, the only splash of color was the short red sleeves on the shirts. She sighed and grabbed what she thought was her size, then moved to the changing area where other girls had gathered. Some of the girls had grouped together, whispering amongst themselves; Fox found a corner and peeled off her sweat-soaked blouse and skirt, changed as quickly as she could, and left without a word. She tossed her worn clothes into a hamper and didn't look back—she hated the fashion in Babel.

"Name?" a Hunter asked once she left the changing station.

Fox blinked. "Uh, Fox Fire."

The Hunter checked her list and then pointed to the left. "You're assigned to Master Jo, that way."

"Thanks."

"Wait." The Hunter blocked her path. "Where are your shoes?"

Fox looked down at her bare feet, dirt stained the bottoms and crusted along her heel. She hardly ever wore shoes, not even when she'd been in Wi and only when she had to here in Babel.

"What's wrong with my feet?" she asked, wiggling her dirty toes.

The Hunter frowned. "Shoes are required."

"But I'm not comfortable in shoes."

"Will shoes interfere with your gift?"

Fox shook her head.

"Then you have to wear them. Period."

"You're holding up the line, barefoot girl," someone over Fox's shoulder complained. She resisted the urge to glance back and instead asked for a pair of shoes from the display table. The Hunter passed her a pair, both of them ignoring the grunting from the angry person over her shoulder.

"Sorry," Fox mumbled, stepping to the side to shove her feet into the white training shoes.

The angry person brushed by, giving her a good look at the complaining boy. He was tall, almost as tall as Roaring, but no older than Fox. She couldn't help but stare as he approached the Hunter, but not because of his height, she stared because he was so striking. Pale skin with white-blonde hair and eyes so angry she wanted to run when he glanced over at her. They were the color of ice, cold and dead and staring right at her now. Fox gulped and looked at her ugly bare feet.

"Name," the Hunter said.

185

"Kohlannis Hunger," he replied.

Fox finished putting on her shoes. *What a name*, she thought as she gave hers to the Hunter. "Fox Fire."

"You mean *barefoot girl*," the Hunter snorted.

Fox deflated. He's *Kohlannis Hunger and I'm the barefoot girl. Great.*

Through the passageway was a host of hundreds of students. White flooded the open field with dots of beige Hunters or black robed Priests waiting for their students. Some raised signs into the air, others shouted their name above the chatter. Fox pushed her way through the crowds, looking for someone named Master Jo. She had expected to find an aged Hunter or Priest with sweeping robes and scars lining his arms; instead, she found a young woman standing idly with a staff resting over both her shoulders. Dreadlocks poured from her head, pulled into a thick ponytail. With her hair pulled back, Fox could see the side of her head was shorn to the scalp. A small sign rested at her feet that read, **Marlo Jo**.

She smiled at Fox when she saw her approaching. "Are you assigned to Master Jo?"

Fox nodded.

"Good, you're my last recruit. Let's get going."

Fox turned to follow Marlo but stopped when she saw white-blonde hair in the crowd of students gathered around her. *The boy from before*, she tried not to groan. Had he really been assigned to the same instructor? She stole a second glance at him and realized he was looking at her, his eyes were so piercing she had to look away but not before she caught the smirk on his dumb face. Hopefully, she'd get the chance to wipe that smirk away during training.

186

Marlo took them through the Academy and out the back doors where they rode a carriage filled with a hundred other students. The ride lasted nearly half an hour before they were dumped at a place called the Training Grounds.

The other students and Masters shuffled off the carriage, going to their section on the Grounds. Fox waited by the carriage with Kohlannis and a handful of other students. Master Jo slammed her staff into the ground as she stood before them.

"This place will be your second home for the next two months," she explained. Her muscles flexed as she swept her arm out. The black Priestly robes she'd been wearing were tied around her waist now, leaving her in a cropped top and baggy pants with the robe hanging around her midriff. The crucifix around her neck gleamed as she spoke. "There are over one thousand students who've enrolled in the Academy. But enrolling is only the first step. Once you're enrolled, you're broken into smaller groups for training. Each Master gets to pick twenty students to train in preparation for the entrance exam. Once you pass the exam, you can finally call yourself a student at the Academy. Until then, you're just trainees." She smiled wide and crossed her arms over her chest. "I'm Master Marlo Jo and I've chosen each of you for my group. That means I'm going to make sure you all get to call yourselves students."

Fox looked around at the others; there were only seven of them—including herself and Kohlannis. Where were the other thirteen?

Marlo took them across the training grounds, past the sparring rings and the obstacle courses, beyond the five-mile running track, and behind the weaponry field to where a small

187

group of students stood with a young Hunter.

She turned to them with a smile when Marlo approached but it was the students Fox noticed first—particularly a student with olive skin and dark hair. He gave her a little wave when she caught his eye; it took everything in Fox not to scream and run to KI.

"This is my training assistant, Master Moneek," Marlo said to the small group.

Moneek nodded to them. "Is this the last of them?"

"This makes twenty," Marlo said.

"That means we're ready to begin. Like … seriously begin."

Marlo smirked. "Indeed."

Marlo Jo did not have the students line up and introduce themselves to the rest of the group. She did not have them play icebreaker games to get to know each other. She did not pass out snacks and start a warm conversation about how nice it was to have her own class now.

Instead, she lined them up and examined them from head to toe. Muttering mental notes aloud—things about their height and muscle mass—or lack thereof. Fox burned with shame under her master's scrutiny, but when the misery was over, Marlo turned to them and said, "Some of you have been here running obstacle courses for weeks." She stood before the line of twenty trainees and slammed her staff into the ground every few words. Fox watched as the earth caved in around the smooth metal. It sounded heavy, at least fifty pounds. She wondered what metal it was forged from.

"But now that my roster is full," Marlo continued, "the real training can begin. The first thing I want to do is assess your individual skills and see how well you've honed your anointing thus far. This assessment isn't a pass or fail sort of thing—it's just going to help Moneek and I decide how to focus your training from this point forward."

"So, you don't have to be nervous. But you do have to try your best." Moneek gave them a wolfish smile, her plump cheeks dimpling as she grinned.

"That means using your gifts to give you an advantage," Marlo said. She turned and pointed to something in the distance—so far away, Fox couldn't even see it. "Your first test is to go retrieve my bandana."

The trainees blinked at her which made her laugh loudly. "Moneek and I left our handkerchiefs on the other side of the training grounds—one for each of us. We want them back. So go get them."

"**NOW!**" Moneek screamed.

A flash whooshed past the two masters, so fast it made Marlo cover her eyes from the dust. "Looks like someone's got the gift of *Speed*," she said.

A heartbeat of realization ticked by before the rest of the trainees took off running. *This is obviously a test of our agility,* Fox thought, sprinting through the field. *That means whoever has a speed enhancing blessing is going to be at an advantage.* She leapt over a bench and pumped her arms to maintain her momentum; there were students on either side of her but, one by one, they pulled away from the group, using their gifts to help them.

One boy leapt over the same bench but landed on all fours, running like an animal. His back bent into an odd angle and his knees buckled beneath him as he let out an animalistic growl.

He's changing! Fox screamed inside, trying to keep herself from freaking out. The amazement was too overwhelming; she lost her footing and stumbled to the side—right into another trainee.

"Watch it!" the boy cried as they tumbled to the ground.

Fox rubbed her knee as she got to her feet. "I'm sorry—" she froze, staring at the boy with white-blonde hair. He glared at her, his eyes cold and filled with anger.

"Great. Let me guess, you can't run because of the shoes, right?"

She couldn't tell if he was mocking her. "I was surprised by the boy. He—he turned into something. Something that wasn't human anymore."

Kohlannis rolled his eyes. "I don't have time for this."

"It's called *Shifting*," a familiar voice huffed.

Fox turned to see KI with his hands on his hips, sucking for breath. She crushed him with a hug. "You're here!"

"I told you I'd be training, too." He hugged her back, glancing over her shoulder to Kohlannis. "Looks like you're making friends."

"More like enemies," "Kohlannis said.

"Give her a break, Ana. It's not like you can't catch up."

For the first time, he smiled. "Why the heck are you so far behind?"

"Tailing Fox." He motioned to her.

"*Fox*," Kohlannis repeated. Coming from his mouth, it sounded like a curse word.

Fox stared between them, her mouth hanging open. When had the two of them met? When had they become so *familiar*? She swallowed, hoping KI hadn't noticed her confusion. More than his appearance had changed; he was making friends; he was training without her. He'd said he was *tailing* her—did that mean she was moving slow compared to how fast he could run?

The three of them had stopped moving but neither of the boys seemed concerned about catching up. They were standing around cracking jokes about Fox's bare feet—Kohlannis had decided to tell KI the story of how they'd met earlier. *What does this mean?* Fox wondered. *What are they capable of?*

Without thinking, she took off running.

"Fox!" KI called behind her, but she didn't stop. She didn't have time to worry about how far behind she was. There was a student who could run faster than the eye could see, a boy who could shift into animals, and what about the rest of them? Who else was stronger? Faster? Smarter than her? All of a sudden, the knot she'd fought for months ago seemed so small and insignificant. She'd been the strongest in her class, had trained for years to get that little cord of thread. And now it all felt like a joke.

She ran in the direction the other students had gone, not caring if KI or Kohlannis caught up or went ahead. This test wasn't about them, all that mattered was getting one of those bandanas.

When she reached the end of the open field, she was gasping for breath. A cluster of trees lay ahead, inviting her into the forest beyond the Grounds. She didn't see any of the trainees from her class, but she had no idea where else to search.

"You're not going in there, are you?" KI had caught up and stood beside her, staring ahead at the trees. He stood a full head and shoulders taller than her, but Kohlannis was even taller than him, standing on his other side.

"We have to find the bandanas," she replied.

"How do we know the other students haven't found them already?"

"We don't," Kohlannis said. "But we have to look."

"*We?*" Fox looked over at him.

He quirked an eyebrow. "You can barely run straight, barefoot girl. You need my help."

She turned to shout at him, but KI cut her off. "Let's go. Altogether."

They walked into the forest, trying their best to keep quiet and move quickly. Fox's eyes darted through the trees, searching for a cloth, a piece of material, anything that looked remotely similar to a bandana. It dawned on her, suddenly, that this handkerchief could be *anywhere*. They might even be on the wrong side of the Grounds—the other students could have found the bandanas already and be heading home. *But we have to try*, she told herself, and just as the thought passed through her, she spotted something hanging from a tree ahead.

"Look!" she shouted, running for the tree. In the branches hung a square stitched cloth; Fox yanked it down and waved it above her head. "I found one!"

Kohl raised an eyebrow at it. "The other one could be nearby."

A jolt of realization hit her. There were only two bandanas. One of them wasn't going to return with a prize in their hands. Fox glanced between them, seeing the stern looks on their faces, watching them come to the same conclusion. Silently, KI turned and raised something in the air. Relief washed over her.

"It's actually right here."

Kohl nodded and turned to look into the woods, letting out a sigh of defeat. He crammed his hands into his pockets and took a step. "I shouldn't have tagged along."

"Master Marlo said it wasn't pass or fail," Fox tried to explain.

He glared at her, blue eyes icy and cold again. "That doesn't mean I didn't want to—" he cut himself off, distracted by something over Fox's shoulder. "No way."

"No way what?" Fox asked.

Kohl walked over to her and reached above her head, he tugged on a branch and pulled back a small cloth. A bandana.

Fox stared at it. "No way."

"What does this mean?" KI asked, looking from one bandana to another.

Kohl peered into the trees, squinting as he walked forward. Fox watched as he stooped and found another bandana in the dirt, then grabbed another hanging in a tree, and found one more tied around a branch.

He held them all up for the small group to see. "It means our agility isn't the only thing being tested."

They searched every inch of the forest; under every rock, in every tree, Fox even dived into a pond to get the bandana lurking at the bottom. Soaking wet, she sat down with her companions and studied the cloths.

"This is pointless," Kohl grumbled.

KI nudged him. "They're here somewhere."

"Ever the hopeful."

"One of us has to be."

Kohl rolled his eyes and leaned against a tree. "I say we just head back. It's been hours. If no one's found the stupid handkerchiefs by now, they ain't worth finding."

"It's a test, Kohl," Fox said. She knelt in the grass with the bandanas on display in front of her. They'd found sixty-two in total, each with a different pattern and design. No two bandanas were the same, which didn't help them at all. Fox had no idea what to look for or where to even start. "Maybe we should just bring them all back?"

Kohl snorted. "You're as stupid as you look."

"*Ana,*" KI scolded.

"I don't see you making any suggestions, except to give up!" Fox snapped. She'd had enough of his chide remarks and bad attitude. She didn't care if KI seemed to like him, Kohl wasn't helping at all.

Kohlannis watched her for a moment, a stiff silence holding them both in place. His eyes roved over her face, down to her shoulders, then her torso and body. She shivered under his gaze, wishing he would say something—even something rude, just to break the sudden quiet.

He pushed from the tree. "This is lame."

Fox watched him go. "What do we do now?" she heard KI ask.

"I guess we can take two and hope for the best," she replied.

Master Marlo and Moneek stood with a small group of students when Fox and KI returned. They'd stayed in the forest a little longer, fussing over which bandanas to choose and take back. Kohl waited in the crowd, emptyhanded and avoiding eye contact. Fox didn't complain. She sat with KI and waited in silence for the last few trainees to scramble back. It took another hour for the rest to show up, when they finally did,

Master Marlo stepped forward with a smile on her face.

"That took longer than I thought it would. Perhaps I overestimated you guys." She laughed at this, like this was all a joke to her. Fox tried hard not to scream out in anger.

"Everyone who found a bandana, hold them up."

The trainees complied; over half the students had found one. *Who got the right ones?* Fox questioned.

Marlo pointed to a boy. "You. Stand up."

He stood and Fox recognized him as the Shifter from earlier. He was shorter than she remembered, now that he was standing upright and not on all fours. His hair was messy, and his tan face was split with an arrogant grin.

"You found Moneek's bandana," Marlo said.

His grin widened.

"How did you know it was hers?"

"It has her scent," he answered plainly.

Marlo pointed to a girl and told her to stand. She followed instruction and Fox watched in awe as a girl with brown skin and snow-white hair rose to her feet. She was elegant, almost regal, with a long neck and eyes the color of seafoam. "How did you know that was my bandana?" Marlo Jo asked.

She smiled and turned over the cloth in her hand. "It has your name on it."

Fox cringed. That was all it took. Her name was written on it.

"Good job to the two students who found the correct bandanas," Marlo went on. "I hope you all learned something from this test. It wasn't all about speed, was it?" A few trainees shook their heads. Marlo looked at a young girl in front wearing goggles with her red hair pulled back in a ponytail. "Terra

Mochett. You've got the gift of *Super Speed*, don't you?"

She nodded. "Yes, I do."

"I hope you learned that your gift can only get you so far." A blush bloomed on Terra's cheeks. "Don't take it personally—everyone here will learn this lesson. All of your gifts are exceptional, but don't forget that you have other skills, too. You needed speed to help you search faster, but it was *observation* that helped claim one of the bandanas." She looked directly at Fox, making her shrink beneath her stare. "Fox Fire, you didn't find the right bandana, but you were one of only a few students who decided to work with others on this test. Good job."

"Thank you!" Fox nearly shouted, desperate for a compliment. She'd gotten tired of feeling pathetic.

Marlo put her hands on her hips. "Here at the Academy, you will learn to master your gift. But I also want to teach you how to sharpen your other skills—that's what our training will focus on, using *everything* in your arsenal. Believe it or not, there are people right here at the Academy who don't have blessings. But that doesn't make them useless." Marlo smiled at her students. "You don't have to be the strongest to be the best. Remember your training and even you can make a difference in this world. I promise."

16

Fox Fire

Training wasn't easy. Master Jo had promised to turn each of her students into hardened warriors, but Fox didn't feel like a warrior at all. The only thing she felt was sore. Marlo's sessions consisted of obstacle courses, five-mile runs through the Grounds, and sparring matches between students. When the class wasn't putting out physical exertion, she worked their minds through hours of seminars and lessons.

"There are only two forces in this world," she explained today.

Fox sat in the grass with the rest of her peers, scribbling notes on a slip of parchment with fingers so raw they were nearly bleeding. She'd worked herself to the bone, just like all the other students around her, but there was still much to learn.

"The force of Good," Marlo went on, "which comes from God.

Or the forces of Evil, which comes from the enemy—Satan and all his minions."

"Like demons?" Terra asked, she adjusted her goggles and smiled at Master Jo as their instructor nodded.

"Demons, evil spirits, anything that isn't of God is of Satan. That includes certain powers and abilities."

A hush enveloped the students.

Marlo nodded at Terra. "You have the gift of Super Speed." She glanced at a boy named Dart. "And you're a Shifter."

Moneek stepped forward, scanning the crowd of studious teens before she randomly pointed at one. "What's your gift?"

A boy with tan skin and jet-black hair pulled into a bun stood and cleared his throat. "My gift is called *Sturdy*." He held his feather pen in the palm of his hand, as the wind stirred, the pen began to float as if it would blow away in the gentle breeze. "I can make things very light," the boy said, and then he grinned and dropped the feather pen to the ground. It landed with an audible *thud*, causing the earth around it to crumble, like he'd just dropped a boulder. "Or very heavy."

Moneek smiled, impressed. Even Master Jo gave him a firm nod of approval before pointing to the girl beside him. "And you?"

"My name is Andor," said the next student, a girl with a short, curly afro. "My gift is called *Light*. It gives me the ability to see in the dark."

Snickers went off in the crowd, unimpressed with her talents, but Master Jo and Moneek congratulated her with the same enthusiasm they'd used with the last boy.

Marlo pointed her staff at Fox. "And what's your gift?" she asked.

Fox swallowed and rose on shaky legs, remembering everything her brother and Lieutenant Diaz had told her about her family's past and their supposed abilities. "My gift is called *Sundancing*. And it gives me the ability to manipulate fire."

The crowd paused. It wasn't until Moneek leaned forward, squinting, that Fox realized they were expecting a demonstration of some sort.

She bit her lip. Even though the lieutenant had assured her that she was a sundancer, Fox hadn't been able to produce any flames yet. Roaring hadn't even addressed the subject with her, wholly consumed with his grand plan to get back to Wi. Fox believed Diaz was right. She hadn't been burned by her brother's flames. But she also couldn't use any fire. And she had no idea how to change that.

"Fire is uncontrollable," Fox muttered, staring at the grass.

"A wise decision, then." Master Jo gave an approving nod and Fox sat without another word. "Your training here isn't to show off to each other. It's to learn and grow. Some of the most impressive abilities are also the most dangerous."

"How is it a gift, then?" asked one student, the girl with white hair and green eyes. Fox stared at her as Master Jo found her in the crowd and answered, "That's the next point I want to make." Marlo gripped her staff. "When your gift comes from God, it's called a *blessing* or an *anointing*. It was given to your bloodline to help humanity fight back against the demonic forces of this world. We wrestle not against flesh and blood; this means our fight is spiritual—*supernatural*—so we fight with supernatural gifts. And we don't use them to fight each other, but there are people out there who ignore the Will of God and use their powers for evil. These abilities are not called blessings, they are called *curses*."

"So people who use their gifts to hurt others—people with bad intentions—their powers are cursed?" Dart asked.

Marlo took a breath, gazing out at her flock as she answered, "Our intentions certainly play a role in how our powers are labeled. But it's much deeper than that. Everything you do with your powers uses *spiritual energy*. Light energy, provided from your Spirit within, or Dark energy channeled through a demonic force or element. Abilities which use Light energy are blessings. Abilities which use Dark energy are curses. But never get complacent, my pupils. Blessings that are used for the wrong purposes, gifts that are abused, or are used with bad intentions, they can *become* curses."

"I don't understand," Terra said, shaking her head. "How can a power be a curse if it's still helpful to people?"

Marlo smiled faintly. "Have you ever heard the scripture; *the devil comes as an angel of light*?"

The students nodded.

"That can apply to this concept, too. Sometimes the abilities and the people we meet in this world may seem good, when they're not. The only sure way to tell isn't by determining how useful their powers are. It's by looking at the world through spiritual eyes. Seeing things as God sees them. Because what is good to man isn't always good to God."

Fox nodded to herself, thinking about the biblical passage from Matthew chapter seven, how those from the world would present their work to Christ for judgment, naming all the good deeds they had done while on Earth. And Jesus would tell them, *Depart from me, you evildoers*.

Because Master Jo was right. What the world sees as good

isn't always good to God. Fox wondered if the Walls of Wi had been good. She wondered what her ancestors had done to cause the Fire Tribe to lose the gift of the flame for two hundred years, then—abruptly—she decided she didn't want to know.

I'll learn how to use this gift the way God intended it to be used. I won't hide behind Walls. I'll protect the people I love. She glanced at KI, studiously taking notes as Master Jo went on explaining how to feed their Spirits.

"The stronger your Spirit, the stronger your powers. Our gifts can grow and evolve, just as our faith does," she said. "The closer we are to God, the stronger we become. Because when we are totally dependent on God, it's truly Him who fights our battles. Not us."

"Does that mean we'll never lose?" Dart asked.

"It means *God* never loses," Marlo said slowly. "*We* can still lose our battles. We can fail during our trials and tribulations. Because sometimes we get anxious. We take things into our own hands and fight in our own strength. And our own strength is never enough." She smiled, pounding her staff into the earth. "But enough of our written lessons. Now that you've learned about spiritual energy, let's see how many of you can apply it."

"We apply it every time we use our abilities," said the boy with Sturdy powers.

Marlo nodded. "That's right, Vinny. But how does it work? I bet most of you use your abilities without even thinking, just like we don't think about placing one foot in front of the other— we simply start walking, right?"

The students nodded.

"Well, there's a method to the madness, if you can believe it. You aren't mindlessly using your abilities; you are tapping into

201

the very power of God. It might seem easier to just act without thinking, the same way that it's easier to walk without staring at your feet. But once you apply a method to it, you can take things to a new level. When you begin to *think* about it, you go from walking to running. That's when you can plan. You can decide how fast to go, when to slow down, or if you even need to run at all."

"*Strategy*," Moneek said, summing things up.

"How do your powers actually work? What's the method? What do you think about when you activate it? What's your limit?" Marlo crossed her muscular arms. "That's the lesson for today."

"Sounds interesting," KI said beside Fox. She turned to smile at him, but Marlo was speaking again, forcing her attention back to the front.

"Pack away your pens and parchment and meet up at the weaponry barn. You have two minutes."

"What do you think we're doing today?" KI asked, standing and stretching.

Fox shrugged one shoulder, watching the rest of the students move toward the weaponry barn. Until now they had only run through the obstacle courses and sparred using hand-to-hand combat. Now, Master Jo would allow them each a weapon. A grin spread over Fox's face as she shoved her things into the sack she'd packed, tossed it by the giant oak she'd been sitting under, and walked toward the barn.

KI walked beside her, his shadow streaking out ahead of them. Fox tried not to stare at his profile as he chuckled, dark hair flowing around his face. He was striking, not just because of how handsome he'd gotten, but because he'd changed at all.

This was not the skinny kid from Wi she'd held in her arms weeks ago. He'd always been an inch or two taller than her, but she had to blink up at him now, the top of her head barely reaching his shoulder.

"You're excited." KI was smiling at her.

"Aren't you?"

"I'm curious. Why weapons? Why now?"

"We would have trained with them eventually," Fox said, moving into the crowd of students. "Why not now?"

Master Jo stood before the barn, holding one of the doors open as she spoke. "You'll each get to pick out one weapon, so choose wisely and choose quickly. We won't be training here."

Fox raised her eyebrow, but before she could ask any questions, Marlo stepped aside, and the mass of students poured into the barn. There were shelves lined with weapons and shields and gadgets Fox had never seen before. Her mouth fell open as she stared at a massive sword the size of her own body. There was a ball and chain propped up in the corner and even a display of bows with quivers full of arrows on the far end of the barn.

One student picked out a set of throwing darts, another took a simple sword sheathed at her hip. Fox saw Terra shaking her head in disapproval before she walked out with absolutely nothing.

"Check this out," KI said, grabbing Fox's wrist and pulling her into a small area.

She gasped, looking up to glimpse the arrangement of spears propped against the wall. Long ones, short ones, each staff with a unique sharpened end. Fox could have spent a full week handling every single one, testing its weight, learning how well it could stand against other weapons, memorizing the feel of it against her palm.

She reached for one, a simple spear with a metal staff and an iron tip, it reflected the sunlight off its bar as she gripped it.

"You look like Master Jo," KI laughed.

She wrinkled her nose. "I guess I do."

"That's your weapon of choice?" asked a voice behind Fox.

She turned to find Kohl watching her. He stood leaning against the beam beside him, his body turned slightly so she could see the way his shirt clung to him, hugging the curves of his chest and arms as he folded his hands into his pockets. He tilted his chin up, wisps of blonde hair falling into his face. "A spear," he said, and his voice was so plain and dull Fox couldn't tell if he was mocking her, but she decided she didn't care. Kohl had made it clear the first day they'd met that he wasn't her friend. And he hadn't done anything to convince her otherwise since then. He was friendly enough with KI—they seemed like buddies, in fact—but he had never been kind to her. Most days, he didn't even acknowledge her presence. But here he was now, staring down at her as he stepped closer, dragging his eyes along the bar of her spear, examining it in such a way it made Fox shift uncomfortably.

He reached for the weapon, his hand brushing hers.

Fox stiffened.

He chuckled, a low, throaty noise.

"Jumpy," was his only response, murmured through full lips as he gazed down at the staff.

"What weapon are you picking out, Ana?" KI interrupted.

Kohlannis was busy studying the spear now, holding it up and squinting at it, like he wanted it for himself. Just as Fox opened her mouth to remind him that she'd seen it first, he passed it back to her, bored.

"Come here, KI. I'll show you."

She hadn't been invited. But she didn't want to be left alone while KI ran off with his new best friend, so Fox quietly followed the boys to a new section in the barn where a collection of daggers sat on display.

KI was beaming, holding up a curved blade similar to the rahkai they'd trained with in Wi. "Look at this, Fox," he said with a smile.

Kohl took the blade and tossed it away. "Look at *this*," he said, holding up a different one.

Fox stared at the dagger he'd discarded, annoyed by his carelessness. And annoyed that KI hadn't seemed to notice, but she refused to whine about it. Instead, she stooped and scooped up the little dagger. As she lifted her gaze, she realized someone else had joined her group in examining the blades.

Vinny had walked over. He was with another boy, one with the same tan skin and jet-black hair as his. They looked similar, *related*, but the other boy's eyes were kinder. Both of them approached KI and Kohl, smiling like they were all the best of friends.

Kohl frowned at them. "Pick out a dagger from somewhere else, Vin."

Vinny bunched his shoulders, made a show of looking around the room like he was in awe. "I want one from here."

"You want *trouble*," Kohl corrected him.

The boy beside Vinny laughed. "We're honestly just here to look."

The area fell silent a moment, everyone staring at each other, trying to see whose smile would falter first.

Kohl let out a sigh, like he knew the fight wasn't worth it. "Here." He passed Vinny the dagger he'd been showing KI. "Check this out."

Vinny's eyes lit up. "Nice," he whispered, hefting the weapon, pricking his finger with the tip of the blade. "Can I take this one?"

"Kohl had it first."

Fox hadn't realized she'd spoken until every eye was trained on her. Why she felt the need to step in and defend Kohlannis, she had no idea, but it was too late to take it back now, so she swallowed and lifted her chin. "Kohl wanted that dagger for himself."

Vinny eyed her, his gaze shifting to the spear gripped in her hand and then to the dagger she'd picked up from the ground. She thought he was going to walk over and take one of her weapons, but he didn't move at all. He threw his head back and laughed.

Fox winced.

Kohl grunted, a muscle in his jaw spasming as he clenched it.

"Are you his mother?" Vinny asked, wiping away a tear.

Fox cursed herself for being so foolish. "Just give him back the dagger—"

"Look," Vinny took a large step toward her, coming much closer than she expected for someone who wasn't very tall and had legs as short as hers. Now that he was a mere breath away, she could see the lines around his mouth as he laughed at her again, his lips stretching to form an amused grin. "You don't know this yet because you're new here, but the Hungers aren't good people." He leaned back, his grin turning predatory as his eyes roved her frame. "A pretty girl like you shouldn't be following around Hunger trash." He shrugged one shoulder, looking over at KI now. "Or demonic freakshows from the Academy."

Fox bared her teeth. "You don't know what you're talking about."

"I'm from the Lin Clan." He patted his chest like he was proud. "My bloodline is small but old. I was born and raised in this city, Fox. I know more about these people and this place than you ever will."

She gripped her spear. "But you don't know a thing about KI."

"I know enough. He lives at the Academy. And so does Kohlannis. You know they don't let you live there unless you're a danger to the people in your own home, right?"

She didn't know that. But she refused to admit that to Vinny. Not that it mattered as he took another step toward her, forcing her to stumble backward or risk him nearly kissing her as he leaned down and said, "KI is a refugee, he doesn't have any other place to go. But Kohl's got family here."

"That's enough," Kohl said behind him.

"The Hungers live in their own sector of the city—and they *still* sent him away to live at the Academy."

"I said that's *enough*, Vinny," Kohl snapped, stepping forward like he was ready to fight.

Vinny turned so fast; Fox hadn't even registered the motion until he was facing Kohl, his dagger raised. He didn't attack. In fact, he twirled the blade around and held it out for Kohl to take.

"No need to get antsy," he said. "We're classmates, after all."

Slowly, Kohl reached for the blade, taking it from Vinny's hand. Then he gasped as the weight of it suddenly took him to his knees. Kohl clutched the hilt with both hands, teeth gritted as he tried to lift it from the ground. His left hand was trapped beneath it, almost crushed by the weight of the little weapon.

Vinny stood right in front of him now, smiling down as he watched him struggle. "Heavy, isn't it?"

"Lighten the dagger," Kohl said darkly.

"Say please."

"You'll break his hand if you don't lighten it!" Fox said.

Vinny rolled his eyes, kneeling to touch the blade. "I was only playing."

Kohl immediately gasped, his shoulders relaxing as he picked up the dagger.

Vinny held out his hand. "I think I *will* take that one."

For a moment, Fox thought Kohl would stab him with the weapon, but after another heartbeat of silence, he simply handed it over. "It's all yours."

Vinny patted his shoulder and then turned to Fox Fire. "You shouldn't stick close to them. They'll only bring you down."

"I should stick close to you, right?" She made a disgusted face when he smiled charmingly.

The smile withered. "I made you an offer. I won't ask twice."

"You need to leave," Fox said, stepping aside so he could pass her without getting close.

Vinny glared at her an extra moment, then he sighed and rolled his shoulders back. Cracked his neck. "I tried." He glanced back at his buddy. "What can I say? I'm a sucker for pretty girls."

The other boy laughed, though nothing was funny. "Let's go,

Vinny. I want to pick out a weapon, too."

Fox watched them leave in silence, letting go of a sigh of relief once they were out of earshot. "I don't know what his problem was," she said, walking over to Kohl. She glanced down at his reddened hand. "Are you al—"

"What is wrong with you?" he snapped, eyes blazing.

She stiffened. "What are you talking about?"

"If you don't understand, then there's no point in explaining." He turned, grabbed a random dagger from the display and stalked off, bumping her shoulder as he left.

Fox blinked, utterly confused. "I don't get it," she said, glancing up at KI.

"Maybe Vin had a point?"

Fox crossed her arms. "What point?"

"All I'm saying is ... Ana could have handled Vinny and Montell on his own. They aren't a big threat to anyone."

"His hand was almost crushed," she said. "Seemed like a big enough threat to me."

KI took the dagger she was holding, sheathed it at his own hip. "Maybe."

Outside the barn, Master Jo split the students into two groups, then she lined up each group single file. One line stood behind her, the other stood behind Moneek. "Stay in line and stay together. I will not be slowing down for anyone," Marlo said, taking off at a slow trot. The groups followed their leaders, trotting, then jogging, then full on sprinting.

They ran for at least a mile, clearing the training grounds and passing into the forest beyond. Fox gasped for breath; she was used to vigorous training; this wasn't much different from what her own uncle had put her through in Wi. But it was hard to run with a long spear in her hand—even harder for the kid behind her who'd chosen a giant two-headed battle axe.

Master Jo led them through the woods, weaving through the trees, running down a steep cliff, and curving into a cave. The walls of the cave were decorated with hanging lights, but after half a mile, the oil lamps disappeared, leaving them in total darkness.

Marlo kept running.

Fox sucked for air, her lungs burning, her legs reaching their limit, but her instructor didn't slow down, not even for a second. Some of the other students began to complain, grumbling as they dropped their heavy gear. Fox tripped over a discarded sword, the sharp blade tearing the leg of her white pants. She screamed and fell forward, dropping her own spear. Panic tore through her as she scrambled, trying to keep up. She couldn't see in front of her, couldn't see beside her. But she could still hear rapid footsteps running ahead and behind.

Kohl had been in line in front of her. She reached forward with one hand, shocked to find him a mere step away. Now that she knew he was so close, she could make out his labored breathing. He was in bad shape, panting like he could drop at any moment. *And*, Fox realized, *he's slowing down.*

"Kohl," she whispered, though the sound seemed to boom through the entire cave, echoing off the dark stone walls. "Kohl, you have to keep up. We can't fall behind."

His only response was the sound of his strangled breathing.

"*Kohl!*" she whispered fiercely.

"I'm trying!" he snapped.

"Here," Master Jo's voice came from ahead.

All at once, the cave lit up in a burst of sudden light. Fox blinked away the stars dancing in her eyes to see the open area, illuminated by a torch held in Moneek's hand. The assistant smiled at the students as they collapsed onto the hard ground.

"It's just a cave," Dart said, looking around. Other than Terra, he was the only student not on the verge of death from their mad sprint through the woods.

How much stamina does he have? Fox wondered. *Probably as much as a horse.*

She glanced over at Kohl, he was leaning against the cave wall, his shirt stuck to his body, drenched in sweat. Fox could make out the shape of his broad chest beneath the material clinging to his flesh, but it wasn't the curve of his muscles that caught her attention, it was the black markings on his skin. If she squinted, she could just make out the swirling pattern, like some sort of design had been tattooed over his entire torso.

It wasn't until someone bumped into her that Fox realized she'd taken a step toward Kohl. She froze and glanced up at the figure beside her—and her heart nearly stopped.

A dead man looked down at her.

His face looked like the work of Satan. Burned and twisted, like he'd been taken apart and sewn back together. For a moment, Fox wasn't sure what the slithering movement of his flesh was as part of his skin bunched and gathered. Then it clicked, *it's his mouth*—a pair of lips folded into cheeks with thick black stitching zigzagging through them. He was smiling at her.

She shivered, staring up at the black holes in his head. His eyes were mere sockets with flesh flapping over them. Eyebrows gone, his nose nothing more than a cavity blowing air through it. He had hair on his head, shining dark waves that

211

touched his shoulders. But it did nothing to hide the monstrosity of his visage.

And, Fox grimaced, *he stinks*. Like the smell of death.

She gasped, covering her mouth as the bitter smell nearly overwhelmed her. Tears burned at the backs of her eyes, and she squeezed them shut, forcing herself to take slow breaths or risk vomiting right there. When she opened her eyes, she stared down at the ground, tracing the lines of the dark green vines that slithered along the cave floor and on the walls. As her eyes neared the white shoes of the dead boy before her, she realized the vines around his feet were dead. Like they'd withered up at the mere sight of him.

She lifted her gaze to meet him again, wondering why he didn't just leave.

"I know I'm not pretty, but I'm not *that* bad," he said, his voice surprisingly calm, surprisingly *charming*. It didn't match the mouth it'd come from. Not at all. Fox could fall asleep to the sound of this young man's voice. She could listen to him read anything all day long. But his face... his *face*. He looked like he was decaying right before her.

"I—I," she stammered, unsure what to say.

"Slaine, you're scaring her." A girl stepped beside him, she was all legs—nearly as tall as the boy, with thick coils of chocolate hair and cocoa colored skin. She turned her golden eyes on Fox, regarding her with little interest as she placed a hand on Slaine's arm. It was covered in long sleeves. And his hands were covered in gloves.

Fox stared at his attire, different from everyone else's short sleeves and cutoff pants. *Is it possible*, she wondered, glancing back down at the dead vines beneath his feet, *that his gift is*

212

death?

The girl slid her elegant hand up his arm to his shoulder, turning his horrible face away from Fox. "Let's go wait over there." She motioned across the cave to another girl. "Kressa is waiting."

Fox watched them leave, startled by the sound of KI's voice as he said, "Slaine... I don't know his surname. But I do know you shouldn't get close to him." He blinked down at her. "He only hangs around really strong students, or ones with healing abilities."

"What are their abilities?" Fox nodded to the two girls across the cave.

KI glanced at the taller one. "Syren Danis. She can share her Light energy with others, it'll heal and rejuvenate them." He squinted at the other girl, small and thin with a noticeably pretty smile. "Kressa Lion. She was born here—I think. Her blessing allows her to turn her skin into Duntell, it's a metal manufactured right here in Babel. Stronger than steel and denser than iron. It also doesn't rot or rust."

"That's why it's safe for her to be around him," Fox mumbled.

KI nodded. "Otherwise, her life might actually be in danger if Slaine ever got too close."

"So his gift *is* death," Fox said.

"I don't know what it is exactly," KI admitted. "I've never seen him use his blessing before. I just know we shouldn't go near him. It's why he wears long sleeves and gloves all the time."

"Whatever his gift is, it isn't a blessing," Fox said. "It's a curse."

213

KI stiffened beside her, like he disagreed, but he didn't get the chance to argue as Master Jo told them all to gather round.

"This is your final task for today," she announced. "It's very simple. Just make it out the cave—but don't use the way you came."

Murmurs went off through the crowd of twenty students. Even Fox had to admit the assignment seemed easy enough, especially considering the cave only went in either direction. Even if they couldn't go back the way they'd come, all they had to do was walk straight.

Master Jo smiled. "Sounds simple, right?"

"Seems so," Dart shrugged. "If not, I can always pick up a trail to get out." He sniffed the air for emphasis.

"Of course you can," Marlo said. "But what about the rest of you?"

The students whispered amongst themselves before Terra stepped forward. "The cave is a straight shot. I'll be out in a matter of seconds."

Master Jo only nodded, remaining silent as Moneek laughed, clutching the torch in her hands. "That's true, Terra. But how fast can you run in the dark?" She snuffed out the torch, pitching the cave back into blackness.

Fox's heart leapt in her chest as she took a step forward, but someone grabbed her arm roughly. "Hey!" she said.

"It's just me." KI's voice was calm.

"What's going?" Fox asked.

"I'm guessing this is part of the final task."

"To get out of the cave without any source of light?" she asked, and as soon as the words left her mouth, the cave lit up in a soft glow. Fox jerked her head toward the source, her eyes widening as she spotted one of her fellow peers standing in the center of the clearing, her skin beaming as if someone had lit an oil lamp inside her.

It was Andor, with a smile on her face. It stretched even wider as her peers circled her, exhaling sighs of relief.

"I thought you could only *see* in the dark," Vinny said, frowning. Still not impressed with her.

"If I store up enough spiritual energy, I can emit light. So others can see as well," Andor explained.

"Why don't you just be grateful she's helping us at all?" Fox asked.

Vinny glowered at her.

"We've got bigger things to worry about right now," KI said. "Like, how do we get out of this cave?"

"*Or*," Vinny stepped into the center of the circle, walking around Andor with his arms up as he spoke. "How about we first figure out where the heck our Masters have gone?"

Fox stepped back and looked around, realizing Vinny was right. Master Jo and Master Moneek were gone. She didn't know if she was more worried about being separated from her teachers or being left without that torch Moneek had.

"This is our final task," Terra said, stepping into the circle with Vinny. He frowned at her, like she should have asked permission before coming in. "We can't expect our instructors to hold our hands through this."

"But they left us here," Dart said, his face pinched in anger and fear. "And without any light, we can't just run through anymore. Besides, we don't even know if the cave really is just a straight shot. We could be standing at the start of a labyrinth."

"The lesson today is about strategy, remember?" KI

reminded everyone before panic set in. "That means we need to figure this out ourselves. We *can* figure it out ourselves, otherwise, Master Jo and Master Moneek wouldn't have left us here."

Vinny smiled at him, wolfish and mean looking. "It's just like the little demon boy says." Fox took a step forward, but KI's grip on her arm tightened, keeping her in place. "We've got to work together," Vinny went on. "So, who's ready to start strategizing?"

17

Fox Fire

"First things first," Vinny said, still stalking the circle with Andor and Terra beside him. "Everyone give their name and gift; we need to see which blessings are most useful right now."

Someone in the crowd snorted. "Absolutely not," said an angry voice as the students parted to let a girl through. She was a heavyset student, round hips, a pudgy belly, full breasts, and a head full of thick curls. Her arms were muscular, like she could twist Vinny in half, and she was tall—a full head and shoulders over him, even without shoes on. Fox glanced at her bare feet, wondering what her blessing could be if she was allowed to walk around like that.

The girl entered the circle and stood before Vinny, arms folded, an angry look etched onto her dark brown face. "I'm not telling anyone my blessing."

"Why not?" Vinny asked.

She rolled her eyes like she was disappointed in him. "I took you for the smart brother."

Fox glanced over at Montell, not missing the little snicker he let out. Vinny was not as amused. "Care to explain what I'm missing, Wunda?"

Wunda sighed. "We're classmates, but that's only for now. When we take the entrance exams, it won't be a group test. It'll be every man for himself. If I reveal my blessing now, you'll just learn how to counter it and use my weaknesses against me when it matters most."

Whispers scattered through the crowd, even Fox understood where she was coming from, but Terra disagreed. "We're in this together, Wunda—"

"I don't need you guys to get through this cave," she cut her off. "Neither the dark nor any twists or turns will slow me down." Wunda turned to leave. "You guys are on your own."

"Wait," Andor called. "The point of this task isn't just to make it out the cave. It's to *strategize*. Master Jo wants us to work together."

Wunda's shoulders tensed, but she didn't take another step.

"If you leave, we'll just follow you," Andor went on. "You can't stop us, so you might as well work with us."

"You already know my blessing," Vinny said. "And Andor's, and Terra's. Don't hide yours if you can help everyone like you say you can."

Wunda sighed and turned back around, crossing thick arms over her chest as she said, "Wunda of the Cyruson Tribe."

Vinny's eyes widened. "No way," he whispered.

Fox glanced at KI for explanation, but her friend only

shrugged.

"She's strong," Montell said beside them.

Fox nodded at him. "That much is obvious."

"No." He shook his head. "You don't get it. The Cyrusons are the founders of Babel."

Fox stopped breathing for a moment. She was looking at a member of one of the founding families of Babel—of the Academy itself. "How?" she said quietly, her eyes scanning the angry teen animatedly arguing with Vinny over why she had to give him more details than just her name.

"My name alone should be more than enough information about me!" she nearly yelled.

"But are you related to him? To Lord Jericho?" Vinny asked.

"Lord Jericho," Fox repeated.

"The Bishop of the Academy," Montell whispered. "He's the one who protects and controls the Walls."

Fox turned to face him; her brows wrinkled in confusion. But somewhere in the back of her mind she remembered the funeral of her fallen brethren, when dozens of men and women in uniform shifted the earth and buried hundreds of coffins at once without using a single shovel.

She gasped. "Lord Jericho is an earthdancer."

Montell grinned, proud of her for figuring it out. "They call him the Stone Guardian, Protector of the Walls of Jericho."

Fox pressed her lips together. "What does that make Wunda?"

"Lord Jericho's niece," she said, arms folded as she stared at Fox and Montell, like she'd been listening the entire time. Fox stirred, feeling anxious all of a sudden, but Wunda's smirk put her at ease. "You're a dancer, too." She glanced to the side, at someone deeper in the crowd. "And so are you."

Fox followed her gaze to another student, the girl with white hair and green eyes.

"Her, too?" she muttered.

Montell nodded. "Vyanna Farron. She's a seadancer."

"How many kinds of dancers are there?" Fox asked.

"Shouldn't *you* know the answer to that?" Montell replied.

"There are six," Wunda said confidently. "And we have four of them right here in this cave."

Four? Fox glanced around, but before she could find the other dancer, Wunda said, "Now that we know my blessing, how about we actually form a plan to get out of this cave?"

Vinny smiled. "It'll be easier to plan if we know exactly how your gift works. Like, how is it that you wouldn't need light or a map to get out of here?"

Wunda glared at him. "You don't need to know every little detail about my blessing. I can just lead the way."

He sighed. "It was worth a shot."

"We need a better plan than just walking behind Wunda," Terra spoke up. "Think about it; Master Jo let us each pick out a weapon. Why would she do that if we didn't need them in here?"

"I dropped my weapon while we were running," someone complained. "It got too heavy."

"So did I," Fox mumbled.

"Anyone have combat-style blessings?" Vinny asked. "You can walk in front and behind to protect everyone."

Dart raised his hand. Fox stared at his fingers, at how sharp his nails were—almost like claws. "My blessing makes me stronger and faster. I've got keen senses, too. And if push turns to shove, I can shift into something powerful." He shrugged. "Maybe a bear."

"That's perfect," Vinny said. "You can help lead the way. One more?" He glanced out at his fellow peers, hands on his hips like he was in charge.

A few students grumbled, but no one spoke up.

Montell bumped Fox's shoulder. "Fox Fire can walk in front!" he said loudly.

Her jaw dropped open. "Wait!"

"Aren't you a sundancer?" Vinny asked.

She nodded. "Yes, but—"

"That sounds pretty combative. And you can use your flames to provide light in case Andor gets tired."

"Well, maybe—"

Vinny smiled. "Then it's settled. Any other volunteers?" He peered into the crowd again, putting together a team. Once he collected enough students, he clapped his small hands together. "Those in the front and rear, meet ahead or behind. Everyone else gather in between. Keep your eyes peeled and stay alert. Anything can happen."

"Why are we *all* taking orders from this little man?" Wunda complained. "Your blessing isn't even impressive."

Vinny clutched his heart like he was hurt. Fox knew better.

"I may not be the strongest of the bunch, but I promise I'm one of the smartest." He grinned, and it stretched wider as Wunda rolled her eyes and stalked off.

Fox slowly made her way to the front of the crowd, aware that Montell and KI were following her. KI inched closer, whispering, "You sure you gonna be okay?"

"I'll be fine," she told him as confidently as she could.

221

"Maybe we won't bump into any enemies," he went on. "Maybe you won't have to use any sundancing—"

Fox spotted Kohl in the crowd, leaning against the cave wall. "Let's go check on Kohl," she suggested, shifting direction to make her way toward him.

KI followed, taking the hint, and dropping their conversation. "Sure."

Fox had used Kohl as an excuse to get away from KI, but as she neared him, she felt glad she'd decided to go over to him. It was hard to tell from a distance, but up close, Fox could see the way Kohl's chest rose and fell like he was still short of breath.

He should have recovered from the run by now, she thought, moving closer. He saw her coming and pushed from the wall to leave, but he was too slow. *Slower than normal.*

"Hold on." She touched his shoulder, and, to her shock, he didn't flinch away. His skin was hot underneath his shirt, she could feel the heat coming off him in waves. And he was still sweaty, the white tee sticking to him like someone had dumped a bucket of water over his head.

"You're still exhausted," Fox said.

Kohl let out a shaky breath. "I'm fine."

"You're clearly not."

"Just leave me alone, Fox." He moved to step around her, and she moved to block him, but it was Montell who intervened.

"I think I can help," he said, extending a hand before the angry boy could protest.

"What do you think you're doing?" Fox snapped, grabbing his wrist.

Montell glanced down at their hands. "I'm trying to help."

"How?"

"If you'll let me go, I'll show you."

"Let him." Kohl's breath was ragged.

At the sound of his hoarse voice, Fox let go of Montell and watched as he pinched the hem of Kohl's shirt. Instant relief flooded the boy's face and he sagged against the stone wall, sliding down to the ground.

"I don't understand," Fox said.

"It seems my brother left Kohl with a parting gift," Montell explained. "He added fifty pounds to the weight of his shirt."

Fox's eyes bulged. "When? Vinny never touched him—"

"He did," Kohl said, pushing to his feet. "He patted me on the shoulder right before he left."

She remembered. And then she thought of how Kohl had been running slow, falling behind as Master Jo had led them on their run. He'd done all of that with fifty extra pounds hanging on his back and shoulders.

"Why didn't you say something?" Fox asked.

"Because it wasn't a big deal." The usual anger was back in Kohl's eyes as he stood up straight. "I was fine, Fox. I didn't need your help."

She crossed her arms. "You would have dropped dead from exhaustion if I hadn't checked on you. You should be thanking me."

"Well, I'm not going to." He made a face, something like a grimace. Like he was sick—of Fox or the Academy, she couldn't tell. "I don't need your help getting through my training. So stop sticking your nose where it doesn't belong."

He brushed by her, moving to take his place amongst the crowd of students, but Fox whirled around to yell at his retreating figure. "I'm the only one here who's nice to you!"

He laughed over his shoulder. "It's *your* fault Vinny ever touched me. Just remember where your niceness gets people."

Fox glowered, too stubborn to admit he was right.

"He'll get over this," KI said coolly. "He's just cranky because he did a five-mile run with a fifty-pound shirt on." He snorted.

Suddenly irritated, Fox walked away from both her friends, shaking her head. *Not that Montell is my friend.* In fact, she had no idea why he'd been sticking so close to her, and she couldn't figure out why he was following her now.

"Don't worry," he told her as she pushed her way to the front of the line. Wunda saw her coming and gave Andor a nod. The group started a slow pace through the tunneling cave.

"Don't worry about what?" Fox asked.

"About your buddies. I'm sure they'll come around."

She glanced over her shoulder, shocked that KI hadn't followed her. Annoyed that Montell had.

"He thought it'd be best if he stuck with Kohl," Montell explained.

Fox grunted. "Well, whatever."

"You know, my brother had a point earlier."

"Your brother said a lot of things earlier."

"But he was right about the Hungers. They're cursed."

Fox felt a coldness wash over her and she snuck a glance at Wunda to see if she was listening. Wunda walked a few paces ahead, chatting with Andor. "Cursed?" Fox said quietly.

Montell nodded. "Their gift. It's dark. So dark, the entire Hunger Tribe is considered a danger to the rest of Babel. That's why they're sectioned off in a gated community."

"Why are you telling me this?" Fox asked.

Montell thought a moment. "I just thought you should know.

224

Since you seem intent on being friends with him."

"It's not that I want to be his friend," she told him, "He's friends with KI. And KI and I are very close."

"Is he your boyfriend?"

Fox tripped over a rock. "Excuse me?"

"It's a joke." Montell snorted. "Though, judging from your reaction, I'm guessing there's something going on?"

"You're pushing it," she huffed.

He held up his hands defensively. "Fine. I'll leave it alone."

"Why don't you go check on your brother?"

"Sheesh, I know when I'm dismissed." Montell fell back in line, finally leaving Fox to herself as she trudged through the cave.

Andor and Wunda led the way in relative silence now, their chatter replaced by the echoes of footsteps and occasional whispers. They walked for what seemed like hours, single file, in one direction. Fox was beginning to think their final task was a little too easy when they came upon a fork in the road.

"Right or left?" Andor asked.

Wunda closed her eyes, pressing her toes into the earth beneath her feet. "Right," she said at the same time Dart exclaimed, "Left."

They stared at each other.

"I smell fresh air coming in from the left," Dart explained.

Wunda squinted. "I feel tremors coming from the right."

"What do tremors have to do with anything?" Andor asked.

"Tremors are the same as vibrations. It means activity somewhere in the cave."

"Activity could be from the enemy." Dart crossed his arms.

"Or it could be from animals using the cave entrance,"

225

Wunda countered.

"I'm with Wunda on this one," Andor said, raising her hand like she was casting a vote.

Fox glanced at Dart. "I think we should take the left."

"What's the hold up?" Vinny pushed his way to the front before Wunda could start an argument. He glanced back and forth between the split group. "Someone want to explain?"

"Left or right," Fox said. "Dart smells fresh air left. But Wunda feels activity near what she thinks is the cave entrance on the right."

Vinny thought a moment, his hooded eyes squinting as he concentrated. "Let's split up."

"What?" Fox said in unison with Wunda and Dart.

Andor shrugged. "Sounds like a good idea."

"What if there's only one way out?" Fox asked.

"What if *both* sides lead to the exit?" Andor replied.

"I just want to go home." Wunda started down the tunnel on the right. "Anyone who wants to follow me should come along because I'm not wasting any more time."

Andor followed, along with Vinny and over half the class. When the rest of the students had cleared out, Fox realized she was the only one left with Dart.

And Montell. And KI. And Kohl.

She sighed. "This is honestly the worst day ever."

"Don't say that," Montell told her.

"Why didn't you go with your brother?"

He shrugged. "I trust Dart's sense of smell more than I trust Wunda's big feet."

"Maybe it would have been smart to follow the rest of the class," Dart said sheepishly. "Wunda is from a strong Tribe.

And," he glanced down the corridor where Andor's light was fading away. "They took our only source of light."

"We have a sundancer with us," Montell scoffed.

Fox withered, her shoulders sagging and her knees feeling weak. "Actually—"

"Actually what?" Kohl said, stepping forward.

"I—"

"I think its best we save our energy in case we need to fight," KI interrupted. He glanced at Dart, his eyes barely visible in the darkness taking over as Andor's group moved further and further away. "You can see in the dark, too, right? Or at least use your nose to guide us out?"

Dart nodded. "But we'd better stick close. Don't want to trip over anything."

They walked single file; Dart in front, followed by Fox, then Montell, KI, and Kohl in the back. Fox kept one hand on the wall beside her with the other swaying out in front, her fingertips gently brushing the back of Dart's white t-shirt every now and then. He kept a fair pace, moving quietly, the only sound he ever made was the occasional sniff.

No one spoke behind him. Fox wasn't in the mood and Montell suddenly seemed distracted. She could hear his anxious breathing as he marched behind her, could feel his hand against her back as he swiped at the air, searching for her presence, making sure he hadn't been left behind. *He's nervous*, Fox realized as she heard him swallow. Every sound in the cave was amplified, echoing all around them as they moved, every footstep like a blunt weapon banging against the ground.

He should be nervous. Montell shared the same blessing as

227

his brother, changing the weight of whatever he touched. It was impressive, but right now, in a dark cave with no exit in sight, Fox wondered if she'd been stuck with the worst of the bunch.

Dart was certainly helpful, he was leading them through this cavern, after all. *But what about the others?* KI was stronger and faster than he'd been in Wi, but he showed no other signs of having a particular blessing beside that. *And Kohl?* Fox frowned in the darkness. She had no idea what his gift was—but whatever it turned out to be, Montell had told her the Hungers used cursed power, so it wouldn't be good.

And then there's me. Fox wouldn't even allow herself to focus on her failures. Montell seemed convinced she was their secret weapon, shooting fireballs at whatever monsters might be hiding around the next corner, and providing light when they'd had enough of the pitch black around them. He would likely die right there on the ground behind her if he knew the truth. KI knew the truth, and he'd done his best to cover for her when they'd first started walking, but Fox doubted he could come up with an excuse for her now as the ground beneath them began to tremble.

"Stop!" Dart ordered, planting his feet firmly.

Fox froze, her eyes blinking through the inky shadows. She couldn't see her hand in front of her face, but she would swear she saw *something* move up ahead. And then she *felt* something moving—a coldness brushing against her ankle.

She jumped, falling into Dart who grunted in anger. "Hey!"

"Sorry," Fox breathed.

"What's going on?" Montell's voice was high and panicked.

"I—I felt something," Fox said, eyes wide open, staring at nothing but the blackness before her. She felt the coldness again, this time it came with sharp bristles scraping against the back of her leg.

"Felt what?" Montell said. "I can't see!"

The ground rumbled again, the same way it had in Wi. When the giant had come for them all. Fox fell against the wall. "What's happening? Dart?"

"Something's moving. I don't know what it is."

"Light!" Montell called.

"Calm down," KI told him.

"I need to see!"

Something ran by, skittering over the walls. "What was that?" Fox shouted.

"*Light!*" Montell was shrieking now.

"Fox, use your sundancing!" The voice belonged to Kohl, an uncharacteristic edge to it.

"I—" she gasped, fumbling in the dark, trying to remember everything Master Jo had said earlier. Light energy, channeling your Spirit within, focusing on something to give you strength. She squeezed her eyes shut, listening to the sound of her breathing, focusing on the beating of her own heart. There was something else alive inside her, she could feel it calling out. Like a flicker yearning for breath, to gasp into a flame.

And then ... light burst forth, crackling in the darkness, illuminating the entire tunnel.

Fox gasped, staring at the flame.

It did not belong to her.

Montell sat on the floor of the cave, a fire dancing in his palm. He didn't look panicked at all. Didn't seem like the frantic boy he'd been moments ago. In fact, as his gaze landed on Fox, she thought he looked eerily similar to his brother. Always planning, always plotting. Always thinking he was the smartest man in the room.

He might be, Fox thought, gaping at him.

Delight danced in Montell's brown eyes, reaching down to tug his lips into a smile. "Did you know," he said calmly, "some people can be born with more than one blessing?"

Fox scooted closer to him, staring at the flame. "You're a sundancer, too?"

He shook his head. "Guess again, Fox."

She had seen him lighten the weight of Kohl's shirt earlier. He obviously had his brother's power, so then how could he— she gasped.

"You can copy blessings."

He grinned. "Only from the people I've touched."

And he had touched her, or, rather, *she* had touched *him*. When he'd offered to help Kohl and she'd grabbed his wrist. He had stared at their hands, slender fingers brushing over his flesh, but she thought he was only insulted by her intrusion.

"I felt it," he said, staring at the flame in his hand. "The fire. The moment you touched me."

"That's beautiful," Kohl deadpanned behind them, "but we've got bigger things to deal with right now." He jerked his chin up, and Fox traced his gaze to the bowels of the cave before them.

She could see what'd been moving around them now. In the light of Montell's flickering flame, a thousand little creatures crawled along the walls and ceilings. They had eight legs, a bulbous bottom, and pincers that could snap a finger off.

"Spiders," Fox said, watching them inch away from their group, afraid to be touched by the light.

230

Dart shook his head. "Not spiders. *Feeders*."

She repeated the word, unsure what it meant. "These things don't look any different from spiders."

"They smell different," Dart told her. "They have a stench. The same stench I've smelled on demons."

She swallowed. "But they're not moving closer. As long as we have the fire, they won't touch us."

"Only problem is," Dart pointed straight ahead, "we've stumbled right into their nest. And that's the only way out."

"Are you sure?" KI shivered beside Fox. "Maybe we can double back."

"We can't." Dart glanced over his shoulder. "The exit isn't far."

"How far?" Fox asked.

"Half a mile, max."

"I'm not walking through a nest of spiders—"

"*Feeders*," Dart corrected.

"I don't care!" KI yelled. "I'm not walking that way."

"He has a point." Kohl inched closer to Montell's flame. "If light is our only protection, we might need a backup plan. All they have to do is snuff it out and we're done for."

"Guys," Dart said.

"What do you think makes a feeder different from a spider?" Kohl interrupted. "It's their diet. They don't feed on other bugs or insects. They eat animals. *Humans*." He folded his arms across his chest. "I'm not walking into a nest of man-eating spider demons."

"Then, what do we do?" Dart asked.

"We get rid of them." Montell stood, still holding the flame in his hand. "I'm sure there's more to sundancing than holding

231

fire in my palm." He glanced at Fox. "Right?"

Her first instinct was to shrug because, what did she know? But she caught herself and pressed her lips together instead, nodding. "Sure."

"Why don't you two work together?" Kohl suggested. "Double the power."

Montell laughed. "You want two novice sundancers to shoot fireballs into an enclosed area?"

Kohl quirked an eyebrow. "Never mind."

Fox watched Montell closely, not missing the knowing look he gave her as he stood and faced the squirming demons. *He knows*, she thought, as he took a fighting stance. *He knows I can't sundance.*

Montell threw a punch into the cave, fire sputtering from his fist and falling onto the ground. It ran along the dirt, chasing away the feeders. Fox thought she heard their screams as they burned away. She shivered, but not at the sight of a thousand feeders dying as Montell threw another weak punch, flames belching from his hand, she shivered at the question that danced down her spine.

Why is he covering for me?

Why had he covered for himself?

He'd told her he had felt the fire the moment she'd touched him. But he'd panicked and cried for her to use her own flames in the darkness—knowing he could have done it all along.

Wunda's words flowed through Fox's mind. *I'm not revealing my blessing ... It's every man for himself.*

Fox had been right before. Montell wasn't her friend. *But,* she watched him throw one more fireball into the cave, smiling as he'd apparently cleared the last of the creatures, *he's not my enemy, either.*

One last feeder ran along the ground, its back alight with sunfire. Kohl stepped on it, hard. He glanced at Fox as she stared at his foot, grimacing at the dead creature beneath it.

"That's the last of them."

"Good," she said softly.

"Dart says it's just a straight shot from here. Not much farther."

"Good," she said again, pushing from the wall. She wobbled, realizing how long she'd been sitting and watching Montell play with fire. A warmth on her shoulder took her by surprise. Fox looked up to find Kohl beside her, his hand on her, stabling her.

"Careful," he muttered.

"Thanks." She slowly stepped away from him, but he slid his hand from her shoulder to her arm, gripping firmly. "Listen," he said, his voice low and serious.

Fox blinked, taken aback by his tone. She wouldn't allow herself to believe it, but she thought—for a second—that he sounded ... *concerned.*

"What is it?" she asked.

Kohl leaned toward her, coming dangerously close. She could smell his scent, like sweat and something masculine— something she couldn't name. "Don't let him touch you again," he warned.

Fox glanced ahead at Montell who was talking with Dart, a flame still dancing in his palm. The Shifter stood a good six feet away, well out of arm's length of the copycat student.

"I don't know how his blessing works," Kohl was saying, regaining Fox's attention. "I don't know how many blessings he can copy at once, or for how long. But don't let him touch you

233

again, Fox."

She nodded. "I hadn't planned on it."

"Don't you think it's weird..." he let go of her arm and she pretended the spot where his hand had been didn't feel cold all of a sudden. "Montell had the chance to touch me earlier. He could have copied my blessing. But he didn't."

It was weird. But not for the reason Kohl was thinking. Montell didn't touch him because he didn't want to be cursed. Fox kept that thought to herself, however, stepping away so she could follow Dart out of the cave.

"I don't know what Montell's after. But it's better for all of us to keep our distance."

Kohl nodded, cramming his hands into his pockets. "Let's just get out of here."

He didn't have to tell her twice.

18

Roaring

When Roaring stepped outside, he felt as if he'd stepped into another world. The roads were gritty, beaten down by horses and carriages and those noisy shoes all the women wore. The buildings towered over him, blocking out the sun, and when he walked past a group of men gathered near the corner of the street, they barely noticed him. *This is not Wi*, he told himself, remembering how his presence could shift the mood in a room. There'd been a time where the Prince of Fire need only raise an eyebrow and silence would veil the room, all conversation hushed to a whisper as his comrades waited for a command. In Babel no one seemed to care about his presence or his royal blood or his raised eyebrows. Roaring Fire was nobody and he had no idea how to change that.

Beside him, Cat tugged at his sleeve, peeling it away from his sweaty arm. "You're going the wrong way," she said with a frown.

That's right, the market was in the other direction. Roaring turned with a grunt and walked back toward their little apartment; a square brick building wedged between two others identical in size and shape. Children ran up the road with balls in their hands, slobbery dogs running beside them in excitement. Chava would have loved to run down the street, but she was cramped up in their home; a three-bedroom space with a living room and kitchen. Talon and Cat had agreed to share a room as long as Roaring kept Chava off the couch; the Prince of Fire didn't care where he slept, he hadn't planned on sleeping here long. But he'd already been in Babel for nearly two months now and was no closer to getting home than when he'd first arrived.

Each day we spend here, we lose a little of ourselves. He remembered the first time Talon had stepped into the living room wearing those awful clothes the hospital had given her; a pale pink blouse and a yellow skirt that stopped just above the ankles, silver rings in her ears and her head wrapped in a white scarf to hide her missing hair. She looked ridiculous; Talon had been the Beauty of Fire—a woman who seemed to glow in her royal robes and wrappings, tribal paint rimming her amber eyes and decorating her brown skin, a headdress covering her waist-length coils. Talon could turn any man's head, even in a plain buckskin dress. But in the garb here in Babel she was just another silly looking lady with her weird makeup and her noisy shoes and her gaudy jewelry.

Cat seemed to like the fashion here, enjoying the ugly shirts with all the buttons, the weird underclothes, and the funky smelling oils she rubbed onto her skin. Roaring stole a glance at his little sister as she walked beside him, holding his arm to help stable herself in those click-clack shoes. Cat fit right into Babel as if she'd been born here; she managed to look charming in her blue blouse and beige vest, in her skirt that only came to her knees, and shoes that made her two inches taller. He wasn't surprised; Cat had made it quite clear that she enjoyed the City of Babel and the simplicity it offered.

"We don't have to hunt for food or fight demons anymore," she'd argued the night they returned from the meeting at the Academy. Though Fox had run off, they'd continued their task at laying out plans for the future. The Council was split; half wanted to stay in Babel, safe and sound and cozy, while the other half wanted to return to Wi—to bloodshed and hard work and outdated tradition, as Cat had put it.

Roaring sighed. It didn't help that he'd been left here alone to care for his sisters while Talon ran off to Wi with the Academy. *Two weeks*, she'd told him, *I'll be gone for two weeks*. And she'd looked at him like it was nothing, with a shrug of her shoulder and a crooked, nervous smile on her face—like she couldn't figure out why he'd been so shocked. It wasn't that Talon was leaving that'd surprised him, it was that she'd decided to go alone without discussing it with him first.

"When did you begin making these decisions without me?" he'd asked, eyes wide in disbelief.

Talon went about her room packing away clothes, keeping her back to him so she wouldn't have to meet his burning glare. "I am the Grand Chief," she said carefully. "I have the right to make some decisions on my own."

"This isn't about you being the Grand Chief," Roaring said,

his anger rising. Did it not matter that he was her dear older brother? Her *favorite* sibling? "Talon, we make these decisions together. You and I."

"I knew you wouldn't agree. I knew you wouldn't think I could handle this—no one does, but I can!"

"Talon," he sighed. "It's just that … maybe you shouldn't be going alone."

"I won't be alone." She turned to him, chewing her lip and keeping her eyes on the floor. The scarf she normally wore was discarded on the bedside table; Roaring couldn't help but stare at her, at the fuzzy growth sprouting on her head, barely an inch of her course curly hair. She'd only had half her hair ripped out but had decided to shave the rest so it would grow back evenly. Roaring wasn't sure if he liked the scarf or not, but this was the first time he'd seen her without it. "I'll be with the lieutenant," she said, catching his gaze. She realized he'd been staring at her—at her shaven head—and reached for her scarf.

Roaring turned away, somehow feeling embarrassed. "I'm a leader of the Hunting Regiment," he managed to say. "It's my responsibility to protect the Village of Wi—I should be going with you."

"It's your responsibility to protect the *people* of Wi," Talon corrected. "And the people are here. So, I need you to stay. Who will lead in my absence, if not you?"

Talon had made that sound quite heroic; *who will lead in my absence, if not you?* For a moment, Roaring had swelled with pride, as if he were taking on a great responsibility—leading the people of Wi while the Grand Chief was away. It was something tradition had denied him all his life, a chance to take charge of his own village, but now the opportunity was right in front of him. How could he not feel honored to stay back and lead and protect his people, watch over them day and night? Roaring was proud. And then he woke up the next morning and reality hit him when Cat complained there was no more milk or cheese or *food at all* and Fox asked for coin so she could purchase lunch at her new training course, and Chava needed to be walked— because she couldn't use the bathroom in the house, of course.

I am not leading anything, Roaring had realized, his pride trickling away as reality washed in. *I am babysitting.*

Cat gasped and tugged on his arm, pulling him toward a merchant's stall. They were in the marketplace now, a sector in Babel swimming with merchants and civilians and the occasional Hunter walking the street, a weapon on her hip, patrolling for riffraff.

"Buy this for me!" Cat squealed, pointing to a golden necklace with a red stone hanging from it.

Roaring squinted, leaning close. "How much is it?"

"Two silvers!" the merchant replied, his chapped lips curling back to reveal yellow teeth.

"I want it!" Cat said.

Roaring opened the pouch of coins he'd stuffed into his pocket before leaving; one gold, two silvers, and a dozen copper pieces lay inside. "If we buy this, we won't have much for the supplies we need at—" he paused, blinking in surprise. He'd almost said *at home*, then again, he didn't know what else to call their apartment.

Cat's wide eyes appeared in front of him, batting her long lashes. "Are we really that low?" she asked.

They'd been given an allowance by the Academy that was supposed to last them at least three months, but everyone had needed new clothes and Cat had insisted on buying all the jewels she could get her hands on and Talon hadn't realized how expensive certain spices would be before purchasing. Of course, Fox's enrollment in the Academy had cost a small fee, and she'd needed clothes to train in. Talon had promised she would get paid for going on the mission with the lieutenant, but they wouldn't see that coin for another two weeks. Roaring closed the pouch.

"We're low," he said, walking away from the merchant and the necklace. Cat lingered for a moment, staring longingly at the stone before catching up to her brother.

"*Fine*," she whined. "Let's get the food, then."

An hour later they left the market with three pounds of goat's meat, a whole chicken, ten pounds of yams, a sack of wheat, a jar of olive oil, and a basket of fresh fruits and vegetables—all of which had been successfully bargained for by Cat Fire. Roaring had almost given away their only gold coin on a half-pound of ground pork, he'd lost two coppers to a poor cut of goat's meat, but Cat managed to smile her way to a better cut and an extra pound. The yams were sold at half price after a great deal of airheaded laughter on Cat's part—the merchant thought himself a handsome comedian by which she'd happily indulged him, listening to every joke and jab while Roaring wasted another copper on just one handful of strawberries. Cat spent fifteen minutes in a shouting match with that merchant, trying to get their coin back—somehow, she emerged the victor and sauntered away with a basketful of figs, berries, and fresh banana leaves.

"You're terrible at this, you know," Cat said, tossing their last coin into the air—a single piece of silver.

240

Roaring shrugged. "We never had to trade or argue for our food in Wi."

Cat poked him in the shoulder. "If it weren't for me, you would've wasted all our coin."

"Says the girl who wanted to throw away almost half of it on a necklace."

She stuck out her tongue. "I don't remember that at all!"

Roaring dumped their groceries onto the kitchen table once they'd gotten inside. Chava greeted them with a lazy yawn and sniffed at the food. "What do we do now?" he asked, staring at the uncooked food.

"We put it away." Cat slapped the back of his head. "Are you really this useless without a weapon in your hand?"

Anger swelled inside but he swallowed it down. "We're all useless in this place."

"Make the most of it," Cat said, moving swiftly through the kitchen, loading cabinets and filling jars. "It isn't like what any of us expected, but we finally have some sense of peace in our lives. We aren't living in fear anymore, wondering when the demons will come for us. Will you at least try to enjoy that?"

Roaring let out a sigh and followed his little sister through the kitchen, putting food where she pointed and following her instruction for making dinner. They were almost done with a pot of stewed goat when Fox opened the front door.

"Welcome home!" Cat shouted. "We made dinner!"

Fox glanced at them, dirt smeared on her cheeks and her clothes stained with grass; she had scrapes on her knees and bruises everywhere else. She'd always been the rowdiest of the siblings, pushing herself in her training and challenging Roaring to duels whenever she could, but even then, she'd never looked this beaten up before. Tears swelled in her eyes, and she rubbed them away with the back of her hand, smearing a trail of snot down her chin before running off to her room. Roaring waited until he heard the door slam before he spoke.

"We can try to enjoy this peace here in Babel. But we cannot ignore the war outside forever."

Fox did not answer when Roaring knocked on her door. He thought about leaving, but he knew Talon would scold him for giving up so easily if she found out what'd happened. He knocked again and waited but when no answer came yet again his patience withered and he kicked the door in.

"Go away!" Fox shouted, leaping from her bed, and bounding toward her brother.

When she approached, she grabbed for the door and Roaring moved to block her, but she suddenly shifted, made a fist, and punched him in the gut. Roaring let out an *Ugh* as all the air in his lungs was forced out; Fox, swifter than he recalled her being, threw another jab, but this time he saw it coming and caught her small hand in his.

She glared up at him, anger bunching her shoulders and wrinkling her features, making her look feral with her wild and unruly hair. She had her brother's uncontrollable locks, thick coils that could stretch down to her butt but stubbornly shrank to form a literal mane of dark hair bunched at her shoulders. He glared at her; Talon was beautiful, Cat was clever, Roaring was a leader, but Fox had always been nothing but trouble. Until now, he hadn't realized that she was exactly like him.

Sighing, Roaring let go of his anger and his baby sister's hand and rubbed the back of his neck. "Calm down, little paws. I'm

242

just trying to help."

"Well, you can't help," she snapped, glaring at him. "Why don't you just go away?"

She was right; Roaring was not fit for giving advice or offering comfort. He had no idea what he was doing. *Why did this have to happen as soon as Talon left?* He couldn't stop himself from rolling his eyes.

"School is hard, right?" he said dumbly. Fox had returned with cuts, scrapes, and bruises every day since entering the Academy; until now, Roaring hadn't thought she might be having trouble.

Anger melted off Fox's face as pain and sorrow took over. "Why am I so weak?" she blurted, tears flowing down her face.

Roaring was shaken. "Fox, you're not weak at all. You've been training your entire life to fight demons." *Is the Academy so difficult?* he wondered.

"I can beat any of those kids hand-to-hand," Fox said with a sniffle. "Even fighting with weapons, I know I can win. But no one fights that way here; no one uses their fists or their blades—everyone fights with their *gifts*, and I don't have one!"

"Fox," he said quietly. "You do have a gift."

"But I don't know how to use it!" She wiped at her tears. "What happened to sundancing? Why did it vanish for two hundred years?"

"I don't know. The Fire Tribe's gift faded over time, just like many other gifts. Once Walls were erected, people were finally able to keep the demons out. But after a while, peace became boring, the Walls became cages, and humans began to turn their powers on each other. Their gifts became curses."

"Wi is one of those villages," Fox whispered, her eyes wide

with realization. "We used our powers to hurt each other."

Roaring nodded. "As quickly as the gifts appeared, they were taken away. God never meant for us to use them for evil."

"Then why have they reappeared?"

"Because we need them again." Roaring looked at his sister, hoping she understood what he was trying to say. "Our powers are meant to protect people; we need them now more than ever. Being members of the Fire Tribe's Head Family, the bloodline from which sundancing originated, it's only natural that the powers would awaken in us."

Fox heaved a sigh. "But how do I use it now that its back? I can't make it through the Academy without a gift. I'm useless."

"You aren't useless, Fox," Roaring said. "You are a Child of God."

She glared at him, as if this were all his fault. "I'm *weak*. I can't use my dancing, so I can't protect anyone."

"Everyone has a weakness, Fox. You aren't the only one struggling in your class, I promise."

"You haven't seen these kids." She shook her head. "They're like nothing I've ever seen before. I feel like I'm wasting my time."

Somehow, Roaring knew exactly how she felt. Shopping at markets, walking dogs, even this talk with his little sister—he wasn't born for this. The Prince of Fire was a warrior; he should have been on a hunt, stalking through the woods right now, maybe even fighting a demon. Instead, he was giving a pep talk, stumbling to find the right words to cheer up his emotional little sister. How could he be useful to Wi, right now? What could he do to help his people?

He glanced at Fox, studying her cuts and scrapes and

bruises. "Maybe I can help you," he said.

"You mean, teach me how to sundance?"

"I remember how our mother taught me. Maybe I could show you the techniques I've learned so far."

Fox's eyes lit up. "Let's do it."

19

Talon

A bird sang outside Talon's tent. Part of her wished time would stop, just for a moment, so she didn't have to get out of bed and the bird wouldn't have to fly away. If time stopped, she wouldn't have to go back to being the Grand Chief of Wi; she wouldn't have to make any tough decisions or settle debates or see the disappointing look on everyone's faces. Since that terrible Council meeting, where she couldn't even control her youngest sister, she'd noticed the doubtful eyes, had seen the tightlipped smiles, and had heard the dejected sighs.

Roaring, Ryko, Kifu Kato—they all knew as well as she did; Talon was not fit for this job.

Roaring should be here, not me, Talon told herself, wrapping up in her blankets. If her brother had gone on this mission in her stead, he would have led the charge with a proud smile. Roaring would know how to rebuild the Walls because he'd gone beyond them more times than she could imagine. *What could I do back home in Wi?* Kifu Kato had asked as much when Talon had told him and Ryko she was leaving.

"Are you sure *you* should go?" he'd asked, eyebrows furrowed in confusion.

Talon hadn't known what he'd meant by that. "I am the Grand Chief," she'd replied. "Why shouldn't I go?"

Kifu Kato bunched his shoulders, searching for the right words. "Well, yes, you are the Grand Chief. But, maybe someone with more experience should at least assist you. If you took Roaring—"

"I am sure I can handle it alone."

She'd spoken out of anger when Kato had approached her, but now, lying in her makeshift bed on the floor of her tent, Talon wished she had taken his advice. The old Council used to listen to Roaring without question, even Lieutenant Diaz had shown interest in the Prince of Fire. Though Roaring envied Talon for her birthright, he would never know the title of Grand Chief was *all* she'd inherited. The respect and command that came with it had quietly fallen on his shoulders.

I can do this, Talon told herself, *I can lead, too.*

Outside her tent, the bird's singing grew louder; its low, mournful cry filling the air. Talon had seen many new animals and creatures she'd never heard of during her journey back home. When she'd first left Babel her group traveled day and night on horseback and had camped in the forest the first few nights. Lieutenant Diaz rode ahead of the main force while the rest of the team kept pace behind. She'd been left in the rear guard.

"My lady?" a voice outside her tent called.

Talon stirred beneath her blankets. "Yes?"

"We're packing up to leave now."

She sighed. "I'll be out in a moment."

Talon splashed water from a basin over her face, chewed on a mint leaf, and changed into her riding clothes. It took only five minutes for the men of the rear guard to break down her tent and have her horse ready. Someone had even saved a bowl of porridge for her to eat while she waited for the commander to give them details about today's travel.

They would spend another day riding. Messages from Lieutenant Diaz's group would determine which path they would take. Since the lieutenant had gone ahead, his team scouted out the best and safest route for them to travel with Talon in their midst. She tried not to feel like a burden as she mounted her horse and began a slow trot.

They traveled in silence, save for the occasional command from Sergeant Boyé, an old Hunter of nearly sixty years. He rode in front, guiding them through the lush forest, giving warning to avoid muddy areas, pitfalls, and even a cluster of resting deer. Greenery had swallowed them whole. Out here, the trees were bigger, the animals shier, and the grass taller. Talon had no problem keeping pace, but when they met the sticky grounds of a swamp, she fell behind. Just when she thought hope was lost, a Hunter grabbed the reins to her horse and smiled.

"You don't have to worry," he said kindly, "we won't leave you behind, Your Majesty."

"Your Majesty?"

He blushed. "I'm sorry, I heard you were like royalty."

Talon laughed. "Sure, something like that."

The Hunter's name was Hemiah and he had a bright smile and a large round nose. He'd been raised in a small village in the Region of the Lion and had moved to Babel after his home was destroyed. Talon had listened intently as they rode side by side, enjoying the stories of his home and his family and even his training. He had a gift that gave him the ability to control plant life; when he wasn't telling her a story, he would point out every kind of tree they passed—and the bushes and the weeds and the flowers, too. During one of their breaks, as they stretched their legs and sipped iced peppermint tea, he leaned over and whispered into the grass. A dozen white roses grew from the soil; he clipped them and offered the bundle to the Grand Chief with a shy smile.

For a moment, it seemed as if this trip would be more leisure than business. At the day's end, lying in her tent with her bundle of roses resting over her backpack, Talon had nearly forgotten her aching limbs and sore muscles from the long ride. Then she heard shouting outside and emerged to find half the camp in an uproar.

A messenger hawk had arrived from Diaz's squad; something called *shadow frogs* was lurking nearby. Talon wondered what the creatures could be, but the sheer panic summoned by their approach quelled any rising curiosity. Hunters scrambled to pack up tents and stamp out fires, horses cried out in fear, throwing their riders to the ground as they reared and stomped their heavy hooves.

The tall grass surrounding the team began to shimmy as the shadow frogs closed in. Talon could hear their gurgling grunts and feel the ground shaking beneath her feet.

249

"On your horses!" Boyé commanded, riding through the grass on his steed. He galloped through the makeshift camp, shouting orders and waving a torch around. The grass was tall enough to tickle the belly of his horse, more than enough for the shadow frogs to hide in. A patch of growth beside the Sergeant shimmied and, before Talon could yell for him to move, a dark creature leapt from the brush and swung at his head.

Boyé was quicker than he looked; defying his age, he reacted with lightning speed, raising a sword to slice the monster in half, its black, fleshy body fell to the ground and convulsed until it shriveled up and turned to dust. Another frog followed the first and met the same fate, but the third one was more fortunate. It attacked while the sergeant was busy hacking at the previous frog, instead of swiping at his head, this shadow frog leapt into the air and opened its mouth. A slick white tongue shot forth and landed on Boyé's shoulder with a *splat!* A single moment of realization ticked by; the Hunter's eyes grew large, his mouth opened as he whispered the words, "Oh no," and then the sticky tongue retracted, yanking him from his horse. He disappeared into the grass, screaming madly as half a dozen black creatures dove into the field to devour him whole.

Talon's eyes stretched wide, filled with fear as she watched the shadow frogs leap back and forth, grabbing Hunters and dragging them into the dark plains. Screams erupted all around her; she was surrounded by death on every side. *I've got to go!* she told herself, taking off into the grass. A riderless horse galloped wildly through the camp, nearly trampling her as it ran by. She reached up and gabbed the reins, holding on for dear life when she was lifted from the ground and dragged through the grass.

250

The horse ran at full speed, panic forcing its legs to surge forward. By the grace of God, Talon managed to swing her leg over the saddle and sit upright; when she did, she saw that the camp was completely overrun. The darkling frogs had come in droves, attacking Hunters, devouring horses, and destroying the tents and supplies. They were ugly creatures; big quadrupedal beasts that looked somewhat frog but also somewhat human, with slimy black bodies, wide round eyes, and sagging jowls that inflated like a balloon every time they inhaled. Instinctively, Talon searched the packs strapped to her horse; first aid supplies, a strip of jerky, a skin of water, and four throwing knives. The weapons weren't the greatest, but Talon had good aim and knew how to ride.

She threw one knife at a darkling as it leapt at her, its fleshy body tumbled through the air, bursting into a cloud of dust as it hit the ground. A second knife went into the head of a frog gnawing on a Hunter's face; the woman screamed in horror, frantically trying to fight it off until Talon's knife split its skull. The force of it knocked the frog away and pinned it to a nearby tree. Talon snatched the blade loose as she galloped by. Calmer now, her horse rode easily and swiftly, trampling frogs and leaping over debris. It was a graceful mare, small for her age, but her speed made up for her lack of muscle.

Talon clutched her last three knives; she couldn't afford to waste these. Most of the fires had been put out but she knew where to ride, even without the light. Her nimble horse took her across the field at lightning speed, dodging the leaping monsters with ease. One frog leapt from the grass and caught her off guard, forcing Talon to surrender one of her precious knives. When she made it to the trampled tents across the camp, she clutched her remaining two blades so tightly her hands went numb.

The tents before her had been destroyed by shadow frogs and panicking horses; bodies of Hunters lay in the grass, dead in their sleep. Talon held onto a shred of hope that Hemiah was alive. She checked the bodies closest to her, holding her breath as shaking hands carefully turned stiff heads. Hemiah wasn't there—*thank You, Lord*, she exhaled. But she still had to find him.

The nearby debris yielded no results; Talon overturned tables, peered into sleeping bags, and even chased a shadow frog away from a corpse to glimpse its face. She'd nearly given up when she heard groaning from the trampled tent beside her. Rushing inside, she untangled the covers and equipment to find Hemiah buried beneath it, bloody and confused.

"Hemiah!" Talon exclaimed, shoving a heavy pole off his leg. He groaned in pain and struggled to sit up. His hand immediately went to his head, smearing blood across his brow.

"Are you hurt?" Talon asked.

"I'll be fine. What's happened?"

"The camp was attacked by shadow frogs."

Fear crossed Hemiah's face.

"You must have been asleep when it happened."

"I heard shouting, but before I could make it out of my tent, it collapsed on me. I was knocked out cold."

"The shadow frogs are still here," Talon said urgently. "If you can move, I need you to help me—I think you can get rid of them."

He nodded and motioned for her hand, gripping it as he wobbled to his feet. "Just tell me what to do."

Struggling to hold Hemiah, Talon guided him to her horse who nervously waited nearby. The sounds of shadow frogs running through the grass haunted her, but she forced herself to swallow her fears and hoped Hemiah didn't hear the worry in her voice.

"You can control plant-life, correct?"

Hemiah nodded, his eyes wide and fearful as he took in the scene around him.

"I need you to clear this field. Get rid of all the grass and we'll be able to see the shadow frogs. If you can do that, they won't be able to hide from us anymore."

"We're the ones who are hiding," he said.

Talon shook him by the shoulders. "Hemiah! We will die here if you do not clear this grass!"

Hemiah shook his head but complied, nonetheless. Extending both his large hands, he inhaled sharply and then pivoted, swinging his arms as if slicing through the air. The grass obeyed his command and withered in seconds. Once the grass cleared, the nightmare became clear; only a handful of Hunters remained while dozens of shadow frogs surrounded them, hunched over in the damp soil.

"Step back," Hemiah ordered. He limped past her and extended his hands, letting go of a deep breath as the ground began to shake.

Talon steeled herself, keeping her eyes on the skittish creatures. A few ran off as the earth trembled, but the more defiant ones remained—encircling them, preparing for another fight. Before any of them could attack, the ground beneath their slimy, webbed feet cracked and giant roots crawled forth to grab the monsters and drag them beneath the earth.

It was over as fast as it had begun.

Talon fell to her knees. "You did it," she whispered.

Hemiah sat down beside her. "I'm sorry I couldn't save more."

* * *

Of the twenty-six Hunters and Priests who'd left the Academy, only thirteen remained; two of them were unconscious, seven injured, and four were so weak Talon was sure they'd be dead by morning. The horses were less fortunate; only six of them survived the attack and one was so frightened it ran off and broke its leg in a ditch. The Grand Chief had a Hunter put it down and butcher it for meat.

While the meat was cut and stashed away, Talon patched up all who could walk and ordered Hemiah to build a wagon to carry the rest; he followed orders, whispering to the nearby trees and watching as they extended their branches, cracking and splitting them to form a suitable wagon. The feeble team would ride through the night, only stopping to refill water skins in a nearby river and check the bloodstained map they'd found on a corpse. Talon tried her best to be optimistic, but she knew their chances of survival were low. Without a messenger hawk, they could not contact Lieutenant Diaz who likely had no idea of their predicament, and without communication with the rest of the squad, they were walking blind.

No one had complained of Talon's leadership when she'd patched them up and bravely set out for the next village ... then the horses grew tired, limbs began to ache, and the butchered horse meat rotted much sooner than expected.

"I'll be taking leadership from here," Mung, a young Hunter, announced when they stopped to rest. "With Boyé dead, I am the highest ranked among us, and I am familiar with this area. Koh Village is the nearest settlement, I can safely guide us there and send a hawk to Lieutenant Diaz."

"I've been guiding us just fine," Talon tried to argue.

Mung narrowed her dark eyes. She was a beautiful woman, perfectly smooth skin—no spots or blemishes, despite being a hardened Huntress of the Academy—full lips, and hair cut short so it stayed tucked behind her ears. "Wasn't your village attacked by a swarm of demons?"

"Yes," Talon replied.

She raised a single eyebrow; it was grey, despite her youth. "How do we know those shadow frogs didn't attack us because of you?"

"You're not serious, are you?" Talon grew angry. "Demons attack *many* villages for no reason other than bloodlust. How can you blame the shadow frogs on me?"

The Hunter ignored her, speaking to the rest of the squad as if she weren't even there. "We've all heard the whispers—Wi was a village of *witches*, cursed for the evils hidden behind their Walls. Some even say they summoned the demons themselves just to lure out Academy soldiers."

"This is insane!" Talon shouted but when she glanced around, taking in the serious faces and angry glares of her squad, she realized no one was on her side. Not even Hemiah. "You don't think I'm responsible for the shadow frogs, do you?" she asked him.

Hemiah could not meet her gaze. "I don't know. Maybe they came looking for you because you survived the attack on Wi.

255

Maybe it was a coincidence." He bunched his shoulders. "I don't know."

Defeated, Talon stood and offered her wrists to Mung. "Why don't you just shackle me and leave me here to die since I'm so much of a threat?"

She smiled, and it was the strangest sight, like watching glass splinter. "You'll keep your horse, Lady Talon. But you will ride in the rear and if I suspect any foul play, I will cut you down myself."

* * *

Getting to Koh Village took longer than Talon would have liked. The men trusted her less each day, only feeding her when they remembered and keeping a guard on her even when she went to use the bathroom.

Talon put aside her pride and lifted her robes to squat over a shallow hole in the woods when she had to go. The only thing she cared about was reaching Koh so she could send a hawk to her brother. Roaring would know what to do. Roaring would come save her. Roaring would make all this go away.

The guard beside her kicked a small rock. "Hurry up."

Talon sighed and reached for the fallen leaves nearby. She hadn't eaten at all, and her thighs and rear ached from riding, and she hated the guard who wouldn't look away, not even when she'd asked him to.

"Mung says not to take my eyes off you," he told her, and then, "How could I anyway?"

Talon ignored the look on his face as he watched her, his gaze following her hand as it slipped beneath her skirts to clean herself up. She ignored the way he licked his chapped lips and ignored the gaps in his smile from all his missing teeth, and the sticky spit that made his mouth shine.

Talon tossed her leaves aside and stood, adjusting her robes. "What is your name?" she asked.

He smiled, pleased by her interest. "Naman of the Heko Clan."

"I will remember your name when I get back to Babel and my brother will remember your name when he comes for you."

Naman's smile melted, and he took a step toward her. Talon realized how big he was up close; a full head and shoulders over her. His lips were pulled back, but he was not smiling. His breath made her nauseous.

"And what will your brother do when he finds me?"

Talon looked him in the eye. She wanted to seem as threatening as he was, wanted him to feel as small as she did, but she was tired from riding and queasy from his bad breath, and she still hadn't eaten. She swayed on her feet and put her hand against a tree to stable herself.

Naman grabbed her by the neck. "Tell me," he said. "What's your brother going to do to me?"

"Let me go," she whispered.

He laughed in her face and his breath made her eyes water. "Aww, have I made you cry?" he chuckled, his grip tightening.

Talon clutched his heavy hand, digging her nails into his flesh but he did not seem to feel it. He backed her against a tree and her head hit the bark with a *thud*. When Naman's other hand reached for the knot on her robes, she titled her head back and screamed.

He loosened his grip, stunned by her shrill cry, then he

257

shoved her to the ground.

Someone rushed through the trees, drawn by the ruckus. "What's going on?" a Hunter yelled.

Naman stood over Talon. "She was screaming. Probably calling for demons to attack us!"

The Hunter's eyes grew wide. "Our scout just returned, there are reports of a wyrm nest nearby."

"No!" Talon gasped. "I was screaming because he attacked *me*! I have nothing to do with the wyrms!"

Naman grabbed her by her garments and wrestled her to her feet. "Get up!" he shouted, dragging her through the woods. Talon did not try to fight him; she had no strength and with the wyrms nearby, she knew she'd already lost.

Mung shackled her.

Her meals grew further and further apart. When she became too weak to sit atop her horse, Mung ordered her to be chained in the wagon with the sick and dying. The wyrms never attacked, but when Talon pointed that out it only earned her a gag.

It took another two days before Koh came into view. Talon cried when she heard the village gates creak open, dreaming of a hot bath and a hot meal and a bed that was more than a pile of dirt or a cloak placed on the ground. But Mung was still in charge, and she would not have a witch treated warmly. The squad leader had Talon dragged from the sick wagon and taken before Chief Ramah, leader of the great Koh Village. He sat on a dais peering down at them through one eye, the other had been taken in a raid months before, while loyal men and women watched in silence.

Talon didn't need to be forced to her knees; she fell on her own and stayed there, too weak to stand anymore. Mung stepped forth and told her tale; how the shadow frogs had appeared and the wyrms after that, trying to connect them to the raid on Wi—a raid that had begun in Koh.

"The monsters who rampaged through this village made their way to Wi days later. I believe it is because of this woman!" Mung pointed to Talon. "This *witch*."

The room fell quiet as Ramah pondered the Hunter's words. Talon could hear herself breathing, shallow and strained. She could hear the fire dying in the great hearth set in the wall behind the chief. He sat on a fat pillow instead of a throne, though he looked every bit a king in his floor-sweeping robes and jeweled necklace and the crown that sat atop his head. It was shaped like a bird's nest wrought in gold, complete with barbs and thistles protruding here and there. It wasn't until Talon noticed the words of the Koh Tribe written above the great hearth that she realized the design was not a nest but a crown of thorns.

Merciful, the words said in the Old Tongue.

A sense of relief washed over Talon; years of studying the Old and New Tongue had finally paid off. Mung had come to the wrong village if she hoped Chief Ramah would treat the Fire Queen unkindly, despite such terrible accusations.

"The punishment for practicing witchcraft is death," Mung was saying. "Cross Academy and Koh Village have been allies for centuries; we have come here seeking refuge and you have given it to us. I will not take a life behind your gates, but I will not try to stop you from carrying out whatever sentence you see fit for this vile woman."

Chief Ramah squinted at Talon, taking in her ragged clothes, her red scarf that'd loosened and hung low to cover part of her face, and her skin caked with dirt and oil and dried blood. She looked as haggard as a witch and when he asked her if she had anything to say, her voice came out harsh and low, like the croak of some dark creature. Of course, she hadn't been fed properly in days and had spent most of her latest travels shackled in the back of a wagon that carried more dead men than living but Mung had left those details out.

"Chief Ramah," Talon rasped, licking her dry lips, "I am not a witch."

Mung growled and snatched the red scarf from Talon's head. Gasps and fretful shrieks ran up the oak walls as the crowd took in her shaven head. The Grand Chief did not speak again, she simply lowered her head and stared at the hard mud ground. When tears fell from her eyes to plop onto the earth, she smiled, surprised she had any water to spare.

"Look at her," Mung hissed. "She has the look of a witch."

What a strange word, Talon thought. When she was young, a man in Wi had been accused of dabbling in witchcraft; she remembered his trial, how everyone shook their heads and marked him a traitor. A warlock was a traitor, someone to be hated. But a witch was a strange thing. A mysterious danger. Something to be *feared*.

Talon was not a witch, and she did not enjoy the thought of being put to death, but if she was going to be accused of practicing witchcraft, she'd rather be a witch than a warlock. If those were the only two options.

Ramah heaved a great sigh and the room hushed. "A squad from the Academy stopped here over a week ago. They told me to expect a second squad soon, and that this squad would be guarding precious cargo." He waved his hand at Talon. "I wonder how this precious gem became the corroded stone before me."

"It is dark magic, Chief Ramah," Mung insisted. "She can summon demons at her leisure."

"If that is the case, I will let the Academy decide what to do with her."

"The punishment for her crimes—"

"Is death. I heard you the first time," Ramah interrupted sharply. "But I was left with instruction to treat this cargo as a gem and so I will until I hear from your commander again. I sent a hawk to him as soon as you arrived, we can expect a response within a day or two. Our birds are quite swift."

"Chief Ramah..." Mung's voice was weak, defeated.

Ramah motioned to his guards, and they moved to grab Talon by the shoulders. She buckled in their arms, her consciousness fading from exhaustion.

When Talon opened her eyes again, she was in a warm bed with furs wrapped around her and birds singing outside her window. She had been scrubbed clean, and a hot meal had been left for her; mushroom soup and a loaf of fresh bread with sliced pears and a pot of tea that tasted like dark leaves and clay. She ate every bite and drank the tea right from the pot, burning as it went down. She sighed and went back to her window to hear the mournful song from the birds, but they had flown away. Her tiresome day had begun.

At least she wasn't a witch anymore. At least she wasn't shackled. At least she was free. Except that she wasn't.

Handmaids arrived moments later to escort her back to

Chief Ramah. He had summoned her. Talon preferred the company of the chief to that of the Hunters who had chained and accused her, but she couldn't stop her stomach from twisting in anxiety as she followed the young ladies through the Village of Koh.

Chief Ramah had honored the words of his tribe; he'd been *merciful* to her, and kind, too. But he made himself very clear when Talon came to a halt before him.

"Do not mistake me," he said, his voice low and rumbling. It seemed to rattle off the high walls, making her tremble where she stood. But Talon didn't let her fear show. This meeting with Chief Ramah was not like the last one. This time she could stand on her own, and this time Mung was not there to snatch her scarf from her head and shame her before Ramah's entire council. Talon stood with her head held high and her belly full of mushroom soup and tried to convince herself that she was brave.

Chief Ramah looked at her as if she were a child. "You are accused of taking part in dark magic. I am taking these concerns quite seriously, but I will not cast judgement on you myself. You have committed no crimes against *me*, you are not mine to judge." His hard, brown face seemed to soften, deep creases smoothing out, clenched jaw loosening as he spoke. "Until I get word from your commander, you will be treated as a guest."

As a guest, Talon was given a bath and a bed and a hot meal. But as a guest *accused of being a witch*, she would not be allowed to leave her quarters. A guard would stand outside her door day and night and the ladies who came to leave her food or pour her a bath would not look her in the eye nor speak.

Talon agreed to Chief Ramah's terms, left with no other

262

choice, really. But it was still better than riding in the wagon with dead men, chains chafing her skin.

The Grand Chief quietly returned to her room and sat at her table, staring out the window. All she could do was wonder when Lieutenant Diaz's hawk would arrive and worry what its message would be. Evelyn would not believe that she was a witch. Evelyn would not let them keep her locked up in this room for long. But she didn't feel certain of that. He had left her in the rear guard. Entrusted her in the care of the very people who'd turned on her and put her in this predicament.

Maybe Lieutenant Diaz would believe she was a witch. Maybe Lieutenant Diaz would leave her to rot.

Lord Jesus, Talon prayed internally, *I cannot take much more.*

She gulped back her tears, trying hard to fight against them. Talon would not cry because Roaring had been right; she shouldn't have gone alone. She would not cry because she was not a coward. She would not cry because she was the Grand Chief and Grand Chiefs do not cry.

20

Fox Fire

The walk to the Academy was long and quiet. Fox Fire stepped into the street to avoid crushing a flower growing through the cracks of the sidewalk. She wiggled her toes inside her shoes, wishing that she were barefoot. She sighed.

Beside her, Roaring gave a grunt. "What's wrong?"

When her brother had said he would teach her how to use her gift, Fox thought he would give her lessons before bed—she never guessed he would pack a lunch and follow her to the Academy. She resisted the urge to sigh again.

"I was just thinking of training with you."

Roaring stood a little taller, his pride swelling. "I'll show you how to sundance, I promise."

Fox pressed her lips into a hard line, trying to force herself to smile.

Training at the Academy was not the same as training in Wi. It was much tougher, with students who were less human than Chava.

She stole a glance at her brother. He was just like them—one of the gifted children she couldn't seem to beat.

"Tell me about your training," Roaring said, wiping sweat from his brow. His shirt had soaked through, sticking to his strong chest and back, and his curly hair relaxed with the muggy heat. He looked beaten.

"You're out of practice," Fox said.

Roaring turned to her, his face curdling in anger, but before he could yell, he tripped on a rock and spewed curses at the ground instead. Fox chuckled. This was not the man who proudly wore his wolf's pelt and commanded a hundred men with just the nod of his head. The Prince of Fire was a stumbling wreck on the streets of Babel.

"I think you'll do worse than me at training," Fox said.

"What makes you think that?"

She shrugged. "I may not have a gift yet, but I know my place."

"What is that supposed to mean?"

Fox smirked. "You still act like a prince."

"Because I am one."

"The kids here aren't like the members of the Hunting Regiment; they're not going to care that you're a prince."

"They'll care that I'm a sundancer."

"No, they won't."

"What are they like?"

There was a girl who could move herself and others to different locations just by thinking of the place—she called her gift *Teleportation*. Another girl had the power of healing. She could repair a broken arm in a matter of seconds, and she could stand beside Slaine without feeling like she was slowly dying. Speaking of the dead boy himself ... Slaine made things die. Sometimes without even touching them. Sometimes the grass around him withered when he sat down.

Fox shivered just thinking of him. He seemed more like a demon than a human. Montell had told her there were myths about people like him—creatures called *zombies*. But she'd never heard of them before, and Monty wasn't sure if Slaine was *actually* dead or just looked like he was.

Either way, it was hard to understand why Babel kept the Hungers locked in their own sector of the city but not Slaine's family. Then again, Slaine wasn't from Babel. He was one of the hundreds of recruits who'd traveled night and day from outside the city—or even the Region—to take the exam. No one knew anything about him, not any more than he'd shared. Which hadn't been much.

"Well?" Roaring said, still waiting for an answer. "What are the Academy trainees like?"

"They're like you," Fox finally said. "Except dangerous."

When Fox and Roaring walked onto the Academy training grounds, they were greeted by Master Jo.

She raised an eyebrow at Roaring, then glanced down at Fox. "You've brought a guest."

"My brother wanted to train with me."

"Are you looking to enroll?"

Roaring eyed her. "I haven't decided yet."

"Well, you're welcome to observe for as long as you need. The entrance exam isn't for another few weeks, that means the grounds are open to anyone who wants to train. If you change your mind about enrolling, just let me know—there's a bit of paperwork and a small fee."

"I know," he grunted.

Fox held her breath, expecting her brother to complain about the fee. He'd gone on a rant about running out of coin after Fox had explained she'd needed to pay to enroll in the Academy before taking the entrance exam. *What happens if you fail? Do we get that coin back?* he'd asked, throwing his hands into the air. Despite all his complaining, he'd pried their last silver coin from Cat's claws that morning before leaving for the Academy.

"My name is Marlo Jo," Fox's instructor said. She had one hand on her hip and the other holding her staff. "I'm a Priest of the Cross, and my job is to help trainees cultivate their talents. I'd be happy to show you around if you'd like."

"That'd be great!" Fox blurted before her brother could refuse.

With her staff in hand, Marlo guided them through the training grounds, stopping to study students sparring and running the track and resting in the makeshift infirmary set up outdoors. Roaring didn't speak but he nodded at all the right intervals and watched raptly every time they stopped to observe a fight.

A pair of students prepped for a duel in the middle of the sparring grounds; Kohl, going against Vyanna Farron. Fox took a deep breath, staring at her snow-white dreadlocks. They were pulled back into a ponytail that fell to her waist, it looked almost as heavy as her thin body. A small group of students moved to gather round the ring—before Fox could protest, Roaring stepped away, shouldering into the crowd to get a better view.

"Roaring, wait!" she called, but he ignored her.

The fight had begun; Kohl charged Vyanna, his legs moving faster than human legs should. Before he could get close to her, she shifted and made a gesture with her hand. Fox's mouth suddenly felt dry, and she blinked rapidly, trying to work moisture into her eyes.

A wave of water had appeared before Vyanna, pulled from the air around her.

"Amazing," Fox heard Roaring say.

The water moved at Vy's command. She sent it at Kohl with a flick of her wrist, coiling it like a whip and cracking it at his head. He managed to dodge but the water grazed his shoulder, instantly turning to ice the moment it touched him. The ice crawled up his arm, making his left side useless.

"No way," Roaring breathed.

"She's a seadancer." Fox stood beside him, her eyes glued to the action unfolding. She had seen Vy spar before, and each time it still amazed her. "Her name is Vyanna Farron, she's heir to her tribe and the top student in our class—she'll likely rank number one in the entrance exam."

"What about the boy?"

"Well," Fox tilted her head to the side. Kohlannis could keep up with most of the students. He was strong and fast and clearly had experience—or at least training. But Fox had yet to see him use his blessing. She had no idea what it was or how it worked. And she doubted she would see it now. This wasn't the first time Kohl had gone against Vyanna. Their matches were fun to watch, but always ended the same way. With Kohl flat on his back or completely frozen.

"His name is Kohl," was all Fox said about the blonde-haired boy.

Despite his arm being frozen, Kohl continued the fight, but it didn't last much longer. Vy watched closely as he awkwardly sprinted across the ring; when the time was right, she summoned a wave of water, drawing it from the air around her, and shot it directly at him. Unable to dodge, Kohl took the full force of the blast in his chest. The wave sent him spiraling back across the ring, landing with a heavy thud right at Fox's feet. She stared down at him, only somewhat concerned.

He groaned, his half-lidded eyes blinking up at her in weak, papery ticks. Though she pitied him, it was Roaring who stooped to offer aid, using his fire to melt the ice crusting his left arm.

Whispers rose through the crowd as students witnessed Roaring's power—a display of mastery through his delicate touch. Even Vyanna could not ignore their presence; her green eyes narrowed on Fox's brother in suspicion.

"I don't think I've seen you before," she said, her voice surprisingly high-pitched—girly, like Talon's.

"He's my brother," Fox began, but Roaring cut her off as he stood to introduce himself.

"I am Roaring Fire, Prince of the Fire Tribe and Child of the Sun—and I challenge you to a duel."

Fox's heart thundered in her chest. Challenging a student to a duel was not just an offer to spar but a display of skill and power. Vyanna spent most of her time on the training grounds locked in duels with other students; Fox doubted there was a single student at the Academy with more combat experience than the Farron heiress.

She glanced up at her brother; Roaring was the Prince of Fire, he had experience in combat, too, and he was incredibly strong. It was foolish to issue such a bold challenge but maybe he stood a chance. *Fire against water.* Fox hoped Roaring's flames could hold up.

Vy stared at the arrogant prince for a long moment, her bright orbs roving over him inquisitively. "Are you in the training program?" she asked.

Roaring harrumphed, crossing his arms. "No."

"Then your challenge is declined."

A vein in Roaring's neck throbbed, anger pulsing through him hot as the fire in his blood. "You'll beat up this weak boy, but you won't fight me—someone who is clearly on your level?" he called after her retreating figure. "You're heir to the Farron Tribe, right? Well, I'm the eldest child of the Fire Tribe's Head Family. That makes us rivals."

Vyanna turned on her heel, her ponytail sweeping with her motion. "And that is exactly why I will not fight you. The students here do not fight to entertain some petty rivalry, we train to get stronger so that one day we can save and protect the people we love."

"You're just afraid of losing to a rookie."

Vy clenched her jaw, her anger surfacing for the briefest moment, but just as quickly as it rose, it was stamped out by her natural coolness. With a sigh, she said, "If you can beat my cousins in a duel, then I will fight you. What do you say?"

Fox bit her lip. Fighting Vy's cousins would not sit well with her brother, he would see her offer as an insult to his name and talent. But Roaring had no idea just how skilled Vy's cousins were. Twin siblings, Toad and Ren of the Ool Clan, a small sister

of the Farron Tribe, were just as deadly as their older cousin—
if not deadlier, Fox thought, watching them emerge from the
onlooking crowd. Two bodies indistinguishable in size and
shape crossed the floor to stand beside the Farron girl. The Ools
were brother and sister but identical nonetheless with
matching green eyes, matching short grey hair, and matching
skin a shade of brown so dark it almost appeared midnight blue.

Roaring barely glanced at them. "My challenge was issued to
you, Farron Princess."

"Those are my terms."

He grunted in reply.

"Two on one isn't very fair!" Fox said. It was a desperate
attempt to get her brother out of the match, but her statement
seemed to push things in the wrong direction.

"You're right," Vy agreed. "Why don't you fight alongside
your brother?"

Fox hiccupped. She'd fought only one of the twins before—
Toad—and the fight hadn't ended much differently from the
duel between Kohl and Vy. The twins could use the same
abilities as their cousin, but they weren't as merciful as she was.
They liked to drag things out or finish things quickly, toying
with their opponent or totally crushing them right off the bat.

A teasing grin stretched across Toad's face. Fox shuddered,
memories of their 5-second fight flashing in her head; him
whipping his hand at her, sending a rush of water in her
direction, her flying through the air, hitting the ground hard.
Everything turning black.

"I don't think I'll be much help," Fox muttered.

Roaring exhaled so hard, steam rolled from his nostrils. Fox
thought she smelled the sharp scent of smoke in the air just

then. "She's right—she doesn't have as much experience with her gift as I do."

"Then get another to fight with you. Three against the twins is very fair—actually, I think four would give you the best shot at winning."

"You call *me* arrogant?" Roaring shouted, steam rising from his body. "But you send two people to fight four—who do you think you are?"

Vy blinked. "I'm a student at the Academy training program; the *top* student. There are few here I have not faced in combat. I know the strengths and weaknesses of almost everyone around you—you should heed my advice when I say you'll need two others to make this a fair fight."

"He'll take your advice," Fox *would* have said but Kohl beat her to it, stepping into the ring beside her brother. "I'll fight on his team."

Toad's face wrinkled in anger. "I'm not fighting Hunger trash."

"You will," Vyanna instructed.

"They still need another teammate," Toad told her.

"I'll fight with them!" a voice shouted.

The crowd parted to let a muscular boy into the ring; Fox gasped. "KI!"

He winked at her.

"That's four," Vy announced. "Is there an instructor who will observe this fight?"

Marlo, who'd been watching from a distance, raised a hand. "I approve of this fight. Competitors have five minutes to prepare."

Standing in the shade of a nearby tree, Fox and her team tried to make a plan.

"What do you know about the twins' abilities?" Roaring asked.

Fox bit the inside of her cheek, swallowing painful memories of her loss to Toad. "They have the same gift as Vy."

"Not exactly," Kohl said, leaning against the tree. Unruly blonde hair fell into his eyes, he swiped it away and planted his gaze on Fox. "It's more like they have the ability to *use* Vy's gift—almost as if it's a borrowed power."

Fox thought of Montell and his power to copy blessings. *Was it like his gift?*

Roaring squinted, confused. "What do you mean?"

"I can't really explain it. That's all I got."

"That's useless."

"I offered more than you did," Kohl snapped.

Roaring turned to argue but Fox cut in. "I don't think we can win, no matter what their abilities are."

"Can we use any sort of weapon?" her brother asked.

Fox shook her head. "We can train with whatever weapons we want, but we're not allowed to use them in duels—unless the weapons are an extension of our natural blessings."

Roaring heaved an agitated sigh. "That's ridiculous."

"It's supposed to keep students safe; better to knock someone out with a blast of water than accidentally stab them to death."

"We have the numbers," Kohl offered.

"But not the skill." Roaring crossed his arms.

"What's that supposed to mean?"

"It means you should leave all the fighting to me."

273

"There's a reason we have four people on this team, genius. You can't fight them alone."

"There's four people on this team because they *underestimate* me," Roaring corrected.

"It's not all about *you!*" Kohl exclaimed.

"Guys, we don't have time to fight with each other." KI exhaled a sigh. "You're both right; Roaring can take the offensive while Fox and I stay on defense. Ana, why don't you shadow Roaring to counterattack?"

Kohl's jaw clenched but he didn't argue, just peeled from the tree, and began making his way back to the ring. "Fine," he said over his shoulder.

"Seems like you two know each other." Roaring eyed KI closely.

He shrugged one shoulder. "A bit."

Marlo called for the teams to take their places; Roaring led the way with an exasperated sigh. "If we stick to the plan, we should win."

At the ring, the twins waited with Vyanna standing close by; Toad with his arms crossed, a stupid smile on his face, as if withholding laughter. Ren gazed into the crowd, staring at no one in particular. When her brother leaned over to whisper something in her ear, she yawned in response.

Instructor Marlo had both teams line up facing each other and shake hands.

"This match will last exactly ten minutes; knock your opponents out of bounds, knock them unconscious, or force them to concede and you will win. If time runs out before any of these conditions are met, the duel will be declared a draw. Does everyone understand?"

Both teams nodded agreement.

"Do you agree this is a peaceful duel amongst allies?" Master Jo asked.

All six students answered *yes* in unison.

"And do you promise not to purposely cause death or major injury to one another, and to maintain the friendly camaraderie established by Cross Academy?"

"Yes!" Fox said, almost too quickly. It wasn't until KI suddenly took her hand that she realized she'd been shaking. *Why am I so nervous?* She'd trained in combat for years in Wi; this was nothing. It *should* be nothing.

Master Jo gave a firm nod. "May Christ hold you accountable should you break your promises. Begin!"

21

Roaring

In Wi, Roaring had fought with a rahkai. Every member of the Hunting Regiment had mastered the curved blade before moving on to any other weapon. Roaring had trained with a battle ax, a weighted club, he'd even tromped through the woods with a bow and arrow for a few months, but his favorite weapon had always been the rahkai. It was lightweight and easy to use; the blade seemed to melt into his hand when he wielded it, becoming part of his body. As he stood in the ring, preparing to fight the Ool twins, he tried to remember what it felt like to have a blade in his hand. How long had it been since he'd battled a demon? How much time had passed since he'd had a good fight?

Master Jo asked them for agreements; Roaring spoke without thinking, itching to begin the match. Heat swelled in his chest, pouring into every part of his body. The smell of smoke tainted the air. The Prince of Fire had no blade in his hand, but he did have a weapon, and this one had been forged of fire.

Marlo slammed her staff into the ground. "Begin!"

Heat exploded from Roaring's fist, bursting to life in the form of fire. His teammates stumbled backward, trying to avoid the heat—even the crowd gathered at the edge of the ring scrambled to escape the searing blaze that danced into the air. Great flames shot forth, surging toward the twins; one swiftly stepped aside—Roaring wasn't sure which one, but it didn't matter, he would defeat them both. The other attempted to dodge but, thinking quickly, Roaring shot another blast, feeling a wave of heat wash over his frame. Sweat bubbled on his brow, his muscles strained against his own skin, the backlash of his brute force hit him hard.

The second fireball caught the other twin off guard; hungry flames hurled across the ring at full speed, but Roaring extinguished them just in time. Instead of burning the twin alive, the attack knocked the Ool sibling flat on their back, leaving only their clothes singed from the extreme heat. The crowd gasped and murmured together, shocked by the easy defeat. Roaring let go of a small breath—but before he could do any more, the first twin was suddenly right in front of him. Instinctively, his feet shuffled backward to evade, but the Ool twin was faster than he thought; a hard jab to his gut knocked the wind out of him, nearly bringing his breakfast up with it.

Roaring stumbled back, shooting another blast of fire to ward off his opponent. He could hear Fox's voice behind him, shouting for him to watch out but before he could react, the twin was on him again. This time he was fast enough to dodge and managed to dance away and regain his footing; the attacks were quick, but Roaring was quick, too, successfully avoiding every jab, kick, and punch thrown his way. He would have been proud of himself except that he knew he was being pushed toward the edge of the ring—stepping out of bounds was just as much a defeat as being knocked out. He had to do something now.

"Kohl!" he called, his voice coming out more panicked than he liked.

The blonde boy proved reliable, running ahead of him and landing a good kick to the Ool's ribs. Roaring used that precious moment to stable himself and opened his mouth wide; smoke billowed forth, pouring onto the ground, and rising to darken the air, casting a black veil over the entire ring.

"Get back!" he yelled.

The Hunger boy followed orders, ducking behind him as he breathed another dark cloud onto the ring. Peering through the smokescreen, Roaring could see his opponent standing a few feet away. The stupid grin on the twin's face was the last thing he saw before the smoke swallowed him whole. *Toad*, he thought angrily.

"You covered the entire ring in smoke!" Kohl shouted, coughing.

Roaring tried to remain calm. "I know."

"You and your sister are the only ones who can breathe and see through this!"

"I *know*. I'm sorry. This was a last resort."

Kohl knelt and rubbed at his reddened eyes, Fox and KI appeared by his side, huddling together in the smoke. "What do we do now? We've still got eight minutes left but I don't think we'll last that long."

"That guy is fast, and he's stronger than I thought," Roaring said. "He was trying to push me out the ring." He looked down at his hands, warm and sweaty from the fight; calluses covered his palms and scars peppered the backs. He closed them into fists, trying to hide the fact that they were shaking. "And he almost succeeded."

"He'll come for you again as soon as this smoke clears," Kohl said.

"Then we'll move before then."

"But how?"

Three pairs of frightened eyes stared up at the sundancer, wondering how they would make it out of this and hoping that Roaring somehow had the answer.

He looked down at them and realized he'd been holding his breath. Though this was only a friendly spar, Roaring felt a very real chill run up his spine. He'd seen these frightened eyes before. This was no different from the hunts he'd taken with the Regiment. The fear they all felt was the same fear his team felt when they'd been cornered by a monster. Despite slim chances, Roaring had always found a way to get his men back home— he'd always found a way to lead them to safety.

I can do this, he told himself, *I can lead them … because I am the Prince of Fire.*

"You guys can't see through the smoke," he explained, "but that means neither can Toad. I can sense his presence and movements, so can you, Fox, if you concentrate." Fox's eyes widened in disbelief, but she steeled herself and gave a firm nod. "That means you and Kohl are switching places."

"Are you sure?"

"I'm positive. You can do this, Fox Fire, you're the only one who can stand by my side right now."

"What do I have to do?"

"Toad is going to come for me as soon as he can; all I need is for you to be ready with a counterattack. Once he's close enough, hit him as hard as you can. I'll do the rest."

"What about us?" KI asked.

"You two should try to stay as far back as possible, but keep your guard up—"

"Roaring, I can sense them!" Fox blurted, her eyes wide again.

"That's good," he said.

"No," she leaned closer, her breath blowing the smoke away with her desperate words. "I can sense *them*. There's *two* people moving in the smoke."

Roaring stood up straight and stared into the black cloud; though he could not see them with his eyes, he could *feel* the twins through the smoke, as if the dark veil were his flesh and the Ools mere bugs crawling on it. Toad was standing in the same spot he'd left him, swaying from side to side, but there was a figure beside him; *it* must *be Ren*.

Suddenly, the figure moved, rushing right at them.

Roaring inhaled sharply. "Move! They're—" before he could finish his sentence a dark form appeared in front of him.

A terrible cry pierced the air, but it was cut off by the sound of another, this one weak and reedy. Roaring's eyes flitted through the smoke but all he could see was a dark blur dancing through the cloud, attacking everyone but him.

Instinctively, his hands balled into fists, but he hesitated. *If*

I use my flames, I'll burn my teammates, too. He exhaled hard, forcing out all the air in his lungs until he felt he would suffocate. Then he breathed in deeply, sucking in all the black smoke.

With the smokescreen gone, Roaring could see clearly; Toad stood in front of him, just a few feet away—exactly where he'd left him. That same stupid grin on his face, stretched wide across full lips. Behind the prince, Kohl was on his knees, while KI stood further back, cradling an injured arm. Fox remained standing but there was a cut across her right eye, blood smeared into her dark eyebrow. Ren stood to the side in her fighting stance, ready for more.

"I thought I knocked your sister out," Roaring said.

Toad let go of an annoying giggle. "I'm not surprised. You seemed oddly confident in yourself. Then again, you have no idea who you're up against."

"We can still win." He held up his fists. "You're the stronger twin; as long as you're focused on me, I know the others can handle Ren. Your water is nothing against my fire."

Toad laughed again, this time it was low and dark. "Is that what you think our gift is? *Seadancing?*"

And then, before he could answer, Toad took off, sprinting toward the young dancer.

They clashed for a few moments, taking turns lunging and defending. The heat in Roaring's body pulsed through his veins, it was all he could do to contain it. If he used his dancing at this range, he risked burning the boy too badly—that would get him disqualified. Toad took advantage of this and refused to back off, leaving Roaring no choice but to abandon his fire and fight hand-to-hand.

281

"You were wrong about us being seadancers," Toad said, charging with a right hook.

Roaring evaded and countered with a kick.

"And you were also wrong about another thing." Toad jumped back, that silly grin stretched across his face again. "I'm *not* the stronger twin."

Behind them, Ren dismantled his team. She knocked down Kohl and lunged at KI, giving him a bloody nose before going after Fox. Roaring could only watch in disbelief as his teammates were pummeled with ease. His heart sank.

Ren traded blows with Fox. *She is fiercer than her brother,* Roaring noted, but her attacks against his sister were weak, almost hesitant. The prince's eyes widened as he caught a glimpse of the very halfhearted jab she took at his little sister. *They don't know,* he realized, *they don't know Fox can't use her flames yet.*

Without thinking, Roaring shouted, "Fox *now!*"

His sister gaped at him, panic and confusion written all over her face, but it didn't matter that she had no idea what he meant because his words had been enough to give them the opening they'd needed.

Wary, Ren backed away from Fox and Toad backed away from the prince—giving him just enough distance to safely use his flames.

With a proud grin on his face, Roaring punched at the air and released a massive wave of fire. He watched with relief as the flames engulfed Toad, but his relief petered out when the boy's hand emerged through the fire and grabbed hold of his fist. Roaring gasped right before he was punched in the face, the force sending him a few steps back.

Toad stood before him, but instead of wearing that silly smirk, his face looked crooked, his features appeared sharp—almost distorted. It wasn't until he took a step closer that Roaring realized his skin had hardened, almost as if rocks had appeared on his flesh. Slowly, the cracks and jagged edges in his face morphed back into his usual smooth dark skin. Toad's stupid smile returned as well, a teasing grin Roaring had come to hate.

"You look surprised," he said.

"You should have been knocked out by that."

"If I didn't have the anointing of the Ool Clan, I would have been."

Roaring squinted.

"It's called *Adaptive Evolution*; it means we adapt to the situation or environment. Throw us in a lake and we grow gills, shoot fire at us and our skin becomes heat resistant."

A dizzying urge to vomit settled in Roaring's stomach. The twins had been toying with them all along.

"You look incredibly surprised," Toad said, but Roaring was not listening. His mind was busy sorting through every action he could possibly take. *There is a way out of this,* he told himself, *it doesn't have to end here.* But KI was nursing an injured arm, and Kohl looked ready to collapse, leaving Fox to fight as best she could. It wouldn't be long before Ren finished them off and came for him next. And Toad would be by her side.

Gritting his teeth, Roaring shifted into his fighting stance; his legs wide apart, his knees bent, hands clenched into fists ready to strike at any moment. *Maybe I will lose here, but I won't lose because I stood still and did nothing.*

Toad grinned. "Let's get this over with."

He's resistant to my heat, but all that means is I don't have to hold back.

Toad charged at Roaring, but the sundancer moved quicker than he expected, blasting him with a ball of angry fire. The flames licked at the boy's body but did nothing more than burn his clothes away. Unashamed of his nudity, Toad fought on, sidestepping Roaring's next attack and closing in with a swift kick to the chest. Roaring stumbled backwards but countered with another fireball—this time, Toad didn't even try to evade. He took the blast full on, but being heat resistant was not the same as being immovable. The fireball itself did not affect the young fighter but at such proximity, the impact certainly did.

Roaring's blast sent Toad spiraling across the ring, landing with an audible *thud!* Even the prince winced as he watched his lanky body bounce on the dirt. Clumsily, Toad struggled to his feet, but Roaring refused to let him recuperate. It was his turn to charge.

Legs moving fast, the sundancer crossed the ring in a few swift strides and balled his fist. Flames flickered to life and seeped between his fingers to erupt into a raging swirl; *he won't try to dodge, because he knows the heat can't hurt him,* Roaring thought. But the flames weren't the only thing Toad needed to worry about. Just before Roaring's fire made contact, he extinguished the flames and simply punched Toad in the face. Knocking him out cold.

A sharp cry rang out, swallowed by the sudden gasp of the crowd. Roaring didn't have to look to know the cry had come from Ren Ool. He heard her quick footsteps before he saw her, but even then, he still had no time to react. Pivoting, Roaring shifted to counter but all he could do was lift his hands to guard his face. At the last second, he realized he'd chosen the wrong guard; Ren's fist was coming from below, attempting a devastating uppercut.

With no time to dodge, Roaring braced himself for the impact but instead of getting gruesomely punched by Toad's angry sister, he was saved by the sudden appearance of a glossy, transparent wall.

In an instant, a shimmering wall of glass had appeared between the fighters, taking the full force of Ren's attack. Her fist banged against the wall, but the impact didn't shatter it, it only left Ren howling in pain as she yanked her fist back and shook her injured hand.

Roaring blinked, stunned.

"Time's up!" called Master Jo. She stood on the edge of the ring with her hand extended and her fingers spread; when she closed her hand into a fist, the wall disappeared.

"Toad Ool was knocked unconscious. Ren Ool is still standing. KI, Kohlannis Hunger, and Fox Fire were knocked unconscious, but Roaring Fire is still standing. Since neither team met the conditions for a win, this match is a draw."

A disappointed groan resounded around Roaring. Though he hadn't lost, he still hadn't won, and he wouldn't get to fight Vyanna Farron. It was hard to hide his frustration, especially when he had to pass the Farron princess as he left the ring.

Roaring half expected her to smirk or jeer at him, but she simply nodded and extended a hand. "You fought well."

Her kindness made him feel worse. "Not well enough," he said, walking off.

* * *

285

Since Fox, KI, and Kohl had been knocked unconscious, Roaring had no choice but to wait in the infirmary for them to rouse. He would have preferred to simmer in his failure alone, but Master Jo had insisted on sitting with him while he waited.

"You fought well," she said, passing him a bundle of ice. "You've got an impressive gift."

Roaring held the bundle, enjoying the soothing coldness against his hot skin. The ice began to melt right there in his hands. "Is that what you used in the ring?" he asked. "Your own gift."

Master Jo smiled, a hint of pride flickering across her face. "The Jo Clan is small, but we've got a pretty interesting anointing, right? We call it *Guard*; the power to summon an unbreakable wall at will. It might seem unimpressive compared to people who can shoot fire from their fists, but I've learned to use it in a way that makes me more useful than even I would have thought."

"It comes in handy for breaking up fights," Roaring said.

"I guess I was meant to be a teacher."

He glanced at her, taking in her dark skin and brown eyes, her long legs that seemed to stretch across the room, and her strong arms folded across a flat chest. "In a place like this, you could have become anything you wanted."

"I can say the same about you and your sister and those boys, too." Master Jo sighed, her eyes gazing over the sleeping children. "Kids and adults come from villages across the Region—even the globe—just to take this entrance exam. Cross Academy is supposed to teach you how to fight demons, but our training is about so much more than slaying monsters. It's

286

about facing your fears and every dark part of this world."

Roaring shifted in his chair. The ice had melted into water now, sizzling into steam as it trickled into his palms. Long dark lashes fluttered when he blinked; he watched his sister, wondering what on earth she could learn here at this school.

"The only fear I have is losing my family."

"Then get strong enough to protect them," Master Jo said. "The Academy can help you do that."

"Are you trying to recruit me?"

She smiled, and he would never admit that it was pretty. "Imagine how that match would have ended if you'd had the right training."

Roaring sighed. "Perhaps."

22

Talon

Talon heard the horses before she saw them. At first, her cup of tea began to shake and then her bowl of half-eaten soup and that's when she heard them. At least a dozen horses running at full speed, their hooves destroying the ground beneath them as they charged. She ran to her window, knocking over her small table in the process, and threw the curtain aside. By then, the riders had neared the front gates of Koh, hidden by a cloud of angry dust.

A young woman ran into Talon's room, panicking as she saw the overturned table and spilled food, brown soup soaking into the hardwood floor. "What's happened?" she gasped but Talon hushed her.

"Riders at the gate."

Talon's room was in Chief Ramah's own home; an

extravagantly designed log house built atop the highest hill in Koh. It'd been constructed with three floors and enough animal pelts to have filled a forest. The Koh Village was known for its expert hunters. From her window in the grand house atop the high hill, Talon could see nearly every part of the little village. Hunters from Koh's Regiment ran back and forth at the gates, shouting commands as they tried to find out who the riders were. Talon already knew.

The cloud of dust surrounding the men had not yet settled but she did not need to see the riders to know they were from the scouting squad of her mission. Talon's heart began to pound at the sound of the gates creaking open. And then she saw him.

Lieutenant Diaz was the first rider through the gates; sitting on a golden stallion, its ebony mane flowing back into his face. He raced through the gates and circled the greeters waiting for his team, hopping down while his steed was still in motion. His eyes were aflame, burning with anger as he approached a guard. The man shrank beneath his glare, though Diaz was much shorter than him. Talon wished she could hear his words and hoped that he was asking about her.

Beside her, the handmaid grabbed her by the elbow. "We should go," she said, pulling her away from the window. Another servant waited by the door, staring wide-eyed at the overturned table and spilled soup. She snapped to attention at Talon's approach and guided them through the grand house around the lush gardens and to the village gates. By the time they made it outside, the lieutenant's team had cleared the area, their horses taken to the stables. Talon bit her lip, her nerves unwinding. If Diaz wasn't here then he was likely with his men, speaking to Ramah and discussing what would happen next.

Mung was probably there, too, whispering curses into their ears.

The ladies brought Talon into the great hall, the same place she'd been dragged to when she'd first arrived. They stopped at the double doors and made sure Talon looked presentable; adjusting the silk scarf wrapped around her head, tugging at the long, wide sleeves of her dress, and dusting the dirt from her soft slippers. She tried to calm herself while they fussed; the lieutenant was here; he would handle the situation. *There is nothing to be afraid of.*

Inside the throne room, Ramah sat on his cushion in a flowing red kaftan and his crown of thorns. He was hunched over in conversation with Diaz, exchanging fierce whispers around the pipe in his mouth. Puffs of smoke escaped his lips with every other word. The lieutenant's face appeared calm, but that look of boredom he usually wore was not there. He was leaning into the chief, hanging on to every word. What emotion he felt, Talon could not tell. All the wild anger he'd had at the gates seemed to have calmed into a quiet storm.

A squad of Academy Hunters stood on the side of the dais with the lieutenant, their eyes watching their leader, waiting for a cue or a signal. Guards from Koh stood sentinel beside their chief, eyeing the men from the Academy, wondering if there would be a fight soon.

Talon walked slowly, keeping her eyes forward. Nobles and officials from Koh lined the walls of the throne room, watching the witch as she approached. She could hear their hisses and whispers, but she kept her gaze ahead, refusing to acknowledge their presence. When she was halfway down the aisle, her slippers whispering against the carpet, the lieutenant glanced up.

His eyes found hers and as recognition set in, he turned from the chief and stepped down from the dais, walking right toward her. Gasps erupted around the room, even Talon blushed as she saw the shock cross Ramah's face. It wasn't every day someone turned their back on the Chief of Koh.

Diaz was in front of her now, one hand extended, reaching for her. Before Talon could react, he was touching her face, holding her chin so he could examine her. Hazel eyes roved over her; he saw the dark circles under her eyes and the fading bruise on her right cheek, evidence of her struggle in the woods. This close, she could smell his scent; grass and soil and something else, something dark. The expression on his face was unreadable but Talon could see something in his eyes; a small spark of anger, flickering every time he blinked.

He pulled away.

"Where is the squad who accused her of being a witch?" Diaz's voice boomed off the high walls, demanding an answer.

Chief Ramah would not let him take control so easily, not in his own village, in his own throne room. He relaxed on his cushion, swinging one foot down to hang over the dais. He took a long drag from his pipe and exhaled through his nose. "We'll call for them."

Diaz returned his attention to Talon, his eyes landing on her bruise. She resisted the urge to cover her jaw; her face tingled where he'd touched her. "Who did this to you?" he whispered. "The Academy Hunters?"

Talon shook her head. "No. It happened in the forest, with the shadow frogs—"

He turned away before she could finish. "Call for my men!"

The agitation in his voice was clear, even the guards beside Chief Ramah shifted, unsure what to do.

A brief moment of panic grabbed hold of Talon as she watched the lieutenant approach the dais, but before he could do anything, the large double doors of the throne room creaked open, and Mung was escorted in. The surviving Hunters trailed after their elected leader but somehow all the passion and anger they'd had days prior was gone. Mung did not look like the confident woman who'd presented Talon to Ramah that fateful evening. Her shoulders were slumped now, her eyes downcast, unable to meet Diaz's scorching gaze. She looked afraid.

Lieutenant Diaz met them halfway down the aisle. "What were you thinking, Mung?"

"I took command and handled the situation—"

"What were you *thinking*?" He was yelling now, his anger coming out in uncontrollable waves. Talon had never seen him so expressive before. "Your men were killed! Slaughtered by demons in the woods and you blamed your own guest? You didn't handle the situation—you let your fear take over."

Mung winced at his words, unable to deny the truth in them. "We thought there was a connection, Lieutenant."

He took a step toward her, closing the distance between them. Despite his height, Diaz managed to make Mung look small, shrinking her with his gaze. "I can tell you right now, there is no connection. Talon is not a *witch*, not a *sorcerer*, and she is not a *summoner*—she's our guest, the Grand Chief of the Village of Wi, and she is here of her own accord to assist us with research on the *actual* demonic threat looming over us!" Spittle flew from his mouth as he hollered at her, his voice rising with every word until he was shouting at the top of his lungs. The onlookers from Koh whispered behind their veils and wrappings, some of the women even shrieked. Talon felt the tension, too, the simmering anger that filled the room, nearly suffocating them all. She had never seen Lieutenant Diaz behave this way, and even though Mung had brought her much trouble, she wished he would calm down a little.

Mung did not speak when the lieutenant finished, neither did the squad behind her. Hemiah stood further back, hiding within the crowd of Hunters, avoiding both the lieutenant's and Talon's gaze.

Diaz heaved a sigh and turned back to the dais. "Chief Ramah, will you spare an escort back to Babel?"

He nodded. "You can have fresh horses and rations, too."

"Good," Diaz said with a nod, and then to Mung, "Pack your things, you're going back to Babel—all of you."

Mung stepped forward to protest, but the lieutenant didn't back down. "I don't want to see you anymore!" he yelled. "And when I get back to Babel, I don't want to see you at the Academy, either."

Anger flashed on Mung's face right before disbelief washed it away. All at once, the fight went out of her; her eyes fell to the floor and her lips parted to speak, almost as if the words were poison in her mouth. "Yes, sir," she said so quietly, Talon strained to hear. Then, without another word, Mung marched out of the throne room with her squad following close behind.

Hemiah kept his gaze locked on his feet.

Lieutenant Diaz appeared in front of Talon again, capturing her attention. He was so close she had to take an involuntary step back. His hand went to her face, gently touching her cheek, but that sweet concern he'd had before was gone, replaced by that familiar, unreadable expression. He looked at her the way he always had before, like he was suddenly bored. His job was now complete. The task had been achieved; rescue Talon, continue with the mission.

"Pack your things," he said softly. "We're leaving immediately."

Talon could only nod as she watched him leave, trying to forget the way it felt to have his hand on her skin.

23
Roaring

He called to the heat within, and it responded, gathering in the center of his chest. It churned and stirred, breathing and expanding before it poured back into every crevice of his body. The red-hot creature surged through his veins, searching for a way out; he concentrated and directed it, forcing it to bend to his will. With a roar, it burst from his hands in a massive ball of blistering heat—and fire was born.

Roaring panted for breath as he watched his fireball fly across the field and dissipate in the air. Beads of sweat prickled on his forehead, and he swiped them away with the back of his hand. Fox stood watching from a distance, entranced by the power she knew slept soundly inside of her.

He straightened and smiled. "That's how you do it, little paws. The heat is already there inside you, just call to it and it will answer."

She hesitated. "I don't know how to call to it."

"Well ..." Roaring wanted to scratch the back of his head. He had no idea how to teach Fox to call to the heat but after their match against the Ool twins, he knew she desperately needed to learn. Had Fox been able to use sundancing, they would have won that match. If Fox had been able to sundance, the Ools and that Farron girl wouldn't be able to look down on them. But Roaring didn't want to put all the blame on his sweet baby sister. She had fought well, even without her dancing.

Fox took a fighting stance; squatting with her legs far apart and her hands balled into fists, ready to strike or defend. She inhaled deeply, trying to call to the heat, to summon it the way Roaring had explained. Her breaths came quickly, almost as if she were panicking, forcing the air in and out of her lungs.

"Calm down," Roaring said. "You can't force the fire to come—just call to it and it will be there."

Fox looked annoyed but started over anyway. She began with her stance, then focused on her breathing, taking slow, deep breaths. Roaring watched her closely, taking note of the moment she left his presence and sank into her thoughts, searching for the fire inside. Her eyes stared blankly ahead but her brow furrowed in concentration; her breathing became rhythmic, as if she were aligning herself with her own power. A smile crossed Roaring lips as he observed, wondering if he looked this strange when he'd first learned how to dance.

Fox's face changed; her concentration remained but her blank stare was gone, replaced by a fixed gaze as she took aim. She shifted her position, sliding her feet across the grass, and then thrust her fist forward with a grunt.

Nothing happened.

"I can't do it!" Fox exclaimed, falling into the grass.

Roaring frowned. "You looked like you were making progress."

"I thought I was doing something, but apparently, I wasn't. It doesn't matter where I search inside or how many times I call; the heat won't come."

Roaring sat beside his little sister. It was the end of the day, they should be heading home, but he glanced at the fields stretched before them, taking in the students on the obstacle courses, the kids locked in dangerous duels, even the trainees who hacked away at the wooden dummies with fresh, glittering blades. Everyone was still here. Working hard. And every day the gap between the Fire siblings and the rest of the students became clearer. Roaring was desperately trying to keep up but hope for Fox and her dancing dwindled every training session. He tried to empathize with her, to remind her that her combat skills weren't bad, but even she knew that would not be enough in a place like this.

Roaring pulled his eyes away to stare at his baby sister; he could reach out and touch her, place a gentle hand on her shoulder, pull her into a much-needed hug. But he knew if he did that, she would only shove him away in anger. Fox was not like Talon or Cat, she did not want to be held, did not want to be told that everything would be all right. She wanted to learn sundancing and Roaring had promised to teach her. So far, they had both failed.

He sighed. "What do you think about when you try to summon your flames?"

Fox shrugged one shoulder, her thick, curly hair bouncing up

297

and down. "I think about fire. About being strong." She looked up at him. "What do you think about?"

"I don't usually think," he admitted. "I dance the way I feel."

"How do you feel?"

"The only times I've ever danced, I've felt angry. Outraged. The first time I discovered my flames was in the middle of a fight; after that, I trained with our mother, but I was always mad. Mad that I had to keep my dancing a secret. Mad that I couldn't use it to protect the people I loved—and when I finally got the chance to use it against darklings, it wasn't enough."

Fox chewed on this a moment, absently watching two students spar in a ring just a few yards away. Marlo Jo shouted at them to stop and marched into the ring to declare a winner. "You're saying I have to be angry to summon my flames?"

"I'm saying you have to find a fuel. Mine is anger, our mother's was a love for her people, her village. Every fire begins with a spark—you were born with that spark already inside you. But you need fuel to give that fire strength, to keep it alive. Find your fuel, Fox."

"What do I do until I find it?"

"You're still a great fighter without any dancing," he told her. "Work on that."

Fox pressed her lips together. "I need more than that—even if I do get better, I need something more to fight against people with blessings."

"Overpowering your enemy through brute strength isn't the only way to beat them."

Her forehead creased as she tried to understand. "How on earth do I beat them, then?"

"You fight their weaknesses. Study your enemy. Find their

298

vulnerabilities and use it against them."

Fox stood up, brushed the dirt from her knees. "All right, then."

He quirked an eyebrow. "All right, then?"

"I'm going to the Academy library."

"Why?"

"Haven't you noticed? The students here don't go around announcing their blessings to everyone. If you want to learn about someone's power, you've got to learn their name and then hope the Academy has information on it."

"They keep records of every blessing that's ever come through this city, don't they?" Roaring asked, a grin sliding across his face.

Fox nodded. "I'm going to study every blessing I can find. I'm going to find their weaknesses and I'm going to learn how to beat them."

Pride swelled in his chest. Fox had never seemed so confident until now. "That's how you do it, little paws.

With his sister headed for the library, Roaring left the Grounds and made his way to the training eatery; a little stand set up with tables and chairs nearby. A small man with golden skin and dark hair happily served lentil soup, flat bread, roasted meats, and fresh vegetables.

"*Shalom*," he greeted in the Old Tongue.

Roaring paused, caught off guard by the greeting. The people of Babel used the Old Tongue far more often than he'd heard it back in Wi. The entire city seemed steeped in the ancient culture; their kosher foods and fresh grains, their elegant clothes and golden jewelry— nose rings and bracelets and headdresses, too, totally different from the sweeping cloaks and tribal paint of the Fire Tribe.

"Shalom," Roaring said, hoping his accent was believable.

The man smiled at him. "I knew you weren't from here."

"Was it that obvious?"

He passed him a bowl of soup and a slice of flat bread. "Not because of your accent. I knew you were different because you hesitated."

Roaring hesitated again, unsure how to answer.

"See?" The man laughed. "You think too much. Relax, enjoy your food."

He forced a smile. "Thank you. Shalom."

At a table by himself, it wasn't difficult at all for Roaring to enjoy his food. Hunger dominated every conscious thought in his mind as he shoveled the soup into his mouth. The man had been generous, giving him a large bowl filled with lentils and meaty chunks of cured lamb. He'd even given him an extra slice of flat bread. With all his training and fighting and dealing with Fox, Roaring hadn't realized how hungry he'd gotten.

"Slow down there," a voice said.

He lowered his bowl and wiped his mouth, smiling when he recognized Master Jo sitting across from him. She returned his smile and passed him a cup. "Either you're really hungry or you really love lentil soup."

Roaring examined the cup. "It's cold tea," Marlo said. "Lemon."

He drank it down. "Shouldn't you be training students?"

"Training ends in the evening. I was heading home. Then I saw you stuffing your face."

He chuckled.

300

"How's your sister?"

"Working hard. Same as everyone else."

Marlo nodded. "She registered as a sundancer. But I've never seen her use her gift before."

"I haven't been here long, but I haven't seen everyone's gift, either."

Master Jo raised an eyebrow.

He leaned forward, pushing his bowl to the side, his hunger forgotten. "Kohlannis Hunger." He didn't know much about the boy, but his was the first name to pop into his head so he said it and waited for Marlo to reply.

She shifted uncomfortably in her chair, brown eyes focusing on everything but his face. "I'm not going to start telling you information on the other students. You'll have to learn about blessings on your own."

"Then what can you tell me?" he said. "Blessings aside."

Marlo let go of a noise, something like a sigh and a grunt. "Have you ever wondered what life was like before the Great Demon War?"

"Um..." The question had caught him off guard. "Not really."

"For hundreds of years humanity has been fighting the demons. But how did we live before the spiritual realm was torn open and the darklings appeared?" Master Jo paused, pressing her lips together like she was trying to decide what to say next. "Before we fought the demons, humans fought *each other*. We battled for land, resources, power—one of the kingdoms who stood out most was the Hungari. They conquered more land than any other nation on the mapped world, and when the Great Demon War broke out, they continued to expand their reach."

Roaring squinted, trying to take in all the information. He'd never wondered about life before the War until now, had never thought about living in a world where demons weren't a physical threat. A world where other humans were the only enemy.

"With the War came the development of the powers we call *blessings*. With their blessing, the might of the Hungari doubled. Some people used their anointing to build walls and simply survive, the Hungari used theirs to establish the Region of Shadows." She leaned back and hugged herself. "Kings rule kingdoms. Chiefs rule villages. But who rules an entire region?"

Roaring felt goosebumps prickle on his skin. He'd thought the Fire Tribe had been the most powerful force in all the Region of Smoke and Ash for establishing the Village of Wi. But the Hungari had established an entire *Region*. One-quarter of the globe. All ruled by just one tribe.

"I've never heard of this," he muttered.

Marlo glanced up at him, peeling her eyes from the table for the first time since she'd started this tale. "It's a history that is well known here in Babel. Maybe because it's tied directly to the Hungers."

"How? The Hungari aren't the Hungers."

"Yes," she corrected, "they are."

Roaring stared at her. "You're going to have to tell me more."

"The Region of Shadows was the first territory to be recognized on the New Map after the Great Demon War began," Marlo explained. "But the Hungari weren't satisfied with ruling just a quarter of the world, they wanted to have it all. By then, the foundations of the Academy had already been set. Babel wasn't a flourishing city within the first hundred years of the

War, but it had a good start. The Academy was backed by a small army of soldiers, and they weren't afraid of the Hungari.

"History calls it The Blessed War; a battle of anointings—superpowered humans fighting to the death in a supernatural war." Marlo surrendered a smile, proud of the Academy's strong history. "Cross Academy stopped the Hungari conquest after seven years of battle. Determined to have peace, the leaders of the Cross created a treaty with the Hungari Nation. They would be allowed to keep all the land they'd conquered so far, but they could not expand any further or ever leave the Region of Shadows again. To make sure the Hungari maintained their end of the treaty, the Academy took in fifty children from their nation. They stayed in Babel as trainees, but the threat was clear; if the Hungari ever broke their treaty, if they ever left their territory or attempted to expand their military again, their own children would pay the consequences."

Roaring stirred, shaken by the revelation. "That doesn't sound very Christlike for the Cross to take children as hostages."

"No," Marlo agreed, "it doesn't. But our faith is not determined by what sounds Christian to *you*."

He swallowed, unable to come up with an argument.

"Besides," Marlo continued, "the Academy never truly intended to harm the children and the Hungari knew this. Despite having their own kin held as hostages, they didn't stop training their military and they never stopped scheming against the Cross. Twenty years of peace passed before it happened, but eventually, the Hungari launched a revolt." Marlo rested her chin on a fist. "They didn't realize the Academy had grown in those twenty years of peace. They'd made alliances with other strong tribes and clans and had established the Region of the Lion. This time, the Academy wasn't alone in their battle against the Hungari. This time, their war didn't last seven years."

"Why didn't they use the hostages, since the Hungari broke the peace treaty?"

Marlo smiled. "Because it wouldn't have been Christlike."

Roaring looked away, slightly embarrassed. "Oh."

"When the dust settled, the Hungari had been totally crushed. Once again, the Academy took in another set of hostages while the remaining Hungari ran with their tails tucked. But then the Academy faced trouble within their own city."

"What do you mean?"

"The tribes and clans allied with the Cross weren't satisfied with simply taking hostages. They feared another revolt from the Hungari in the future; by this time, the world had come to know of the troublesome people and the terror of their abilities. Their anointing gave them dark powers, it was not a blessing at all, but a curse."

Roaring let out a little gasp. He'd heard Fox say something like that before. That the Hungers were cursed. That something was off about Kohl. He had wondered why she continued training with him, then. Why she didn't shun him the way the rest of the trainees seemed to. Then he realized they shunned KI as well and he knew there was no chance Fox would abandon her friends. Neither one of them.

"How much havoc did the Hungari cause?" Roaring asked.

"Enough to leave the citizens of Babel unsure if they should fear them or the darklings." Marlo shook her head. "Fear like that sows deep seeds of hatred. Hatred that buds over time."

Roaring made a face. "This was all hundreds of years ago. Hardly relevant today."

"It is relevant," Marlo informed. "When the Hungari Revolt had been settled, the tribes and clans allied with the Academy threatened to break their alliance if something wasn't done to restrict the cursed powers of the Shadow Region. The Academy was cornered. The Hungari hostages weren't little children anymore; they had grown up and multiplied into a viable clan within the city. The fears and concerns of the allied tribes weren't unfounded." She looked away, like this was the worst part of the story. "With no other choice, the leaders of the Cross decided to restrict the Hungari to a small sector within the city. They limited their travel so they couldn't leave Babel and when the Hungari pushed back against their restrictions, the leash was tightened."

"Tightened how?"

Marlo took a shaky breath. "They were forbidden to leave their sector. Forbidden to get certain jobs, and even forced to change their name. As an attempt to distance them from their violent cousins in the Shadows, the Hungari hostages of Babel surrendered their surname and became known as the Hunger Tribe."

He blinked, slowly putting the pieces together. "The Hungers today are descendants of the original Hungari hostages."

Marlo nodded. "But it doesn't end there. The Hungers *did* attempt an uprising here in Babel. Fed up with their restrictions, they tried to overthrow the Academic Council, but their plans were ruined when a spy turned on them. Since their betrayal came to an end without any bloodshed, the Academy was willing to forgive their mistake. But the allied tribes spoke up again, outraged by the boldness of the Hungers." She shrugged one shoulder. "They argued the Hungers needed to be punished harshly for their attempted revolt. The Academy gave in to their wishes. This time they placed a seal on every Hunger in the city. The seal severely limited their powers, blocking their spiritual energy so they couldn't reach their full potential."

Roaring stared at his hands, thinking of his sundancing. All his life he'd had to hide his abilities for fear of how his own people would react. He couldn't imagine having something placed on his body to forcibly quell his power. Now, for the first time, he understood why his mother had insisted he keep his dancing a secret. *When people are ruled by fear, they act out in hatred.* His heart broke for the Hungers, wondering how much more powerful Kohl would be if he didn't have a seal on his body.

"But," he said aloud, "Kohl seems strong even with the seal."

Marlo nodded. "It's been over one hundred years since the Revolt. Hungers born today are still sealed, but things have changed. The seal isn't as strong, restrictions aren't as tough as they used to be." She gave him a smile that didn't seem very happy, but something in her eyes let him know her next words wouldn't be as depressing as the rest of her story. "The leaders of the Hunger Tribe and the Academy have finally agreed, it's time to give the Hungers another chance."

"What do you mean?"

"For the first time since the original hostages were taken in, members of the Hunger Tribe have been allowed to enter the Academy for training."

He blinked at her. "Well, that's a big chance to give them."

"Believe me," she snorted, "I know. I remember the outrage from the city when the announcement was made. But the decision had been set in stone; the Hungers would have their chance—though they could only submit one student. The choice was unanimous. The student who would represent the Hunger Tribe at the Academy would be Kohlannis Hunger."

"Why him?"

"Good question," Marlo sighed. "Kohlannis is not a member of the Hunger Head Family. In fact, his father died in a work-related accident when he was a child, and his mother is just a baker. There is nothing particularly special about him."

"Then why?" Roaring asked.

She gave him another sad smile. "Because the Hungers knew whoever they enrolled would have a target on his or her back. They sent an insignificant kid with no father and a poor mother into the Academy so they wouldn't lose much if he didn't survive the exams."

Roaring exhaled slowly, unsure how he felt about the news. He understood the concept of sacrifice quite well, but Kohl was only a kid—just a year older than Fox—it wasn't his responsibility to make these sorts of sacrifices. It wasn't fair that he was being thrown to the wolves just because he was unimportant. And it was worse that his own tribe didn't have much faith in his survival. He was alone on the Grounds. Except for KI and Fox Fire.

Roaring made a fist, not surprised by the ribbons of smoke curling between his fingers. He would need to learn to control his anger now that he was using his flames more often. They seemed to come alive whenever he got emotional.

"Don't get overly involved." Master Jo was looking at him, her eyes dropping to his smoking hand. "Kohl could have refused when his elders approached him with the opportunity. But he decided to join the Academy, anyway, knowing he was nothing but a pawn. He agreed to their terms. Agreed to move on campus and be monitored in case his seal ever weakened. He agreed to go through the program, knowing from the start that he would never fight on even ground. He would enter his training with a mere fraction of his true strength. But he did it anyway. He wanted this. He wanted to bring honor and respect to his tribe, no matter what."

Roaring sighed, some of his anger ebbing away. "I see."

"And besides," Marlo said. "Kohl's spiritual energy is potent. Even with his seal, he's a talented student."

"He isn't a very popular student, though." Roaring couldn't help but think of how the other trainees avoided him like he was poisonous.

Marlo agreed. "He is a Hunger. He comes from a tribe with a bad reputation and a blessing many still believe is a curse. But he doesn't let it stop him; everyday he shows up and trains regardless of the looks and stares. I'm actually surprised you guys made friends with him."

"I'm not his friend," Roaring corrected.

Marlo chewed her lip. "KI and your sister seem to get along with him."

"Apparently, KI stays at the Academy with him. And Fox is friends with anyone who's friends with that kid."

Marlo looked uncomfortable. "KI isn't very popular here, either."

"Because he stays at the Academy. Which makes everyone

think he's either cursed or a demon."

She blew air through her lips. "Kids are cruel. They hate KI and Kohl because they're different."

"No," Roaring said, standing from the table, "they hate them because they're alike."

KI was being kept at the Academy because his powers were unknown. He was a danger to everyone around him, even the Hunters and Priests who studied him. Kohlannis was there because his family had a history of trying to take over the world—and almost succeeded. He was an excellent student, despite being sealed and having his powers impaired.

Roaring let go of a sigh, goosebumps prickling his skin again. A wicked excitement stirred inside him, a wild desire to train and work with the best—to test his own limits—unfolded within. Fox had been right. The children at the Academy were nothing like the members of the Hunting Regiment.

"And how are KI and Kohl alike?" Master Jo looked up at him, blinking away the brightness of the setting sun.

He glanced down. "They're both powerful."

24

Fox Fire

Danis Tribe, currently of the City of Babel in the Region of the Lion.

Origins: Village of Tawe in the Region of Ice.

Reasons for relocation: Tribe formed alliance with Babel and sent members to live in new city.

Date of resettlement: Year 75 ABD (After Black Day).

Anointing: Healing abilities.

Sigil: A serpent erected on a pole.

Words: *Rapha.*

Jo Clan of the City of Babel in the Region of the Lion.

Anointing: Create indestructible walls.

Sigil: A brick wall.

Words: *You shall not pass.*

Fox paused, hunched over her large book, pen in hand. She leaned her back against the cracked tree trunk behind her and thought of Marlo Jo. The image of how she'd stopped their fight with the Ools by summoning a transparent wall was vivid in her mind's eye.

What would have happened to Roaring if the timer hadn't run out?

I was useless, Fox gripped the pen in her hand, ink stained the tips of her fingers. Getting stronger was the only way she could stand by her brother's side. *If I could dance, that fight would have ended differently.*

Fox sighed and flipped to a different section.

Hunger Tribe, currently of the City of Babel in the Region of the Lion.
Origins: Region of Shadows—specific village unknown.
Reasons for relocation: Unknown.
Year of resettlement: Unknown.
Anointing: Void.
Sigil: Plain black flag.
Words: *Fear us.*

Fox squinted, thinking of her blonde companion, but her thoughts didn't drift very far. The next moment, a body suddenly crashed into her pile of books and papers, spilling her pot of ink onto her notes and into the grass.

Startled and angry, she yelled, "Don't you guys see me trying to study?"

KI, who'd been thrown into her books, stood and apologized.

311

"I'm sorry, Foxy. Roaring doesn't know how to go easy." He rubbed his back and winced. Bruises covered nearly every inch of flesh Fox could see; his arms, his shoulders, and there was a new one forming on his jaw. She envied him.

"Why do you two get to train while I'm stuck reading books all day?"

KI shrugged sheepishly. "Ana isn't fighting, either."

Behind them, Kohl sat in the shade of a bush, lazily watching from a safe distance.

Fox huffed. "He never joins us." That was true; whenever they weren't training with Moneek and Master Jo, Kohl would limit his activity to lying around and complaining about everyone else's performance. Fox tried her best to ignore his critiquing, reminding herself that most of the time, he was just cranky. Sometimes he could be friendly. Sometimes he could even be *nice*. Like the time he'd warned her about Montell. And when he'd volunteered to fight with her and Roaring against Vy and her cousins.

"Well ..." KI said, scratching the back of his head. He turned to Kohl. "Why don't you join us for a bit?"

"That's not the point," Fox said. "I never get to train with you guys!"

"I thought the reading *was* training?" KI cowered. "And besides, Ana never gets to fight anyone. It's hard to find people here who are willing to train with him."

"Vyanna's always willing to fight," Fox said, then she crossed her arms and smirked. "But he's probably tired of losing. So here he is." She waved her hand at him.

"He can train with us, if he wants to," Roaring offered.

Kohl propped himself up on his elbows. He watched them a

moment, blue eyes squinting, then he chuckled. "No thanks."

"See?" Fox made a face. "He doesn't want to train with us—even though no one else will come close to him."

Kohl's gaze slid over to her; despite their distance, Fox could feel the heat of his glare. "Do you know why no one wants to train with me?" he asked.

"Because you're a jerk."

A boorish laugh filled the air. "Because they think I'm dangerous."

Now Fox was laughing. "They think you're *dangerous*? Even though you got your butt kicked by Vy and her cousins *again*?"

He narrowed his eyes. "That was only because I wasn't using my blessing."

"Sure. Alright. You didn't use a blessing in that match, and you haven't ever used one in training with us. I don't think you actually have an anointing."

He sighed. "Not that I have to explain myself to a weakling. But I don't train with you guys or those guys," he gestured to the rest of the training field, "because I *choose* not to fight. You don't train with them because you can't."

If she could sundance, Fox would have exhaled steam. If she could sundance, she'd be training with her brother instead of poring over ancient texts or fighting with her friends. Roaring had told her studying the clans and tribes of the Region would help her learn their weaknesses. It'd been a good idea at first, and still was, if she was being honest, but Fox would rather be sparring than reading.

Kohl let out a laugh, regaining her attention. "Just to make things clear—I don't use my blessing because I don't know how." He made a show of looking her up and down. Fox felt her ears begin to burn. "I choose not to use my anointing because I don't need to. Everyone thinks the Hungers are cursed. The Hungers *themselves* even believe it." He glanced away, a shadow of hurt flickering over his face for just a moment. "They fear us because of our powers. They think the only reason we're strong is because we have an unfair blessing. Well," he took a breath, shook his shoulders, "I'm here to prove we're just as powerful *without* our gift. I don't need it to pass the entrance exams. And I don't need it to become the strongest Hunter in the Four Regions. I'll reach my goals without *ever* using my blessing. Not once."

A moment of stillness suspended over them. Fox blinked at Kohlannis, unsure if she felt angry at him or sorry for him. When she didn't respond, KI spoke up, "Why don't we all just train together?" He nervously looked from one friend to the other. "It'd be nice for you to spar with us, Ana. And Fox could use the extra training, too."

"She has to study," Kohl said, a smirk crossing his face.

"I can't study anymore since KI spilled ink all over my notes," Fox said angrily.

Roaring sighed. "I can't help you get better with sundancing, Fox—"

"This isn't about dancing," she insisted. "I still need to train, even without my flames. You fight with KI, why can't you fight me?"

"KI is … different."

Fox balled her hands into fists. Roaring had been feeding her that same excuse for a week now; at first, he couldn't train her because she couldn't sundance, now he couldn't train her because he was obsessed with KI. Not that she could blame him; KI had gotten taller, faster, and stronger since arriving in Babel. It was hard not to notice how easily he countered Roaring's moves while they sparred. KI was a better partner for her brother than she was.

When did he surpass me? Fox wondered.

She glanced up at her companions, anger threatening to summon tears. *I can't cry in front of them. They'll never forget it if I do.*

She turned away. "I'll train alone today."

Roaring called after her, but she did not listen. Fox walked until she cleared the sparring rings and obstacle courses, and when she made it to the infirmary, she kept walking. Dozens of tents lined the edge of the Academy training grounds; foreign flags and sigils and tribal colors flying over the growing camp, some Fox recognized from her studies, others she'd never seen.

There were only four Regions on the mapped world; beyond the Region of the Lion lay the Salt Sea and beyond that, a cluster of islands called the Lord's Pews. No one had sailed beyond the Lord's Pews and if anyone had crossed the Open Sea to the west of the Region of Shadows, they hadn't lived to tell of it.

"Checking out the competition?" KI asked behind her.

She couldn't keep herself from smiling, she had hoped he would come after her. "Master Jo says people from around the world will be competing in the exam."

"Are you nervous?"

She shrugged. "I don't know. There are so many people out here with so many different powers."

Months ago, Fox had never even heard of blessings; there had been stories and legends passed down from her grandparents and tribal elders, but those were wild tales about dark powers and dangerous battles, some even claimed the founders of the Fire Tribe could tame the Sunriders birthed of the volcano beneath their village. Fox didn't believe much from the stories. But blessings were real, and if people had come from around the world for this exam, she would certainly be in over her head.

"I could barely hold my own against the Ools," she said. "And I was absolutely useless in the tunnels with the feeders. Montell was more help with *borrowed* power than I was with my natural born ability."

KI stood beside her, rubbing the back of his neck. "You did better than the rest of us."

"No, I didn't. And I won't do well in the exam if Roaring doesn't train me."

He shifted uncomfortably. "Roaring is trying his best."

Fox let out an exasperated sigh, turning to walk along the edge of the field. She stopped at a small creek the students used for drinking and knelt to wash her face. The fresh water separated the tents from the facility, forming a natural border between the herds of travelers and the students running the courses. Each and every person out there would become her enemy in a short time.

"Kohl is right," she said, staring into the water. "I can't sundance. My combat training is all I have to rely on for the exam. But if Roaring won't help me with that, I'll be torn to pieces out there." She dug her fingernails into her palms, ignoring the pain. In Wi, she would have her red knot tied to the spear she'd designed. She'd just earned her braid, had finally gotten her uncle to acknowledge her strength. And then everything changed. For a single day Fox felt the strongest she'd ever been; since then, she'd only felt weak and left behind.

Beside her, KI's reflection appeared in the pond, his eyebrows crinkled and his eyes full of something she couldn't describe. "I won't let you be torn to pieces," he said.

Fox glanced up at him. "You've changed."

"It isn't something I asked for."

"You have to live at the Academy where you're monitored constantly and prodded by doctors. The students here avoid you like something's wrong with you."

"I know."

"They look at you the same way they look at Kohl."

KI pressed his full lips together but did not respond.

"You're close to him," Fox pressed.

"I see him around the Academy."

"With Lieutenant Diaz and the rest of the research team?"

KI swallowed. "He's in a complicated situation."

"So are you."

A pained expression crossed his face and Fox knew what he was thinking. *Please don't ask any more.* The look made her chest tighten. When had they started keeping secrets from each other?

"No one here likes him," she said. "No one wants to be around him except you. Some people say he has dark powers— that he's cursed. I can't even find anything about the Hunger Tribe in my studies. What sort of blessing is called *Void*?"

KI winced. "People just don't understand him."

"But you do? He said himself that he's dangerous."

"He said they *think* he's dangerous," KI corrected sharply. He turned and knelt in the creek, avoiding her gaze while he leaned over to scoop a handful of water into his mouth.

"Maybe you know Kohlannis better than the rest of us," Fox said. "But *I* don't know him and when the exam comes, he won't be my ally."

KI shook his head, wiping water from his mouth. "No one will be an ally. You remember what Wunda said, it's every man for himself."

"*Every man for himself*," Fox repeated, staring at the tents.

"Maybe that's why your brother won't train with you," he suggested. "All these people out there and all those people training in here are your competition. *I'm* your competition and so are Roaring and Ana."

"That's why Roaring should be helping me."

"Maybe he doesn't think you need any help."

"But I do," she insisted. "I can't sundance yet."

"Maybe he thinks you're good enough without it."

"I'm not." She laughed to herself. "All of this happened because I can't sundance. If I'd had this power back in Wi, I would have killed that demon before it ever touched you. I would have protected Talon when she was nearly killed. I would have been able to save everyone. But I couldn't."

KI placed a hand on her shoulder, large and warm and comforting. His touch called her attention and she gazed up, enjoying the sight of his handsome features, of his strong jaw and heavy brows, his large, muscular frame. He looked almost nothing like the fourteen-year-old boy she remembered from Wi. If she didn't know any better, she would swear he looked as old as Roaring now.

"Fox," he called her name, "you don't have to put this sort of pressure on yourself."

"Yes, I do. I lost both of my parents," she whispered. "But I would have been able to do *something* if I'd had my flames."

"I know what it feels like to be powerless. I know what it's like to wake up an orphan one day."

She swallowed thickly. In her obsession with power, she'd forgotten how much grief KI had faced—grief he'd been holding on to for years. "I'm sorry. I didn't mean to throw myself a pity party."

He shook his head. "You have every right to mourn and worry about getting stronger. But don't think you have to face this worry alone. You have three awesome siblings; Talon is the Grand Chief of Wi, Roaring is an incredible sundancer, and Cat holds down your new home all by herself. Don't overlook how much love and support you have, and don't forget they're fighting to get stronger, too."

She nodded, letting go of a sigh. "I just don't want to lose anyone else."

"You won't lose anyone else," KI assured. "I've gotten stronger, too, Fox. I don't need you to protect me anymore; so, let me be the Shield I should have been when you'd needed me most."

As much as his words hurt, she had to agree. KI was stronger now, stronger than he'd ever been. Though he still had a lot more training to do, she couldn't ignore his progress or ability. But she also wouldn't ever forgive herself for changing his life so much. If she hadn't dragged him beyond the Walls that day, none of this ever would have happened. If she had put him first, they'd still be at home. They'd still be safe.

"Well," she said softly, "even if you don't need me, I will never stop trying to get stronger and I'll never stop trying to protect you. I owe you that much."

319

KI smiled. "Fine, then. Let's race to the top. See who can master their abilities first."

"Let's see who can shut Kohl up first," she snorted. "He never misses a chance to remind me of how weak I am."

KI kicked a rock into the creek. "We only have a few weeks left before the entrance exams begin. Maybe I can convince him to spend that time training with us. I think he would get along with everyone better if he fought with us again."

She made a face. "I don't think anything will make him get along with other people."

"Why not?"

"He's rude, for starters. And he doesn't like anyone besides you."

KI took a long breath. "I can't exactly argue with that. But let's give it a try. Roaring could teach all of us some new moves—and maybe you'll learn to sundance. You never know."

"Sure. You never know."

PART III

25

The Red Face

He waited until night. When the sun had finally disappeared, he crawled from beneath his blankets and found his clothes; a pair of black pants and a long-sleeved black shirt, black boots and a belt loaded with small weapons. His gloves were black, too, with hard knuckles to help him pack a more powerful punch. He tucked small knives into both of his sleeves and tucked a blade into each boot. His mask came last, tied tightly so it fit snug against his face. Then he stepped into the cool night air.

He'd studied the camp when he'd first arrived; days of hard training left everyone too tired to care about a masked man running through the rows of tents at this hour. He wasn't afraid of being seen before making it out, but even if someone did happen to spot him, he knew how to take care of them.

Clusters of tents stretched on for over a mile with flags and banners of respective tribes flapping gently in the wind. He moved swiftly between them, silent and unseen, until he came to a clearing leading deeper into the city. This would be the hard part; while the training camp was tired and asleep, the rest of Babel was still wide awake. Lanterns hung from poles, dotting the streets, leaving the city veiled in a lazy golden hue. Guards marched up and down the roads, horses trotted along the pavement, pulling carts and wagons behind, merchants called for customers to buy just one more item before going in to rest.

He climbed up the nearest building to avoid walking along the roads. The inner city was filled with high structures carved from thick slabs of stone; apartments stacked on top of each other, crammed beside each other, packed in to make room for the next wave of refugees. Rickety wooden bridges swayed high overhead, connecting buildings and forming clusters of neighborhoods. He climbed high enough to see everything below, taking in the weaving and winding roads, the patches of open land where small farms unrolled and cattle grazed, the large temple with a white gleaming cross steepled at the top.

Moving quickly, he used the overpasses to take him toward the center of the city, jumping from bridge to bridge, building to building, avoiding people when he saw them and trying to keep as quiet as possible. When he neared his destination, he climbed lower, swinging to the ground in an alley behind a merchant selling biscuits; he had a cart set up with freshly baked bread and a variety of toppings—gravy, jam, even ground meat simmered with peppers and onions. Though he hadn't eaten, he didn't stop moving. He hadn't come here for food.

Two streets over he saw the guards he knew would be on duty

tonight—he remembered them from hours spent hiding in the shadows, observing and learning as much as he could about this sector of the city ... about the Academy. In the dark, the giant cross-shaped building glowed brighter than the temple just a few blocks away. Though it was made from jet black stone, he could see the structure clearly—glimmering against the night sky as if the stars themselves had settled on its surface.

In Babel, they said all the city's roads led to the Academy tower, he knew this wasn't true—most of the roads directed citizens to the great Christian temple—but as he took in the sparkling black stone, it was easy to see how it'd become the center of Babel.

Covered by the veil of night, he moved in closer, keeping an eye on the guards. He needed them to separate and walk alone, that way he could take them down more easily; but as they continued walking side by side, chatting about nothing, his hope began to dwindle. He would need to make a distraction. This wasn't a difficult job, but he would have to be careful. One of the guards was a Priest with a blessing that allowed him to see through the dark. He'd seen this blessing before at the Grounds; it wasn't a gift built to take lives, but it was perfect for a security guard walking the beat. The other guard was a woman with no blessing, but her training as an Academy Hunter still made her quite a match when it came down to brute strength. He would have to take her out first, then the other.

He moved in closer to get a better view and then stopped to check the weapons packed in his belt; flash bangs, throwing knives, poisonous darts, and more. His hand closed around a smoke bomb before he ducked into the shadows and got into position. The guards were further down the street now, walking their normal patrol; ten yards ahead, he threw the smoke bomb close enough for them to see and moved to begin his attack.

The guard with the blessing of Light stepped forward first, squinting into the darkness. When his companion stepped beside him, he waved her off, volunteering to check it out himself. As soon as the guard was far enough away, he swooped in and silently approached the female Hunter from behind. She was tall and muscular with smooth skin the color of polished wood. Her head was shaved so there wasn't any hair covering her ears; he saw the moment she heard him approaching, when her ears pricked in curiosity, and she began to turn around. But it was too late. He had his arms around her head and neck before she could react, dragging her back into the shadows behind him.

He left her body in a dark alley nearby and raced to find the other guard before he noticed his missing companion. The Priest was deep in the cloud of smoke now, squinting as he moved. He had anointed vision in the dark—but he couldn't see what wasn't right in front of him. Slowly, he moved in from behind, sliding a small blade from his sleeve as he stepped into the smoke.

The Priest took another step but stopped suddenly when the moonlight from his blade reflected against the wall. There was no time now; the Priest pivoted, moving quicker than expected, and a throwing knife slipped from his wide, black sleeve, *just* missing him. Without thinking, he threw the blade in his own hand and lunged just as the Priest moved to dodge. Caught off guard, the Priest received a swift kick to the ribs that took the wind out of him and undoubtedly left a few broken bones.

The Priest stumbled backward, holding his side. He fell

against the wall and looked up at the man, his eyes growing large and round. "I know you," he whispered, seeing clearly in the darkness. "*Murderer* ... Two robberies last week, another body found the week before that—all of them committed by a man in a red mask."

He calmly stepped forward and slid a small blade from his sleeve. The Priest gasped and fell to his knees. "You—you're the *Red Face!*"

He'd had more to say, but his words died on his lips, choking him along with his own blood. He searched his body, looking for anything that would make it easier to get into the Academy. He found a single key and stashed it in his pocket. As he turned to leave, he caught a glimpse of his own reflection, illuminated by the moonlight against the glossy wall beside him; his mask was the image of a snarling man with heavy eyebrows—his expression outraged, as if shouting in anger. The leather skin was a deep shade of red, stained even darker from all the blood he'd shed.

He stood in the alley a few seconds more, thinking of the Priest's last words. The Red Face *was* a cool name, but he hadn't robbed anyone. He'd knocked them out and searched their bodies for anything useful ... but he hadn't robbed them. And he was not a murderer. *Assassin* was more like it—though, even that word was too harsh. He hadn't come here to kill anyone; he knew people would inevitably end up dead because of him, but he hadn't *come* to kill anyone.

He'd arrived with one goal: Get the boy and get out.

The Red Face moved swiftly through the streets; those guards were the only two who patrolled this area, leaving him free range of the next few blocks. If his timing was right, the guards on the next shift wouldn't be here for another hour. That meant he had to get in and out of the building in less that forty minutes, then out of the city in less than twenty. He sighed behind his mask.

At least the first part was over. With the Hunter and Priest taken care of, the back entrance to the Academy was left unguarded. The Red Face used the key he'd taken off the Priest to unlock the door and quietly slip inside. It was dimly lit with torches lining the ebony stone walls; doors stretched on in both directions. Swiftly, he made his way down the hall, careful to remain silent. Anyone could open any door at any moment, anyone could round the corner at any moment. He had to make this quick and he would have to deal with anyone who saw him.

According to rumors going around the camp, the boy lived at the Academy—likely in the quarters reserved for quarantined patients. He didn't have a map but there were directories pasted at the end of every hall; a scroll unrolled and spread on the cool stone. Nothing about quarantine was listed on the rooms but he knew they wouldn't advertise something that was supposed to be a secret. Despite the massive size of each floor, the nineteenth floor had only three rooms listed, every other floor had dozens. *He must be there somewhere*, the Red Face thought, running toward the nearest staircase.

When he reached the sixth floor, he heard voices at the top of the stairs and paused to catch his breath. He could duck onto the fifth floor and hope the voices kept moving—but what if the fifth floor was their destination? He could hide in a room, but what if there were people inside?

He grunted in frustration and glanced up the stairs. The

distorted shadows slithered along the wall, trailing down ahead of the approaching voices. They would be on him in a matter of seconds.

Moving silently, the Red Face ran a few steps down to the landing platform, putting out the torches along the way. He could hear the voices above him, switching from casual to inquisitive as they noticed the light fading out below. Two Hunters dressed in uniform descended the stairs; their approach slowed once they neared him, questioning the darkness, cautiously inching forward.

They hadn't realized they'd passed him until he stepped from the shadows. One of the Hunters stole a glance over his shoulder at the very last second and caught him moving toward the stairs. He had no choice but to attack.

The one who caught him went down before he could even fully turn around. The Red Face got him with a sudden jab to the back of the neck, strong enough to snap it. But the second Hunter put up a fight; he lunged at the Red Face, drawing his sword and taking a wild swing. He missed, raking his blade along the stone wall; sparks lit up the dark stairway for a moment and he gasped as he realized who he was up against. That single pause of surprise gave the Red Face the opening he'd needed; he pivoted and got in close—too close for the Hunter to use his sword. The sudden nearness made him lurch backward, instinctively trying to dodge the next attack, but it was too late. His sword was twisted from his hands, his feet swept from beneath him. He hit the ground with a yelp, gasping just before his own blade went through his chest.

There was nowhere to stash the bodies, so the Red Face dragged them into the shadowy corner of the dark staircase and kept moving. Someone would eventually stumble across them, he had to move twice as fast as before.

He sprinted up the next few staircases without a problem, stopping on the thirteenth floor to wait for a young-looking Priest to pass by. He scanned the directory pasted on the wall, searching for a room he could hide in if this floor was her destination, but then he thought, *if this isn't where she's going, she'll keep descending and eventually find the bodies*, and he had to keep them hidden for as long as possible. So he stepped into the torchlight as the Priest came near, and lunged without hesitation.

She had tried to scream but that was hard to do with a hand around her throat. Small hands clawed at his larger ones until her eyes rolled to the back of her head and her body went limp. He couldn't leave this body on the staircase, too, so he chanced a door that should have been a closet, according to the directory, and let go of held breath when he found the small room empty. He placed the Priest's body on the floor and turned to leave but paused when he caught a glimpse of her face. Her brown eyes weren't rolled to the back of her head anymore—they were wide open now. And they were looking right at him.

Great.

He'd bumped into a Priest with the *Reanimation* blessing. He'd heard of this anointing before—a gift that granted the power to bring oneself back to life. Now he had to kill her again and hope there was a limit to how many times she could die before staying dead.

The Priest took a deep breath, seemingly sucking all the air out of the room. The Red Face stared in shock as she stood and faced him, cracking her neck loudly. Her expression was blank; he didn't know if he should be afraid or angry. It didn't matter. He slipped a small blade from his sleeve and ran at her.

The lady Priest was stronger than she looked, and fast, too. Confined to the small closet, the Red Face couldn't move as freely as he wanted; he slashed at her head with his blade, but she shifted and managed to land a hit to his ribcage. He hissed beneath his mask and took an involuntary step back. The small Priest moved in swiftly, knocking him against the heavy door with a *thud!* and reaching for his mask.

Her hand snaked past the arm he threw up in defense and grabbed hold of the carved red wood, slamming his head against the door. "Who are you!" she yelled, her voice darker than her brown skin. Her fingers gripped his mask and began to pull. Panic arrowed his heart and he reacted without thinking.

If she hadn't been so focused on his mask, she might have seen the blade before it opened her throat. The Priestess stepped back, shock clear on her face, and clawed at the skin of her neck. Blood gushed between her fingers, flowing in rhythm to the beat of her heart. He watched her die. Stumbling backward and falling into a pile of boxes, her bloody hands striking out at nothing, reaching for help that would not come. She dropped to her knees, her eyes wide open, a cry on her lips, smothered by the gurgling of her own blood. And then she stopped moving.

He knew she would be back, but he didn't know how long that would take. Recovering from a slit throat wouldn't be as easy as coming back from strangulation. Either way, he didn't have time to wait, and with only a few thin throwing knives, he didn't have time to cut out her heart to keep her dead. He had to keep moving.

The directory had listed only three rooms on the nineteenth floor but when he stepped off the staircase onto the landing platform, the Red Face realized that was a terrible understatement. Dozens of doors lined both sides of the hallway, punched into the walls, hiding secrets from the world. The boy was here somewhere, he had to be. But which door was he hiding behind?

Two Priests patrolled the hallway; the Red Face waited for them to get close before he snatched the first one by his long sleeve. He squealed in shock, but it was quickly silenced by a knife gliding over his throat. The second Priest whistled just as the Red Face lunged at him; he didn't realize the whistle was an attack until he was lying flat on his back with a blade pointed at him.

"Who are you?" the Priest said calmly. Every word he spoke felt like a hurricane roaring in his ear, pounding against his skull. *A sound-dancer*, the Red Face realized. *He's throwing off my equilibrium.*

"If you won't tell me who you are," the Priest said, "I'll just find out for myself." He extended a hand, reaching for his mask.

Fear shot through him like a bolt of lightning. The Red Face sat up, ignoring the sting of the Priest's blade as it slid over his skin. A piercing sound threatened to burst his eardrums, but he grunted through the pain, twisting the Priest's blade from his hand, and forcing himself to his feet. When he stood, he felt as if he were standing on a boat; his feet wobbled, and his legs buckled. He dropped to one knee with a gasp.

The Priest smiled and then opened his mouth to speak. The

331

Red Face never heard the words, he only felt the stabbing pain of a thousand knives cutting into his flesh. His vision began to blur, and his body felt heavy, he could feel his mind losing its grip, slipping further away from consciousness.

It could not end here.

He was so close to getting the boy. If he didn't do something, he would end up failing his mission and find himself in custody of the Cross. He dropped to both knees and lowered his head; there was no other choice.

Energy flickered to life within him. He called to it, and it answered with a clap of power, expelling heat from his body, directly at the Priest. The surge of energy hit him head on, knocking him off his feet. It electrified the air, crackling as it travelled along the stone walls. When it kissed the hanging torches, sparks sputtered to life and rolled onto the floor, igniting in a streak of bright red fire.

The Red Face watched as the flames ate up the floor and ran down the hall; angry and hungry and desperate to burn. Technically, he hadn't started the fire. He'd only provided the heat that'd sparked into the blaze. Still, he hadn't wanted to use his power; it would only be a matter of time before anyone linked it back to his real identity. But as long as no one lived to tell of what he'd done; he knew he'd be all right.

Smoke woke the sleeping residents. The door directly to the right of the Red Face opened to reveal a teenage boy. He was taller than they'd said he would be, with unruly dark hair sticking straight up, like he'd been tossing and turning in his sleep. His face scrunched in confusion when he spotted the dark assassin. The Red Face lunged before he could even speak, grabbing the boy roughly by the arm and holding a knife to his throat.

Calmly, the boy held up his hands and said, "I'm guessing you're not here to save me from the fire."

The Red Face responded by shoving him toward the stairs. He walked without a problem, obeying the pull on his arm until they reached the top of the staircase. He'd finally gotten his target; all he had to do was get out of the city. He heaved a sigh of relief as he turned onto the stairs—that's when he was knocked off his feet.

The attack had come from behind; one violent shove that'd sent him tumbling down the steps. The boy had fallen with him but when the Red Face rolled over, his ribs and muscles crying out in pain, he saw the young boy standing beside a companion.

The assailant stood at the top of the stairs, his pale skin and white-blonde hair standing out in the black smoke. Kohlannis Hunger. The Red Face knew that boy. He didn't like him very much, but he knew enough about him to figure he would be here and that he would give him trouble.

Kohl's face twisted in anger as he said, "Who are you?"

The Red Face did not answer. He rolled to his feet and released a throwing knife from his sleeve. Kohl evaded, giving the Red Face time to rush in; but he was injured and fighting uphill; to no one's surprise, Hunger dodged his follow-up and blocked his next attack, too.

"KI, go!" He turned and shoved his friend away.

But KI refused. "I'm not leaving!"

The Red Face sighed behind his mask, watching in silence as KI and Kohlannis stood their ground together. He would have to kill Kohl and then take KI. But he'd already taken a beating from the lady Priest and the sound-dancer and a tumble down the stairs. He couldn't afford to drag this out.

He slid a blade from his belt and charged at KI; when Kohl leapt to his defense, he feinted and attacked him instead. The boy choked on a gasp but regained his composure and dodged every jab and slash from the Red Face. The dark assassin fought his way back up the stairs to level ground, dancing around the boys, trying to keep them both in his sights.

KI was strong but he was also predictable and sloppy; it was Kohlannis who gave the Red Face the most trouble. He was quicker and deadlier, striking out with all his strength. But he was also unarmed and in his night clothes; a dark pair of pants and a long tunic that came down to his knees. It also didn't help that he was barefoot and struggling to breathe in the smoke.

It's only a matter of time.

The Red Face pushed hard, ignoring the pain in his muscles and his ribs and the ringing in his ears. With a grunt, he threw himself at Kohl, sending them both tumbling to the ground. The floor burned with the heat of the flames so close; the Red Face rolled so he was on top of Hunger and brought down his blade, but KI kicked him, and he fell sideways, the knife only grazing his cheek.

"Ana!" KI screamed, turning to land another kick.

The Red Face caught his leg but before he could twist his ankle, a sharp pain bloomed in his abdomen. He let go of KI and glanced down, panting behind his mask; Kohl held his blade in his hand, smirking as he shoved the sharp end deeper into his flesh.

He had trained for hundreds of hours; trained to handle himself calmly in the most stressful of situations. Trained to remain in the shadows, to move in silence, and to be unseen, unheard, unbroken. But with his own blade buried in his stomach and his own blood seeping between his fingers as he grabbed at his wound, the Red Face was not an assassin. He was just a guy who wanted to go home.

Kohlannis yanked the blade out and tried to stab him again, but the Red Face shoved him back down and rolled away. He backed up as the boys pushed him together, his blade twinkling in the black smoke. Behind him, he could hear a troop of Hunters scurrying up the stairs, drawn by the fire. KI was right there in front of him—just a foot away. He could have grabbed him and ran, he could have used his blessing and risked being caught, he could have fought through the pain. But he saw the look of determination in Kohl's eyes, and he felt the power come alive inside him.

It was just a flicker, like the spark of a match being struck; but that spark took a breath and crackled into a raging storm of spiritual energy, aching to be released. The Red Face knew Kohl. Knew about the terrors of the Hungers. But he had no specific information on their blessing, had no idea what to expect if Kohl released the power surging through him right now.

Wounded and afraid, the Red Face released a throwing knife at him. When Kohl moved to dodge it, he charged the boys but instead of attacking, he pivoted and threw himself down the nearby steps. The group of approaching Hunters shouted in surprise but with the fire and the smoke and the young boys screaming, the Red Face shoved through the crowd and escaped down the stairs in the midst of all the chaos.

26

Fox Fire

Fox smelled the smoke in her sleep—the foul odor of soot and ash and fear. Then she heard the bells and opened her eyes. Shaken from her slumber, she ran to her window and took in the scene; the people running back and forth, horses pounding down the road, voices crying out, calling for water.

Roaring shoved open her door, his eyes wide open. "The Academy," he said, "it's on fire."

Fox gasped. "KI!"

Her brother turned and ran down the hall, she followed without hesitation. "We have to go! We have to make sure he's all right!"

"I know," Roaring said, marching through their small apartment. He stopped in his room for a shirt and Fox realized he must have woken suddenly as well. His hair was loose, tumbling over his shoulders in a mess of thick coils, and he was barefoot. He yanked a brown tunic over his head and tied back his curls with a ribbon Cat had made him. "Put something on and we'll leave together," he said, stepping into his boots.

Fox ran back to her room and grabbed her training uniform from the floor, yanking her clothes on as she moved to the living room. Cat was waiting for her, nervously clutching the hem of her nightgown as Chava paced back and forth.

"Are you coming?" Fox asked her older sister.

Cat shook her head. "I'm staying in case someone sends a messenger hawk. I've sent one to Kato—I know he doesn't care for KI, but I thought he should know in case ..." her voice trailed off as she glanced away. "In case something bad has happened to him."

"The Academy is a huge building. The fire could have started anywhere. KI could be perfectly fine," Fox said, concentrating on shoving her feet into her shoes.

Roaring whistled for Chava to sit, she happily obeyed, leaning into his hand as he rubbed her head. "Protect Cat." Then he turned to his little sister, his face stony, his voice firm. "Stay inside. Do not open the door unless you know it's us or someone from Wi."

Cat nodded and then hugged him, tilting her head up to kiss him goodbye. Fox sighed impatiently. KI could be burning alive and Cat wanted hugs and kisses right now. Her sister offered a small smile and said, "Be safe." Fox grunted and yanked open the door in response.

When she stepped outside, she felt the claws of the city's panic grip her violently. Raw fear settled on her shoulders like deadweight, smothering all the hope she'd had locked in her heart. In the center of this great city was a burning cross; Fox could see the fire even from her stance outside her home. She watched in awe and horror as the flames danced in the sky, shining brighter than the moon. A chill went up her spine, though she felt warm all over.

Without a word, Roaring took off at a sprint. Fox followed without needing the order, jogging down the road and whipping through the crowds of panicked onlookers as they neared the Academy.

Roaring slowed to an urgent walk, his strides long and determined. "I don't know what to expect," he said, pushing through the crowd.

Fox walked beside him, panting. "Let's just get as close as we can."

The fire sat atop the Cross, bursting from its top floors, exploding out the windows and swirling into the sky. Smoke billowed from the structure, coating the city below in a black smog. It was hot up close; Fox's face began to sweat as she stared up at the burning building.

Members of the Cross with healing abilities waited on the sidewalk to treat any injured while a team of Priests guided panicked onlookers to a safe zone. Fox followed the crowd to the safe zone and craned her neck to get a better view. In the mass of Hunters and Priests gathered around the Academy, she spotted Marlo Jo with members of her clan; they summoned their indestructible walls to block off the building and keep the fire from spreading. More walls went up through the crowd to keep them from getting too close.

Two strong Hunters hauled giant urns of water down the pathway created by the Jo Clan. They set the water at the entrance to the Academy where a group of white-haired Tribesmen waited. Fox recognized them right away; the stark white hair of the Farron Tribe. They were dressed in various uniforms; Hunters, Priests, workers, some even wore their tribal colors—snow-white and seafoam green. Fox watched them with a growing smile on her face. The Farrons could manipulate water—*they can help put out the fire!* she thought happily.

They moved swiftly and elegantly, guiding the water from the urns to splash over the flames escaping out the windows overhead. Others dunked the water over themselves, soaking them from head to toe, then they turned and ran into the burning building. Fox gasped and grabbed her brother's arm. "They're going to look for survivors."

Roaring was busy scanning the crowd around them. "I don't see KI."

"Maybe he already got out?" Fox said, pushing through the mass, trying to get closer to the Academy doors.

One of the walls from the Jo Clan blocked her way, transparent and shimmering with flecks of silver and gold. She slapped her hand against it and the wall absorbed the impact. "Please!" she cried, pressing her palm to the glass, willing it to break and let her through. "My friend is inside!"

Roaring appeared by her side, towering over her like an angry shadow. "Fox, we can't get through here," he said. The crowd pressed around them, panicked and full of fear. "Let's try to find another way."

Fox ignored him, staring through the transparent wall. The Farrons were right in front of her, guiding water into the flames. Hunters ran in and out of the building, carrying people in their arms, rescuing as many people as they could. Fox's eyes grew wide with each person who passed—hoping to find KI. Then she spotted a familiar face.

Vyanna Farron ran out the front doors, her white hair blackened by soot and smoke, her clothes burned, and her face covered by a cloth tied around her head. She stumbled to the urns and guided the water over her body, sighing in relief as it washed over her.

"Vy!" Fox screamed, her palm slapping hard against the shimmering wall. "Vyanna!"

Roaring stepped beside her; for a moment she thought he would stop her, but he placed his hand on the wall, examining it. Then he took a step back and said, "Watch out."

He inhaled sharply and released a surge of energy into the wall. A bolt of lightning struck the transparent barrier, crawling over the surface in a display of sparks and crackling light. The crowd screeched in fear, stepping away from the structure; on the other side, the Hunters and Priests turned in shock, their mission momentarily forgotten.

Right in front of them, Vyanna Farron stared into the crowd. Confusion crossed her face before melting into recognition. "Roaring Fire?" she said so loudly her tribesmen stepped closer to see what was going on.

Roaring pressed his hand against the wall. "Princess, you need our help."

Vy nodded.

At the urging of the Farron Princess, the Jo Clan made space for Roaring and Fox to pass through. Fox gasped with relief when she ran to Vy. "I have to get inside!" she blurted, voice cracking with fear.

Roaring tried to explain. "You know we're sundancers; we can't be burned by the flames, and we won't be harmed by the smoke."

"Will you be able to put out the fire?"

He hesitated, caught off guard by the question. "I'm not sure, actually. We were hoping you would let us go in and search for survivors."

"Have you rescued KI?" Fox said, her eyes darting around.

Vyanna stared at her. "I think you may be in shock. It might not be a good idea for you to go inside—"

"I am not standing out here and doing nothing—"

"Calm down, little paws," Roaring interrupted before she said something she shouldn't. He grabbed her by the shoulders and turned her to face him. "We'll find him. But we can't do that if we're all worked up. Remember your training. Remember what you learned in Wi."

Fox's shoulders dropped. She exhaled and looked at her brother, an apology in her eyes. He nodded, understanding the words she couldn't speak. "Ready?"

"Yes," she told him.

Vy stood watching beside the urn of water. Up close, Fox could see the sweat staining the collar of her shirt. It was hot this close to the building, but Fox welcomed the heat, called out to it with an ache in her heart.

"What do we need to do?"

Vyanna passed them both two leather pouches of water and then secured one to each of her hips. "Just follow me and point out anything dangerous I can't see. Stay close so I can use your sacks of water to put out as much of the fire as I can."

Fox nodded as she marched behind the Farron Princess. A

341

Hunter waited by the Academy doors, a cloth tied around his mouth and nose, his sleeves rolled up to reveal pale skin stained black from running in and out of the burning building. He shouted for them to stay low and stay together as they passed him by. "We think most of the people trapped inside are on the upper floors!"

Vy nodded and calmly walked into the building.

All the screaming and the shouting and the church bells ringing from outside came to a sudden hush as soon as Fox crossed the threshold into the Academy. It was totally black inside, heavy smoke moved slowly through the halls like a living creature. Fox shivered.

"The stairs are this way!" Vy said, jogging toward the end of the hall. "We've already cleared the first nine floors."

The heat intensified with every floor they climbed, the smoke grew thicker and every now and then Vy stopped to catch her breath, pouring water over her face mask and inhaling the cool liquid. When she caught Fox staring, she laughed.

"Sundancers cannot be burned; seadancers cannot be drowned. The air in here is tainted by smoke, breathing in water helps clear my lungs—as strange as that sounds."

Roaring appeared by her side. "If you need to go back—"

She shook her head. "We're almost there. Out team has to clear the twelfth floor."

Roaring nodded and motioned for her to take the lead.

When they reached the twelfth floor, they cleared the rooms together, one at a time. Roaring would open the door, kicking it off its hinges, and check through the smoke before letting the others inside to help search for any survivors. On this floor, the rooms were only filled with black smog; thankfully, they didn't

342

find any bodies but that didn't ease Fox's worrying at all.

She could feel the heat kissing her cheeks on every floor they cleared but it wasn't until they reached the fourteenth floor that they saw actual flames. The fire had destroyed part of the floor above them, leaving flaming debris to fall below. Vy had nearly been crushed by a falling chair before Roaring yanked her out of the way.

She fell against the wall with a grunt, extending her hand, feeling for support in the darkness. "I can't see anything now," she said, embarrassed. "The smoke is too thick for me."

"Can you guide your water straight ahead?" Fox asked. "The staircase is on fire."

"Wait." Roaring approached the collapsed stairs. He knelt by the flames and stuck his hand into the fire; when he pulled away, a single flame danced in his palm, flickering in the hazy smoke.

Fox stared at it, feeling its pull, as if the heat were calling out to her. All her training told her to call to the fire, it never mentioned the fire calling out to her. Without thinking, she stepped forward and extended her hand.

Roaring hesitated when he noticed her reach, but he passed her the flame without a word. For a second, Fox wasn't sure she would be able to hold the fire. She hadn't been able to produce her own flames at all, but maintaining an existing flame was different. *I already have the spark*, she remembered, *I just need to add my own fuel to keep it going.*

Fox held her breath and took the fire in her hands; it called to her, and she answered, watching power dance and hiss, begging for some of her strength. This fire was alive—all flames were—but it wasn't the same as the fire her brother used or even the fires that'd burned in Wi on the night of the attack. The flame in her hand was angry, greedy, and hungry for blood. She could feel it seeping into her skin, searching her body—her *soul*—for energy, for her own flames. It raced through parts of her she didn't know existed, searching the void inside for her internal light. And when it found it, it burned in her chest, anxiously trying to devour the fire within.

Fox gasped and let go of the flame. It sputtered out before reaching the floor.

"What's wrong?" Roaring said, watching her through the smoke. "You held the flame, Fox. You did it."

No, she thought, *I didn't. I didn't add fuel to that fire—it took fuel from me.* She looked at her brother. "Something about that fire isn't right."

Roaring's eyebrows furrowed. "I thought the same thing. This fire is hotter than usual—hot enough to burn through the Academy's stone floors."

"Can you extinguish it?" Vyanna asked.

Roaring pressed his lips together, concentrating on the blaze. He sighed. "I can't. It isn't natural, but it isn't from a dancer, either."

"I can put it out," Vy offered. "My water isn't what you'll find in a lake or stream. Its collected and blessed by our Priests. It will put out any flame—natural or otherwise." She stepped forward and removed the small cork on the water pouch secured at her hip. "Just tell me where to aim."

"Straight ahead, waist level," Roaring instructed.

Vy guided the water from her pouch right at the flames. It went out with a wicked hiss before fading into darkness.

"Let's go," Roaring said.

Carefully, they made their way up the stairs, climbing over debris and clumsily guiding Vy through the pitch-black smoke. On the next floor, they found the smoldering hole where the chair had fallen through; Vy put out the flames around it and sighed. "We have to be careful, there may be more holes like this ahead."

Fear of falling through the floor slowed them down but they pressed on together, putting out all the flames on the fourteenth floor. When they went to climb higher, Vy sank to one knee in a fit of coughs. Roaring caught her by the arm, but she waved him off and staggered to her feet. "I'll be fine."

"You've inhaled too much smoke."

She flicked her wrist and the cork on his water pouch popped. He jumped in surprise, watching curiously as the water danced from the sack to her face mask and she inhaled with a gasp of relief. "I said I'll be fine."

"You don't have much water left and we still need to climb back down fourteen floors. We need to turn around."

Vy let out a frustrated sigh, but she didn't protest when Roaring pulled her toward the stairs, gently guiding her away.

Fox balled her hands into fists. "I'm not going back."

"Don't be stupid—"

"I'm not leaving until I find KI."

Roaring stared at her and for a few tense moments, Fox held his gaze. He was her older brother, the greatest fighter in her village, and a master of flames—but she was not going to let him stop her from seeing KI, not when they were so close.

"I don't need to worry about the smoke or the flames," she reminded him.

Roaring looked like he wanted to argue more but his will

345

blew out of him with a sigh and he gave her a curt nod. "I'm coming back for you as soon as I get Vy to safety. Be careful, little paws."

Fox raced up the stairs with Roaring's warning ringing in her ears. *Be careful*; something he rarely said to her—maybe to Talon who wasn't built for fighting, maybe to Cat who'd never even finished her Regiment training back in Wi, but never to Fox. She shivered despite the heat and turned the corner. Then she froze in place.

The hallway was consumed by fire; the strange flames that'd tried to snuff out her own heat swirled in a vortex throughout the building. For half a second, Fox hesitated, fear creeping up her spine. *I cannot be burned*, she told herself, but she could fall through the floor if she wasn't careful. The ceiling above was pocked with holes, some so small they were barely noticeable, others big enough for a man to fall through.

Fox ran through the flames, feeling the heat brush against her skin with every step. "KI!" she screamed, running as fast as she could. She broke into a sweat but did not feel the burn of the fire, instead she felt the burn of her muscles as she kicked in doors, ran through rooms, and sprinted down the massive halls of the crumbling Academy. The fire roared around her, and though it'd frightened her earlier, she enjoyed the feel of its power swelling and flowing through the halls. For the first time, Fox felt connected to fire, felt it tugging on her, drawing her near. She came to a stop in the middle of the hall and stared at the flames crawling along the black stone. As if in a trance, her legs carried her toward the blaze, giving in to their pull.

Fox held out her hand, reaching for the fire—but she stopped short when a cry cut into her thoughts. "Fox Fire!" the voice

346

said.

She gasped, whirling around in search of the sound. "I'm here!" she hollered. "Where are you?"

There was a pause, so long Fox thought her heart would explode, and then she heard him again. "Fox!"

She took off running, kicking down every door she passed until she found him. In a small office near the end of the hall, the door crashed to the floor to reveal two teenage boys huddled together. Fox cried a string of incoherent words before she crumpled to the floor, tears streaking her soot-stained face. KI was in front of her now, his strong arms wrapping her in a fierce embrace.

"You came," he said, his voice hoarse.

She pulled away. "Of course."

"We tried to get out when the fire started but then the floor collapsed and took us down with it. We couldn't see through the smoke and Ana couldn't—" he broke off in a violent fit of coughs, doubling over to vomit when Fox tried to help.

"We need to go," she said, panic rising in her voice. "Now."

KI wiped his mouth and reached for the wall. "Ana's hurt."

Fox peered over his shoulder and noticed Kohlannis sitting on the floor for the first time. He was watching her through the smoke, his white-blonde bangs curtained over part of his face. Fox's eyes trailed his body, from his burned chest to his pale legs resting on the floor in front of him, his hands clutching one of his ankles.

"Can you walk?" she asked him.

He grunted and grabbed the desk to pull himself to his feet. He managed to stand upright but when he tried to take a step he winced and lost his footing, his knees buckling beneath him.

347

Fox ran to his side and held him up. "Here," she said, but he jerked away angrily.

"I don't need your help. Just give me a minute."

She frowned. "We don't have a minute."

KI wiped sweat from his forehead. "Let me do it, Foxy."

With a huff of annoyance, she turned away and marched back into the hall; she had bigger things to worry about than Kohl's attitude. Her friends had managed to survive the fire by hiding in a small room; closed off from the flames, they'd been kept safe from most of the smoke and searing heat, but the fire still raged outside and only Fox could walk through it unharmed. Maybe if they moved quickly, they could run and take minimal damage from the fire—maybe they could hunker down and wait for Roaring to return with Vy or another seadancer. But she'd kicked in the door, exposing them to the smoke and the heat pouring in. They had to move now.

Fox glared at the flames, angry and confused. *What do I do?* she wondered, thinking of her brother, trying to figure out how he would handle this. She could feel the fire pulsing around her, begging for energy like before. *God*, she whispered inside, *Jesus ... What do I do?*

Hesitantly, she called out to the blaze and ... like always, the flames did not respond. So she held out her hand to the wall and collected a single flame in her palm; the fire called to her again, but she ignored it, refusing to let the strange heat into her mind again. Instead, she took a breath and closed her hand, snuffing out the flame. Then she blinked at the walls, an idea blooming in her head.

With both hands extended, Fox let the fire crawl over her flesh; her skin tingling as it kissed her, searching for an opening. She took a shaky breath and instead of calling out to the fire, she slowly let it in. The heat rushed through her, filling her body with its strange energy, searching for her inner flame. Before it reached her own fire, she let go of her held breath and forced the flames out. Heat expelled from her body in a cry of defeat; Fox didn't let go, she forced the flames not just out of her body but away from the walls, off the floor, and down the hall. The fire went out with a hiss, screeching as it died and faded into smoke.

Fox fell to her knees with a laugh. She had done it—*controlled* fire, forced it to bend to her will. Fire was a living thing; it took immense strength to master it, summon it, and manipulate it. Roaring made it look so easy but not even the Prince of Fire had managed to put out the strange burning blaze.

Fox felt the drawback of this new ability weigh down on her as she struggled to her feet. Instead of calling out to the fire and controlling it, she'd answered fire's call and let it in. Forcing it out of her had taken all her strength, strength she needed to get back down to the first floor.

She exhaled hard and turned back to the office; KI stood with Kohl leaning against him, both of them gaping at her. "What just happened?" KI breathed.

Fox stared at her hands. "I don't know."

"Whatever, we need to get out of here. The rest of the building is still burning," Kohl said angrily.

Fox ignored him. "The smoke will get thicker from here. Just stay close to me and move as quickly as possible."

It was hard to rescue her friends. In her head, Fox had imagined she would find KI and they would run out the building together, leaping over debris and sprinting through smoke. But reality was not as pretty. They moved painfully slow; choking on smoke and tripping over rocks, stumbling into dead bodies of Hunters trapped beneath piles of debris. The building was sweltering—even by Fox's standards—but they had to keep going.

Thankfully, Fox didn't have to battle the flames anymore; she'd put out all the fire on the fifteenth floor and Vyanna and the Farrons had extinguished all the others. All they had to do was escape through the smoke and hope the ceiling didn't fall down on top of them. Fox kept a burning pace, pushing through her exhaustion. Mercifully, her friends never complained. Even though they moved slower than Fox liked, it was obvious from their grunts and pants that they were trying as best they could.

KI supported Kohl, dragging him through the blistering heat. Fox had expected an earful of hissing complaints from him, but like a tamed wolf he only sulked and grunted in pain whenever he had to hobble over debris or bodies. He kept his mouth shut but the hot anger never left his eyes; they found Fox through the black smoke, glaring at her, somehow blaming her for all this, as if they hadn't been helpless without her. *Maybe*, she thought, stealing a glance at him, *that's why he's angry*.

Fox breathed a sigh of relief when they reached the tenth floor. The fires on this level had been cleared before she'd even entered; there was still smoke lingering in the halls, but the air was breathable and easier to see through. Behind her, KI touched her shoulder.

"Slow down a bit?" he panted.

Fox bit her lip. "Alright, but we can't keep a slow pace for long."

"It's just that Ana isn't doing so great."

"I'm doing fine," Kohl said, his voice gravelly. He shoved KI away and used the wall to hold himself up. "Keep moving. We don't need to slow down."

"If you need a break—"

"I don't," he clipped, limping past her.

Fox stared at KI, trying to keep her anger in check.

He shrugged. "I guess we don't have to slow down, then."

She could have yelled at him; shouted that his friend was a jerk even though she'd saved him, but she knew it was pointless. No matter how irritating Kohl seemed to be, KI was always there to defend him. Fox eyed him for a long moment, letting the silence settle, then she turned to leave but as soon as she reached the first step, her legs buckled, and she tumbled down.

She opened her eyes at the bottom of the stairs; KI knelt beside her; concern etched onto his features. Kohl leaned against the wall, no emotion on his face whatsoever.

"What?" Fox said, wincing as she sat up.

"You fell down the stairs," KI explained. "I think putting out the fires took a toll. Maybe you should rest for a moment."

Kohl peeled from the wall, staring down at both of them. "No. We don't need to slow down—we've wasted enough time already."

"Half that time was wasted on you." Fox jabbed a finger at Kohl's injured leg.

"You're the one lying on the floor right now," he said plainly.

She struggled to her feet, waving off KI's extended hand. "What's your problem? I *saved* you."

Piercing blue eyes watched her quietly. The silence went on

351

for so long Fox wasn't sure Kohl would respond until he pulled his gaze away and said with a shrug, "Nothing."

The reply baffled her so much she stumbled over her words. "A—are you—you're not serious, right?"

"Guys," KI said but Fox ignored him, yelling at Kohl's back.

"Who do you think you are?" No one else had come to help him—no one else would even *want* to help a Hunger kid. "Get over yourself!" Fox yelled. "You should be happy I even bothered to come in here!"

He turned to her, his face curdling in anger. "Every time you stick your nose into my business, you want a reward. *You...*" he looked down at her, "someone who can't even use their own blessing, thinks I should be thanking them for anything at all." He shook his head. "And your reason behind all this is because of who I am. Because you think no one else would ever bother to help me, talk to me, or save me but *you*." He scoffed. "The audacity."

Fox blinked. "I don't get it." He had fought alongside Roaring, had trained with KI daily, had leaned on him for support as they made their way through the building. "You accept help from everyone else but me."

Kohl glared at her. "No one else acts like I *need* their help except you."

She wanted to scream, but she hadn't the energy to do it. Instead, she shook her head and took a shaky step forward, ignoring KI as he offered a hand to stable her. That was it, then. Kohl hated her because she wanted to help him.

No, she blinked, *he hates me because I think he needs help.*

She pushed away her thoughts, there wasn't any time to focus on Kohlannis, anyway. She still had to get out of the

352

building. Through the smoke, she could make out the distinct floor-sweeping cloaks of Academy Priests, she could hear the sound of their approaching footsteps.

Relief rushed through her as the men and women neared them, turning into pure joy when a familiar face stepped into view. Roaring Fire.

He was beside her before she knew it, offering to carry her the rest of the way, but Fox shook him off. She would not let Kohl see her carried down the stairs by her older brother. So she shuffled along as best she could, ignoring her exhaustion and listening to Roaring's details of the situation outside.

When they finally cleared the building, she wanted to faint, but she held her composure and hobbled to the clearing where the Priests with healing abilities waited. Kohl received treatment for his ankle, sulking and huffing the entire time, while KI was treated for minor burns and smoke inhalation. Fox listened as he recited what'd happened, her stomach twisting as he described the masked man who'd come to get him.

"You were targeted," she said aloud.

KI stopped talking to the Hunter who'd been scribbling down his story and turned to Fox. "Yeah, I was."

She didn't even have to ask why. Fox knew there was a demon inside her friend, growing, feeding on his spiritual energy, slowly taking over his body. Of course there were people who wanted KI dead. But this masked man hadn't tried to kill him. He'd tried to *take* him. Just like the giant who'd crushed her village. Just like the silver-haired demon with her wind swords.

Lieutenant Diaz had warned them that someone would be

coming to get what was theirs. Fox never thought it would be so soon. They had only settled in Babel three months ago. Had the enemy regrouped so quickly? Had they found KI already? Or was this someone else?

Fox replayed KI's story in her head. A masked man lighting the Academy on fire. Was that his blessing? Was he a sundancer?

She chewed her lip. No, Roaring had said he couldn't extinguish the flames because they weren't from a dancer. But what sort of gift allowed one to manipulate fire without it being sundancing?

Maybe it's someone with a similar blessing...

Fox jerked forward, shaking her head in disbelief as the thought flowed into her mind. Maybe it was someone who had *copied* a blessing.

She thought of Montell and how different his sundancing had looked compared to Roaring's. Fire didn't shoot from his fists when he'd used his borrowed powers; it'd belched from his palms and fell to the ground like he was pouring out heat—not directing and controlling it. But had the flames been different? Had they felt hungry and dark like the ones engulfing the Tower?

Fox couldn't remember. She hadn't gotten close to the copied flames. Hadn't studied them. Hadn't answered their call.

She squeezed her eyes shut. *And ... would Montell really do something like this?*

No. It wasn't possible. He wasn't her friend, but he wasn't her enemy, either. Besides, how long had it been since he'd touched her? Nearly two weeks. And he'd came in contact with plenty of other students since then. Fox remembered him trying to earthdance after he high-fived Wunda when her team had finally made it out the tunnels. And he'd touched Terra during a different training session—ran himself into a tree and had to ask Syren Danis to fix his broken nose.

There was no way he still had her blessing in his cache. There was no way he would hold on to it for this long. Fox huffed, irritated. There were thousands of people in Babel with gifts she'd never heard of—not to mention all the new trainees traveling from outside the Region.

Maybe, Fox glanced over at KI, *maybe it wasn't Montell*. It was too obvious, anyway. He had revealed his blessing to her before. If he was the masked man, he had to know she would immediately suspect him. And he'd also told her something Master Jo hadn't even mentioned.

Did you know, some people can be born with more than one blessing?

Why did he tell me that? Fox wondered. Was it simply Monty showing off how smart he was? Or was he planning something? Sowing seeds of doubt for this very moment.

It could be him, she acknowledged, or it could be one of the thousands of others in Babel. It could be any other student she trained with every day. Using one blessing on the Grounds while keeping a second one secret.

The Priest tending KI's injuries instructed him to shift position so she could cut away his burned shirt. Fox glanced over at them; her attention stolen by his movement. KI calmly stood and peeled away his tattered pajama shirt. That's when Fox saw it for the first time; the twisted black lines stained onto his skin, forming a dark pattern across his back.

The bold black lines were a code for something, that much

was obvious, but Fox could not decipher them. They seemed alive, glowing against his olive skin, feeding off his energy.

Amber eyes blinked in shock as Fox stared at her friend, trying to find something to say. She felt fear zigzag through her, and for the first time since she'd arrived in Babel, Fox felt afraid that maybe everyone had been right. Maybe there was something wrong with KI. Just as quickly as the fear had formed it was washed away by guilt—because if there was something wrong with him, it was all her fault.

But that's okay, she told herself. Because she'd finally gotten stronger, if only a little. It hadn't been much, but she had held a flame when she stood in the burning Tower. She had extinguished the blaze that even her brother couldn't put out. And she had done it for KI.

It was KI who'd fueled her wild fighting the night her village had been destroyed, KI who'd inspired her to join the Academy, and KI who'd made her brave enough to run into a burning building. She didn't care what was inside him or what was wrong with him. She didn't care about Montell or a masked man or whoever thought they could take her dear friend away.

I'm going to protect him. Fox stared at KI's back, her gaze tracing the inky black markings, memorizing every line and swirl. *I won't let them have him—not the monster inside or the ones outside, either.*

27
Evelyn

Lieutenant Diaz shifted in his chair, trying his best to stifle the yawn creeping up on him. The tent smelled like roasted boar, Captain Payne's favorite. Her team had apparently enjoyed a very successful hunt while he'd been gone. She stood over the fire, rotating the fat pig over the crackling flames as she spoke. He watched her absently, trying to stay focused. He hadn't slept since he'd left Koh, pushing his horse to maintain a brutal pace—even by his standards. Going back for Talon had derailed the mission more than he'd liked, now he was making up for lost time. But the trip had been worth it. He'd rescued the Grand Chief. He'd dealt with his insubordinate team. And then he'd raced back to the frontlines.

"Where is she?"

Diaz glanced up. "What?"

Captain Payne put the fire poker down. "The Grand Chief—where is she?"

"Oh ... I left her behind."

"In Koh?" She put a hand on her heavy hip, cocked her head to the side. "After going through all that?"

"No, not in Koh. I left her with a different squad so I could ride ahead."

"So, she's still coming here?"

He nodded lazily. "She's riding in a carriage, so it should be a few days."

"How comfy."

"I didn't think she could handle the ride on horseback."

"Is that the only reason you left her with Squad Two?" She gazed at him inquisitively, hearing all the words he hadn't spoken. Lieutenant Diaz had never liked Payne very much, but he'd spent enough time fighting beside her to know she could read him more easily than he was willing to admit.

He shifted uncomfortably in his chair, unease inching up his spine. "I left her so she would be comfortable and safe."

"Alright," she said, seemingly satisfied with that answer.

"When will we be ready for the next phase of the mission?"

"Another day or two."

"You said I could choose my own team."

She gave a slow nod, trying to figure out where he was going with this. "Yes, I did."

"I want Lieutenant Kotaro off the team."

Captain Payne stared at him; she looked menacing with the fire flickering behind her, making her shadow shimmy and blink. "You want your second lieutenant *off* your team?"

"It isn't what you think—"

358

"Then explain what it is because you're not making any sense right now."

Diaz exhaled, annoyed. "You got the report on what happened in Koh."

"About the crazies holding that poor lady hostage?"

He nodded. "I want to make sure someone will be able to protect her while I'm gone."

"Protect her from what?"

He looked at her seriously. "From anyone else who might harm her."

Captain Payne left her roasting boar to stand behind her desk. She splayed her hands on the smooth wood, eyeing Diaz closely. "And by *anyone else*, you mean someone on this squad."

"It was members of the last squad who held her captive in Koh," Lieutenant Diaz said hotly. "I want someone I trust to stay behind and guard her while we move into phase two."

"How noble of you. But if you're so worried, why did you let her ride alone in that carriage with Squad Two?"

He hesitated, giving Captain Payne the answer she needed. With a snort of amusement, she pushed away from the desk and crossed her arms. "You didn't ride for three days, nearly killing your horse, so you could preach to me about how much you want to protect this woman. You rode ahead because you couldn't stand to be around her anymore."

Diaz didn't answer.

She cackled again, making him squirm. "I've always wondered what it would take to get some emotion out of you. You're so distant—*completely* focused on the mission, on the team, on the objective." She shook her head, a smile spreading across her plump face. "I thought maybe Lieutenant Kotaro could bring out your sweet side one day, but you look at her the same way you look at a cold chicken sandwich."

Lieutenant Diaz winced. "You're point, Captain?"

"You care about this woman," she said bluntly. "You care about her so much she's become a distraction to you, hasn't she?"

Diaz tried his best to ignore her claims, keeping his face calm and steady as he replied, "I care about keeping Lady Talon safe, Captain Payne, like anyone else here should."

She smirked and shrugged one shoulder. "Whatever you say, Lieutenant Diaz."

"Are we done here?" He pushed his chair back.

"You'll have to tell Kotaro she's off the team. I'm not doing your dirty work."

"Fine."

"And you'll replace her with Lord Izzy."

Diaz stared at her, trying to make sense of her orders. "Captain," he said quietly.

"Izzy is the only one skilled enough to replace her—even better, if you ask me."

"I hadn't."

Captain Payne squinted. "Careful, Evelyn."

"You said I could choose my own team for the mission."

"Now I'm reconsidering."

"May I ask why?"

"No."

"*Please?*" The word came out as more of a sigh than a question. He knew what Captain Payne was doing; she loved getting under his skin.

Then, without notice, she set her joking aside. "Your judgement may jeopardize this mission, Diaz. I won't have that. You don't have to take Kotaro along, but you won't walk into that forest without a strong ally by your side and Lord Izzy is the only one suited for the job."

She stared at him, suddenly seeming much taller than her 5'6 height, though he was still three inches taller. Her back straightened and she held her head high; her kinky hair was pulled into a slick bun and her sharp eyes were focused on him. In the firelight they seemed to glow, though not with malice; Captain Payne did enjoy picking at the lieutenant, but he knew from the fierceness in her eyes that her remarks were fueled by a strong sense of duty—not her usual childish games. While he would never say he liked the captain, Diaz had to admit he couldn't think of someone better for the job. He just wished he didn't have to work for her.

"All right," he agreed. "Izzy goes with me."

"I don't see why it's such a problem. I thought the three of you grew up together."

"Something like that."

In his tent, Diaz shut out the sounds of the camp around him; Hunters and Priests sharpening weapons, muttering prayers, getting ready for the next phase of their mission. It wasn't supposed to be this difficult; they were supposed to ride out to the destroyed Village of Wi, examine the remains, and determine when reconstruction could begin. Then they'd spotted the herd of shadow frogs, then Lady Talon had been taken and held against her will, then Lieutenant Diaz sent half his team home, and now he was left facing his worst enemy. The only foe he had yet to defeat.

In the basin by his bed, he stared at his reflection. His features twisted and shifted with the ripples of the hot water. Hazel eyes, a square jaw, and golden-brown skin. A scar went through his left eyebrow, a souvenir from a fight he couldn't remember. The only thing he could focus on right now was trying not to focus on the words of his superior. They rang inside him, echoing through the chambers of his mind, winding their way into his heart.

You care about this girl.

He gritted his teeth, trying to swallow his anger. It had been far too long since he'd cared about anything beside his mission. He'd held his own mother as she lay dying, watched his father bleed out on the cold winter floor, and had witnessed the death of countless comrades. He'd numbed himself—not just to the pain of loss but to the joys of companionship. Because every time he let someone in, they seemed to slip away.

He slapped the water and let go of his resolve with a sigh. He was too tired to think about this now. A bed of furs waited beside him, blanketed in red and brown and chestnut warmth; he kicked off his boots and climbed in fully dressed, surrendering to a fitful sleep.

That night, he dreamed of his mother. The day she died. He saw himself holding the bow and arrow, staring at the darkling that emerged from the trees, twisted and broken to match the jagged bark all around them. With shaky aim, he set loose a single arrow and held his breath. The darkling dodged and ran at them. He thought his mother had lost too much blood, he thought she was weak—had *always* thought she was weak; hiding behind her curtain of hair like a shield to protect her

362

from glaring eyes, hurtful words, and his father's anger. She had never stood up for herself against him, let alone a darkling. But that day she surprised him.

Evelyn felt the impact of the ground before he realized his mother had shoved him out the way. She hovered over him, propped up on her shaking arms and knees; her thick hair stuck to her face, tangled in her sweat and the melted snow. Her eyes were wide open and wet with tears; as they ran down her face, they dripped red onto his. That's when he realized she'd been stabbed.

Protruding from her backside was the demon's branch-like hand; it had lunged at him, but she'd shoved him to the ground and threw her body over him to protect her only son. Mercilessly, the darkling had stabbed her instead, a wound so deep Evelyn thought its hand would force its way through his mother's abdomen.

There was so much blood. Wicked crimson stains splattered onto Evelyn's heavy coat, blotting the snow in dark streaks. He looked up at his mother, trying not to burst into tears. Despite the pain she must have felt, his mother smiled at him, her full lips parting to reveal bloodstained teeth. Her tears spilled down her cheeks and fell onto his face, mingled with her own blood, as if she were crying red. He gasped. His mother was going to die.

"M—Mama," he whispered.

"Don't," she smiled ruefully. "Don't let it in."

The demon shifted, trying to retract its hand. His mother yelped in pain, squeezing her eyes shut. Evelyn wrapped his arms around her neck, holding on for dear life. If this demon was going to take her away, it would have to take him, too.

His mother let out a shaky breath. "Don't let it in, Eve," she said—she always called him that and he always hated it, but right then he wished he could hear it over and over again. "These emotions you feel right now—fear, anger, hatred—don't let them in, Eve."

The demon roared and yanked hard, tugging its hand free from his mother's body. She let out a horrifying scream and collapsed into Evelyn's arms, sagging into the snow as her blood gushed out. Evelyn sucked in a gulp of air and exhaled a scream, clutching his mother's lifeless body, but there was no time to mourn.

The darkling shook the blood from its hand and came after him. Before he could register any thoughts or formulate a plan, Evelyn yanked his mother's dagger from the sheath secured to her hip and crawled to his feet. The demon's arm shot forward, whipping at him like a crooked branch snapping in the wind; he rolled out of its path and held up the blade to parry the demon's counter. It's branch-like arm splintered against the metal blade, and it stepped back with a howl, cradling its limb, and glaring at young Evelyn.

Anger told him to stay and avenge his mother. Hatred told him to stay and destroy this creature. Fear told him to run.

With a sorrowful gasp, Evelyn dropped his knife and sprinted into the woods with a demon hot on his tail.

"Lieutenant Diaz!" a shrill voice called his name, and he opened his eyes, waking suddenly—violently. It took him a moment to blink back his sleepiness before he realized what was happening.

A girl cowered beside him, leaning over his bed. Her dark eyes stared at him in fear. "What," he whispered, confused.

"I came in to check on you, sir," she explained quickly, the words leaving her mouth in a panic. "You were yelling in your sleep. I tried to wake you, but then—" her words cut off in a gasp of pain. That's when Diaz realized he had her by the wrist, gripping so tightly she'd begun to bruise red.

He let her go. "I'm sorry."

"It's all right."

"Who let you into my tent?"

She rubbed at her wrist. "I let myself in—"

"Get out," he ordered, throwing his covers back. Morning had come and gone, leaving a searing afternoon heat in its wake. The lieutenant was soaked in his own sweat, his hair brushed all to one side, as if he'd rolled over in his sleep. He stood at the water basin by his bed, it was chilly now and with a splash to his face, it slapped the grogginess of sleep right out of him.

The young lady cleared her throat. "Captain Payne ordered me to check on you when you didn't show up for the briefing this morning—"

He paused, wiping his face with a towel. "There was a meeting this morning?"

"Yes. Captain Payne received a messenger hawk."

"What did it say?"

"I—I don't know. I'm just a disciple—"

"Never mind," he said, brushing past her toward the exit.

"Wait!" The young disciple scrambled to gather her bag of supplies. "I'm supposed to give you a checkup before you leave!"

Diaz stopped at the entrance to his tent. "What do you mean, *before I leave*? The next phase doesn't start until tomorrow."

"I don't know, sir. I'm just telling you what Captain Payne told me."

He exhaled hard. "I don't have time for a checkup."

"She said I couldn't come back until I gave you one," the girl said pleadingly.

Lieutenant Diaz grunted; if he weren't pressed, he would have felt bad for her. He knew the stress of working under the captain better than anyone, he could only imagine the sort of struggle Payne was putting this young disciple through.

"Come with me, then," he said, walking out his tent.

Overnight, the camp had gone from peaceful resting grounds to a frenzied panic. Hunters and Priests didn't roam the grounds packing weapons and muttering the sacred Script. The smell of roasted boar no longer penetrated the air; it had gone sour—sweat mingled with fear and worry.

Lieutenant Diaz pushed aside the flap to Captain Payne's tent. He was met with two-dozen pairs of eyes, one pair belonged to his superior and she was not happy to see him.

"Look who decided to roll out of bed and join us." She put a thick hand on her hip. "Do you have any idea how late it is?"

"What did the message say?" Diaz asked, crossing the room. He ignored the prying eyes of the Hunters and Priests gathered in the captain's tent. Their stares made him very aware of his shabby appearance, but the information of the message was far more important than his looks.

Captain Payne harrumphed. "You would know if you had bothered to wake up on time."

"Captain—" he swallowed, trying not to let his emotions get the better of him. If the message wasn't urgent, the camp wouldn't be in a frenzy. His mind couldn't help but drift,

366

wandering into the horrible darkness and speculation that something might have happened to Lady Talon.

Don't let it in. His mother's last words echoed in his head, and he squeezed his eyes shut, trying to block them out. How could he not let in the pain and the anger he felt? He'd wondered that ever since she'd muttered the words to him, her mouth stained with her own blood.

Darklings had taken the only person he'd ever loved. And they had taken so much more after that. His father, his home, his comrades. If he couldn't allow himself to feel his own anger, bitterness, hatred—then he wouldn't allow himself to feel anything at all.

Slowly, Lieutenant Diaz exhaled a sigh. His panic and frustration washed away almost immediately, replaced by the stiff detachment that defined him. He clenched his jaw, realizing Captain Payne had been talking that entire time.

"You may be Major Marshall's favorite," she was saying, "but you aren't mine. You don't get special treatment here, lieutenant."

"Are you going to tell me the message or not? We're wasting time," Diaz replied, unbothered by her comments.

Captain Payne narrowed her eyes. "Out. All of you."

Without a word, the onlooking crowd stood and exited the captain's tent. Lieutenant Diaz couldn't help noticing those who remained, Lord Izzy and Lord Razzle, high-ranking Priests of the Cross.

The young girl from his tent turned to leave but Captain Payne stopped her. "You stay," she ordered. "I'm guessing Diaz didn't let you examine him."

"No, captain."

"Do it now."

Diaz bristled. "That isn't necessary."

"Yes, it is."

"Don't touch me," he said to the girl.

She backed away with a gasp, glancing at Captain Payne.

"If you don't allow her to examine you, I will remove you from this mission and transfer it to the Priest's division."

"This is an Academy sanctioned mission; you don't have the authority to transfer it to the Cross."

Payne smirked. "Maybe not, but I do have the authority to take you off of it."

"Over something so petty?"

"The health of my men isn't a small matter, lieutenant. You came here exhausted and hungry, you overslept without knowing, and look at you—" she waved a hand at him, emphasizing his appearance. "I just want to make sure you're in good shape, that's all. If you accept the checkup, I'll tell you about the message."

The lieutenant clenched his jaw but began unbuttoning his shirt anyway. The young lady watched him timidly, unsure what to do. She was a young Priestess, wearing all white instead of black, a disciple who'd just graduated from the Academy. *What a terrible first mission*, he thought, looking her up and down. Her hair was sectioned into two thick braids that brushed past her collar bone; a rosy blush veiled her light brown cheeks as she watched him undress. Her full lips parted wordlessly, an echo of surprise forming over her face as she took in the scars and markings on his flesh.

He left his shirt hanging open and held his arms out at either side. "Well," he said, annoyed.

368

The young disciple approached him carefully, keeping her eye on him as if he might attack at any moment. He amused her with a grin which made her hands visibly tremble as she splayed them on his skin. With unsteady fingers, she exhaled, and he suddenly felt a rush of vitality as she poured her spiritual energy into his body.

There were many tribes and clans with healing abilities in the City of Babel, Lieutenant Diaz usually received his treatments from a member of the Danis Clan. They had a blessing that gave them the ability to speed up a person's recovery—a knife wound could be healed in minutes, a broken bone in an hour. The young disciple before him now did nothing like that. She poured her own energy into his body and siphoned out the injuries, sifting through his flesh and working out any weakness or pain.

He didn't like it. It felt invasive and strange; the sensation of having someone else's spiritual energy inside you seemed somehow wrong. Spiritual energy was unique, like the winding lines of a person's fingerprint, each one was different.

Diaz closed his eyes and his body reacted to the energy flooding through him. Injuries he hadn't been aware of melted away; the lingering numbness in his burned hand, an ache in his back, soreness from riding all night. The energy pulsed through him like blood in his veins, searching for an ailment to heal. It went through his chest to his abdomen, all over his body, and when it was done healing his physical wounds, it began to search deeper.

Diaz felt the moment her energy seeped into his mind—his soul—poking curiously at the darkness he'd kept so carefully hidden in his heart. The place where all those unfelt emotions

369

remained locked up inside.

His eyes shot open, and he grabbed her hand, startling her.

She gasped and looked up at him.

"Don't do that," he said quietly, but he knew from the look on her face that she'd already gone too far. Had she touched his heart? Felt the rage and the hatred inside him? Could she heal him if he'd let her?

He didn't want to know.

"Is he good?" Captain Payne called over his shoulder.

Slowly, the disciple pulled her hands away from Diaz's bare chest, untangling her fingers from his. He hadn't realized he'd still been holding her hand. "H—he's fine," she said, eyes glued to his.

"Thanks," he muttered, buttoning his uniform again. He turned to Captain Payne. "The message?"

She snapped her fingers at the disciple. "Out." When she left the tent, Captain Payne explained, "We got a hawk—*Lord Razzle* got a hawk, to be specific."

The massive Priest stood, towering over everyone in the room, and unrolled a scroll that seemed tiny in his large hands. He was a giant, like all members of the Shoren Clan, nearly ten feet tall with smooth skin stretched over inhuman muscles. Lieutenant Diaz had worked with Razzle plenty of times, fighting side by side with his devastating war hammer, but he had never gotten used to his size. Looking at him now, he felt thankful the Shorens were on the Academy's side.

"The message was from my wife, Lady Shakira. She told me the Academy was attacked."

Diaz's breath hitched for a moment, his emotions suspended between horror and relief. The Academy was attacked—but

370

Lady Talon was okay.

"They don't know who the perpetrator was. Witness testimonies were vague, but he caused significant damage," Lord Razzle said.

"How significant?" the lieutenant asked.

"He set fire to the Academy tower."

They were gripped by a tense silence. Even Captain Payne, who'd already heard the news, glanced at the floor in dismay.

Lieutenant Diaz took a moment to register the message. "How could someone set the Tower on fire?"

"There weren't many details. The damage was extensive but only a few casualties." Razzle glanced pointedly at Lord Izzy who'd been silent the entire time. His face was hard, lines and creases molded in anger distorted his youthful face.

"Who was it?" Diaz asked.

"It was my apprentice," Izzy bit out. "He killed her. Twice."

Diaz blinked. If he remembered correctly, Izzy's apprentice was a young Priestess named Vehenort of the Benjamin Tribe. Her bloodline held a blessing which gave them the ability to bring themselves back to life. Stronger members of the tribe were said to have the strength to bring others back from the dead, too—some whispered it was this very reason that Lord Izzy had sought out the young protégé, making her his apprentice at the age of fifteen. Diaz hadn't witnessed it himself, but he'd heard stories of the young Priestess resurrecting her master on the battlefield. It was no surprise; Izzy was an elite member of the Cross, not even Captain Payne had clearance to accompany him on certain missions. Lieutenant Diaz couldn't even begin to imagine the dangers he'd faced on behalf of the Cross. Lady Vehenort was perhaps the only human alive skilled enough to accompany him; her blessing, and exceptional mastery of it, made her the perfect companion.

But Izzy had left the young girl alone in Babel while he went ahead on this mission. And she'd died ... "Twice," Diaz said softly. Reanimation was an incredible blessing but there was a limit. Some could only bring themselves back once, others a few more times—but Diaz knew this hadn't been Vehenort's first or second or *fifth* death. He dared a glance at Izzy. "Is she...?"

"She's alive," he said tersely.

"Then she wasn't a casualty. Technically."

"Technically not," Captain Payne agreed. "But the attack happened all the same and she was not the only victim or the target."

"Who was the target?"

"We don't know. But I assume we'll find out more information when we return to Babel."

"And when will that be?"

"After we've completed this mission."

Lieutenant Diaz raised an eyebrow. "*After?* Why aren't we turning back now?"

"Because we have a job to do."

"There was an attack on the Academy—"

"And it's over now." She pointed to the paper in Razzle's hand. "That message did not call for reinforcements, it was sent as a courtesy so we wouldn't be surprised when we return."

Diaz sighed, resisting the urge to massage his temples. He wished the disciple would return and stop the pounding headache he felt coming on. "So, what's the plan now?"

"We've bumped up the second phase in the mission. You and

your team will be leaving immediately."

"Are you sure we're ready for that?" he questioned.

Payne smiled. "You're the only one we're waiting for."

Lieutenant Diaz suddenly felt very aware of how disheveled he looked; his hair swooped to one side of his head, his uniform wrinkled from sleeping in it, and his skin oily from days without a bath.

He ran a hand through his hair. "Give me fifteen minutes."

"Take an hour; I doubt you've eaten yet," Captain Payne ordered.

"Fine." He hesitated. "May we talk privately?"

Without a word, Izzy and Razzle excused themselves, offering curt nods as they left.

Payne sat at her desk, heaving a sigh as she fanned herself with her fat hands. "What is it?"

"My team."

"Ah, yes. You're very fortunate, lieutenant. Since we've bumped up the second phase, you won't have to worry about breaking the news to Kotaro. She won't be here in time to join you."

He swallowed, hoping his relief didn't show on his features.

"Only problem now," Captain Payne continued, "is you'll have to use men from this squad to replace anyone else who's with Lieutenant Kotaro."

"That won't be a problem," Diaz said. "You still want Izzy on the team."

"Of course."

"And what about Razzle?"

"He's staying here with me to deal with the second squad arriving today. The plan is for your team to go ahead, clear out whatever demons you find and gain entrance to the village. The rest of us will catch up once you send the signal that it's safe."

Lieutenant Diaz made his way to the exit. "I'll be ready to leave in an hour."

Back in his tent, Evelyn noticed his water basin had been refilled and a plate of hot food left on his desk. Sitting on his bed was a familiar figure.

"Lord Izzy." Diaz sighed, going to the basin. He removed his shirt and splashed water on his chest and face. "What do you want?"

"We need to talk."

"Go ahead."

"Why are you here right now? Ahead of your team."

"I wanted to ride out to make arrangements for the second phase of the mission."

Izzy hesitated, digesting the information. Diaz could feel his eyes planted on his back and suddenly felt the urge to turn around, but he resisted and focused on his wash. He scrubbed his face and hair with a bar of soap that made his skin burn and then rubbed the bar over his bare chest and back. The bumps and ridges of his scars brought back memories he'd tried to forget, fights he'd won—some he'd nearly lost. It'd been Izzy who patched him up back when they were in the Academy together and it was Izzy who'd placed the thick black markings on his body, just as he'd done for the boy.

In the polished mirror hanging on his wall, Diaz caught Izzy's reflection and realized he was still staring. His bright eyes roved over the markings painted across his back, wrapping around to his chest, studying them closely.

"How long has it been—"

"A few months," he grunted, trying to avoid the topic.

"I could take another look."

Lieutenant Diaz splashed water over his frame and then wiped himself down with a towel. He dropped his pants, started washing his lower half. "You don't need to do that. I'm fine."

"Then why are you here instead of with Kotaro?"

"I already told you."

"I don't believe that."

"Well, that's too bad," Diaz said, walking naked to an open chest. He pulled out a fresh set of clothes and jammed his leg into a pair of underpants. Black marks lined his thighs and his calves, too, disappearing beneath his clothes as he slid into his military uniform.

When he finished dressing, he grabbed his plate from his desk; leftover boar with fire roasted onions and a crust of stale bread soaked in the pig's fat. A cup of ice-cold water washed it all down; the lieutenant leaned against his desk when he was done, looking at his old friend.

A look of concern had taken over Izzy's delicate features, but Diaz was not fooled, he knew there was anger hiding behind those hazel eyes; he'd seen it released on the battlefield. The two had grown up together in Babel, raised side by side as orphans until Major Marshall took Diaz under his wing. Reunited at the Academy, Diaz realized the only thing that had changed about his young companion was his hunger. Where there had once been a hopeful light there was now a burning fire, a quiet storm raging inside him. Izzy held as much anger as the lieutenant; the only difference between them was what fueled it. Izzy burned to right the wrongs in the world, to defend the friends he loved and honor the family he lost. But Diaz's anger stemmed from a raw and potent hatred.

He glanced away. "I left Kotaro behind because I needed to get away."

"I thought so." Izzy stood to leave. "You'll never get over things if you don't address them, Evelyn."

"Is this your way of making me address them?" he asked.

Izzy stopped in his doorway. "It's my way of warning you not to slip up."

28

Roaring

Roaring took a deep breath. The air felt chilly, a cold wind that left a dull ache in his chest. Training had been postponed indefinitely, which meant the Fire siblings had to find other ways to practice sundancing. Roaring had been fine with skipping the gym altogether, but Fox had insisted on training. They'd gone into the woods beyond the Grounds, sparring until their muscles screamed. Fox still couldn't produce her own flames, but she could work with the fire Roaring passed to her.

Their fights were exhilarating. Trading searing blows, exchanging scalding hot punches. It never burned them, but they felt the rushing heat coursing through their veins, and it left them breathless and tired when the day was up.

The Prince of Fire glanced over at his little sister, watching her stretch and pack her things. She hadn't spoken much the last few days, not since the Tower went up in flames. Academy officials had thanked her for her role in rescuing KI and Kohl and extinguishing some of the fires inside, but that was all the gratitude they showed. Fox hadn't been allowed to see her friends since then. The lack of communication had begun to take its toll on her. Roaring could sense her frustration in their match. Every punch, every blow, dealt with a bit of rage. It was better than locking herself in her room to cry, so he didn't question her about it, but he did wonder.

What if they don't let KI out again? What if the Academy decides his presence is a danger to the entire city?

Roaring exhaled, shaking away his thoughts. There were other things he needed to worry about. Like his sisters and their safety. If assassins were out looking for KI, then Fox's life was in danger, too. She was close to the boy, almost stubbornly attached to him. Roaring would never ask her to leave KI behind, but he had to start thinking about the bigger picture. Something—or *someone*—was after him, and even the Academy wasn't sure what for.

The assassin had gotten into the Tower. Had nearly burned it to the ground.

If they can't protect them, then we can't, either. Roaring closed his eyes. Now would be a good time to remember his goal. He had never planned to stay here in Babel. Had never planned to enroll in the Academy. Since training was postponed, there was no reason to delay. It wasn't like he had anything better to do. Maybe this was a blessing in disguise, an alarm ringing, telling them it was time to go.

He opened his eyes again, stealing another look at his sister. She'd wanted to return home, too. But that was before she'd enrolled in the Academy. After all this, would she still be willing to leave?

Roaring already knew the answer—*not without KI.*

She was standing in front of him now, her head tilted to the side, a question on her lips.

"You there?"

He nodded. Sighed. Then he palmed the back of his neck. "Ready to go, little paws?"

She turned and walked away without looking back.

Cat was finishing dinner when Roaring and Fox arrived home. Smells of simmered mustard greens and fluffy cornbread, sweet yams cooked until tender, assaulted him so violently his mouth began to water before he'd even stepped inside.

He opened the door with a smile and immediately lost his train of thought. Cat stood over the table, setting down plates and napkins, in the living room sat the entire new Council of Wi. Kifu Kato rested on the sofa between Ina Modon and Ryko. Thunder Bolt took up the chair beside them with Chava resting peacefully at her feet. The giant hound lifted her head as she spied Roaring in the doorway, and every pair of eyes followed her gaze to the Prince of Fire.

Roaring swallowed. "Uh—"

"You're here!" Cat exclaimed, rushing across the floor. She grabbed Roaring and Fox by their arms and dragged them into the house, whispering fiercely as she moved. "There's a Council meeting today. I'm guessing you forgot."

He had. "No, I'm just tired."

"Well, you'd better go to your room and get energized because they've been waiting for an hour."

"What?"

She shoved him toward his bedroom. "Just go! You have five minutes before the tea is served."

In his quarters, Roaring leaned against his heavy wooden door. For all his whining over wanting to be the Grand Chief, he had to admit he didn't feel like dealing with the Council today. With a grunt, he swallowed his irritation and changed his clothes, then he made his way back out to his guests.

The Council had left the living room by the time he emerged, joining Cat to sit on cushions around the floor-table. His sister glanced up at him as he arrived and patted the cushion beside her. Roaring took his place between Cat and Fox and noticed, with a start, that he sat at the head of the table. His entire life he'd sat beside Talon and she beside their mother, at her right hand. Though he was the oldest, the head of the table was not his place and could never be ... until now.

Cat led the family in prayer, whispering *in Jesus' name, Amen*, as she raised her head and began shoveling food onto plates and passing them around.

"Sorry for making everyone wait," Roaring said, accepting a glass of chilled lemon tea from his sister.

Thunder set down her slice of cornbread. "It wasn't long, Grand Chief."

The words took him by surprise. He sat up straighter and cleared his throat. "Let's get down to it, then."

Kifu Kato leaned forward; his food was untouched. "Where is your sister? We thought she would be back by now."

She should have been back over a week ago...

"She's still away on her mission."

Cat chimed in. "We got a letter today. Lady Talon will be

380

gone for another week or so."

"She needs to be here," Kifu Kato complained, though, in his thick Wi accent, his grievance almost sounded like a threat.

"I'm sure I can handle things while she is away," Roaring said. He reached for his cornbread and started on the black-eyed peas and stewed meat.

Kato narrowed his eyes. "Do you think you'll have time? The Grand Chief has left for an *Academy* mission and the acting Grand Chief can't even make it to Council meetings on time because he's busy on his own adventures with the *Academy*. Does anyone remember the Village of Wi?"

Roaring slowly set his cornbread down, brushed the crumbs from his fingers. His eyes landed on his uncle with the heat of the fire burning inside. "I remember it, *Kifu*. I remember every brick of every Wall. I remember every Hunter of the Regiment. I remember every Magus, every Council member, every man and woman who died in the attack."

"Then why are you sitting here in those wretched clothes after training with those wretched people?" Kato motioned around the table. "You sit here and speak about a village you don't even represent. Who are you?"

Roaring glanced at the Council members one by one; Kifu Kato, shirtless and covered in tribal tattoos, Thunder and Ryko in their warrior's garb, and Lady Ina in a hand stitched kataa designed in Wi fashion. They looked completely different from the men and women who'd traveled to the Academy with him weeks ago; he still had a silly picture of Kifu Kato in his head, wearing a buttoned shirt and noisy shoes. Roaring resisted the urge to look down at himself, to take in his pressed shirt and creased pants and his hair tied back with a ribbon Cat had woven together with his tattered red knot—the only piece of Wi he carried with him everywhere he went. Suddenly, he ached for the large bangles that'd once decorated his arms, the beaded necklace that'd clapped against his bare chest, and the rahkai he'd kept strapped to his hip.

He stared at his plate, thinking of Talon, wondering what she would say right now. "I am the acting Grand Chief," Roaring spoke slowly, hoping he sounded like his little sister.

"I think you *act* more like a student at the Academy, if you ask me," Kato said.

"Did I?"

His uncle looked confused. "Did you what?"

"Ask you what you think."

Silence hung over them as the tension stretched taut in the air. Beside him, Fox snorted and then tried to cover it with a cough. She hadn't been very fond of Kifu Kato since he'd abandoned KI.

Kato leaned over his plate, his voice came out cold and dangerous. "You should care what I think, *nephew,* because everyone else here does."

"Everyone else is free to speak," Roaring said.

Ryko cleared his throat. "We think you've been spending too much time at the Academy."

"We just don't see how your studies benefit the village," Thunder added.

Roaring nodded, trying to think of what to say next. The Council didn't believe he was dedicated to his own village, they didn't believe he cared about his own home.

"Are you going to say anything?" Kato asked, his patience wearing thin.

No, there was nothing left to say. No speech would convince them of his loyalty to Wi. He would have to show them.

Roaring extended his hand, palm up, and exhaled slowly. He felt the spark of power flicker in his chest and then burst to life, surging through his veins. Heat rushed throughout his entire body; he guided it to his hand, to break free in the form of fire crackling against his skin.

Kifu Kato jumped back so fast his knee bumped against the table. Cat lunged to keep her cup of tea from spilling over, but the shock was clear on her face as well. Around the table, everyone wore the same surprised expression, everyone except Fox Fire.

"This is the true power of the Fire Tribe," Roaring began. "The gift of the flame has been in our bloodline for generations, waiting for a spark to bring it back to life. That spark happened when my mother was born and again when I was born." The fire danced in his hand, sending shadows across the room; the black streaks shimmied across Kifu Kato's face as he watched, mesmerized by the flame.

"The Academy has hundreds of students with abilities I can't put into words. They specialize in training people to use their gifts for fighting demons. That's what I've been training for; to master my abilities so I can take what I learn back to Wi." He closed his hand, snuffing out the flame and wrinkling his nose at the smoke wafting out between his fingers. "I have never forgotten about Wi. Every day I look forward to returning and rebuilding."

"Rebuilding Wi is the reason Kifa Talon left with the Academy," Cat chimed in. "She's going with a team to scout the land and make sure it's safe to resettle."

Kifu Kato shifted uncomfortably, unsure what to say. "I ... I don't understand."

"You know the legends of the Fire Tribe, we've all heard them," Roaring said.

"I always thought they were children's stories," Lady Modon breathed, her eyes still glued to Roaring's closed hand.

Thunder crossed her arms. "There are similar stories about the Bolt Clan as well. Our ancestors were rumored to have the power of lightning—though no such abilities have manifested in anyone as of late."

Kifu Kato pinched the bridge of his nose. "Those powers are what got my sister killed. They fooled her into thinking she could take on every demon that made it past our Walls."

Roaring's gaze drifted to his closed fist. "Lady Reign of Fire died defending the village. She used her gift the best way she could. If she'd had the proper training, she might have been able to survive that battle."

"What are you saying?" Thunder asked.

"In Wi, my mother and I kept our blessing a secret," Roaring explained. "We were afraid if anyone found out about our abilities, they would think we'd gotten our powers from a dark source. Here in Babel, these strange abilities are normal; Fox and I fit right in."

"Can you do that, too?" Lady Modon pointed to Fox, who'd been busy sucking the meat off a turkey neckbone.

Fox put down her food and stared at her plate. "No, I can't."

"She has the ability," Roaring interjected. "She just hasn't been able to summon the flames yet."

"So you both plan to train at the Academy so you can return home and teach the rest of us?" Kifu Kato asked.

384

Fox spoke up. "I plan to stay here until KI is better."

All the wonder and awe from before fizzled out at the mention of the boy's name. Kato grew angry. "I thought the Academy was handling his situation?"

"They are," Fox said.

"Then why are you involved?"

"Why *aren't* you?"

"Because that boy is an abomination!"

"No, he isn't!"

"An assassin tried to kill him!"

Roaring held up his hands. "That's enough! We shouldn't be fighting each other."

Kifu Kato took a sip of his tea to calm himself. "I don't think it is wise to stay involved with the child."

"KI isn't a threat," Fox said.

"You don't know what he is," Kato replied tartly.

Fox narrowed her eyes at her uncle. Roaring recognized the look; it was a glare that said her respect for their blood ties had reach its limit. The Prince of Fire had worn the look plenty of times himself.

"I am *not* abandoning KI," Fox said firmly. "I don't care if we rebuild Wi tomorrow, I won't leave him here. He needs me now more than ever." She stood from her cushion. "I'm tired." Then she stomped to her room and slammed the door.

Kifu Kato let out a sigh. "Will you try to change her mind?"

Roaring shrugged one shoulder. "I have bigger things to worry about."

"Agreed," Ryko spoke up. "If I may speak freely, Grand Chief, your gift is impressive, but what about those of us who aren't in the Fire Tribe? How do we benefit from your training at the

Academy?"

"Why don't we just join the Academy ourselves?" Thunder asked. She unsheathed her dagger and examined the blade. "I've been itching to put this to use."

"Training and the entrance exams have been postponed," Roaring said.

"What does that mean for you and Fox?" Kato asked.

"I can't speak for Fox, but I've decided not to take the exam. I won't be continuing any training with the Academy."

Thunder put her blade away. "Why not, Grand Chief? You made it sound so beneficial."

"It is beneficial. But you all have a point. I need to be focused on returning to Wi, and with training postponed, now might be the right time to concentrate on getting back home. Once Talon is back with a report on the damage to the village, we can start making plans."

"And in the meantime," Thunder went on, "what should we do? How should we make coin to survive in this city until we can return home? Where should we go to train and stay in shape until the Regiment is reformed?"

Ryko scratched the back of his head. "I've been getting work as a personal guard for an old lady a few houses down from me. It isn't the same as the Hunting Regiment, but its coin."

Lady Modon clapped her hands together. "That's wonderful, Ryko. I've been making and selling traditional Wi-style jewelry in the market. The ladies here love our fashion."

"Sounds like everyone is handling themselves well enough," Roaring said. He glanced around the table. "If there are any other concerns..."

"Grand Chief." Thunder shifted on her cushion. "I apologize

for coming here with such a negative attitude toward you. I didn't understand your intentions with the Academy."

"Even though I am only the acting Grand Chief, Wi is always my top priority," Roaring said tiredly. "Now, if you will excuse me—"

Kifu Kato stood. "We'll be going, nephew."

Ryko, Thunder, and Lady Modon stood to follow him, nodding their goodbyes. When Kato reached their door, he glanced back at Roaring. "We look forward to the next Council meeting."

Once the door closed behind them, Cat sighed. "That wasn't as bad as it could have been."

Roaring stared at his half-eaten food. "They don't trust me."

"That isn't true. Thunder apologized for everything."

"Thunder did. Ryko, Kifa Modon, and Kifu Kato remained silent."

"Lady Modon is innocent; she probably had no idea Nuncle and the others had planned a confrontation. And Ryko is a follower, you really can't blame him."

"But I *can* blame Kifu Kato."

Cat fed Chava a leftover turkey bone. "You can also ignore him. He's just an angry old man."

Roaring clenched his jaw. "He came into my home and confronted me at my table while eating my food."

"He did."

"He has no respect for me." Strong arms crossed over his wide chest. He felt the heat inside him swelling and he tried to swallow it down. Letting his anger get the best of him now would do no good.

"He has even less for Talon," Cat said. "You should be happy

387

Nuncle chose this time for an argument. I don't know how things would have ended if she had been here."

"Things wouldn't have ended well for him," Roaring told her plainly.

Cat leaned back on her elbows and stared up at her older brother. From this angle, he could see how pretty she looked in the candlelight; the way the shadows moved over her face, highlighting her high cheekbones and full lips, her sharp eyes and perfectly arched eyebrows. Talon had always been known as the Beauty of Fire, but Cat had never been far behind.

Roaring smiled at her, enjoying the way she blushed because of it. Even though she wore a silly pink blouse and a long skirt that didn't match, she still looked like the little sister he remembered in Wi.

"What are you looking at me that way for?" Cat asked, suddenly shy.

"Just thinking that I'm glad you haven't changed."

"But I have," she said. "We all have. It'd be weird if we hadn't."

"That is true."

"But changing doesn't mean you've stopped caring, Roar." She touched his arm, a delicate gesture that immediately drew his eyes to her small hand. "I know your goal is to return home and I'm not going to sit by and let anyone say otherwise."

Roaring stopped staring at her slender fingers to cock his head to the side, his ponytail flopped onto his shoulder. "What do you mean?"

"I know I'm not a warrior like you, or a leader like Talon. I don't even want to return to Wi—but I also don't want Kifu Kato to have his way." Cat squeezed his arm. "You're busy with the

388

Academy and Fox and KI. Talon is gone for who knows how long? Someone's got to put our uncle in his place or else he will turn the rest of the Council against you two."

Roaring smirked at her; he had seen his little sister determined before, but only in arguments over who their parents had picked for her in many of their failed marital arrangements. When it came to the politics and regulations of the village, Cat had rarely offered an opinion or shown any concern. This was a side of her he hadn't known existed. "What do you plan on doing?"

Now it was her turn to smirk. "Don't you worry about it." Then her smirk faltered as she realized what her brother was doing. "You—you're mocking me! You don't think I'm capable!"

"No, no, I do." Roaring raised his hands defensively. "It's just that I've never seen you like this. I didn't know you had it in you."

She harrumphed, crossing her arms. "Well, I do. Who do you think has kept this household together since we arrived here? If things were left up to you, we'd be broke and hungry."

"You don't have to be so honest," Roaring said.

"You remember how you nearly wasted all our coin at the market? If I hadn't been there—"

"I get it," he said quickly.

"Look," Cat reached for his hand. "All I'm saying is, I can take care of this. Don't worry about anything but training Fox and getting back to Wi. I don't understand everything about this world—or even this city—but I do understand how much your dancing will make a difference in rebuilding and protecting the village in the future. Let me handle Kato and the others, at least until Talon gets back."

Roaring retracted his hand, feeling her small fingers slip away. "Whenever she gets back."

"Her letter said another week or so. She also sent some coin, which is good, and more is to come since the mission has been extended." Cat retrieved the small letter from her pocket, a tiny scroll with a broken seal. She passed it to her brother. "You can read it, if you'd like."

Roaring took the scroll and leaned over, gave her a peck on the lips. Then he stood. "Thanks, I'll do that."

"Roar?" Cat called to him.

He paused mid-stride, headed to his room. "Hmm?"

"Get some sleep tonight. You look tired."

Roaring chuckled. "I'll try."

29

Talon

The sun peeled through the trees before it kissed Wall Yamina. Then it rolled over the massive structure, illuminating the broken village below. Homes built by hardworking hands were crushed into dust, stables destroyed, the great temple toppled over. Standing atop the Wall, Talon blinked back tears. This ruin was not her home. It couldn't be.

"The winch is ready," Second Lieutenant Kotaro said. She appeared beside the Grand Chief, her eyes downcast behind her round glasses.

Lady Talon nodded, she had no words for the lieutenant, though she was thankful for her presence. Gentle Kotaro had been kind to her; had kept her well fed and warm since leaving Koh. Made sure she had a fresh set of clothes and stopped every few hours for a bathroom break—whether Talon had requested it or not. But what she really appreciated was Kotaro's distance.

The young lieutenant didn't pry, even though there were questions written all over her face. Other than exchanging necessities, conversation was brief—never more than a small comment about the weather or the pace they were keeping. One time, Kotaro stopped the carriage and climbed inside to offer Talon parchment and pen to write her family. Talon remembered the way her voice sounded, sweet and shy but to the point. She used that same tone of voice now as she directed her to the contraption set up at the far end of the Wall.

"The ride won't be more than a minute or two, Grand Chief."

Talon glanced at her, wanting to correct the title for the first time. She didn't mind being *Lady* Talon in Babel where there were no Grand Chiefs or councils or tribesmen. But she was back in Wi now, standing atop the great Wall Yamina. She was the Grand Chief of the greatest village in the Region of Smoke and Ash. Her ancestors had tamed the Sunriders, her elders had breathed smoke from their lungs. Her own brother had mastered the dancing flame. But this ... this pile of ash and ruin before her did not look like the home she remembered, and she did not feel like the Grand Chief she was supposed to be.

Talon sighed and climbed into the metal cage without a word. The ride down was loud, metal gears screeching as the crank worked. When she looked down, she could see the men at the levers below, heaving up and down in time with the bumping of the giant crate. The sun poured over their bent frames; two Hunters in full uniform, despite the heat.

"Is Lieutenant Diaz here?" Talon heard herself asking.

Kotaro glanced up, the smallest hint of surprise shadowing her face. "Yes. He arrived about a week ago. We got a hawk from him giving us clearance to escort you inside. The area is safe."

Area. Talon was careful not to glower as she repeated the word in her head. The *area* was the Village of Wi. Her home. Or what was left of it, at least. It had changed in more ways than just being destroyed. Even the air in the village was different. Darker. Heavier.

"It feels odd," Talon said, peering through the safety bars of the door.

Kotaro blinked at her. "What does?"

"The air."

She narrowed her eyes in thought. "It's likely the demonic activity. The village needs to be cleansed as well as rebuilt."

"Will the Academy truly help us rebuild our home?"

"Of course," the lieutenant said. "Once we take a look around, you'll be able to assess the damage and we can come up with a plan for how this will play out."

"We will repay you—"

Kotaro shook her head. "We're not doing this for money, Grand Chief. We're doing it because it's right."

Talon smiled, murmuring, "Treat others the way you want to be treated."

"Wise words." Kotaro returned the smile.

When the cage reached the ground, a Hunter opened the door for the women and gave Kotaro a report on where their living quarters had been set up and which parts of the village were off limits.

"What do you mean the innermost ring is closed?" Talon interrupted.

The Hunter glanced at her, then nervously returned his attention to Kotaro. The lieutenant placed a gentle hand on the

393

Grand Chief's shoulder. "There was extensive damage to that ring. It's where the giant and the silver-haired demon fought with your brother. We'd like to study that area without anyone disturbing the scene."

Talon frowned. "I lived in the innermost ring. My own home was less than twenty yards from the spot where the silver-haired demon appeared."

"I understand, Grand—"

"No, Lieutenant Kotaro, you don't." She turned away, the gown of her dress sweeping the scorched earth around her. She'd been given a few dresses as a parting gift when she'd left Koh. Kotaro had made sure they were kept clean and tucked away in her carriage during their ride to Wi. Now, the hem of Talon's dress was stained with dirt and grass and black smudges—lingering bits of soot and ash from the attack on Wi. It had been months, and the debris and damage still clung to the village as if it'd all happened two nights ago.

Talon shouldn't have been surprised. It's not like anyone had tried to clean things up until now. Still, as she glanced around at the destroyed homes, the toppled over cabins, the uprooted trees. Talon felt tears pricking the backs of her eyes.

Please don't cry, she willed herself. *Please keep it together.*

"I want to see my home." The words came out weak, a light tremble to her voice.

Kotaro hesitated. Even the Hunter beside them seemed uneasy, glancing back and forth between the women and the winch he should have been working.

The lieutenant heaved a sigh. "All right. But I'll have to escort you—"

"Lieutenant Diaz gave strict orders," the Hunter began, but

Kotaro stopped him with a gentle pat on the arm.

"Tell Diaz I'll be in the inner ring with the Grand Chief."

They walked together along a path presumably cleared by Diaz and his men. Kotaro offered Talon a horse to ride so the trip wouldn't take so long, but the Grand Chief refused. She wanted to see everything. Wanted to pass through every Gate. They went by training cabins and the small shacks that'd once been used to store smoked meats. They walked by destroyed sheds and what used to be small pens to keep goats and cattle inside. Clusters of Hunters peppered each ring, some cleaning up debris, others bent or squatting by what Talon guessed was something of interest. Perhaps remains of a demon, or other evidence they could take back to the Academy.

"I wonder how many demons Lieutenant Diaz found here when he first arrived," Talon said.

Kotaro walked a few paces in silence before answering, "Likely hundreds. Most of them would have been drawn by the Dark energy you're sensing."

"And he cleared them all out himself?"

"He had a team with him. Though I'd bet he could have done it alone."

Talon smirked, unsure if the second lieutenant was joking or not. When she stopped walking to turn and look at the Hunter, she realized the young woman wasn't kidding at all. Kotaro was smiling at nothing, stars dancing in her eyes as she praised her superior.

"Lieutenant Diaz is one of the most talented men I know."

Talon had never seen him fight before, but she had been more than thankful when Evelyn had ridden back to Koh for her.

"He is special," she admitted.

When they made it to her old home, Talon paused, staring at the wooden structure. It'd been large enough to house the Head Family and a few servants, too. The home hadn't been a luxury mansion, like some of the great buildings Talon had seen in Babel, but it'd been hers.

Most of the house had been left relatively intact. The western side of the building crushed and falling apart, the front doors kicked in. Scorch marks trailing up the sides. But it was in far better shape than the other structures. The Chief's Way had been totally destroyed, the gardens were burnt black, the temple smashed—as if the giant had stomped directly on top of it.

Talon took a step forward, but a hand on her arm pulled her back. "I wouldn't recommend going inside," Kotaro warned.

"Are there still demons?"

She shook her head. "But we don't know how stable the building is. It could collapse on you."

"I'll only be a minute," Talon said, pulling away.

She heard Kotaro sigh, but the lieutenant didn't try to stop her. Talon walked the great halls, peered into rooms, and even tiptoed through what was left of Fox's bedroom.

"Are you looking for something in particular?" Kotaro asked behind her.

Talon shook her head, but she stopped midstride as she came upon the room where the village Council used to meet. "I'd like to go in here, actually."

Before Kotaro could protest, Talon pulled aside the animal pelt still hanging in the doorway and stepped inside. The room was dark, void of any life or color, but largely unscathed. The

396

firepit still decorated the center of the floor, the flag of the Fire Tribe still hung on the front wall, the statue of the great Sunrider remained intact, protruding from the far wall.

A small grin worked its way onto Talon's lips as she walked over to the statue and knelt before it. Underneath the cushion where the late Grand Chief usually sat, was a small compartment where a change of robes and a flaming veil was usually kept. Talon lifted the cushion and then the board in the floor, sighing in relief as she found the garments and the crown. They had taken no damage, not even the smell of smoke had tainted them, hidden underground.

Talon didn't hesitate to shimmy out her dress and slide into the tribal clothing. Kotaro kindly turned her back when she realized what she was doing. When the flaming veil was in place over her short curls, Talon sat on the cushion beneath the stone Sunrider and smiled. "Take a look."

Kotaro turned, gasping when she saw the Grand Chief. A red and gold kataa, designed to match the scales of the great Sunriders, flowing around her body, pooling onto the floor. The flaming veil, gleaming bronze—even in the dim room, with strips of material hanging low to cover the top half of Talon's face. Her smile was the only thing visible to the young Hunter.

"Traditionally," Talon explained, "I would hold a cross in one hand and a flame in the other."

"You would hold a flame?" Kotaro asked.

"The First Flames did, back when they wielded the power of the sun."

"As your brother does?"

She nodded, the veil dipping low with the movement. "Over time, the flame was replaced with a candle or a burnt roll of

397

sage."

The lieutenant chuckled. "We burn sage in Babel, too."

"It's a pleasant fragrance, isn't it?"

"It certainly—" The sound of hooves pounding outside cut her off. Kotaro pivoted and ran for the door without another word.

Talon would have run behind her, but she was clumsy in her floor-sweeping robes and the flaming veil made it difficult to see, especially in the dimness of the partially destroyed house. She made her way through the halls, listening to the sound of Kotaro's voice outside. She was yelling—no, she was being yelled *at*.

Talon tripped out the front doors and into the harsh heat of the afternoon. Her hands went up in front of her to meet the ground before her face did. The sound of her cry silenced the shouting in the open field. When she looked up, brushing the veil aside to see, Talon saw Lieutenant Diaz staring down at her. He was beside his horse, that same golden stallion he'd ridden into Koh days before, a hook-sword gripped in his hand, his eyes ablaze.

The anger melted away as he stared at her, and after a horribly long moment of silence, he swallowed, sheathed his weapon, and cleared his throat. "Lady Talon—"

"I told you she was fine," Kotaro said.

He moved to offer Talon his hand so he could help her to her feet, glaring at the second lieutenant as he did so. "You were given strict orders to avoid this area."

"I understand—"

"No, you *don't*, lieutenant." His tone was sharp, clipping out each word like they hurt to say. "This entire village is teeming with Dark energy—most of it is concentrated *here*. You could have gotten hurt. *Lady Talon* could have gotten hurt."

"Evelyn!" Talon gasped.

He turned, shocked to hear his given name, and even more stunned when he saw the look of pain on Talon's face. He hadn't let go of her hand since he'd helped her up, but what'd started in kindness had turned into a crushing grip in his rising anger.

Talon bunched her shoulders, clutching at Diaz's wrist as she blinked up at him. "You're hurting me," she whispered.

He jerked away, running that same hand through his thick hair. "I—I'm sorry."

"It's all right." She cradled her hand, staring at him as she tried to think of something else to say. It was the strangest thing, watching his nerves unravel. Talon had somehow gotten used to the stoic look he always wore. She had convinced herself that he was always in control because she never seemed to be. But now Lieutenant Diaz was shaken and stumbling for words, anxiously running his hand through his hair. Dark brown strands fell into his face, the very ends curled up, like little swooshes plastered to his skin. Talon stared at them, smothering the sudden urge to touch his hair, twirl a curl around the tip of her finger.

"I'll be all right," she said softly.

He turned away from her, his shoulders bunching together as he took a deep breath. A dark brown splotch bloomed on the back of his beige uniform, right between his shoulder blades, where the most sweat had gathered. The three of them stood there that way for a few moments, Diaz breathing, calming himself down, Kotaro staring through wide eyes, and Talon massaging her sore fingers.

Then, as quickly as the outburst had occurred, it was suddenly wiped away. The first lieutenant rolled his shoulders and turned on his heel. When Talon looked up at him, he was the same man from the Academy; passive expression, a dead look in his eye. Like he didn't care whether anyone here lived or died—not even himself.

"Do you need medical attention?" he asked her.

She shook her head.

"I'm sorry for yelling at you, Second Lieutenant Kotaro."

The apology took her by such surprise, Kotaro actually gasped. Then she composed herself and saluted. "No worries, sir!"

He rolled his eyes, giving her only half a smile. "At ease, soldier."

Kotaro snorted.

Diaz glanced at Talon. Took a slow step toward her. "Lady Talon. I shouldn't have hurt you."

"It was an accident. And you only did it out of concern. I shouldn't have convinced Lieutenant Kotaro to come out here with me. She'd warned me the inner ring was off limits, but I had insisted."

He shook his head. "It's actually a good thing you insisted. There's something I want to show you."

Lieutenant Diaz grabbed the reins of his horse and led both women away from her home. They walked across the scorched gardens to the infirmary and then wrapped around the back of the partially destroyed building. Talon's eyes went wide when she turned the corner and saw what the Academy had been doing in Wi.

The small cabin that'd been used to house KI during his

coma had been completely enclosed in a red and white tent—the colors of Cross Academy. Lieutenant Diaz escorted Talon into the tent and stood beside her as she blinked in awe. There was a giant, scorched black hand sitting in the corner of the room, big enough for Talon to lay in the palm and wrap the fingers around herself.

"Is that..." Talon breathed.

"The hand of the giant demon that walked through your village," Diaz told her.

Even Lieutenant Kotaro stared in shock, though her surprise held an air of excitement. Talon couldn't really blame her. She knew why the Academy had done this—as if the team of Hunters hovering over the fleshy limb, poking and prodding it with tools wasn't evidence enough. They were studying it.

A young-looking Priest walked from around the hand, his bright eyes landed on Talon almost immediately. "Grand Chief," he said, walking over. "I was told we wouldn't be seeing you today."

"We weren't supposed to," Diaz said. "But Kotaro broke protocol."

Izzy glanced sideways at her, but Talon stole his attention as she extended a hand, nervously clutching her veil with the other. "It's nice to see you again, Lord Izzy."

He took her hand like they were old friends. "I'm glad you came."

"Is this the source of all the Dark energy I've been feeling in Wi?"

The Priest tilted his head to the side. "You can sense the Dark energy here?"

"I can sense it everywhere," Talon said, blinking. "It's

401

palpable. Almost like a stench in the air."

"Amazing," Izzy muttered.

Lieutenant Diaz stepped forward. "Lady Talon, you're right. The hand is the source of all the Dark energy you've been sensing. It was cut from a powerful demon, so it's lingering evil is seeping out."

"Are you going to burn it?" Talon asked, stepping closer.

Diaz stood beside her, examining the black appendage. "Technically, your brother already burned it once during his fight with the silver-haired demon. The hand wasn't totally incinerated—which was a good thing for us because right now, we're using it."

"Using it?" She'd thought they were studying it.

He nodded, though it was Izzy who explained, "Spiritual energy—whether Light or Dark—is like a fingerprint. It's unique to each person. Which makes it traceable."

Talon said, "Ohh," her mouth forming a perfect circle. "You're trying to locate the monster who left its hand behind."

"We've already done that," Diaz said.

Izzy's eyes went wide, like the lieutenant had said too much.

Diaz waved him off. "Lady Talon should know this."

"Know what?" she asked, glancing back and forth.

"We traced the Dark energy back to the beast who lost this hand." Diaz kicked its index finger. It made a squelching noise. "And then we traced the beast back to its owner."

"Back to *its* owner?" Talon raised a dark eyebrow.

"The giant who destroyed your village was summoned by a witch," Izzy cut in. "We found her."

"Did you kill her?" Talon asked.

Diaz laughed like she'd just told a joke. "We watched her."

"And what did you learn from watching her?"

Now Diaz looked away, glancing back at the hand. "Unfortunately, Lady Talon, that's information we can't tell you."

She felt like she would faint. "You can't bring me in here, show me this, tell me you caught one of the parties responsible, and then say that's all I get to know." She shook her head. "Don't do this to me. What sort of message am I supposed to give to my people when I return home?"

Lieutenant Diaz met her gaze. "Tell them they will be avenged."

Lady Talon laughed, though she truly wanted to cry. Her shoulders sagged as the fight went out of her. "That sounds very cool when you're a strong man speaking to a distressed woman. But when you're the Grand Chief talking to a room full of disgruntled villagers who've been waiting weeks for answers," she laughed again, clutching her veil, "those words will offer no comfort."

She didn't wait for Lieutenant Diaz to reply or for Izzy to explain. Talon turned and walked out the tent, heading nowhere in particular but desperately wanting to get away from that giant hand. Footsteps followed her, hurried and heavy, and she turned to tell Diaz she didn't want to talk anymore, but her words died on her lips as she saw Lieutenant Kotaro approaching.

A very small part of her heart sank as she realized Evelyn had not gone after her. She hoped it didn't show as she offered a tense smile and said, "You don't have to escort me everywhere, Kotaro. I'm sure you've got a lot of work to get done."

"Actually," Lieutenant Kotaro exhaled a heavy sigh, "I've

been charged with escorting you home."

"Oh, I'm done looking at my old house now."

"No," Kotaro shook her head, "I meant home ... to Babel."

Anger swelled in Talon's chest. Was Diaz getting rid of her now? One little outburst—one disagreement—and he was packing her up?

"If Lieutenant Diaz thinks he can just send me away—"

"I'm going with you." Diaz's voice was deep and sure as he emerged from the tent. "You are not being punished, Lady Talon. I assure you."

"Then why?"

"Because you have a message to deliver." He returned to his horse and untied the reins. "I hadn't realized your people have been waiting for a word all this time. This mission shouldn't have taken this long. I'm sorry."

She fiddled with the ribbons on her veil, childishly refusing to acknowledge his apology. "Why are you returning to Babel?"

"Because I have a message for my people as well." He mounted his horse and looked down at her. "My men will provide you with fresh horses. The horses don't enjoy riding up the Walls in a cage, so we'll have to leave the village through a hole in the southern part of the Wall."

Kotaro stepped beside Talon. "We'll meet you at the exit in thirty minutes, sir."

He nodded and then rode off. Talon watched him go, unsure if she was angry or sad or relieved. It seemed her emotions were all over the place lately.

"What can I tell my people about their home?" she asked Kotaro. "When will we be able to rebuild Wi?"

The second lieutenant paused and stole a glance back at the

tent with the giant hand inside. It would be hard to move in with that thing sitting in the middle of the innermost ring.

"Well, the damage is extensive. But the village isn't beyond repair. We can start rebuilding within the next few weeks since the demons have been cleared out."

"And what about the hand?" Talon asked.

"It might be best to focus repairs on the outer rings until its removed."

The Grand Chief nodded. "I hope the villagers won't be bothered by the Dark energy it's giving off."

"Without training, they likely won't be able to sense it at all. It's beyond impressive that you can sense it, Lady Talon."

She glanced over at her. Kotaro wasn't the first person to compliment her on being able to pick up the presence of the Dark energy flowing around them. Izzy had said it was 'Amazing.'

Kotaro smiled. "The Kotaro Clan has mastered a technique called *Imbue*. We can pour our spiritual energy into objects to empower them." She pointed to a burned tree ahead. "I could imbue a branch from that tree and use it like a sword if I had to. In our hands, anything becomes a weapon."

"That's incredible," Talon admitted, unsure why she was sharing this.

Kotaro blushed. "My family has produced generations of blacksmiths since we settled in Babel one hundred fifty years ago. My grandfather runs our shop back home." She glanced at Talon, her eyebrows raised over the rims of her glasses. "He's looking for an apprentice."

The Grand Chief squinted. "Are you offering me the position?"

"You have a talent for sensing spiritual energy. You could really find a place at the shop, if you wanted." Kotaro shrugged her shoulders. "My grandfather made the hook-swords Lieutenant Diaz fights with. We're good at what we do."

Talon didn't doubt that. But she was the Grand Chief. And she had plans to return to Wi and rule as its queen. Learning how to channel her spiritual energy sounded incredible, but she couldn't get distracted. The Flaming Veil had to come first.

She slowly shook her head, but Kotaro spoke before she could give her an answer. "Just think about it. I know you're the Grand Chief, but you don't have to be in Wi during the reconstruction. While it's being rebuilt, you could intern at the shop and strengthen your skills." She leaned toward her with a smile. "The coolest thing about Imbue is anyone can learn it. The Kotaro Clan simply specializes in it. Imagine all the weapons you could design if you learned Imbue."

Talon only sighed. She didn't want to think about it, because then she would have to admit it sounded intriguing.

Kotaro touched her shoulder. "Consider it. You can think about it during the ride home."

"Yes," Talon said quietly.

"Don't worry, Grand Chief," the second lieutenant told her. She'd returned her gaze ahead, staring at the cloud of dust left behind Diaz's horse. He was out of sight now, too far in the distance to see, but Kotaro seemed fixed on the path he'd taken. "The journey home will not be the same as the one you took to get here. Not with Lieutenant Diaz there."

Running into shadow frogs and getting accused of witchcraft again was the very last thought on Talon's mind. But she didn't say this, instead, she nodded and let out a shaky sigh. "Do you trust him?"

"With my life." Stars danced in Kotaro's eyes again, shining so brightly, the Grand Chief wondered how she'd missed it before.

"When did you fall for him?" she asked.

It was a bold question. One that overstepped boundaries and threatened to shatter the fragile sense of friendship Talon had formed with the second lieutenant. Her large, round eyes blinked at the Grand Chief, mouth parted in shock as she sucked in a gasp.

"I'm sorry," Talon began, but Kotaro's chuckle cut her off.

She removed her glasses and wiped the sweat from around her eyes. "Is it that obvious?"

"Not to him."

"Well of course." The words almost sounded bitter.

"I shouldn't have pried."

"I've always loved him," Kotaro admitted. "We grew up together in Babel. We trained together. We fought together. You grow to love people after you face death with each other, you know?"

Talon nodded, wishing she hadn't asked such a personal question and unsure of why she even wanted to know. She stared off in the direction Diaz had gone. He'd long disappeared into the haze of the afternoon sun, but Talon couldn't pull her eyes away. She thought of the last time she'd seen him racing on his stallion. When he'd arrived in Koh. When he'd come for her. When he'd checked on her. When he'd touched her.

"I've always loved Evelyn," Kotaro spoke into her thoughts. "But I didn't fall for him until a few years ago, when one of his missions went horribly wrong and I thought I'd lost him."

Talon swallowed, letting silence take over. She didn't know how long she'd been standing there, staring down the road where Diaz had gone when she heard Kotaro's question.

"When did you fall for him?"

The Grand Chief closed her eyes, unsure how to answer.

30
Evelyn

He tightened the laces on his leather boots, made sure each pant leg was tucked in. His belt was next, looped around his lithe hips, then he knotted his red tie—ascot style—and buttoned his beige shirt, groaning as he worked his sore arm through the sleeve. Gold pins gleamed on his shoulders; chocolate brown hair shined on his head—combed back away from his face in a flow of gentle waves. He hoped his sweat didn't make his hair curl up as he entered the humid conference hall.

"Left your weapons?" Major Marshall waited by the door.

Lieutenant Diaz glanced up at him. "Didn't think I'd need them for this."

The major looked him over and then reached out to straighten his tie. Evelyn tried not to look annoyed. Major

Marshall always found a way to remind him that he was his adoptive father. He never felt so young until he was near the grey-haired man, especially now with him adjusting his clothes like it was his first day of school at the Academy.

Less than a foot away, Diaz could see how sturdy Marshall was, despite his age. The lines in his face and the grey hairs on his head told one thing, but the lean muscles on his arms and shoulders said another. And he was tall, too. Tall enough that Diaz had to tilt his chin way up to give him access to his necktie. He stared at the ceiling as the old man's hands worked. It was uncomfortable, being this close with his chin up and his head back, but the lieutenant refused to stand on his tiptoes. Major Marshall was around six feet tall, but Diaz wasn't *that* far behind—not far enough to subject himself to that sort of humiliation, at least.

Marshall finally released him and gave an approving nod. "I guess you don't need the hook-swords. But since you went through all the trouble of wearing the fancy tie, you might as well have completed the look."

Evelyn gave in and rolled his eyes, stepping to the side to glance at the shiny gold decoration on the wall. He could just make out his blurry reflection enough to see how much better Marshall's tie was than his own. He frowned.

"Are they ready for me?"

"You're the one who sent that urgent messenger hawk and then rushed back from Wi." Major Marshall raised a single eyebrow. "We've been ready."

Lieutenant Diaz had spent almost a week in Wi clearing out the demons and studying the giant hand before he'd sent word to Captain Payne that Squad Two could move in. He'd learned all the information he'd needed by then, but it wasn't until Lady Talon showed up that he'd made his decision on what to do with the information.

Miraculously, Lord Izzy had been able to track the Dark energy seeping from the giant's hand, then he'd proved the true mastery of his skill and traced the great beast back to the witch who'd initially summoned it.

Her name was Elsa Attra, a practitioner of the Moon Coven. Lieutenant Diaz hadn't heard of the witch before, but he knew of the coven. Everyone at the Academy had heard of the Moon Coven at some point. They were an infamous band of witches and warlocks whose dark crimes rivaled that of the Nine— mostly because they often worked hand in hand with the Nine.

But for the very first time in Academy records, the Moon witches and the Births of Carnage were in opposition. That couldn't have been any clearer with the testimony of the Wi villagers. The Moon giant was trying to take KI for its witch masters, but the silver-haired demon—a Birth of Carnage—was trying to take KI for the Nine. Each demonic entity wanted the boy for themselves.

But why?

That was the question Lieutenant Diaz had rushed back to Wi to answer. Because Lady Talon had been right. Her people needed answers, as much as the officials of the Academy.

The lieutenant spotted the boy as he entered the conference hall. This room was much larger and grander than the small meeting area Diaz and his associates had met in when KI had first arrived in Babel. There were a lot more people present for this meeting and the topic of discussion went beyond where to house a few thousand refugees.

The Academy had been infiltrated, the Cross nearly burned to the ground. Responders were able to put out the flames and rescue those inside, but when the smoke had cleared, reports detailed a loss of thirteen Academy soldiers—five Hunters and eight Priests—and extensive damage to over 60 percent of the structure. The first ten floors were relatively unscathed, left in good enough condition for Diaz and a number of officials to have this meeting in the conference hall on the sixth floor right now, but everything above that would need to be gutted and restored. It could take years. And only after an extensive investigation took place.

Evelyn's testimony was part of that investigation.

KI sat on a bench between two large Hunters with two Priests sitting behind him. At first, Diaz thought the Hunters were there to protect the boy, but as he spotted the shackles on his wrists, he realized it was the opposite. They saw KI as a threat now. A true danger to all of Babel.

Evelyn wasn't sure how he felt. It was hard to ignore the fact that the Cross had burned all because of this child, but he couldn't bring himself to blame KI. It wasn't as if the boy had doused the Academy in tar and struck the match himself. He'd been targeted.

Somehow, Diaz would have to get the officials seated at the long table across the room to see his point of view if he wanted to help KI at all.

He took a deep breath as he approached the center of the room. It was built like a cathedral, complete with a stage and a small scattering of chairs for an audience. Sometimes the Academy used this room for graduations, though the lieutenant wasn't sure when the next graduation would be, all things

412

considered.

The table at the front of the room sat right below the stage. There were fifteen people sitting all on one side, so they faced Diaz as he stood before them. Lady Shakira was present, along with Lady Vehenort and a few other high-ranking Priests of the Cross. Major Marshall crossed the floor to take his seat with the Hunters on the other end of the table. Beside him sat two generals of the Academy military and a few Hunters the lieutenant didn't recognize.

In the middle of the table was a face Diaz had never expected to see in person—not until he'd made the rank of general, or had been inducted into the Academy's *Shadow*, the league which handled their most sensitive missions. Rumors said Lord Izzy was a Shadow, but he had never confirmed nor denied those claims. Not that Diaz had ever expected him to. The whole point of being a Shadow was to remain anonymous. Hidden.

His Excellency, Bishop Jericho Cyruson sat in the middle of the long wooden table. He was between two Cardinals who sat stoic and draped in velvety red robes instead of the ebony cassocks of the Priests. Despite being sandwiched between two superiors, Jericho managed to look powerful; a tall, strong man with wild hair and calm eyes. He was big, a full head and shoulders over everyone at the table, except Lady Shakira—all meat and muscle, like his chair felt weak beneath him. His seat was made of stone. Which wasn't surprising, considering his blessing. He was responsible for keeping the Walls of Babel alive—constantly shifting to open and close, to thicken or grow thinner or stand taller when needed. He warded off demon hordes all on his own. He was working even now; Evelyn could see the tiny cracks in his skin as he gazed at the older man who wasn't a man at all. It was a stone statue, infused with His Excellency's spiritual energy and sent to take the Bishop's place in this meeting.

The statue would act, behave, and even *think* as Lord Jericho did. It was a living part of him, given the breath of life by a portion of the Spirit the Bishop had shared with it. That life would return to Lord Jericho when the meeting was over and the stone statue crumbled in its chair, returning to dust, and transferring the Bishop's spiritual energy and all the knowledge it'd gathered back to him. It was an ability unique to the most elite of the Cyruson Tribe, reminding everyone of how powerful the founding families truly were.

Diaz didn't let his disappointment show as he realized he *wouldn't* be meeting His Excellency in person today. That should have brought him a bit of relief. The fact that Lord Jericho didn't think the matter was dire enough for him to attend in the flesh spoke volumes to KI's chances of getting those shackles removed by the end of Diaz's testimony.

"Good afternoon," the stone statue of Lord Jericho said. Its voice was human but had an edge to it, like someone talking with a very dry throat.

Lieutenant Diaz nodded at the statue, then at the Cardinals sitting beside it. "Good afternoon."

"You sent a message to the Academy ahead of your arrival," Jericho said. "It was urgent. Yet cryptic."

"Yes, Your Excellency."

"We were hoping you could explain things to us."

Diaz glanced at the Cardinals again.

"They are here on behalf of the Academic Council," the statue of Jericho said. "As you know, there is more than one Cross

414

Academy. What happened here on our grounds might impact the other Academy. So these Cardinals are here to observe and report."

Evelyn gave them a very tightlipped smile. He had nothing against the Academic Council, but he also wanted nothing to do with it.

"Not long ago, Cross Academy was attacked by an assassin seeking to kidnap the refugee you see there," Jericho motioned to KI. "We know the refugee is a target because of the demon stirring inside him. But we didn't know anything about the demon inside or the ones who put it in him." The Bishop's statue inclined its head. "But you have information that can clear the air."

"I do," Lieutenant Diaz said. "While I was in the Village of Wi, I studied the remains and the rubble left behind the attack on the stone village. My team discovered the witch responsible for placing the demon inside KI."

Everyone at the table shifted, even KI jerked forward in his seat across the room, his chains clinking together. The Hunters seated next to him turned to glare at him, one yanked on the chains, and Diaz realized there was a thick metal collar around his neck as well as the cuffs on his wrists. The Priests behind KI exchanged glances, like they weren't sure if the aggression was okay. No one at the Bishop's table seemed to notice.

"Who is responsible for putting that monster inside KI?" Lady Shakira asked. She was the first to refer to KI by his initials. Like he was still a human being.

"The Moon Coven," Lieutenant Diaz answered.

The room filled with grumbles.

"I thought the Moon Coven was allied with the Nine Births

of Carnage?" one of the Cardinals leaned forward as the question slipped from his mouth.

Diaz could barely make out his dark eyebrows from beneath his heavy, red hood. "They were. Right up until the day the giant appeared."

"Are you saying the Moon Coven wants KI for themselves?" the Cardinal asked.

Evelyn nodded. "And so does the Nine."

"But why?" His Excellency asked.

Finally, the lieutenant thought. The question he'd been waiting to answer.

"Because the demon inside KI is one of the Nine."

The silence that followed was deafening. Diaz couldn't even form thoughts around its choking presence. He was relieved when Bishop Jericho's statue shifted on its stone chair and said, "How do you know this?"

"I don't know for certain," Evelyn explained. "But it's the only thing that makes sense."

The statue squinted. Diaz could hear the sound of its carved eyelids crunching together.

"Moon witches are siphon feeders," Diaz said. "That means they get their power by siphoning it from other objects or other people. They perform their feeding ritual once every full moon, so whatever they siphon their energy from must be powerful enough to sustain them for the next twenty-nine days." He shifted his weight from one foot to the other, letting the officials digest his words. "I believe the Moon Coven knows there is a Birth inside KI. And they want it for themselves. To feed on it."

Lady Shakira spoke first. "It makes sense. The Moon Coven would want to feed on someone powerful. As far as demons go, the most powerful are all part of the Nine."

"But how do the Moon witches know the identity of the demon inside the refugee?" Bishop Jericho asked.

Diaz took a breath. Everything he was saying was speculation, but it fit together like pieces of a dark puzzle. He'd sat with Izzy after he'd traced the beast back to Elsa Attra. He'd listened to Izzy's report after the Priest had spent days tracking her whereabouts. There was no doubt in the lieutenant's mind that the Moon Coven knew all about KI and what was really going on. Because Izzy's report didn't include mundane details about a witch stirring a concoction in a bubbling cauldron or riding her broomstick through the night sky. He had reported movement. Witches gathering in preparation for something—something big. And with the Cross half destroyed and the city in a frenzy, it didn't take much to guess what their goal was.

To finish what they'd started in Wi.

"They know the demon's identity because they're the ones who put it inside him," Diaz explained.

The stone statue frowned. "Sealing a demon inside something is a tricky thing to do. I don't doubt the Moon Coven has that power, but you must understand that a demon can only be sealed away if it goes willingly or if it has been exceptionally weakened. If the Moon witches want to get KI back to feed on the same demon they locked away, they could have simply fed on it in the first place, instead of sealing it away."

"The demon was weak when it was sealed away. Otherwise, it wouldn't have subjected itself to being locked inside a child," Evelyn agreed. "But nine years ago, the Moon Coven and the Nine were allies working together. Whatever the reason behind the demon being sealed away doesn't matter. All that matters

417

now is that the Moon Coven and the Nine have both simultaneously decided it's time to get the demon back."

"But why wait this long? And why simultaneously?" the same Cardinal from before asked.

"There's nothing special to the timing. In fact, it's all coincidence." The lieutenant glanced over at KI. He was watching through wide eyes, his raven hair falling into his face, sticking to his olive skin. There was probably no one in the room more anxious than him. Diaz didn't have to wonder why. He was just a kid at the center of a spiritual battle that could change the course of the Academy for the next decade. Half the people in the room didn't see him as human, and every person in the room saw him as responsible for the attack on Wi and Babel at least in some way.

Sympathy worked its way into Diaz's caged heart. How could it not? He bore the same black markings that covered the boy's body. He'd had his own home destroyed by demons and had been forced to live through a witch's ritual just as KI had. And he had woken in the custody of the Academy under suspicion and scrutiny, too. But Lieutenant Diaz had been blessed with the protection of Major Marshall. He'd been taken in by a kind man with a gentle heart who knew young Evelyn had been telling the truth when the Academy officials had questioned him—even without using his gift of discernment.

KI was alone. Abandoned even by his own villagers—all except Fox Fire. Major Marshall could confirm that he knew nothing, that his testimony and statements about his past and everything that'd happened in Wi had been truthful. But Marshall could not confirm that KI wasn't a danger. He could not verify that the young boy's presence didn't threaten the destruction of the entire Academy and the city of Babel.

"The Moon Coven and the Nine want KI now because they finally know where he's at," Evelyn explained. "KI showed up outside Wi one day, naked and bleeding and hysterical. My guess is, he somehow escaped the clutches of the Nine and the witches as well."

Bishop Jericho's statue nodded like he was following.

"The villagers took KI in," Diaz went on, "realized he was deeply possessed, and then placed a seal on him to keep the demon locked away. That seal cloaked the boy's Dark energy, preventing the Nine and the Moon Coven from finding him for nearly a decade. But when KI was attacked by a demon in the woods outside Wi, that seal was broken, and the cloak was snatched away."

"Letting everyone know exactly where KI was located," Lady Shakira finished.

"Somehow, over the last nine years, the Moon Coven and the Nine broke their alliance. The witches want KI to feed off him. The Nine want KI because he's one of theirs. No matter which group decides to come after him, we cannot allow KI to fall into their hands." Diaz folded his arms across his chest. Finished with his explanation.

The Cardinal who'd been silent all along wrinkled his nose. "Of course we can't let that happen. If the Moon witches capture the refugee, they'll extract the demon and siphon its power— making them the most formidable Coven in the entire Region. They wouldn't have to feed again for years. But if the Nine gets KI, they'll reclaim one of their lost members." He leaned forward, his hood tilting up just enough to reveal the wrinkled bronze skin of his chin. "We simply cannot allow that to happen."

"The only thing that must happen," the other Cardinal spoke up, "is the death of the refugee."

Whispers echoed off the high stone walls at the sound of his suggestion. Even Lieutenant Diaz swallowed, nervously opening and closing his burned hand. The injury had long healed, but he found the action soothing now, almost therapeutic. He stole another glance at KI, immediately regretting that decision when he saw his eyes wet with tears. He didn't want to die. Of course, he didn't want to die. He was only a boy. And he hadn't asked for any of this. But Evelyn couldn't overlook the wisdom in the Cardinal's words.

"Killing the refugee will solve all our problems," said the red cloaked man. "When a demon is sealed inside a person or object, their life is linked to that vessel. If you destroy the object, the demon will also be destroyed. If you kill the person, the demon will also die."

His words rang through the air for longer than Evelyn wanted to hear them, echoing off the walls, bouncing through the room.

General Ferris rested her elbows on the table. Steepled her fingers together. "I agree with the Cardinal."

"Be ashamed," Lady Shakira hissed, but the general spoke over her.

"The Academy was attacked—*burned*—because of this young demon—"

"He is a *child*," Shakira corrected sharply. "And his name is KI."

Bishop Jericho's statue held up a hand. "That's enough." The room fell silent again, only disrupted by the grating sound of

His Excellency's statue shifting in its chair. "Lady Shakira," it said calmly. "You have sympathy for the refugee."

"For the child," she said, not afraid to correct her superior. Lieutenant Diaz smiled. He'd always liked the tall Priestess.

The statue nodded toward KI. "Does he look like a child to you?"

He didn't. Not even Evelyn could pretend that he did. KI had arrived in Wi as a stick-thin boy of fourteen with blonde hair and hardly any talent. Now he was tall and lean and dangerous. He looked like a young man, at least eighteen, with dark hair and a square jaw and a build more befitting of someone about to graduate from the Academy, not take the entrance exam.

And every day he seemed to mature. To get stronger. His voice to grow deeper. His body to become leaner. He was changing, and it wasn't because of puberty. It was the demon inside, pumping its Dark energy into his body. Pouring his essence into every part of the young boy. KI looked less like himself and more like the visage of the Birth growing inside him. He was being taken over. And the only way to stop it was to remove the demon or kill the boy.

"No, he doesn't look like a boy," Lady Shakira said quietly. "But that won't justify killing him."

"No, it won't," His Excellency agreed. "We will not be taking the child's life. That is not what the Cross does."

Neither Cardinal seemed to agree with his decision, but they respected his authority and nodded in silence.

"Would we be able to perform an exorcism?" the Bishop's statue asked.

Lady Shakira pressed her lips together before she said in a regrettable tone, "Lord Izzy would be the only one strong enough to do it, but he isn't confident."

The stone man shook his head. "I see. Our only option is to move the boy, then."

"Move him where?" the first Cardinal questioned. "An assassin infiltrated Babel and got into the Academy. If that could happen here, then nowhere is safe. Wherever that child goes, death and danger will follow."

"Why don't we just cloak his presence again?" General Ferris asked.

"There's too much Dark energy present to cover up, at this point," Lady Shakira replied. "But that doesn't mean it's a bad idea to move him."

General Ferris frowned, but the Bishop's statue cut off whatever response she had planned. "If we move KI, death and danger will follow. But it doesn't have to follow him to another unsuspecting city. We can take the child to a location that will leave innocent lives out of the matter. And use him as bait to catch those who would try to take him."

The room was silent for so long, Diaz thought to say something just to fill the quiet. But Major Marshall cleared his throat and said, "We'll need a strong team to protect him and fight whatever forces may come."

The statue nodded agreement. "We have plenty of talented men and women from both the Cross and the Academy sects."

"Many of those talented soldiers are busy helping with the reconstruction of the Tower," General Ferris said. "And helping with the project to rebuild Wi. And helping clear out and study Wi. And helping—"

"Your point, General?" His Excellency cut in tersely.

"We may not have the men."

"Exams aren't far away," the Bishop said with a shrug that crunched. "You'll have new men soon enough."

"Your Excellency, exams and training have been postponed," said a Priest at the far end of the table. Lieutenant Diaz squinted at the young woman. He hadn't seen her before, apparently, neither had the Bishop because he turned and said, "Your name?"

She paused, almost insulted. "Marlo Jo. A Master at the Academy and instructor to KI."

All eyes shifted to Marlo, suddenly curious. She didn't shake under all the powerful stares. "I have been training with KI for a few weeks now. I can testify that he is quite strong, but he is also in control of himself. And he is not a danger to anyone around him. But I would not recommend continuing with the exams or with training until we solve the issue of this mystery assassin."

The statue frowned, dirt crumbling on its face. "We are lacking in manpower. We need to continue with the exams."

"My students are strong—"

"Are they ready for the exam?" he interrupted.

She hesitated. "I believe they are."

"Then we will continue with the program. The entrance exams will be held as soon as possible. We cannot afford to postpone it any longer. The new manpower is necessary."

"Your Excellency," Marlo swallowed, "I don't know how much help new recruits will be—"

"When you need all the help you can get, they'll be more than enough," the statue replied.

Marlo wasn't done. "My concern is not just the *talent* of my students. I am also worried for their safety."

"We cannot spare many soldiers," General Ferris said, "but we will provide the best we can to ensure the students aren't placed in any unnecessary danger. If anything, we can leave them here to help rebuild the Tower while our more experienced soldiers leave with the child."

Master Jo took a slow breath. "And who will protect them from the assassin we haven't caught?"

General Ferris looked like she wanted to reply, but she ground her teeth together instead and glanced at the Bishop's statue, hoping he would say something. He did.

"They won't need anyone's protection. The assassin is only after KI. No one else."

"They will defend their classmate if the Red Face strikes again," Master Jo insisted. "I will defend him, if he comes for my student again."

Diaz smiled. He had never met Marlo Jo before, but he was glad the kid had at least one ally at the training grounds beside Fox. He worked his face back into a neutral expression and listened for His Excellency's reply.

"What would you have us do, Master Jo?"

She seemed surprised by the question, like she hadn't expected him to do anything but disagree with her. "I would ask you to postpone the exams—"

"That will not happen."

"Only until the assassin is apprehended."

"The assassin will never be apprehended without the exams." The statue took a long breath, as if it needed it. "Whoever the Red Face is, he will not come out of hiding again until he thinks he has another opportunity to capture KI. That opportunity will be the exams."

424

Another unsettling cloud of silence unrolled over the room. Understanding weighed down on the officials present. Diaz felt tension gathering between his shoulders, he ached to massage it away.

"You want to use the exams—my *students*—as bait to catch the man who nearly burned down the Cross?" Master Jo asked, her voice filled with controlled anger.

"We catch the assassin and gain a class of new recruits to help get KI to safety," His Excellency explained. "We'll be killing two birds with one stone."

It was daring. And absolutely dangerous. Lieutenant Diaz wasn't sure how he felt about it at all. Then again, he was part of the Academy's military force, not their teaching staff. This decision was out of his hands. After this meeting, he would likely be sent back to Wi to gather more information with Izzy, or he would be assigned to the team that would escort KI out of the city after the exams.

"Why don't we just take KI and go immediately?" Master Jo said. "There is no need to get the other students involved in this plan."

"If we take KI and go," General Ferris began, "the assassin will likely recede back into the shadows and slip away. We need to *catch* the Red Face, not run away from him."

Master Jo stared at the table. Defeated. Diaz wouldn't forget the fight she put up and, glancing at KI and the way he rubbed at his red eyes, neither would he. The plans being laid out weren't pretty. Children would be put in danger—including KI's closest friends, Fox Fire and Kohlannis Hunger. The village still faced a threat of attack at any given moment, from an infamous coven of witches and from the Nine themselves. Not to mention the fact that KI was changing before their very eyes. He could wake up next week as the living incarnation of the Birth inside him. Or he could wake up and get ready for his entrance exams, because they were happening with or without Marlo Jo's approval.

At least he gets to live, Diaz thought grimly. Though that seemed like a punishment in and of itself. The lieutenant didn't know how much of KI even remained inside him right now. If he still had all his memories. If he could hear the voice of the demon inside whispering curses against his soul as he slowly claimed his body for his own. His physical appearance had changed, it was only a matter of time before the Birth began to affect him mentally as well.

"This is what's happening," Bishop Jericho said, loudly enough for everyone to hear, "the exams will be scheduled for the earliest date. The Academy will provide the measures for catching the Red Face, and recruits who pass the exam will be divided into appropriate forces for protecting Babel or protecting KI on his escort." He paused, scanning the faces of his associates. "This will not be easy. This will not happen quickly. The Moon Coven or the Nine could attack at any given moment. But we will stand our ground. Now that we've done all we can for the boy and the city, the only thing left to do is stand." He glanced around the room like he was waiting for someone to voice a reply. When no one did, the hulking statue lumbered to its feet. "Meeting adjourned."

ACKNOWLEDGEMENTS

I still remember when the idea for this story first was first given to me by God. I remember when He whispered to me in my bedroom that He wanted me to self-publish it. I also remember doggedly fighting against the self-publishing, haha.

That was nearly fifteen years ago—before The Rebel Christian even existed. It is because of this book that TRC is even around today. I am so thankful to Christ Jesus that He saw me worthy of this book and this journey. I could not have asked for a greater adventure, Lord. You have taken me above and beyond my wildest dreams. This book is for You and You alone. Because Your vision for me was greater, bolder, and far bigger than anything I could ever ask or imagine.

Thank *you* for reading this book that God has given me. I hope to see you in the next installment. To stay updated on releases and other books published at TRC, visit our website; therebelchristian.com and join our monthly newsletter! Don't forget to follow us on Instagram @TRC_Publishing

The Rebel Christian Publishing

We are an independent Christian publishing company focused on fantasy, science fiction, and YA reads. Visit therebelchristian.com to check out our books!

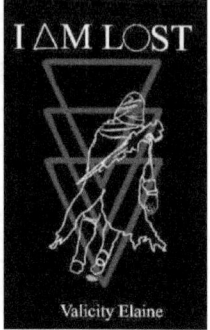
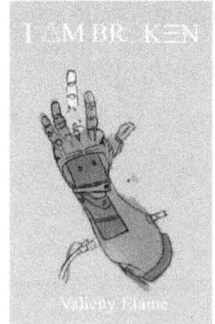